BOUND
BY
SWORD
AND
SPIRIT

ALSO BY ANDREA ROBERTSON

THE NIGHTSHADE SERIES

Rift

Rise

Nightshade

Wolfsbane

Bloodrose

Snakeroot

THE INVENTOR'S SECRET SAGA

The Inventor's Secret

The Conjurer's Riddle

The Turncoat's Gambit

Invisibility (with David Levithan)

THE LORESMITH SERIES

Forged in Fire and Stars

Cast in Secrets and Shadow

BOUND
BY
SWORD
AND
SPIRIT

A N D R E A   R O B E R T S O N

PHILOMEL BOOKS

PHILOMEL BOOKS
An imprint of Penguin Random House LLC, New York

First published in the United States of America by Philomel Books,
an imprint of Penguin Random House LLC, 2023

Philomel Books is a registered trademark of Penguin Random House LLC.

Visit us online at PenguinRandomHouse.com.

Library of Congress Cataloging-in-Publication Data is available.

Printed in the USA

ISBN 9780525954132

10 9 8 7 6 5 4 3 2 1

BVG

Edited by Jill Santopolo and Kelsey Murphy
Design by Ellice M. Lee
Text set in Amerigo BT

For Jill.

Thank you for over a decade of adventures
on the page and the priceless gift of friendship.

Fjeri
Well of the Twins
Ice Coast
Elke's Pass
Ice Mountains
Fjeri Highlands
Senn's Fury
Rill's Pass
Teth's Camp
Wellseeker's Landing
Darkfern
Silverstag
Port Pilgrim
Wuldr's Grove
Alderspring
Shepherd's Rest
Fjeri Lowlands
Bridgegate Cross
Westport
Oakvale
Foxgate
Hunter's Rest
Echir
Siva
Daefrit
Aerindross
Zeverin Gorge
Dothris
Marik
Ghost Cliffs
Ofrit's Cavern
Zeverin Delta
Punishing Desert
The Bone Forest
Butcher Crow
Fortress of the Sands
Handur
Southern Sea
The Great Mines
Isar
Zyre
Salt Coast
Blinding Cape

Forgotten Coast
N
Kelden
Nava's Ire
Fenmyr
Liflamyr
Kaenmyr
Allomyr
Five Rivers
Port Amber
The Great Market
Nava's Bounty
Sola
Nav~Nias
Tribridge
Nav~Horsa
The Gash
Nomis
Mer
Jun
Vijeri
The Tangle
Last Landing
Erlaon
Serpent Coast
Shrouded Cape

❈ FIFTEEN YEARS EARLIER ❈

he Hawk watched the Loreknights fall, one by one. Though he'd expected the war would end like this, the sight of it still speared his soul. The king's ten chosen warriors had ridden to meet the Vokkan army without fear. Armor of silver and gold, ornamented elaborately, threw bright rays back at the sun like coins carelessly tossed from a treasure chest. By contrast, the Vokkan imperial troops were an endless sea of black-and-red tabards, highlighted by glints of silver that crested like waves when the light struck their blades.

Imgar marveled at the way they charged toward the oncoming force. Somehow, the Loreknights still believed they were the invincible heroes of legend. That they were chosen by Saetlund's gods instead of agents of a corrupt king. They had embraced the lie and rode eagerly toward death.

The Hawk—as Imgar's followers had taken to calling him—had long known otherwise, as all those who still honored the gods did. Those who pledged themselves to fight at Imgar's side followed the old ways.

And yet, though he despised King Dentroth and all who toadied to him, in his heart of hearts he'd hoped for a miracle. That the Loreknights might somehow wield the power of the gods and drive away the enemy as they had in battles long ago, and serve the very purpose for which they were created.

But Imgar knew the history that made victory this day impossible.

Decades of corrupt monarchies had transformed the Loreknights from legendary warriors to courtiers.

Emperor Fauld had a special fate awaiting Dentroth's favorites. Champions picked from his own forces to meet them. The gargantuan warriors—the famed giants of Morvadin, one of the empire's earliest conquests—wielded weapons taller than the average man. The first Loreknight to reach them was swept from his saddle by a Morvadin's halberd, then literally pounded into the dirt by another's war hammer. The second Loreknight to fall was caught by two other Morvadins and ripped to pieces.

To their credit, the eight remaining Loreknights didn't balk. They entered the fray, a fury of shouts and steel. A third Loreknight fell. A fourth. Saetlund's champions managed to take down one Morvadin before they finally floundered, fear overtaking any bluster or bloodlust. The fifth Loreknight went down. The sixth. The seventh.

Imgar shook his head, gazing at the bodies broken like toy soldiers on a child's play battlefield.

He watched as the three survivors attempted to flee. The Morvadins let them run. Imgar could hear the Loreknights shrieking as the Vokkan infantry engulfed them. A long groan of horror spread through the lines of Saetlund's small remaining army. Most stood their ground as the Vokkans marched on them; others broke ranks and fled.

Some would call those who ran cowards, but Imgar didn't condemn them so. They'd been led into this war with lies. Why should they be expected to throw themselves on Vokkan swords and spears?

Of course, there were those who would likewise call Imgar a coward—a traitor, even—for what he was about to do.

The Hawk didn't care. History would judge him with its long gaze, but in the present he cared only for the lives and futures of his followers.

Imgar had never thought of himself as a warrior, much less a leader of warriors, but he had also never let a weapon nor a piece of armor leave his shop without thoroughly testing it himself. Over the years, he'd become proficient in the use of daggers, swords, and shields, and more than proficient with war axes.

His smithy sat at the center of town and had become a gathering point of friends and neighbors. Imgar had gained a reputation for shrewd and fair judgment. Disputes were brought to him. In the beginning, they were petitioners from his own village or nearby homesteads. Over time, his reputation drew visitors from across the Fjeri Highlands and even the Lowlands, too. When the call came from King Dentroth to form a militia in Fjeri, Imgar was named their commander. He accepted the position humbly, but not reluctantly, because he went to war expecting the fall of the kingdom. He trusted no one else to do what was necessary to prevent the slaughter of his people.

At a signal from Imgar, his gathered warriors melted back down the hillside. This open plain would be a sea of slaughter. The only place to meet the Vokkans and survive would be rugged terrain, where numbers couldn't overwhelm with sheer force. Even there, the Hawk knew victory wasn't possible. Only resistance. Only survival.

But that was enough. For now.

1

s far as lost brawls went, Teth's scuffle with the Vokkan soldiers could have been worse.

Yes, his left eye was swollen shut, but he still had all his teeth. His body was a map of mottled blues and purples, but none of his bones were broken.

All in all, Teth had come out of the fight in fairly decent shape.

Except for the fact that he was now a prisoner.

No matter how he tried to spin that outcome, which he could usually do to make the best out of bad situations, he couldn't find an upside to his capture.

Throughout the journey from the Great Market to Five Rivers, Teth looked for any opportunity to escape. None came.

He had presumed his time on the road with the soldiers would be rife with regular patrols and patterns that he could exploit. They would make camp for the night. There would be changes in the guard. Distractions would draw the soldiers' attention from him.

He searched for anything that would give him the chance to flee his captors. But by what must be some of the Vokkan wizards' magic, the guards had preternatural constitutions. They didn't sleep. They rode at a relentless pace, stopping only briefly to change horses. During these short breaks, Teth was always accompanied by two guards and his shackles were never removed.

The brutal slog of the journey wore him down, but something more nagged at his mind and mood as they traveled north. The sight of the Vokkan soldiers surrounding him. The flapping of their tabards in the wind. The *ching* of their armor as their mounts trotted over the dusty road.

It was all . . . familiar. But that was impossible. Teth had never been in Vokkan captivity before. So why did his gut churn in a way it never had when he'd found himself in a tight spot? What were these flickers in his mind's eye, like shadows darting in and out, trying to draw his attention? A part of him wanted to focus on the strange feelings and puzzle them out, but another instinct warned him to turn away from the invasive thoughts as if there were something monstrous crouching behind those shadows.

At the beginning of the journey, Teth had been hopeful he'd only be in the Vokkans' clutches a short while. A day, maybe two. But by the time the soldiers marched him down a long hallway in the Temple of Vokk, he wondered if he would even survive the next handful of hours.

When he'd separated from Ara and Nimhea in the catacombs beneath the Great Market, he knew there was a good chance he'd be captured. His instincts whispered that the path Ara and the princess took led to a way out of the tunnels. He didn't have a bad feeling about the other two passages, but there wasn't the tingle of awareness—a quirk of sensation that always served him well as a thief.

He could have gone with them, but he wanted to give the Loresmith and the future queen of Saetlund the best chance of escape from the Vokkan soldiers. So he was the diversion.

Teth hoped by now Ara and Nimhea had reunited with Joar and Lahvja. He took it as a good sign that he was the only captive being dragged back to Five Rivers—at least he assumed that's where he was being taken. If he'd been your run-of-the-mill lawbreaker, Teth might have ended up in a local stockade, but as a companion of the Loresmith there was no way he'd be so lucky. All agents of the Below knew how to spring themselves from the average holding cell, but Teth had no idea what awaited him in Saetlund's capital or who he'd be interrogated by.

Their group crested a hill, and in the valley below, Teth took in the glittering surface of the Lake of the Gods, that massive body of water that was fed by and itself fed into the five great rivers of Saetlund. The Isle of the Gods nestled like a dark green gem at the center of the velvet blue waters, its mysteries hidden from the outside world.

Teth's gaze didn't linger on the beauty of the lake and the island, instead shifting to the walled city on the lake's northeastern shore. Five Rivers, home of the River Throne—the seat of Saetlund's kings and queens. From this height and distance, he could see the towers and parapets of the royal palace, but he couldn't stop himself from staring at a dark spire that pierced the sky. The Temple of Vokk.

His chest flooded with a cold certainty. He was being taken to the temple. There would be no tarrying in a military guardhouse—Teth was bound for the Wizards of Vokk, no matter how desperate he was to go anywhere else. He fought back a sudden wave of nausea. Closing his eyes, he drew a long breath through his nose and waited for his stomach to settle. If he gave in to the dread that clawed at his insides, he was already lost.

Teth hunted for an image in his mind. A face. Dark hair, pale skin, windburned cheeks. Eyes that were by turns warm and gentle or filled with an unyielding purpose.

Ara.

In his world of thievery and deception, Teth was accustomed to ever-changing circumstances, and he thrived on the surprises and twists each day threw at him. But never had he anticipated that someone like

Ara could appear in his life and shatter everything he'd believed about himself—and his fate.

It wasn't that Teth considered love a fool's errand or a myth invented by poets. He'd seen love from a watcher's perspective—his profession required hours of reconnaissance, and he'd witnessed every human action and emotion that existed. Love was real. People hoped for it, grasped at it, were trampled by it. Only the luckiest few found ways to hold on to it and encourage it to thrive.

He knew enough about love to be wary of it; even so, he'd never expected to be ensnared by it.

But he loved Ara. At the first he'd been fascinated by her. She was by turns strong and vulnerable, determined yet somehow lost. He wanted to find the key that would unlock her secrets. She tried so hard to keep them hidden, but she couldn't disguise everything she wanted to with him.

All his training told him that personal attachment to someone as legendary as the Loresmith was a terrible idea, one to be avoided at all costs. And he'd tried—oh, he'd tried—to keep himself in check, to regard the situation with professional distance. But holding himself apart from Ara was like telling his lungs not to draw breath. His body and soul yearned for her.

When he finally kissed her in the sea near Marik, when he held her in his arms, he knew he was lost. He wouldn't have called it love yet—his mind was still wrapping itself around the idea that he could be susceptible to that snare—but he couldn't deny that something significant had happened. He'd crossed an invisible line that marked Before and After.

In the After, Teth's priorities had rearranged themselves. His understanding of who he was, who Ara was, and, most soul-shaking of all, who the gods were had compelled him to take a different path from Ara in the catacombs of Nava's hidden temple. He had an uncanny knack for risk calculation—without it, he wouldn't be one of the best thieves in the Below. He knew he was putting himself in a position of greater risk than he ever would have considered Before, when self-preservation shunted all other considerations aside. But even when captured, he had no regrets. In the After, there were no other choices he could live with. Only protecting Ara. Only serving the Loresmith. Only keeping faith in Saetlund's gods.

It would not be long before Teth's captors took him through the gates into Five Rivers, then on to the temple. He would face more choices. Harder choices. Risking his freedom had been no small sacrifice, but he feared giving himself over to pain would be harder, and he hoped he had the strength to remember who he was now, what his purpose had become, no matter what happened.

Teth gritted his teeth and closed his eyes. He knew he could reach a point where enduring torment for his life alone might not be possible, but he swore to himself and to the gods that he would not be broken. He'd bear the pain for her. For the woman he'd fallen in love with. For the Loresmith. He would follow her to the end of the world.

No matter what horror that temple contained, Teth would survive it. And he would be with Ara again.

By the height of the moon, Teth judged it was close to midnight when they at last reached the city. Once upon a time, even at this hour, the streets of Five Rivers would have shown some signs of life. Yes, there might mostly be evidence of the Below—denizens of Saetlund's underworld—but there would also have been laughing gaggles of drunken fools, stumbling their way home after a night of revelry. There would have been whispers and furtive promises passed between lovers tucked into the shadows. There would have been life.

From what Teth could judge, that life had been snuffed out. The streets were empty save patrols of Vokkan soldiers. Windows were dark. Even rats that should have been scuttling in and out of sewer grates were absent.

The eerie emptiness of the city took on a weight, a life of its own, as they drew closer to Vokk's temple. It was as though some great menacing creature crouched atop the obsidian structure, causing all light, all goodness to flee from it.

His captors appeared to feel it, too. They glanced around nervously, jaws tightening, hands reaching for their weapons. He heard a few swears under their breaths. The horses began to prance and toss their heads, giving sharp whinnies of panic.

Teth swallowed hard. Could there be an evil beast residing in or around the temple? Could it be Vokk himself? As far as Teth knew, the Vokkan god remained with Emperor Fauld, far across the seas. But perhaps that wasn't true. Perhaps the simple fact of Vokk's wizards residing in the temple manifested echoes of their evil god. Whatever the cause, Teth pulled his thoughts away from such questions because the more he wondered about it, the more the dark power became palpable around him, to the point that he could feel its cold, dry scrape against his skin. Its tendrils slid over him, looking for ways to burrow inside. He glanced at the soldiers around him and almost pitied them. It was *their* god who filled the hardened men with so much fear.

As his thoughts lingered on Vokk, those gnat-like shadows began to swarm at the corners of his vision. Flickers became flashes, images shimmered to life, sounds crept into his ears. The creak of wagon wheels. Soft, frightened whimpers.

Teth gave his head a sharp shake to rid himself of the unbidden sensations. Though his hands were bound, he placed them against his chest so he could feel the outline of his pendant through his shirt's fabric.

Calling up the image of Fox, Teth focused hard on the clever, playful creature in his mind's eye.

Eni, Traveler, watch over me as I am forced along this hard road.

Warmth suffused Teth's limbs and quieted his pounding pulse. The tendrils stopped pressing against him, then retreated, and while he could have imagined it, Teth would have sworn that they hissed.

He held on to visions of Fox when they reached the temple's entrance and he was pulled from the saddle and handed off from one set of captors to another. As soon as he was in the charge of the temple guards, the soldiers he'd traveled with returned to their horses and set off at a fast trot. Teth thought they would have charged away at a gallop if they hadn't feared punishment for doing so.

Two guards led him into the temple, one at each of his arms. On the other side of the temple doors was a long hallway. He took in his surroundings, curious to learn more about this heart of the enemy's power. The interior of the temple was dark and sleek. Doors set into the walls were carved ebony offset with red lacquer. Sconces flared on either side of the hall, though the light they gave was weak, emphasizing the shadows rather than driving them back. The dim light forced Teth to squint as he searched for any details that might later be important—one never knew when a chance at escape might present itself.

After a few seconds, he decided not to look too closely. Everything about the place, particularly the walls crawling with black slime, filled him with a sick sense of foreboding that even gazing upon the strange and twisted features of the space would allow its power to seep inside him and plant a corrupting seed.

Teth kept his eyes ahead as they approached the tall ebony doors at the end of the hall. When they reached the doors, one of the guards stepped forward and knocked. A moment later, the door swung inward and Teth was led inside.

The room was large and well appointed, a sort of study or personal library, from what Teth could tell. Thick rugs broke up the monotony of the polished black floor. Fire jumped in a large hearth on one wall, filling the room with far more light than in the hallway. Fine furniture upholstered in silk and velvet sat grouped near the fireplace, a setting that would have been welcoming if not for the rest of the room. The sitting area appeared as almost an afterthought compared to the massive desk that dominated the space. It stretched as long as some dining tables, carved of a heavy wood. Teth surmised it would take at least four strong men to move it. Tall cabinets flanked the desk, and he wondered what secrets were kept hidden inside them.

There were two men and one woman in the room. The woman and one of the men wore dark robes that denoted they were Wizards of Vokk. Though their presence was not a surprise, Teth still fought a shiver. Up to this point in his life, he'd avoided any direct contact with Vokk's wizards, and he had hoped to keep it that way. There were no good stories about the wizards. Those who dealt with them tended to return from their encounters changed, and not for the better; most who were summoned by the wizards were never heard from again.

Two wizards were bad enough, but it was the third person Teth truly dreaded meeting, because from the way the others deferred to him, there was no doubt it was ArchWizard Zenar who stood behind the desk. He was very tall and very thin. His straw-blond hair was pulled back in a severe knot, which further emphasized his already narrow face. His features were pointed, cut at sharp angles.

Teth's mouth went dry as the ArchWizard came closer. Something was wrong with this man; his skin was pulled too tight across his flesh, giving it a glossy, almost translucent appearance. There was a light in Zenar's eyes—a vivid reptilian green—that unnerved him, a sinuousness to his movements that made Teth uncertain that what stood before him was completely human. Perhaps it had been at one time, but something had altered this being to a sickening effect.

"So you are a companion of the Loresmith." Zenar walked around him in a slow circle. Teth wondered what exactly the ArchWizard was looking for. "Tell me, how does the Loresmith choose her fellow travelers? What service have you provided?"

Teth had to clear his throat before he could answer. He'd briefly considered not speaking at all but decided against it. Stubborn silence might cost him more than trying to talk his way through, if not out, of this situation. "Nothing another couldn't provide. I was in the right place at the right time, found her when she'd been set upon by bandits. I helped her, so she was inclined to trust me. She needed a guide. I was happy enough to show her around Saetlund . . . for a fee. Though at this point I have to say it's not been worth the trouble."

Zenar's quiet laugh made Teth's skin crawl. "You didn't find it odd to be guiding a young woman into the jungle in search of hidden places, looking for the gods' secrets?"

"I don't know what you mean," Teth replied, keeping his voice neutral. "I came across her in Fjeri and brought her to the market, that's all."

Teth was sure Zenar knew two things: he'd been captured in the catacombs under the Great Market, and the wizards' hounds had attacked them in Fjeri. The ArchWizard had traced their steps to those locations, but there was no way of knowing what else Zenar had learned about Ara's quest through Saetlund. He was fishing for information.

"As for the gods"—Teth made a dismissive sound—"that's nothing to do with me. As long as her coin made it to my pocket, I didn't care much where she wanted to go."

Zenar tsk'd. He brought one finger under Teth's chin. The fingernail scratching his skin was so long it was almost a claw.

"Even if those places flouted Vokkan law," Zenar said. "You were discovered in a place of idolatry and heresy. Its very existence is an affront to the empire, and your presence there demands severe punishment."

Teth kept his expression neutral. "Like I said, not worth the trouble. Bad call on my part."

Eyes narrowing, Zenar dug his nail into Teth's flesh until it stung. "Heretics are executed. No exceptions. Is that what you are? A heretic?"

"Like I said—"

Zenar cut him off. "Your claims, true or not, matter little, and your actions to this point will not determine your fate so much as what you can offer me now. If you have the answers I desire, you may even earn yourself more of the coin you covet so much."

"I'm listening," Teth said. It was difficult not to jerk his chin away from Zenar's touch when it felt like evil was crawling from the wizard's fingertip onto his skin. He also had the sense that Zenar was very aware of his discomfort and enjoying it.

"The girl and her companions." Zenar finally turned away from Teth, dropping his hand. "Where did they want you to guide them after the Great Market?"

Teth had to fight not to draw a deep breath of relief when the contact between them was severed. His mind quickly riffled through options of how to reply to Zenar's question.

Here was a rare circumstance where the truth might be the best answer. Days had passed since he'd been separated from Ara and the others. They may well have already made the journey to Nava's Ire in northern Kelden. If they were already gone, no harm would be done in sending Zenar after them. But there was no telling how long it would take for Ara to find Nava's Ire and complete the trial there. No, he couldn't take that chance.

Claiming ignorance, while obvious, was also foolish. Zenar was unlikely to believe he knew nothing of Ara's next destination.

Misdirection, on the other hand, had its merits.

"How much coin?" Teth asked. Since he was playing the mercenary, he'd make a good show of it.

Zenar smiled slowly. "Enough to spare you from having to bother selling your services ever again."

Teth forced his working eye to widen. "Generous . . . And considering that you're not sending me to the gallows on a heresy charge, I'm thinking I should accept."

"That would be wise." Zenar nodded, though Teth could tell the wizard was growing impatient.

After hemming and hawing for another moment, Teth said, "Zyre. The university there. She said something about needing to consult a scholar."

Zenar held Teth's gaze. Frustratingly, he could pull nothing from the ArchWizard's expression. Zenar walked back to his desk and exchanged words with the woman. She bowed and left the room.

"We shall investigate your claim," Zenar said, returning to Teth. "Though I must insist on holding you in the temple until we know whether you have misled us."

Teth felt a lurch of disappointment, though he'd known it would never have been so easy as to offer an answer and be given his freedom in return. But cells were made for escaping. There were worse places to be sent. Admittedly, he would have preferred somewhere other than within the temple.

The door opened and someone entered. Teth assumed it was the woman returning, but he kept his focus on the ArchWizard, the most dangerous man in the room.

Zenar turned to greet the new arrival. "Welcome, Your Highness. We have a guest with whom I believe you're acquainted. I wonder how he'll feel about this little reunion."

Your Highness. A frisson of alarm traveled through Teth's body.

Teth shifted his gaze away from the ArchWizard, needing to know what kind of "reunion" his captor meant.

When Teth saw who had entered the room, he experienced a flash of relief, then sorrow, quickly drowned in a nauseating rage.

Prince Eamon came to stand beside ArchWizard Zenar. Teth watched as the wizard rested a hand on Eamon's shoulder.

"Teth," Eamon said.

It didn't matter that a guard had accompanied the prince into the room or that Eamon's appearance was haggard. He'd lost weight, his skin had a sallow cast, and shadows nested beneath his eyes. If he had been suffering, he had no one to blame but himself.

Teth saw panic rising in the prince's eyes and smiled. Eamon was right to be afraid.

2

unlight was their friend. It was early summer, but in the far north the days lingered for long hours, keeping the night at bay and making it possible for Ara and her companions to spend those hours traveling where treading in darkness over difficult terrain would have been too perilous. Yes, sunlight was their friend, and summer's warm breath was very welcome. Each day brought them closer to their goal.

Ayre's light, Ara thought, reminded of their destination. *Ayre's breath*. The Well of the Twins.

Two yet one, the god known as Ayre/Syre was that of duality. Light and dark. Summer and winter. Day and night.

They ruled over the mysterious domains of life: magic, spirit.

Their holy site, the Well, was hidden in the western peaks of the Mountains of the Twins. Ara had spent her childhood in the shadow of those mountains, but pilgrimages to the holy site had been forbidden by Vokkan conquerors, so her knowledge of it resided only in the stories told by her grandmother and Old Imgar. Those stories were vague, full of abstraction. The Twins liked to keep their secrets.

Ara didn't know what she'd find when they arrived at the Well. She glanced over her shoulder at Lahvja, grateful that the summoner would be with her when they reached the holy site. As Lahvja was one of the

Wanderen, her patron god was Eni, the Traveler, but as a summoner, Lahvja had a deep connection to Ayre and Syre. Her magic was drawn from their power. But Ayre/Syre existed in a world of signs and symbols so esoteric Ara doubted she'd be able to fully understand any exchange with them without Lahvja's assistance.

They'd been traveling for a week, keeping off main roads and often riding at night until they were certain no Vokkan patrols were in pursuit. After leaving the fens of northern Kelden, Ara, Nimhea, Lahvja, and Joar had ridden with Ioth to the Ice River, where they split into two parties. Ioth and Nimhea would continue south and west to the location of a hidden rebel stronghold in western Kelden. Ara, Lahvja, and Joar turned north, making their way to Elke's Pass and into the peaks of Saetlund's northern mountain range.

Bidding farewell to Nimhea had been difficult, most of all for Lahvja. They all agreed that splitting up best served their mission, but that truth made the parting no easier. With reluctance, Ara handed care of Dust and Cloud over to Nimhea and Ioth. Daefritian horses had no business climbing mountains. The warhorse Joar had purchased in the Great Market would serve him well in northern climes, while Ara and Lahvja secured two of the sturdier Keldenese mounts available in the village stables.

Ara had hoped returning to her homeland of Fjeri would bolster her spirit, but as they crossed the Ice River, moving west from Kelden's fens to the Ice Coast of northern Fjeri, her heart felt as cold as the ice floes jammed up at the river's mouth. The mountains familiar soaring heights should have offered comfort, but now thoughts of home only reminded her of what she had lost.

Teth.

Letting go of Dust and Cloud had felt like losing another piece of him, another link to him through shared memories. A vise closed on her torso and tightened whenever her mind returned to the thief, the Loreknight, her friend, her lover. When she envisioned his teasing smile and mischievous eyes, a kindling warmth tried to grow in her heart, only to be overshadowed by new visions, visions in which Teth's face was bruised and battered, his body broken. Or worse, his eyes wide and glassy, seeing nothing.

First, Eamon had betrayed them, then Teth had been captured by the Vokkans in a bid to help Ara and Nimhea escape the catacombs beneath Nava's Bounty. His ploy succeeded, but at the price of his freedom—possibly his life.

Ara tried to keep that thought out of her mind. When she failed, she could swear her heart stopped. She couldn't give in to the sorrow that wanted to wrap itself around her. If she did, Teth's sacrifice would be for naught.

She reminded herself of that fact as she, Lahvja, and Joar traveled deeper into the mountains. They'd abandoned the main pathway and its more temperate valleys a few days ago, turning onto a smaller track that took them on a steady climb up the slope. The path wandered toward the twin peaks between which the Well of the Twins was nestled.

The farther they traveled into the mountains, the more inhospitable the environment became. Today they'd reached an elevation where snow still blanketed the increasingly rocky slopes. Trees still grew here, but only pines, and in much sparser numbers. In the next few days, they would pass beyond the tree line and be surrounded by only rock, snow, and ice.

A sharp crack echoed through the valley, snapping Ara's attention to the present moment. Joar, a few steps ahead of her, reined in his mount and held his fist up, signaling a halt, and went still. Lahvja pulled her horse alongside Ara's, but otherwise stayed quiet. Huntress lifted her head, sniffing the air. A quiet growl rumbled in the ice wolf's chest, making the horses snort and stamp. They tolerated Huntress's presence but didn't appreciate it whenever she acted particularly wolfish.

Ara surveyed the trail ahead and the snow-covered slopes that rose steeply to either side of them. Other than the startling noise, nothing seemed amiss. A starkly clear early summer sky offered an unimpeded view of the frozen, jagged peaks of the Mountains of the Twins, their black shapes cutting through the sharp blue of the horizon.

A second crack split the air, this time followed by a rumble, and the snow covering the slopes appeared to shiver. Huntress snarled and stalked toward the right side of the path.

Ara's gloved fingers gripped her mount's reins tighter as the horse tossed its head, shying from the startling sound.

Avalanche. A moment later, she choked out the word. "Avalanche."

Joar, who'd been watching Huntress pace, the wolf still growling and staring at the slope, turned in his saddle to look at Ara.

"No," he said. "Something else."

"Something else?" Ara said, on edge. On the one hand she was relieved that a torrent of snow, rock, and debris wasn't on its way. She could see no way of escape from an avalanche. But the stern set of Joar's jaw and the hackles raised on Huntress's ruff told Ara there was another danger.

The wolf's snarls grew louder as Joar pointed to a disturbance high up on the slope. A long band of snow and ice sluiced downward, like a narrow river snaking down the side of the mountain. Joar pointed again, and Ara spotted a second current a few yards away from the first.

Not an avalanche, but what would cause the snow to move like that? As Ara watched, something arced up from the sliding snow, then disappeared. It happened so fast she wondered if she'd imagined it, but a moment later the snow was pierced again by something fan-shaped and iridescent blue, crowned with slender spines.

A very old story floated into Ara's mind, one Old Imgar had told her when she was still a small child. A story he claimed hunters told one another around campfires whenever their quarry took them high into the mountains.

The day after hearing that story, Ara's grandmother had chased after the blacksmith with a spoon because Ara had woken twice in the night due to nightmares. Nightmares full of glowing white eyes and sharp black teeth.

No. It can't be.

Beneath the snow a shape undulated, two shapes, traveling alongside each other. Ara caught sight of the blue spines again.

Even as her mind fought to deny what her eyes were seeing, Joar shouted:

"Ice wyrms!"

Leaping off his mount, Joar slapped the horse's rump, sending it farther up the trail. As he drew his axes, Ara and Lahvja dismounted and pushed their steeds after Joar's. The horses were all too happy to gallop away.

"Get up the opposite slope as much as you can," Joar called to them. "They use the snow- and icefall to catch prey. If we become mired, it will be a struggle to fight them off."

Ara and Lahvja turned and scrambled up the mountainside. As she climbed, Ara dared to look over her shoulder. While not a true avalanche, the surging white cloud pouring down the other side of the valley certainly looked like one. The heavy weight of snow, ice, and debris drowned the path they'd been riding on only moments ago. It would have buried Joar to the waist and Ara to the shoulders had they been caught unawares.

Ara watched as the two moving ridges snaked beneath the glittering cover of white and silver, twisting, searching for trapped prey. A labyrinthine pattern formed as the two wyrms slithered just under the thick layer of snow.

Not finding what it sought, the first wyrm's head crested the frozen surface, its long snout emerging, nostrils flaring. The story about their eyes was true. Large and set on either side of the creature's head, its eyes glowed pure white with no discernible irises or pupils. The wyrm raised its head and opened its mouth, revealing obsidian fangs. A purple forked tongue flicked out as it rose, head lifted by a long, serpentine body. Whether it scented them or simply sensed their body heat, in an instant the wyrm swung its head in their direction, its eyes glowing brighter. The second wyrm remained hidden beneath the snowdrifts, the only sign it was there an occasional swelling or caving of the white surface. Its near invisibility made it almost more frightening than the wyrm Ara could see.

Letting out a cry like a shrill birdcall that was also somehow sibilant, the first wyrm surged toward them. Spine-tipped fins rose like sails on its back. They glittered pale blue against the stark white snow and propelled the wyrm through the ice and snow at incredible speeds.

Joar answered the wyrm's call with a shout. The beast whirled to meet his attack. One of Joar's axes sliced through a fin, but the wyrm twisted away with a shriek of pain. It dove beneath the snow, then surged up again. Joar met the wyrm's strike with a glancing blow against the side of its head. The creature backed off, momentarily dazed, and Joar pressed his advantage, moving forward, axes whirling. The wyrm hissed and dodged each swing.

As Joar fought, the wind began to swirl around the warrior. He was cocooned by driving snow and pummeling ice while a song rose in the air. StormSong's power had been called to battle. Ara could feel the axes' magic surging within her, the blades imbued with Wuldr's strength and force of will, a gift for his chosen Loreknight and a reminder that though the weapon belonged to Joar, she would always be connected to it.

Ara freed Ironbranch from its harness and took a defensive stance, holding the stave at a diagonal across her body. She and Lahvja had scrambled about five feet higher up the slope, casting nervous glances over their shoulders as they climbed, but the second wyrm remained cloaked beneath the snow. Lahvja stood slightly behind Ara, alert, her fingers flexing as if she could trace the shape of the danger to come by touching the air.

Without warning, the wyrm burst from the snow directly in front of them. It hissed, body rising above them until it gazed down, eyes blazing so bright Ara couldn't look directly at them. The wyrm began to weave back and forth, stare fixed on Ara, its movements sinuous, hypnotic. Ara sensed it was trying to draw her gaze back to it, wanting to mesmerize her.

"I can fight it, but I need a moment to prepare." Lahvja spoke with urgency. "Defend me."

Ara gasped as Lahvja dropped to her knees on the slope, making herself totally vulnerable to attack. Something must have been wrong. Had she been injured in the climb? But then Ara saw that while the summoner's head was bowed, her arms were raised and she was speaking rapidly. She was calling something.

The wyrm saw Lahvja fall and took the opportunity to strike. Ara lunged to block it, and the wyrm's teeth closed on Ironbranch. Frost spread along the stave's surface. Ara suddenly felt a terrible cold seeping through her gloves, onto her skin, under it. Her teeth clenched as the wyrm jerked Ironbranch, trying to wrest the stave from her grasp—but Ara held fast.

With a hiss, the wyrm released the stave, and the cold in Ara's limbs faded. But the beast had only given up its grip so it could strike again. The wyrm's black fangs flashed in the sunlight as its head dove toward Ara once more. She braced herself and struck out with her stave again, but this time the force of the wyrm's attack drove her to one knee.

Holding Ironbranch in its jaws, the wyrm hissed furiously. Frost spread over the stave again. The cold hit Ara's skin, more painful this time, and she cried out. She struggled to keep her hold on Ironbranch. Frigid cold crawled beneath the skin of her fingers, the first hints of numbness much worse than any pain.

Then a flurry of motion came from her left, and the wyrm suddenly released the stave as its snakelike body jerked. Huntress slammed into the creature, driving it to the ground.

Ara dared a glance at Joar. He was still battling the first wyrm. Vicious cuts crisscrossed its body and black blood spilled from the wounds onto the snow, but its attack on the hunter continued, unrelenting.

The blizzard and chorus Joar called with StormSong fought along-side him, but the barrage of ice and snow didn't drive back the wyrm the way it had the swamp creature in Vijeri. Ara briefly wondered if weapons born of the cold were ineffectual against the ice wyrms.

She braced herself, holding her defensive position in front of Lahvja, readying for another attack if the wyrm came back for her instead of the wolf. The second wyrm recovered before Huntress could lunge a second time, swinging its long neck up and out of the wolf's reach. It hissed again, head swaying as it tracked Huntress, who darted around it, snarling, holding its attention.

Light flickered behind Ara. Unlike the harsh white of the wyrm's eyes, the glow at Ara's back had the orange and red hues of flame. Intense heat bloomed behind her, and she whirled to see Lahvja bathed in fire. She had no idea how Lahvja could withstand it. She stumbled away as steam belched into the air and the snow and ice nearby evaporated.

Then Lahvja shouted, "Ara! Huntress! Down!"

Ara threw herself away from the pillar of flame surrounding Lahvja. Huntress dashed away, the wyrm's jaws snapping at the wolf's tail.

Lahvja cried out again, but this time in a language Ara didn't understand. A fiery spear flew from the light around Lahvja and hit the wyrm, scorching its way through scales and flesh until it left a gaping, smoking hole in the wyrm's side. The wyrm screamed, turning away from Huntress and toward the summoner. Lahvja's spellwork answered Ara's lingering question—fire, not ice, was their destroyer.

Lahvja screamed as another flaming spear sailed out of the light. Then another. The spears found their marks, fire boring through the wyrm's body as it twisted and writhed, blood boiling out of its wounds. The stench of its burnt flesh filled the air. It screamed then gave a long shudder. Its long body slumped onto the ground and didn't move again.

Hearing the other wyrm's death shriek, the first creature turned to see its companion writhing in the snow. Joar seized on its distraction. Taking two great strides, he leapt into the air. For a moment he seemed to float, as if held aloft by a gust of wind. Then he brought both axes down on the wyrm's neck, severing its head from its body.

Though the head fell to the snow, the body continued to flail, blood spurting from its neck in wide arcs that hissed and steamed as they landed, creating narrow trenches in the piles of snow and ice.

Ara didn't let her guard down, searching their surroundings and calling to Joar, "Will there be others?"

"No," Joar answered, and set to cleaning blood from his axes. "They always hunt in pairs. There are few of them, and each pair claims a wide territory. It's doubtful that we'll encounter any more on this journey."

She took a little comfort in his words and turned to Lahvja, who was struggling to her feet. Ara reached out to help her up. The summoner was shaking.

"Are you all right?" Ara asked, gripping her arm.

"I will be," Lahvja answered with a weak smile. "I've never used my magic to create an elemental weapon. It was more draining than I anticipated."

Ara's eyes widened. "You've never tried that before?"

Lahvja shook her head.

"Thank Nava it worked," Ara said with a nervous laugh.

"Indeed," Lahvja replied dryly.

They exchanged a long look, and Ara knew the summoner's mind was filled with the same fresh worry as her own. Their focus had been on the challenges Ara would face at the Well of the Twins. But how many unknown perils would rise up to keep them from reaching the holy site? The attack of the ice wyrms felt like a harbinger of troubles she hadn't anticipated.

Joar trudged back through the snow to them. "A good fight! Bracing!"

"That's one way to put it." Ara returned Ironbranch to its harness. She tried to take comfort that he was unfazed while she and Lahvja remained shaken by the fight. "Where's Huntress going?"

The wolf was dashing up the path at a breakneck pace.

"She will make sure the horses do not run too far, else we may never catch them," Joar replied.

Lahvja frowned. "The horses won't like being herded by a wolf. They'll be even more skittish around her now."

"Would you prefer to walk the rest of the way?" Joar grinned. "Because I would not."

3

s the spear tip flashed toward her, Nimhea stepped toward the weapon's thrust and twisted to dodge it. Coiling energy into her core, she launched her body up just as the spear pierced the space her stomach had occupied only a moment before. Nimhea flipped through the air, landing behind her opponent. Straightening, she pivoted around and brought her blade up to the side of her attacker's neck, who went very still.

"Yield," Nimhea said.

Despite the sharp steel at Xeris's throat, she began to laugh. "Yes, Your Majesty, I yield . . . again."

Nimhea stepped back and returned her sword to its scabbard.

"I almost had you," Xeris said as she turned, the Vijerian woman's long braids of blue and ochre whirling with the movement.

"Almost." Nimhea smiled.

The two warriors stood at the center of what had been a horse paddock but was now used as a sparring arena for Resistance fighters.

"I call next." Ioth had been watching the contest, perched on the paddock fence. "I think I've come up with a strategy to finally best our queen."

Xeris laughed. "I'd like to place a wager on that."

"For me or Her Majesty?" Ioth asked.

"Who do you think?"

Ioth winced, placing a fist over his chest. "You wound me."

"Not I." Xeris laughed, nodding at Nimhea. "But doubtless she will."

Nimhea sheathed her sword. "Another time, Ioth. I'm due to meet Suli, and I don't want to keep her waiting."

"A wise choice." Ioth grinned. "Xeris? Care for another bout?"

"Always happy to oblige, Ioth." Xeris whirled her spear around her body in a series of graceful, complicated movements. "Ready whenever you are."

Ioth hopped down from the fence and drew his sword.

Nimhea left the paddock and headed for the old barracks where they ate, slept, and gathered for meetings. This Resistance hideout was nestled in Drover's Redoubt—an ancient ruin buried in the hills of western Kelden. It had been a fortress in Saetlund's earliest days, but had been abandoned and left to decay as the kingdom's great cities rose to prominence. The redoubt relied on its natural environs as its primary defense. The barracks, meeting hall, and armory had all been hollowed out of a cluster of hillsides. Aside from the paddock, the only signs that a fort had once existed in the place were a few piles of stones, the remnants of lookout towers. The entrance to the redoubt was tucked among boulders and bore close resemblance to a cave.

This location, Nimhea had learned, was one of many such places scattered around Saetlund that served as meeting and training grounds for the Resistance. By necessity the sites were isolated, usually repurposed places that had fallen into disuse, whether forts or farmsteads, and could be quickly abandoned should the Vokkans ever show interest.

The Resistance leaders—Suli, Edram, Xeris, and Ioth, who collectively were known as the Circle—moved among hideouts to ensure that no place went too long without personal attention from the movement's leadership. A representative from each of Saetlund's provinces, with the exception of Fjeri. The Hawk—the mysterious warrior Nimhea had yet to meet—hailed from the northwestern province.

When Nimhea had arrived at the hideout, she was determined to establish two things. First, that she was ready to assume her leadership role within the Resistance as the future queen of Saetlund. Second, that said role would in no way be ceremonial. Nimhea was no figurehead. She would win her crown with her sword, sweat, and blood. Hiding behind the sacrifices of her allies while they fought and died—their bodies paving a path to the River Throne—was unthinkable.

No matter how precious a treasure Suli and the other rebel leaders believed her to be, how much they wanted to shelter her while others risked their lives, Nimhea would not allow it.

In the early days at Drover's Redoubt, Nimhea had expected at best a civil alliance between herself and the Circle, and at worst competition and conflict between those who had been with the Resistance from the beginning and the newcomer, her royal inheritance notwithstanding. Instead, she'd been treated with respect and a surprising amount of deference. She wondered why—maybe it was the way she had defied them at their first meeting in Silverstag. When Suli had insisted Nimhea accompany them and leave her brother and the Loresmith behind, Nimhea had refused. No argument the Circle put forth could sway her. To her surprise and relief, she hadn't encountered strong objections to her assertiveness now. It also didn't hurt that she now wore a crown forged by the Loresmith, given to her with the blessing of Nava. The confidence of a goddess did wonders for one's sense of authority.

At least, Nimhea hoped that was the reason. In quiet, secret moments, when the strain of long days and the ache of Lahvja's absence became overwhelming, she secretly worried that she was simply being pitied after the betrayal of her twin brother, Eamon. Or perhaps they were feeling guilty for plotting to have Eamon assassinated without Nimhea's knowledge. When such thoughts hounded her, she steeled herself and drove them off. Doubt had no place in the days to come.

As time passed, her doubts about the motivations of the rebels' inner circle faded. They drew her into their fold. She ate with them, trained with them, traded tales with them. Whatever the reason for her welcome, Nimhea needed to prove herself as a leader and a fighter. Not only to her new companions, but also to herself. She threw herself body and soul into every aspect of life in the Resistance. She spent the most time with Suli and Edram, the elder members of the Circle who mentored her, going through the history and current status of the rebel movement, ensuring she understood its composition, strengths, and weaknesses. She also worked through strategies for the imminent attack. Where their attack should take place was less an issue than when. While the Vokkans had military forces spread throughout Saetlund, the majority were located in Five Rivers. It was clear the attack would be concentrated there, while smaller offensives would strike at key sites in each province of the kingdom.

When she wasn't studying maps and memorizing plans, Nimhea sparred with Ioth and Xeris, honing her martial skills. She committed to each bout with a brutality born of necessity and desperation. Exhausting her body was the only way to still her mind enough to sleep through the night. Even so, she was too often plagued by restless dreams, in some of which she was back in Nava's Ire, forever lost in the fens while she heard Lahvja's sorrowful voice calling to her. In others, she wandered a battlefield strewn with bodies until she came to the one body she searched for: that of her brother, Eamon. But the worst was a nightmare where she stood in front of a cave, knowing her friends were inside waiting for her aid, yet when she stepped into the darkness the cave began to collapse, and she realized it was in truth a giant maw filled with rows of sharp teeth that sank into her flesh while powerful jaws crushed her bones.

Most nights she simply startled herself awake from the dreams, shaken, but sometimes the visions were so vivid—particularly those of Eamon—that Nimhea woke sobbing. As much as she tried to keep her fear and grief regarding her brother tucked safely away in her waking hours, she couldn't hide from the rawness of the emotions while she slept. When she did allow herself to think of Eamon, she wondered if the attack on Five Rivers would bring them together again. And if it did, what would that confrontation mean? Would she face her brother as an enemy? It made her a little sick to realize that encountering Eamon that way might be worse that finding him already dead and lost to her forever.

Better to keep him from her mind as much as she was able. Keeping busy with preparations for the coming conflict did most of that work for her.

Today provided even more than the usual distractions of her existence at Drover's Redoubt. A special guest awaited Nimhea and Suli in the refectory. Royalty, as it were, though of an unusual sort.

Of course, Lucket, the Low King of Fjeri, had situated himself at the head of the long table where the rebels gathered for their meals and where Nimhea usually presided over the Circle's meetings. Nimhea had assured Suli that she needn't give up that place of honor; in her mind, leading the Resistance didn't mean displacing those who'd been fighting the Vokkans since she was a child. Suli, however, insisted that Nimhea take the chair.

Lucket rose to greet the two women. "Your Highness, Suli. I hope you don't mind that I've made myself comfortable."

"Not at all," Suli answered. "And I'm impressed you found wine. Our rations are limited, and I thought we'd run out."

"You have," Lucket answered. "Fortunately, I always travel with my own supply. I'm rather particular when it comes to vintages. Happy to share if you'd like a glass."

Nimhea managed to swallow a laugh, though she didn't necessarily think the Low King would have been offended by her show of amusement. Still, better to err on the side of restraint.

"No, thank you," Nimhea said with regard to the wine.

Suli likewise declined the offer.

While Lucket was dressed and groomed in the same immaculate way he'd been when Nimhea first met him in the ruined fort on the northern edge of the Gash—neatly trimmed silver hair and expertly tailored clothing—she could see changes beneath the fine facade. He'd lost none of the sharpness in his gaze, but new lines branched out from the corners of his eyes, and his expression barely masked a sorrow and weariness that ran deep.

"What news do you bring?" Nimhea asked, seating herself to Lucket's left while Suli took the place to his right.

The Vokkans' attacks on the Below across Saetlund had compromised most of their strongholds and sanctuaries, sending many underworld denizens to seek refuge among the Resistance. Yet Lucket and his ilk had shown incredible resilience in the wake of the attack.

"Plenty," Lucket replied with a mysterious smile. "I'm happy to say that I'm feeling quite optimistic about the future at this moment."

"What of King Fergin?" Suli asked, sounding irked at Lucket's vague reply.

"Ah, my former brother from Kelden." Lucket's smile was chilling. "I gutted the swine myself. He was a fool to think the Vokkans would protect him after their attack. I found him in his hideout in Sola; the idiot didn't even bother to relocate. He was, of course, celebrating with his toadies. That didn't last long after I arrived."

"Aren't you worried the Vokkans will take his death as a sign that the Below hasn't been subdued?" Nimhea leaned back in her chair and folded her arms across her chest. Like Suli, she wasn't sure what to make of the Low King's nonchalant manner.

"I was a bit surprised they didn't kill Fergin themselves after he'd served his purpose," Lucket told her. "Gods know he wouldn't have been of much use beyond identifying our sanctuaries. Fergin was always an idiot, and it always amazed me that he managed to climb his way onto a throne—if he hadn't been so adept with poisons, he or never would have gotten there. Kelden has effectively been a nonoperative sector of the Below since he took the throne, and the fact that Fergin wasn't privy to the most valuable information we hold limits the extent to which we've been undermined."

He sighed, giving his head a little shake. "I don't believe his death will alarm the Vokkans. They don't believe the Below is gone, but they are convinced we've been sufficiently broken. They are wrong. We are hurt, badly, but we're not out of this war."

He paused, savoring a sip of wine, then said, "They will suffer for their miscalculation."

"I'm sure," Suli said quietly. The solemnity of her gaze conveyed just how deeply she believed the Vokkans would regret having crossed the Low Kings.

"On that note, I bring you a proposal from my three remaining counterparts." Lucket paused, glancing around the room. "Do you happen to have any bread and cheese? And perhaps some dried fruit? I convey ideas better when I'm not peckish."

Without waiting for an answer, Lucket pushed back his chair and stood. "You know, I think I spotted some in the larder on my way to this room. Don't trouble yourself, I'll just fetch it."

"On your way to this room?" Suli's eyebrows went up. "Did you arrive so early to our meeting?"

"Early enough that I could enjoy a meander . . ." Lucket replied smoothly.

"And assess our operations?" Suli finished with a wry smile.

She and Nimhea exchanged a look. While the Low King was an ally, the Below served its own interests. Lucket could be trusted . . . but only to a point.

With a grin that told them he knew exactly what they were thinking, he shrugged. "If you'll excuse me for a moment."

Once he'd gone, Nimhea let her laughter gush out.

"I know," Suli said with a long-suffering sigh. "He is who he is."

Nodding, Nimhea said, "I suspect he uses his quirks to belie how shrewd a mind he has."

"I agree."

Lucket returned quickly, bearing a small wheel of cheese, a loaf of dense black bread, and two more wineglasses. He sat and began slicing the bread.

"Now I must insist you join me." He gave a brief, dry chuckle. "I know as a rebellion, you're expected to be downtrodden and struggling, but this is the sole surviving bottle of southern Solan red from the once-renowned, sadly destroyed Nav-Horsa vineyard. Those Vokkan brutes smashed through my wine cellar like stampeding cattle. If they'd had any sense, they'd have taken the bottles for themselves. I spent years building up that collection. It was priceless."

He filled the two additional glasses and set them in front of Nimhea and Suli. "To savor this wine, to truly appreciate how rare, how precious and singular it is, it cannot be mine alone."

Nimhea began to sense that while Lucket was speaking about wine, his heart was broken by another loss. Several losses. He had been betrayed by Fergin. The raids on the Below had left the underworld kingdom ripped apart and scattered.

"Then you shall not enjoy it alone," Nimhea said, picking up her glass.

Suli lifted her glass as well. "Indeed."

"To what has been lost." Lucket brought the edge of his glass to meet theirs and intoned, "It will be ours again."

Nimhea's heart pinched and her throat tightened. She felt the burn of tears in her eyes. The echoes of so many emotions, and history—recent and years past—became a palpable weight in the room.

Lucket met her gaze and held it. She saw the storm in his eyes, roiling beneath his easy facade, and something passed between them. Understanding and, more than that, a ferocious resolve akin to a blood oath.

What had been lost?

A kingdom, yes. That was what they all fought for.

Two kingdoms, in truth.

But closer, more pressing, more painful: For Nimhea, a brother. For Lucket, a son.

She took a sip of the wine. The Low King hadn't exaggerated; it was extraordinarily good.

Teth, Nimhea hoped, prayed, could be redeemed. But Eamon? It was difficult to believe he wasn't lost to her forever. As if reading her thoughts, Lucket said, "I would speak to you about your brother, Your Highness."

Suddenly finding it difficult to breathe, Nimhea nodded for him to continue. She put her wineglass down, worried she'd spill it because her hands were threatening to shake.

"My asset infiltrated Five Rivers to assess the situation," he told her. "While they were not entirely certain of the terms by which Eamon has secured his . . . safety . . . in the captivity of ArchWizard Zenar, they do not believe your brother to be in league with the enemy. At least not any longer."

Nimhea barely kept herself from gasping at Lucket's words. If he was telling the truth, not only was Eamon alive, but he might not be totally lost to her. She didn't know if that was enough to merit forgiveness, but it was far better than learning of continued betrayals.

"They believe Eamon could be cultivated into an asset," Lucket finished.

Heart thundering, Nimhea waited for the Low King to say something more to qualify his remark and dash her hopes, but he simply watched her. She thought she spotted a smile ghosting over his lips.

The ache in her chest was so sudden and deep she pressed her hand to her ribs. Her brother. Her twin. The person she'd loved and trusted above all others until . . .

If he could be restored to her, if he could be redeemed, the hollowness in her heart might be filled again. And if Eamon was truly an ally within enemy territory, then he might also be able to help Teth. No doubt Lucket weighed that possibility as well.

Suli set her wine aside, a stern expression overtaking her features. "Is that wise?"

Nimhea stopped herself from glaring at the other woman. She knew Suli's question was more than reasonable, but it was difficult to restrain her emotions. Resentment and outrage flared that anyone might stand in the way of Nimhea and Eamon's reunion.

"Wisdom rarely dictates the actions of the Below," Lucket replied easily, making Suli's frown deepen. "We prefer to rely on opportunity and instinct. Eamon is ideally situated to help us. He is remorseful, desiring redemption. Who are we to deny that when it serves our purpose?"

Suli opened her mouth to reply, then closed it. She looked at Nimhea.

"Your Highness, you know your brother better than anyone else, yet his betrayal still came as a shock. Do you believe we should take the risk of trusting him once more?"

Nimhea frowned, biting back a knee-jerk reply. She took several moments to consider the question. Lucket watched her closely, his eyes alight with interest.

"It would help if I understood what made him betray us in the first place," she said. "No matter how hard I've thought about it, I can't imagine why he would ally himself with the Vokkans."

Lucket sipped at his wine, then said, "I can offer some insight." His gaze slid to Suli. "Though you won't like it."

Suli raised her eyebrows.

"Eamon didn't believe the Resistance would succeed in defeating the Vokkans," Lucket explained. "And he was desperate to save you from death when the rebellion was eventually quashed."

"He bargained to protect Nimhea?" Suli asked.

"Yes." Lucket plucked a bit of lint from his velvet coat. "Zenar assured Eamon that the princess would be installed as a puppet monarch. He thought that a better outcome than forfeiting her life for a hopeless cause."

Suli scoffed and took a large gulp of wine. Nimhea hated that her heart was pounding as she tried to sort through the emotions that assailed her. She resented Eamon's misguided choices, but her heart ached that he'd been so determined to protect her.

"Why has Prince Eamon abandoned his original plan?" Suli asked tersely. "Has he suddenly decided we can defeat the Vokkans?"

Lucket smiled wryly. "That doesn't seem to be the case."

Suli rolled her eyes. "What then?"

"He has reassessed his opinion of Vokkan rule in general and ArchWizard Zenar in particular," Lucket said. He paused, his smile vanishing. "He hadn't grasped how truly evil Zenar is before . . . and that brings me to another issue that concerns us all."

"Another issue?" Nimhea leaned forward.

"For some time, the Low Kings have been investigating the regular disappearances of children throughout Saetlund," he told them. "Most of the children were taken from impoverished families, those who had no recourse with local authorities. They came to us for help, but we'd been unable to discover why the children were being taken or what happened to them. We didn't suspect a repetition of the Embrace because the empire makes that practice very public to enforce its authority."

Grim lines appeared on either side of Lucket's mouth. He drained his wineglass before continuing.

"Prince Eamon found them."

Suli drew a sharp breath. "But he's . . ."

"A prisoner in the Temple of Vokk," Lucket finished for her. "So are the missing children. Alive, but in captivity. Zenar is behind the disappearances. We don't know why he's taking them, but we know where they are."

"Nava's mercy," Nimhea whispered as dread curled in her belly.

"The remaining Low Kings will continue to support the Resistance," Lucket said. "But it is a personal priority of mine to rescue these children. Prince Eamon will be useful. He's in a position to discover what

Zenar is up to. The information he provides will allow us to strategize and execute a recovery operation."

"I won't argue against that," Suli told him. "Though I don't know what kind of assistance we can offer."

"I don't expect assistance," Lucket replied rather sharply. "Just don't get in the way."

Suli straightened in her chair, bristling at his tone.

Nimhea studied the tension in Lucket's face. The Low King was on edge. Nimhea suspected the rawness of his response was rooted in something more than the fact that Zenar was preying on innocents.

"Has there been any word about Teth?" she asked softly.

Lucket fixed a quelling gaze on her, but she didn't flinch. Suli shot a surprised look at Nimhea.

After holding her stare for several breaths, Lucket said, "Not yet."

"There will be," Nimhea said, her voice steady. "He's too valuable a prisoner for Zenar to treat him recklessly. And that means that like Eamon, Teth will be in a position to help the children."

Lucket averted his eyes, but not before Nimhea saw the flash of pain in them. "I know."

Suli cleared her throat. "Lucket, you know of our mole, the one called the Dove."

"Yes," Lucket replied. "Only a few of my most trusted associates know of their existence, and only myself and the asset I have in Five Rivers are aware of the Dove's identity."

Nodding, Suli said, "Then you also know the Dove may have substantial influence over what happens to Teth. Do you think they might be able to work together for our common purpose?"

Lucket stroked his chin. "Yes. I like it. My agent can act as a go-between."

"Good." Suli laced her fingers together and rested her hands on the table. "Now, returning to the Below's commitment to assisting the Resistance. Do you still have the resources to participate in the attack after the raids?"

"We do," Lucket replied. "When you're ready, we'll hit the Vokkans in ways they won't expect."

"How so?" Nimhea asked. As much as she'd come to appreciate the support the Below had offered and the ways Lucket had assisted them during her journey with Ara, she had a hard time envisioning how a collective of criminals could make a serious impact when it came to actual warfare.

"One of the reasons the Vokkans were eager to attack the Below is that they resented how much control we had over trade across Saetlund," Lucket said. He sent a smile at Nimhea as if he detected her skepticism. "And particularly military supply lines."

Suli nodded.

"What they've failed to consider is that while they have—temporarily, I assure you—wrested this power from us, we still understand the operations of those lines much better than they do."

He paused to cut another slice from a wheel of cheese, the pungent odor filling the air again. "And how aware we are of the vulnerabilities of those lines."

Nimhea blinked in surprise. "You can cut the supply lines?"

"Yes," Lucket replied smoothly. "And we have other ways to undermine the Vokkan army."

"Such as?" Suli asked.

One corner of Lucket's mouth turned up. "Most see the Below as a muster of thieves, assassins, purveyors of illicit goods, and the like, but what they don't understand is that we are the ones who hear the cries of the fallen, of society's castoffs. We help those whom no one else will. The shunned. The forgotten. Where the rest of the world would let them fade to naught, the Below helps them rise again."

"And because they were forgotten by the world," Nimhea murmured, "they do not forget the Below."

"No." Lucket turned his wineglass in his hand. "They do not forget. And when we ask for their assistance against the Vokkans, they will give it without hesitation."

As Nimhea contemplated what the Low King described, a newfound and deep respect for Lucket settled within her. She'd underestimated him and the Below—and was chagrined to admit she'd once done the same thing to Teth. She promised herself she would not make that mistake again.

"A great error made by so many to allow those who serve to become invisible, to consider them passive participants rather than creatures with will and agency. Cooks. Cupbearers. Maids. Tailors. Stable hands. Farriers. Each person a thread without whom the basic pattern of each day could not be woven. We will pull those threads, and the Vokkan armies will unravel."

He spoke with such cold confidence that Nimhea shivered.

"If what you say can be done, we'll be deeply indebted to you," Suli said, and Nimhea caught a hint of awe in her voice.

"Yes." Lucket examined his fingernails, buffing them on his shirt. "You will. And it would serve you to remember the Low Kings always collect on their debts."

He picked up the bottle of southern Solan red. "Now, who'd like more wine?"

4

 eth.

Eamon's breath whooshed out of his lungs. Beneath the bruises and swollen flesh, there was no mistaking the thief. His first encounter with Teth in the woods of Fjeri felt as distant as a dream. But now Teth was here, a captive of the Vokkans. He'd been beaten badly, but he was alive.

But for how long? Eamon swallowed a sudden hard lump in his throat.

Where are the others? he wanted to blurt.

If Teth was here, what had happened to Nimhea and Ara? Had they been taken captive, too? Did Zenar have them bound and beaten, waiting in the wings to be revealed?

Instead, Eamon simply said, "Teth."

What other greeting could he offer?

Looking at the young man he'd once considered a friend, Eamon detected subtle changes in the thief. Teth seemed older, but that wasn't quite it. There was a seriousness in his expression, a resolve that hadn't been present before. And there was something else, something . . . more that Eamon couldn't name.

Teth's good eye caught Eamon's gaze, then flicked away just as quickly. Judgment and dismissal.

Heat crawled up Eamon's neck as he realized how he must appear to Teth. Eamon was free, unchained and unharmed. In this scene he played Zenar's collaborator, with no evidence present to suggest he'd ever been anything but.

Though he felt sick about it, Eamon knew he must keep himself in Zenar's favor. He had no way to fight the Vokkans except by insinuating himself into the wizards' ranks and finding ways to undermine whatever Zenar's endgame was.

Teth presented both opportunity and danger. The thief offered the means for Eamon to further align himself with Zenar. But it would be hard, if not impossible, to make Teth see him as an ally again.

Zenar beckoned to Eamon, signaling he should stand alongside the ArchWizard. He couldn't bring himself to look at Teth as he walked to Zenar.

Eamon kept himself from shuddering when Zenar gave his shoulder a squeeze. "Do you have nothing else to say to your friend, Prince Eamon?"

Forcing himself to face Teth, Eamon took his time before replying. "Where did you find him?"

Zenar's pause was long enough to convey he'd noticed Eamon had not directly answered his question.

"He was discovered in the Great Market while in the company of the Loresmith and your sister, Princess Nimhea." Zenar gave a long sigh. "I'm sorry to say the girls eluded capture. But this one fell right into our hands."

Eamon had to hold back a gasp of relief.

Teth gave Zenar a glare of pure hate, which was impressive given one of his eyes was swollen shut.

"So," the ArchWizard murmured in a silky voice. "Who is he?"

"I already told you," Teth spat. "I was hired to guide the girl and her friends through Saetlund. Nothing more."

Zenar laughed. "I do admit, you are rather unremarkable, but I believe Prince Eamon might offer further insights."

Teth was smart, Eamon thought, to admit some truths while keeping others concealed. Now he had to make that same choice. But how could he know what to say?

"And one can hardly miss the way you are gutting the prince with your eyes, Teth," Zenar continued. "Would a mercenary bear so much animosity toward a relative stranger?"

Teth didn't miss a beat, nor did he stop glaring at Eamon. "He stole from me."

"Ah, yes." Zenar clucked his tongue. "I suppose it would follow that if Prince Eamon took something of yours, you'd not be very fond of him. Though perhaps you'd find a little joy in knowing you may have the opportunity to collect what's owed you."

A threat. And hardly a veiled one.

Eamon had stolen from Teth—or rather from their group when he'd abandoned them. He'd taken one of Ofrit's scrolls, and he'd broken their trust.

What did Zenar expect to happen here?

Teth pulled his gaze from Eamon. "He's not worth it."

Those words of disgust were worse than his anger.

"Teth tells me that the Loresmith will journey next to the University of Zyre," Zenar said to Eamon. "Do you believe this is true? If so, why would she go there?"

Eamon frowned. He was surprised at Teth's cleverness.

"It's plausible," Eamon told the wizard. "She only has one of Ofrit's scrolls and no map."

Teth's face briefly lit up with interest at the mention of a map.

"Without my assistance," Eamon continued, "she may need to consult the archives at one or both of the universities to find the remaining hidden sites."

He could feel Teth's frown. No doubt he was interpreting Eamon's behavior as complete collusion with Zenar.

Zenar turned a broad smile—a horrifying spread of lips and teeth—on Teth.

"So we shall search for the Loresmith in Daefrit." Zenar drummed his fingertips on his cheek. "But we shall also send troops to intercept her at the Well of the Twins and Senn's Fury."

Eamon thought he saw the slightest twitch in Teth's jaw, but otherwise the thief gave nothing away.

"I'm afraid there is another matter of concern," Zenar said, signaling to the wizard hovering near the ArchWizard's desk. "If you would, Elder Tich."

Elder Tich collected two objects from the desk and carried them over—a bow and a quiver holding five arrows.

"This weapon was in your possession when you were captured."

Teth shrugged, looking almost bored. "Roads are dangerous. Plus, a bow's more useful for hunting than a sword. I spend more time fending for myself in the wilderness than I do in towns."

Zenar's hideous smile vanished. "I've enjoyed your performance, boy. But it ends now. This weapon is too fine for a mercenary. Not to mention that my wizards tell me it's carved of no wood they can identify."

Eamon's gaze moved from the bow to Teth. His eyes widened and his pulse sped up.

It couldn't be. Could it?

The change in the thief was very subtle. Teth still wore a lazy expression, but something new simmered beneath the mask of disdain.

Though Eamon found it hard to accept what was right in front of him, he couldn't deny the truth: Teth was a Loreknight.

Though he'd already been stiff-backed, Teth straightened even further and leveled a hard gaze on Zenar.

"Well then, wizard." Teth smiled like a cat. "Let's play for keeps."

Zenar recoiled slightly, but in the next moment he looked pleased. "Much better. I do so hate to waste time. Now tell me: Where did you get this weapon? Did you find it in one of the holy sites?"

"It was a gift," Teth replied.

Zenar scowled, but Eamon knew Teth was telling the truth. He had been given the bow and quiver by the Loresmith. She'd crafted the weapon at the Loresmith Forge.

Zenar glided past Teth, stopping to gaze at the bow. The ArchWizard stretched out his hand and let his fingertips hover over the bow's surface. A viscous black substance seeped from beneath his cuticles, covering his fingernails, then spreading to coat his entire hand like a glove. It moved as it clung to Zenar's skin. Eamon realized it was the same crawling slime that covered the temple walls.

Teth drew a hissing breath as streams of the dark sludge stretched from Zenar's fingertips, wriggling like worms toward the bow.

When the slime made contact with Teth's weapon, Eamon felt a surge of power. The hairs on his arms stood up.

With a sharp cry, Zenar snatched his hand back, the slime swiftly retracting into his skin. He shook his fingers as if he'd been burned.

"Impossible," he snarled, glaring at the bow.

"I don't think it likes you," Teth commented.

Zenar's lips curled back in a sneer. "Whatever petty magics your gods toy with are nothing in comparison to that of the Devourer. I relish the day when you will be on your knees before almighty Vokk. I shall drink your screams and savor them like the finest wine."

"You really enjoy the sound of your own voice, don't you?" Teth replied in a bored tone.

"Such insolence." Zenar's slow smile didn't seem to have an effect on Teth, but it made Eamon's skin crawl. "When Vokk arrives on these shores and you look upon his face, you will do naught but cower."

"Looking forward to it," Teth said, then glanced at the guards standing on either side of him. "Could you ask one of these guys to scratch the bridge of my nose? I've got this crazy itch."

Eamon's eyes widened.

Did the thief want to die? Because he seemed completely unafraid of provoking Zenar. Perhaps it was a shield against Teth's true feelings. Eamon wished he could draw on such a well of resilience. He only felt guilt tinged with fear, both the fear of suffering at Zenar's will and fear that he would never be able to make amends for his betrayal.

He had little control over the former. He had to attempt the latter—even if he failed. Teth's arrival might offer a way to some redemption. He didn't know what he could do for the thief aside from trying to keep him alive. But for now, that's what he would do.

With a long, disdainful look at Teth, Zenar waved his hand to the guards. "The weapon has power, but this boy is refuse."

Eamon cast a sidelong glance at Zenar, surprised the ArchWizard hadn't noticed the subtle waves of power that rolled off Teth.

"He's older than my usual fare, but he'll do," Zenar said in a careless tone. "Throw him in with the children. He'll be part of the next cull."

"Yes, my lord," one of the guards replied.

In the same moment, Teth said quietly, as if to himself, "Children."

Zenar was ready to cull Teth, dispose of him like garbage. Perhaps he was simply pretending not to see the magic, feigning ignorance to gain advantage over his prisoner. But quickly Eamon realized that the ArchWizard truly didn't or couldn't observe the change in Teth. He tucked that thought away to examine at a later time. The fact that the magic of Saetlund's gods was seemingly invisible to the most powerful wizard in the Vokkan Empire mattered. He didn't understand why yet, but he knew it was important.

He also knew that he was the only person who could save Teth's life. Eamon wouldn't let his former friend be slaughtered when it could be stopped.

"Wait." Eamon stepped forward. "You'd be throwing away a priceless opportunity. He wasn't simply guiding the Loresmith. He's a Loreknight. That means he's the only one who can call upon the magic of his weapon. It was crafted for him and only him."

Teth's jaw tightened. The thief had to consider this revelation a further betrayal.

Frowning, Zenar looked Teth over, glanced at Eamon, and then gazed at Teth again. "Why do you believe this?"

Eamon had to choose his words carefully. If he insulted the ArchWizard's ability to discern Teth's gift, he could be in as much danger as the thief.

"If you look closely," Eamon said, "there are signs of magic. They're very subtle; I almost missed them."

Zenar caught Eamon in a sharp gaze.

"I don't believe I would have noticed the change in him," Eamon continued quickly, "if I had not met him before now. It's not only that, it's the weapon. As you said, it's not made of a material you recognize, but I've seen it before. Ironbranch, the Loresmith's stave, is crafted of the same."

The ArchWizard pursed his lips. He nodded slowly then turned back to Teth.

"Of course. Yes, I see it now. So very subtle," Zenar said.

Zenar was lying. For whatever reason, he was unable to detect the magic that was obvious to Eamon.

A slight narrowing of Teth's eyes told Eamon that the thief could see that, too.

With a scoff, Teth said, "Do I look like a knight to you? How do you know I didn't steal that bow, knowing it was magical and likely worth a fortune?"

"You said it was a gift," Zenar reminded him.

"I did," Teth replied. "I often think of stealing as giving gifts to myself."

The ArchWizard scowled at him before gesturing to one of the guards.

"Draw your sword and keep it at his back. If he attempts to attack or escape, run him through."

To another guard, Zenar said, "Unshackle the prisoner."

The first guard's sword hissed out of its scabbard, its point leveled at the middle of Teth's back.

"Give him the weapon, Elder Tich," Zenar said, then to Teth, "You will demonstrate its power."

"You mean I get to shoot you?" Teth grinned. "I can't wait."

"I'm afraid I can't indulge you on that point," Zenar replied. "Perhaps I will volunteer Prince Eamon for your target?"

Teth's face went blank, unreadable.

Zenar scrutinized him for several breaths before saying, "No. I think for now that chair will do."

He pointed to a leather upholstered chair near the hearth.

"I've always wanted to kill a chair," Teth said wistfully as he took the bow from Elder Tich and slung the quiver over his shoulder.

"I grow tired of your chatter, boy," Zenar snarled.

"I'm not exactly enjoying your company either." Teth pulled an arrow from the quiver and notched it, sighed, and then drew the bow.

The arrow flew across the room and hit not the chair but the portrait of Emperor Fauld that hung above the hearth, right at the center of the emperor's forehead.

"Sorry," Teth said. "I'm not a very good shot."

If Eamon weren't so terrified for Teth, he might have laughed. The thief might have been named Loreknight by the gods, but it was obvious that in the essential ways, Teth remained himself.

Teth could be courting his own death. Perhaps he'd prefer to give up his life rather than give up Ara's secrets. The thought made Eamon sick again at the knowledge of his own treachery.

If Zenar was angered at the insult to his father, he didn't show it. He simply frowned at the arrow that stuck out of the painting.

"Again," he said.

Teth shrugged and loosed another arrow. This one lodged in the painted emperor's heart.

Still frowning, Zenar crossed the room and stared up at the arrows. "I see no magic here. I believe you're wrong about your thief, Prince Eamon. He's no Loreknight."

Eamon couldn't blame the ArchWizard for making the accusation. From where he stood, he didn't see anything magical about Teth's bow and arrows either. He didn't understand.

The guard whose sword was leveled at Teth's back cleared his throat before speaking. "ArchWizard."

Zenar whirled around, leveling a hard stare at the guard. Eamon noticed the other guards in the room exchange alarmed glances. Perhaps they were forbidden from addressing the ArchWizard directly.

"Begging your pardon," the guard continued. "But I've noticed something strange."

Zenar walked slowly toward Teth and the guard, giving the impression of a cat stalking a bird. "And what is that?"

"Well, sir." The guard had to pause and swallow. "It's just that, this man shot two arrows."

"I'm aware of that."

"Of course, sir, of course," the guard said. "But there are still five arrows in his quiver."

"So?" Zenar practically snarled at the man.

"There were only five arrows to begin with." The guard was visibly trembling now.

Zenar drew close and looked at the guard sharply. The man actually took a step back.

"Does he speak true?" Zenar turned to ask Teth. "Were there only five arrows?"

Teth smiled. "I don't know this man, so I can't say whether he's honest or not."

"It's the truth, ArchWizard," the guard said. "I swear it."

Elder Tich spoke up. "I can confirm there were only five arrows, my lord."

"How interesting," Zenar murmured.

What happened next was so fast, Eamon could barely track it. Teth pivoted around, notching another arrow as he turned. Eamon heard the twang of the bowstring as Teth released the arrow.

Zenar drew a sharp breath, lifted his hands, and spoke a single word in a language Eamon didn't recognize. The arrow—just an inch from the ArchWizard's heart—slammed into an invisible shield and clattered to the floor.

"Senn's teeth," Teth growled, and reached for another arrow.

The once distracted guard gave a shout and drove his sword at Teth's back.

Eamon didn't remember beginning to move, but in the next moment his body slammed into the guard's side, knocking him off-balance. Eamon and the guard fell to the ground as the sword flew out of the guard's hand. The guard swore and shoved Eamon aside, taking a moment to kick him in the ribs, leaving Eamon to clutch his chest and wheeze as he struggled for breath.

The guard retrieved his sword while Eamon pushed himself to his feet.

"Sorry," Eamon pretended to splutter. "So sorry. I tried to run but tripped over my own feet."

The guard simply offered him a look of disgust.

The two other guards had restrained Teth. The Loreknight's bow and quiver were back in Elder Tich's possession.

Zenar wore a cold smile as he gazed at Teth. "Almost, Loreknight. Almost."

"Gods take you," Teth spat.

"Your gods will not save you." Zenar reached out to grasp the pendant resting against Teth's chest. "And their petty symbols have no power here."

With a jerk of his arm, Zenar snapped the leather cord around Teth's neck and threw the pendant aside. "You're mine now, and you will rue the day you tried to kill me."

Eamon's eyes followed the path of the pendant; he took note of where it landed.

Whirling on Eamon, the ArchWizard hissed, "Your fear means nothing. Your death would mean little. Do not try to leave my presence without my permission again."

Zenar shook his head and turned his attention to the guard Eamon had knocked down. "Sloppy."

The guard paled, and his sword fell from his hand. "Please."

"What shall we do with you?" Zenar rubbed his chin. "There are so many possibilities."

The guard shook his head, then suddenly drew a dagger from his belt and shoved the blade into his own throat. He dropped to his knees, blood bubbling from his mouth, then slumped onto the floor. Eamon gagged, and even Teth gasped.

"Pity," Zenar said. "I was looking forward to some entertainment."

Facing Teth once more, the ArchWizard flicked a dismissive hand. "I require time to decide what I shall do with this one. Take him to his cell."

The guards nodded and escorted Teth from the room. Eamon watched them leave, his mind reeling. What else could he do to keep Teth from harm?

"Study these." Zenar was speaking to Elder Tich and gesturing to the bow and quiver. "I want the power that resides in them. Find a way to draw it out."

Elder Tich bowed deeply.

"And you." Zenar looked at Eamon. "Why did you stop the guard? Your thief tried to kill me."

"I know." Eamon hurried to find an answer that would earn the ArchWizard's approval. "But he wanted to die."

"Explain."

"As you've told Elder Tich, you want the power of the weapon. But that power, perhaps to a greater degree, also resides in Teth. He doesn't want you to take that power, and he knows you'll find a way to do it. Better for him to die than let you have it."

Zenar tilted his head.

"Interesting," he said after several moments. "You may return to your cell."

Zenar signaled a guard to escort him from the room. Eamon dipped in a slight bow to the ArchWizard. He needed to gain as much favor as he could. Zenar appeared pleased by his obeisance.

The guard walked ahead of Eamon toward the door, paying him no mind. Eamon risked a glance over his shoulder and saw Zenar deep in conversation with his wizards. Crouching swiftly, Eamon picked up Teth's pendant and slipped it into his pocket.

s the Vokkan armies pursued the Hawk and his fighters, the rebels retreated into the forests, slipping into the nooks and crevices of the rough Fjerian Highland landscape. For months, the hard features of the hills and forests had kept them out of the Vokkans' grasp. Any attempt at attack would have to be made via the rugged paths that twisted among crags, between boulders, beneath waterfalls, and across raging rivers. Every point of access created a bottleneck where the Vokkans could be picked off by archers or cut down by the axes and swords of waiting warriors at the end of a narrow passage.

It was a strategy that would allow them to avoid defeat indefinitely.

That realization was both good and bad. Imgar's forces proved both elusive and dangerous enough that the Vokkan army no longer wished to hurl its men at a wall of inevitable slaughter. However, the hard truth was that though the Hawk's method of resisting the Vokkans was effective, he still didn't have the numbers to meet imperial soldiers in open battle.

But Fjeri's towns and villages remained undefended, and Imgar could do nothing to stop his homeland from being swallowed up by the empire. Any resistance shown by civilians was crushed mercilessly. Men and women were murdered in their homes, while working their fields and tending their shops.

And the children. The children were taken.

When word of the Embrace reached Imgar, his chest had seized up and he'd fallen to his knees.

Even at the worst moments of the conquest, the Hawk had not despaired. As long as he could fight, he had hope, but the Embrace tore into his soul.

The endless war he could bear. Saetlund had fallen because for years its rulers had served themselves instead of the people. They had allowed the gods to become myths. Histories turned into legends, marvelous but without verity.

The kingdom had been punished for those sins. But children . . . children were innocents, and yet they, too, suffered.

Broken in spirit, Imgar had abandoned his hidden refuge and wandered into the hills. Fear and doubt plagued his mind. What did resisting the Vokkans matter if the thing worth fighting for was lost?

As he struggled with grief and rage, he made his way south and into the forested hills there. Gathering together the scraps of his shredded faith, Imgar pleaded with Wuldr, begging the Hunter for some sign of hope, a reprieve from this scourge of despair.

He leaned against the trunk of an ancient pine and pressed his forehead into the rough bark to distract himself from the yawning pit of sorrow in his chest.

That was when he heard the sound.

A soft cry, then silence.

It came again. More than a whimper, but less than a whine. Raw, bringing to mind a wounded animal.

Imgar pushed himself away from the tree and tracked the sound, treading gently so as not to alert the source of the cries to his presence and frighten it into silence. The sound became louder. So frightened, so pained.

He found the mother first—a warrior woman. Deep slashes across her thighs and belly had ended her, but she'd died with her dagger in her hand, taking her killer with her into the afterlife. The Vokkan soldier lay a few feet away, stabbed in at least five places.

Looking more closely at the woman, Imgar was surprised to discover she wasn't Fjerian. Her impressive height and pale coloring marked her as Koelli, one of those from the northern isles who'd established an outpost on the Ice Coast. There had been Koelli warriors among his fighters who'd remained in Saetlund to fight when the Vokkans invaded, but most had returned to their home islands. He didn't know this woman personally, but she wore the armor of her people—crafted from the scales of awesome sea beasts. He had no doubt she'd been ferocious in battle. An ally. This woman had been one of those who'd stayed to fight, but from whence had she come? Where were her brothers- and sisters-in-arms? Was she the lone survivor of a band of warriors who, like Imgar's, continued to strike at the Vokkans? Saetlund's forces had splintered against the onslaught of Vokkan forces, but he knew there were pockets of resistance like his own scattered throughout the kingdom.

Perhaps she'd been on her way to the highlands, hoping to find sanctuary. Guilt took a moment to claw at Imgar that he, or some of his followers, hadn't reached her before this tragedy.

With a brief prayer that the woman had gone to her ancestors, Imgar continued his hunt for whatever or whomever made the sound that led him to the bodies.

He found his quarry in a hollow beneath a great oak. Imgar was reminded that oaks populated Wuldr's sacred grove in the Fjeri Lowlands. The child wept, curled in on itself. The Koelli warrior had given her life to protect her child.

Imgar wondered how long it had been hiding here, frightened and alone. Hungry and cold. With soothing words and gentle hands, he drew the child from the hollow.

The Hawk had little experience with children and couldn't be sure of the little one's age but guessed that it was old enough to have been weaned. A small blessing.

As Imgar gathered the child to him, it whimpered, then gave a little sigh as it snuggled into the warmth of his arms. A piece of himself he didn't know had been missing suddenly fit into place. The gods had brought him to this place of sorrow to give him new purpose. This innocent laid out his path. For with this discovery came a message: If this child had escaped the Embrace, others might have. And the surviving children could be reared in secret, kept safe.

Saetlund's future was not lost. Hope remained.

5

oar reined in his mount and swung down from the saddle. Turning to face Ara and Lahvja, he pulled down the heavy wool wrapping that shielded his face from the cold and said, "The trail ahead is too steep and narrow for the horses, even if we lead them."

Ara dismounted, patting her horse's shaggy neck. She dragged her own wrap away from her mouth to speak. The frigid air immediately bit into her skin, scratching at her throat when she drew a breath. "We'll have to make camp then and decide how to proceed."

Even as she spoke, prickles of wariness traveled down her spine. They were vulnerable anytime they stopped to seek shelter. But they had no other choice. They needed rest and protection from the elements in these harsh climes. That didn't stop Ara from worrying that at any moment a Vokkan patrol could ambush them or a sudden storm could block their path. Nothing was certain, and danger was all around them.

"I saw a rock shelf and what might be a cave a short distance back," Joar said. "I will scout to see if it would be a suitable place to take shelter."

He handed off his reins to Ara and headed back down the slope with Huntress bounding alongside him.

Ara brought her horse closer to Joar's and surveyed the trail before her. What had already been a challenging climb continued at an even steeper pitch. The path narrowed to a barely discernible game trail, strewn with scree and icy patches. Joar was right. There was no way the horses could continue the journey up the mountain, but she didn't know what that meant for their plans.

At this altitude, even close to midsummer with its nigh-endless days, the air was burning cold. They'd piled layers of clothing on to hide their skin from frostbite. Ara worried for the horses, which didn't have the protection of thick winter coats. So far, the mounts had endured, but rime covered their mouths and noses as each breath they blew out instantly froze in their hair.

Returning to Lahvja, Ara relayed her assessment to the summoner.

"Unsurprising," Lahvja said with a nod. "The Well of the Twins isn't meant to be easily reached." Her expression grew distant, thoughtful. "And some who make the journey do so knowing it will be their last."

Ara frowned at Lahvja's cryptic words. "My grandmother told of travelers who underestimated the demands of the pilgrimage. They paid for their ignorance with their lives."

"Not those," Lahvja replied. "Of course they came, and failed, but they are not whom I speak of. The Twins are the keepers of mystery. What greater mystery is there than death?"

"I don't understand."

Lahvja smiled slightly. "When we reach the Well, I will explain as best I can."

A shout from Joar drew their attention. The hunter waved them down. When they reached him, he led the way to a rock shelf that hung over a wide, shallow cave. It wasn't much in the way of shelter, but it provided ample cover from the wind as well as enough room to house both humans and horses.

Joar relieved the horses of their packs and unsaddled them, then gave each a vigorous rubdown to help warm them. The horses whickered their appreciation, but Joar frowned as he went through the ministrations.

"It isn't safe to leave them here alone," he said. "There are predators that are always seeking prey, and these horses are unfamiliar with the dangers of this landscape."

Ara shuddered at the memory of the ice wyrms. During their trek through the mountains, she'd considered asking what other creatures she'd believed were myths lurked in the snowdrifts, but had decided against it. She was tense enough as it was.

Lahvja nodded. "Our stalwart companions need a protector, and you are best suited to that task, Joar. You and Huntress must remain here to guard our steeds and keep watch for enemies while Ara and I continue to the Well."

Ara went wide-eyed at Lahvja's declaration. Something in Lahvja's expression made Ara suspect Lahvja had been anticipating this turn of events.

Joar seemed likewise taken aback, but he only glowered at Lahvja. "I cannot abandon you. I serve the gods and the Loresmith. My place is at her side."

Ara opened her mouth to thank him, but Lahvja spoke first.

"It is not abandonment, hunter," Lahvja told him. "The survival of our horses is paramount to our success. By keeping them safe, you are protecting the Loresmith and her quest."

Lahvja and Joar stared at each other, unyielding. Ara unhappily realized that she would need to break this stalemate.

"Joar, we know you would never abandon us nor forsake your mission," she said gently. "But neither would Lahvja suggest our separation lightly."

Looking at the summoner, Ara asked, "Do you make this suggestion because you know it is what the Twins require?"

"Indeed." Lahvja nodded. "The pilgrimage to the Well demands the shedding of worldly trappings, of those things we've come to depend on, in order to seek deeper meaning. The more we leave behind, the more likely we will soon find what we seek. We should take nothing beyond what we now wear for basic protection from the elements."

Joar grumbled, kicking at an ice chunk with the toe of his boot. It was the gesture of a sulking child. Ara wanted to laugh, but she didn't blame Joar for not wanting to stay behind.

In this place of spirit and magic, however, Lahvja had the most experience, and because of that, Ara would defer to her judgments. Also, if any hungry beasts showed up wanting to eat the horses, Joar had the best chance of fending them off.

"Joar, we will miss your company and the comfort of knowing your strength and courage are with us," Ara told him. "But in this matter I defer to Lahvja's judgment. She is a servant of the Twins and knows more of this place than either you or me."

Though he looked unhappy, Joar nodded. "If it must be so."

He glanced at the horses, and in his face Ara read a mixture of remorse and relief. He wanted to continue up the trail, she knew, but he would have been equally unhappy to leave the horses unguarded.

"I'll divide the rations," Joar said, crouching to open a pack. "And provide enough to cover you for a few days in case you're caught in rough weather."

Lahvja held up a hand. "No. The supplies stay with you."

Joar stopped digging through the pack and frowned at her.

"The final journey of the pilgrim is the offering of the self," Lahvja explained. "You can bring nothing to the Well but the clothes on your body."

"That is ridiculous," Joar scoffed. "Surely the Twins don't demand you starve yourselves while you seek their holy place."

"We will be provided for," Lahvja replied. "You need not fear for us, but should we fail to heed the requirements of the pilgrimage, we would indeed put ourselves in danger."

Ara chewed her bottom lip. She'd been told pilgrims seeking the Well of the Twins endured hardship and sacrificed much, but she had never learned the specifics of the journey.

"How long will it take us to reach the Well?" Ara asked Lahvja.

"I don't know for certain," the summoner replied. "But I do know that the less we bring with us, the shorter our journey will be."

Joar grunted out an irritated noise. "Strange magics at work. I don't trust it."

"But you follow the gods." Lahvja smiled gently at his words, chiding.

"Indeed," Joar said with a shrug. "But I prefer Wuldr's hunt to Ofrit's riddles and the Twins' mysteries. My god does not ask to play games with my mind."

"It is no game to the Twins," Lahvja said. "It is simply their nature."

Joar shrugged again, then swore under his breath. "Are you permitted a tent to shelter you at night?"

Ara's body gave an involuntary shudder at the thought of spending the night, however short, without protection from the harsh mountain climes.

"If we bring a tent, it will guarantee we spend a night on our way to the Well," Lahvja replied. "If we forgo shelter, I believe the Twins will allow us to reach the Well before darkness falls."

Frowning, Joar looked to Ara for support.

"I can't say I'm happy with the sacrifices you're suggesting, Lahvja," she said. "But you serve the Twins. If our journey will be aided by forsaking food and shelter, that's what we should do."

She threw Joar an apologetic glance. He muttered unintelligible words that were no doubt unpleasant, but he didn't voice further objection.

"If it must be this way, then I will take the horses back to our last campsite. This place serves as temporary shelter, but if you are away for long, it would be best to have the protection of trees and a ready supply of firewood."

His tone was grudging, and Ara could tell he'd had a difficult time coming to that decision.

She rested her hand on his forearm, realizing with slight shock it was so wide she didn't know if she'd be able to encircle it using both hands. She did have small hands, but still. Joar's sheer size continued to astonish her.

"You know better than anyone how to survive here," she told him. "Take the horses and yourself to the best place to wait. We'll find you."

Ara forced a smile, but her heart was heavy. Another separation. Another farewell. She could only hope they wouldn't be parted for long.

6

t least she didn't catch me in bed this time, thought Liran.

Dagger lounged in an armchair near the fireplace in his chamber while Liran stood a few feet away. Her sudden appearance set him on edge, though it wasn't as though he expected her to send word first. That wasn't how she operated.

Liran stood stiffly, his arms crossed, his stance belying the little thrill of relief he felt at seeing her again. It was an odd, unsettling realization, to find himself happy to be in the company of an assassin. And yet, here he was.

"I trust you're well," Liran said gruffly, then chided himself for purposefully adding a rough edge to his voice. For reasons he hadn't yet untangled, he let this woman get under his skin too easily.

That she'd concluded their last meeting with a kiss was definitely part of it, but Liran suspected she'd kissed him only to keep him off-balance.

It had worked.

"Why, Commander." Dagger smiled at him. "Have you been worried about me?"

Liran elected not to return the smile. "Your profession carries considerable risk."

"I wonder if your concern has less to do with my vocation than the recent tragedy that befell my employer and colleagues," she replied.

Biting back a sigh, Liran moved to stand beside her.

"I regret that I wasn't able to offer more of a warning to the Low Kings before the raids," he told her. "My reports say that your losses were devastating."

Her easy facade slipped for a moment, her body giving a little shiver, and Liran found himself reaching for her hand and taking it in his own. The reflexive reaction surprised him, but he didn't fight it. "I'm sorry."

Dagger's fingers curled around his for a moment, and Liran felt his chest tighten. It was the first time he'd held another person's hand since his childhood. Even then, such contact had been fleeting. He felt a wrench of loneliness he hadn't realized he was hiding.

Suddenly uncomfortable, Liran gave her fingers a light squeeze and withdrew his hand.

"You don't need to apologize," Dagger told him. Whatever vulnerability he'd glimpsed a moment before was gone. "Without you, we would have had no warning at all. And your reports are exaggerated; the empire loves to exult in its perceived victories."

Liran raised one eyebrow, not convinced by her bravado. "I have a casualty count and a record of confiscated property, goods, and coin. They are not insignificant. How badly compromised is the Below?"

"We are wounded, but not dead," she told him. "And you know how dangerous a wounded beast can be."

He nodded.

She watched him for a moment before her gaze went flat in a way that made Liran's gut clench. "What have you heard of the new prisoner?" she asked.

Frowning, Liran ran his mind through the recent report Zenar had sent. "He's a companion to the Loresmith, and supposedly a Loreknight."

Dagger nodded. "His name is Teth; he is also the son of Lucket, the Fjerian Low King."

Liran stared at her in shock. Zenar could have chosen to keep that information to himself, but Liran thought it more likely that his brother didn't know his new captive was a prince of Saetlund's underworld. Had he been aware, Zenar would already be looking for ways to exploit that connection.

"Does Prince Eamon know that?" he asked.

Dagger nodded, then waited.

"Zenar does not," Liran said, answering her unspoken question. "Is Eamon intentionally withholding the information, or does he assume my brother already knows?"

"Still unclear." She shrugged. "But I'll find out. If he is keeping it to himself, it's another sign that he could be a useful player in the game to come."

When Liran didn't reply, she said ruefully, "I take it you have yet to approach His Highness about allying our interests."

Liran scrubbed his hand down his face. "There hasn't been an opportunity."

"If I may," Dagger said. "You must create that opportunity. And you should do it soon."

"You don't need to remind me," Liran complained.

"Apparently I do," she countered.

When he scowled, one corner of her mouth curved up.

"I'll see to Prince Eamon," he told her, his irritation fading at the sight of her amusement. "And I'll look after the other royal son's welfare as best I can."

"Keep him alive and in one piece," Dagger said.

"You're not planning to break him out of the temple, then?"

She regarded him in silence for several breaths. Just when he'd decided she wasn't going to answer his question, she said, "I'm investigating several options. But until the Resistance makes their move, Lucket wants to exploit our assets that are already in the capital. Now that Teth is in the temple, he's become one of those assets."

"I see." It was calculating, perhaps cold, Liran thought, but also impressive and intelligent.

"The other assets are myself"—she leaned toward him, resting her chin on her hand—"and, if you do your part, Prince Eamon. And you, of course."

"I prefer to consider myself fighting for the greater good rather than being exploited by someone else," Liran said.

She shrugged. "Semantics."

Liran cut her a sardonic look, and she laughed. "I do so enjoy our talks, Commander."

"Delighted I can entertain you," he muttered, but a smile chased over his lips. "So how do you propose to best exploit these assets?"

"The Resistance is nearing the time when they will openly challenge the empire," Dagger told him. "They have amassed the number required to attack Five Rivers, though they hope to engage the majority of Vokkan forces in open battle rather than lay siege to the city."

"I'm aware of that," Liran said.

She arched an eyebrow at him. "I suspect if you play the role the rebels have cast you in, a siege won't be likely."

He replied with a thin smile.

"Still holding your cards close, Liran?" She laughed quietly.

"I will make my move at the appropriate moment," he said,

unaccountably warming at her use of his given name. "And I am the only one who knows when that time will be."

She held his gaze briefly, then said, "If it amuses you to be obtuse, I'll allow it."

He bared his teeth at her in a dangerous smile. "I don't recall being told by anyone that you're in charge of what I do and do not do."

"I'm not." She smiled sweetly. "But I was hoping for a collaborative effort. After all, I'll be in the city with you."

"You're staying?" His pulse skipped as his mind darted to the question of where she would be staying and how often he would see her.

"For the most part."

Liran moved from his place beside the chair to stand near the hearth, where a low fire burned. He turned away from her, looking into the embers as he wrestled with unwanted impulses. "I'll consider that as you tell me what kind of collaboration you have in mind."

He startled when he felt a light touch on his arm. Dagger stood close. He hadn't heard her leave the chair, much less cross the room.

"Lucket wants us to strike at your brother," she said quietly. Her gaze searched his face, ready to gauge his reaction.

"You think I'll hesitate to do so?" he asked. "I'm already betraying the empire and my father. My course is set."

"Betraying the empire isn't the same as effecting treachery in close quarters," she told him. "People underestimate how difficult it can be."

Liran turned to face her, his voice cold. "Unless you're asking me to murder my brother, which I freely admit I would prefer not to do, I will do what it takes to undermine him. Zenar is evil. We may share blood, but I have no love for him nor loyalty to him."

Averting his gaze at a sudden sharp twinge in his chest, he said quietly, "In the past, I wished it were otherwise, but I've accepted that will never be the case."

She surprised him by reaching up to touch his cheek, the light press of her fingers urging him to look at her. When he did, he found compassion in her eyes.

"Your burden is heavy," she murmured. "And you've had no one to shoulder it with you. Until now."

Her words shook Liran to the core. Even on the darkest of sleepless nights, he hadn't admitted to himself how isolated his existence was. The stark truth of it was almost too much to bear. He turned his face toward her hand, letting his lips touch her fingers briefly before he took hold of her wrist and pushed her away. He released his hold, and she let her hand fall to her side.

"Thank you," he said, conscious of the hoarseness in his voice.

"You shouldn't thank me," Dagger replied easily. "Before this is over, you'll likely rue the day I came into your life."

Grateful for her levity, he smiled. "I expect so."

"With regard to our mission," she said, pivoting to her professional manner. "Lucket believes Prince Eamon is uniquely positioned to offer intelligence on Zenar. Your brother currently considers you an ally, but there are limits to his trust in you."

Liran nodded. "Zenar is only using me because he needs me."

"We need someone who can get close to Zenar in a way you cannot," she said. "Eamon can do that."

"Can he handle that level of subterfuge?" Liran asked.

"He's already managed to withhold more from Zenar than I would have expected."

Liran considered that, then said, "I know Zenar has far more planned than what he's revealed to me. If Eamon could share those plans with us, it could prove invaluable. And I can help him by controlling who's assigned to guard him, have them provide false reports to Zenar about Eamon's state of mind and loyalties."

"The next time I visit, let's discuss whatever secrets he's managed to glean from the ArchWizard, and I'll inform him of the ways you're assisting in these matters," she said. "You see, we're already working together so beautifully."

She stopped his reply by lifting onto her tiptoes and kissing him so softly it was like a whisper. Before he could react to the tender caress, he was alone, once again bewildered by both her kiss and her sudden departure. It took him a moment to realize she *had* whispered something against his lips.

"My name is Maira."

7

eth didn't understand why he hadn't been thrown in a dungeon. Surely the Temple of Vokk had one. Certainly there would be a room more suited to holding a prisoner than the one he currently occupied.

The room was spare, its only furniture a narrow cot against one wall, but it was clean, lacking all the odors usually abundant in a prison. Scents like blood and urine that did as much work to terrorize a captive as the pressing walls of a small space.

In all honesty it was more respectable than any number of places Teth had been forced to shelter during his years as a thief.

He didn't like it at all; not that he longed to suffer, but surprises like this were unwelcome. They made it difficult to anticipate what would come next, and he needed to be ready for whatever ArchWizard Zenar had planned.

He'd also been freed of his bonds. He would have considered the Vokkans complete fools had they not taken his clothing along with his weapons.

Given the dirtied and ragged state of his wardrobe when he arrived in Five Rivers, perhaps its replacement had been intended as another inexplicable kindness. Sadly, the plain linen shirt and black trousers he wore now lacked the spare set of lock-picking tools and folding razor he had sewn into his old clothes.

If he planned to escape, he had to find something to help. A quick scan of the space didn't offer any immediate possibilities, but perhaps closer examination of the cot and its frame would serve him.

Getting out of the cell was the first step. He anticipated fleeing the temple itself would be the most challenging part of his escape, but he knew he could and would do it. That was something Teth had learned early on while thriving in the dark corners, back rooms, and alleys of Saetlund—force of will counted for as much as aptitude.

When escorted to his cell, he'd paid close attention to the layout of the temple and the number of guards. He would have to study their movements, their shift changes, and their habits at any opportunity. One could always count on a few guards to be less than enthusiastic in their duties and prone to laziness, traits Teth was eager to exploit.

Assuming he made it out of the temple, the next stage of his escape should be easy. Five Rivers had several points of access to the Below—safe houses, caches, bought merchants, and allied tavern keepers—all of which offered means to secret himself from Saetlund's capital with fresh supplies and plentiful coin.

Although whether those resources would be available was uncertain. Locations changed. Alliances fell apart, new arrangements brokered.

The sound of footsteps descending the stairs caught Teth's attention. The steps halted outside his door. Keys rattled and one was inserted into the lock. Teth listened carefully to the sounds the lock made as the key turned; they would be helpful in understanding how to later pick it. The door swung open. Teth couldn't decide if he was surprised or not when Eamon stepped inside.

Eamon, conversely, was shocked to see Teth. Teth kept his focus on the guard, not sparing so much as a glance at Eamon. Only when the cell was locked again and the guard had disappeared up the spiral stairs did Teth turn his attention to his new cellmate.

Eamon had so many questions he felt like they would simmer up and boil over out of his mouth, but the look Teth gave him kept him silent.

"What are you doing here?" Teth asked. He stayed where he was, watching as Eamon moved to sit on the narrow cot.

"This is my cell," Eamon told him.

Teth gave a snort of disbelief.

"It is," Eamon said, feeling suddenly deeply tired. As much as he wanted Teth to believe him, he had no idea how to persuade his former friend to trust him.

Teth moved into a crouch. "If you're a prisoner here, why was the ArchWizard so friendly upstairs? He didn't treat you like an enemy, and you didn't act like one." Teth waved a hand toward his bruised face. "And you don't have any of these."

"Zenar isn't interested in breaking my body; he's well aware of the punishing nature of my illness. My frailty," Eamon replied softly. "He needs my mind."

Teth muttered something unintelligible, but Eamon caught the thief's quick scan of his face and form and thought he glimpsed a flash of pity in Teth's narrowed gaze.

"Is everyone okay?" Eamon asked, unable to stop himself. He needed to know. Needed to.

Teth remained silent.

"You're here," Eamon blurted, desperate. "But my sister, the others . . ."

Teth's jaw twitched, then he said, "You've done nothing to suggest you care about their well-being."

Eamon stared at him for a moment, then slumped against the wall behind the cot. "You're right."

They were silent for a few minutes. Teth brooded and scowled, while Eamon despaired.

Teth said at last, "Why are you in a cell?"

Eamon gestured toward the stairs. "What happened in Zenar's office was a test. Everything he does is a test."

"To what end?" Teth asked.

"To see where my loyalties lie," Eamon said. "Or perhaps just to entertain himself. To watch what happens."

"What do you think he expects to happen here?" Teth folded his arms across his knees. "A reconciliation?"

Eamon shook his head. "I'm a traitor. He knows you won't forgive me."

Teth didn't comment on that statement.

"He wants me to convince you to cooperate," Eamon told him. "To make you fear what will happen if you don't."

Pausing, Eamon continued, "Why haven't you asked me where my loyalties lie?"

"Because I have no reason to believe whatever you tell me."

Eamon winced, hating that Teth was right. He didn't know how he could make him believe otherwise.

Teth fingered the leather cord that laced up the deep neckline of his tunic. "You'd be surprised how many mundane things can be used as a garrote."

Eamon couldn't stop his hand from going to his throat. Teth watched the motion with an empty smile.

When he could find his voice, Eamon said, "You don't want to kill me."

"No," Teth replied. "But I'm wondering if I have to."

It was several breaths before Eamon could answer. "I've earned vengeance. I know how wrong I was. More than a fool, I was a coward. I couldn't bear weakness, and in search of power gave myself to the enemy and promises I should have known to be built on evil. I wanted so desperately . . ."

He broke off, seeing Teth's flat stare.

Eamon sighed. "You're right. There is no reason. No excuse. I was wrong. I failed my sister. Myself."

He turned his face away. His eyes burned, but no tears came. His throat was dry, breath raw. There was nothing to plead. No reason to argue. It was right, he thought, that it should be Teth he faced. Someone whom polite society might dismiss, might cast aside as corrupt—but Eamon knew otherwise. Teth saw truth; he ripped through facades in order to survive. There would be no persuading with pretty words or feigned regret. Teth traded in deceit.

Swallowing against the hard, rough lump in his throat, Eamon choked out, "I was so afraid."

Teth looked at him for a long while, then said, "We're all afraid."

"Yes," Eamon replied softly. "But I allowed fear to rule me, and greed to bind me to Zenar."

Teth's eyes narrowed. "What did the ArchWizard offer you?"

Shifting his weight on the cot, Eamon avoided Teth's searching gaze. "He promised that Nimhea would be protected, that she would become queen, ruling as a puppet for the emperor.

"He said . . . he would heal me. Make me whole again."

"And you did not question the emptiness of such a reign?" Teth asked with a wan smile.

Rage spiked through Eamon when Teth would not even acknowledge his long sickness, would dismiss his suffering as if it had never mattered. "Do you know what it is to feel pain with every movement of your body, to know your strength will ebb with the slightest exertion and leave you breathless? Have you felt your limbs shiver and shudder after a leisurely stroll through a garden?"

Teth frowned at him. "I don't—"

"Have you searched every tome and text for the means to relieve your suffering?" Eamon couldn't stop himself. He'd faced so many nights of wracking pain and slogged through days on trembling limbs all while it felt as though nails were being driven into his skull. "Have you honed your mind, desperate to prove your worth?"

"I cannot claim to have searched tomes and texts," Teth said. "But I was an orphan on the streets with nothing . . . I was starving, desperate—"

"Yes," Eamon said. "Desperate. And found by a Low King. Where would you have been without Lucket's intervention?"

Teth drew in a hissing breath, and Eamon's pulse stuttered. He'd intended to be apologetic, ameliorative. Instead he was picking a fight with the friend he'd lost and longed to regain. Yet he couldn't seem to stop himself. His heart was raw. His spirit broken.

"No one helped me. No one searched with me. The focus of our allies was on Nimhea, making her into a weapon, a warrior queen. I could have resented her, but I didn't. She is my sister. My twin. She's all I've ever had, and despite my weakness, she loved me. All I wanted was to help her; my illness made me a burden," Eamon sobbed. "I couldn't bear to see her fail. I'm nothing without her. But how could I serve her when I was so broken?"

"You've done nothing to help Nimhea." Teth was on his feet, stabbing a finger at Eamon. "You undermined everything she's fought for."

"I know!" Eamon shouted. His voice cracked, then faded. "I know."

Teth turned away, his hands fisting. Eamon's heart pounded, another sob welling in his throat.

No one would understand why he'd done what he'd done. And why should they? He wasn't well. His pain remained; it was worse even, exacerbated by the emotional strain of his betrayal. Zenar dangled the promise of magic that could heal him, but had yet to bestow any such gift. Every night continued to be filled with pain, every day greeted with exhaustion.

"Please," he whispered. He didn't know if he was speaking to himself or making one last attempt to sway Teth. "Please believe me. I need to make this right."

Teth turned back, but slowly lowered himself to the floor until he was sitting cross-legged. "How could you possibly make it right? The damage is done. You've allied yourself with Zenar. With the Vokkans."

"I have not," Eamon snapped. He knew he should be more apologetic, but he refused to agree that he was a puppet of the empire when he was not. His mistake was real, but it had limits. His treachery, he hoped, wasn't beyond redemption.

Teth gave a dry laugh of disbelief.

Eamon ignored it. "What I did was wrong, and my choices were foolish, but I only hoped to protect Nimhea and relieve my own suffering. Or try to. That's still all I want. She belongs on the throne, and only the Loresmith, by the will of Saetlund's gods, can bring her the crown. I know that now . . . I should have always known."

He closed his eyes, giving his head a shake. "And Ara—"

"Don't speak her name," Teth snarled. "After what you've done, I don't want to hear you so much as whisper it."

Eamon sat back. He'd expected Teth's anger, but this was something else.

Teth rested his head against the wall and closed his good eye, his throat working as he swallowed hard. His face was tight with pain.

"You're in love with her," Eamon murmured.

Without looking at Eamon, Teth answered. "You're very eager to have me choke the life out of you, Your Highness. It would be faster to snap your neck, but then I'd miss your suffering."

Eamon blanched, but he refused to be silent. "Do as you will. I deserve death."

Teth's eye opened slightly, and he peered at Eamon beneath his lashes. "You do."

With a sigh, Eamon nodded. This time he didn't have words to offer.

Teth pushed off the wall, coming into a crouch.

"Do you want to die?" Teth asked, searching Eamon's face.

Eamon shook his head. "Sometimes I wish I did. It would make it easier to be here. Hope can be cruel."

Teth moved slightly closer. "And what do you hope for, Your Highness?"

Though he felt it was shameful to cry in front of Teth, Eamon didn't try to stop the tears that leaked from his eyes. Nor did he wipe them away as they trailed down his face.

"Tell me." The words Teth spoke were a command, but not a threat.

Eamon's voice cracked when he said, "Forgiveness."

Teth watched him quietly, then returned to his seat against the wall. "After what you did, only the gods can grant that boon."

Nodding, Eamon didn't voice his thoughts: he wanted the gods' forgiveness, but more than anything he wanted his sister's.

He knew he was asking for punishment, but he couldn't stop himself from saying her name. "Nimhea . . ."

Eamon couldn't manage anything further, but Teth seemed to understand, because he fixed his gaze on Eamon and lifted his chin in response.

"You want to know if she'd forgive you."

Eamon nodded and his stomach twisted.

The thief considered the question, then said, "She didn't want you to die."

It wasn't the answer Eamon was looking for, but it was something. "No?"

In some of his nightmares, it was Nimhea who killed him, not Zenar. He preferred the former. He would rather die facing righteous anger than pure sadistic evil.

"The Below sent an assassin," Teth said. "And while the Resistance wanted you dead, Lucket gave orders to assess you first."

Eamon smiled weakly. "She was very polite. I was very surprised she didn't kill me."

"Nimhea was furious that an agent was dispatched at all," Teth continued. "That's all the answer I can give you."

"It's answer enough," Eamon said, the tension in his body easing slightly. "And whether you believe me or not, I will do all I can to help her now."

Teth gave him a long look, then shrugged. "And how do you propose to help her, Your Highness?"

Eamon offered a wan smile. "For one, I plan to save your life."

Teth flinched, though he tried to mask the reflex.

"Beyond that, I'm still working it out," Eamon said. He reached into his pocket and withdrew Teth's pendant, letting it dangle from his fingers.

Teth stared at him for several breaths, gave a shake of his head, stared again. He stretched his hand out and Eamon dropped the pendant into Teth's palm. The thief's gaze focused on Eni's symbol, and he murmured what Eamon thought must be a prayer before tucking the pendant into his boot for safekeeping. Then the thief tipped his head back to rest against the wall. He smiled, and a deep, throaty laugh spilled out of his chest.

It was the most beautiful sound Eamon had ever heard.

8

ahvja's advice had proven wise indeed, Ara thought, when after only a half day's hike, albeit a strenuous one up the steep slope, a tall and wide stone arch came into view. Carved at the center of the arch were a sun and moon. The arch, Ara knew, marked their arrival at the sacred site of the Twins, Ayre and Syre. The site of the tall curving span of stone brought her some relief. Unlike Nava's temple hidden beneath the Great Market, which the Vokkans no doubt considered conquered territory, the mystery and magic of the Twins' holy site might give them pause. Even keep them at bay. It was a thin strand of hope, but Ara nonetheless grasped it.

The moment they passed through the arch the temperature changed. No longer frigid nor thin, the air became soft and warm enough that Ara was soon shedding her heavy wool cloak and coat. As they walked on, she peeled off her sweater as well. Lahvja likewise emerged from a cocoon of winter clothing.

And then there were trees. *Trees.* They'd ventured beyond the tree line of the mountain heights hours ago, yet here was a forest. Admittedly it was a forest unlike any Ara had ever seen.

The strange wood was composed of crystalline trees, their trunks and branches glistening like clear quartz. Half the trees were tipped with leaves of gold, the other half leaves of black. A gentle wind stirred the woods, and the air was filled with the silvery rippling of chimes.

"The Forest of the Equinox," Lahvja murmured. "A place of balance, stillness."

"In the stories, the Well lies at the center of this wood." Ara looked to Lahvja for confirmation, and the summoner nodded.

Though she'd completed three of the Loresmith trials, each new wonder astounded Ara. When Nimhea and Eamon kidnapped her from Imgar's smithy, she'd been full of doubts and resentment about her supposed fate. Now each day brought her into the realms of the gods, in the footsteps of legends.

As they moved toward the center of the wood, the trees became taller, the forest denser. Here and there Ara spotted fruit on the trees' branches. The black-leafed trees bore golden fruit in the shape of large eggs; the gold-leafed trees bore black fruit of the same shape.

The farther they walked and the larger the trees, the more fruit appeared on the branches.

"What happens at the Well is a secret held fast by those who make the pilgrimage here," Lahvja said.

Nodding, Ara replied, "My grandmother said those who received the Twins' blessing at this site would lose it should they reveal what transpired at the end of their pilgrimage, so no one tells the tale. I never knew whether to believe that story."

With a rueful smile she added, "For a time I thought pilgrims invented the secrecy just so they could be smug about it."

The Bone Forest and its butcher crows had taught her otherwise. Only those true of faith could visit the hidden holy sites of the gods and survive. Braggarts and fortune hunters found their doom rather than glory.

With the butcher crows in mind, Ara glanced around the woods, wondering what hidden guardians might be watching them. The thought made the hairs on her arms stand to attention. As she looked around, her eyes were drawn to the luscious fruits hanging from the tree branches. Her stomach rumbled, but she frowned.

"I don't suppose that fruit can be eaten?" Ara asked Lahvja.

"They can," Lahvja replied. "But they should not be consumed without understanding the gift and the cost each offers."

Walking to one of the trees, a black-leafed tree with golden fruit, Lahvja said, "This tree offers the answer to life's greatest question: What lies beyond the veil?"

Ara came to the summoner's side, gazing at the fruit. Its skin gleamed, and she thought she'd never seen anything so exquisite, so beautiful, but Lahvja's words gave her pause.

"Beyond the veil," Ara murmured. "But to know such a thing . . . would that not mean death?"

Lahvja nodded. "That is the cost. Look closely at the ground."

Ara took several steps back from the alluring fruit and peered at the base of the tree. Its tangled roots were covered in thick moss of vibrant green. Ara drew a sharp breath as she comprehended that she wasn't looking at roots, but piles of bones.

"But who would willingly eat this fruit if it's deadly?" She couldn't take her eyes off the gruesome tangle surrounding the tree.

"It is not something I can claim to fully understand," Lahvja said quietly. "But I have known some among the Wanderen who left the caravan to make this pilgrimage, knowing they would not return."

"Why?" Ara asked, forcing her gaze back to the summoner.

"One woman had three children stolen during the Embrace and then lost her husband to a ravaging disease." Lahvja reached up, her fingers following the shape of the fruit without touching it. "A man suffered an injury that left him in unbearable pain and chose to come here. And others simply reached very old age and wanted to cross from this world into the next on their own terms."

Ara rubbed her arms, uneasy. She could understand the desire to end grief or pain, but she didn't know that she thought such decisions should be left to humans. Life and death belonged to powers beyond the mortal realm. Not only that, but she wondered about those left behind when pilgrims made this final journey; did their sorrow not matter?

"Is it right that the Twins offer an answer like this to those who seek it?" Ara murmured.

Lahvja shook her head. "I cannot say that it is right or wrong; it simply is."

Ara turned, her gaze finding a golden-leafed tree with black fruit. She walked toward it to examine the fruit more closely. These fruits were the same shape as their golden counterparts, but where the glimmering gilt of the former had been tempting, the obsidian skin of this fruit was beautiful but seemed somehow ominous.

"What happens to the person who eats this fruit?" Ara asked.

Lahvja joined her beside the tree. A gentle sigh of a breeze stirred the branches, filling the air with more tinkling chimes.

"This is the fruit of fate," Lahvja said. "To eat it is to know one's future."

Ara swallowed against the sudden tightening of her throat. While she'd been uncomfortable with the idea that anyone would choose to seek their own death, the thought of seeing her fate unfold filled her with temptation.

She found herself reaching for the dark fruit without thinking, then bit her lip and snatched her hand back.

"Can a person's future be changed if they don't like what they see?" she asked Lahvja.

What a boon it would be to know how the next days and weeks would play out, to foresee mistakes and correct them, to go forward with confidence in the successes foretold. If she'd known Vokkan soldiers would raid Nava's temple, she could have prevented Teth's capture. And before that, Eamon. The true cost of his betrayal was being revealed slowly, excruciatingly. She couldn't change what he'd done, but this magic might allow her to limit the damage.

"Only the gods know the answer to that question," Lahvja replied, watching Ara closely. "But for most, knowing the future is a curse rather than a blessing. Too many believe otherwise and pay dearly for their miscalculation."

Indignant at this declaration, Ara said sharply, "How could that be? If I could know what I need to do and not do as the Loresmith, it would guarantee our victory."

"Would it?" Lahvja asked in a calm voice.

Ara usually found the summoner's serene demeanor comforting, but in that moment it made her bristle.

"Of course it would! I would know what I'm supposed to do. How I can protect you and the other Loreknights. How I can save Teth!"

"And if you see yourself fail?" Lahvja replied. "What then?"

"Then I'll know I have to make different choices than what I saw in my future," Ara answered.

Lahvja shrugged. "But the future might not be malleable."

"You just said no one knows if fate can be changed but the gods." Ara crossed her arms over her chest, frustrated. A few inches away was a gift. A chance to know more than the enemy. Why would Lahvja want to deny them that? She was on the verge of tears. All the sorrow of losing Eamon and Teth that she'd buried deep erupted with a violence that left her shaking.

Lahvja looked away from Ara and at the tree. "I know it appears to be a miraculous offering, but consider this: What if you see a future that is terrible beyond imagining? A nightmare of fate. Knowing there is a chance that outcome is irrevocable, would you still have the strength to move forward?"

Ara hesitated. What was seen could not be unseen. Were there things so awful that even the possibility of their happening would be too much to bear? Would she have the will to put aside horrors she might witness, knowing she might not be able to stop them?

"And consider the reverse," Lahvja continued. "Say you eat the fruit and see triumph, joy, the fulfillment of all our hopes. Would the confidence instilled in you guarantee your success, or would pride in your ability to win make you careless? Would you fight as hard, knowing you could not lose?"

Turning away from Lahvja and the tree, Ara chewed on bitter resentment. Before her was what appeared to be a wonderful opportunity, an advantage over her enemies. But Lahvja's words rang true.

Letting out a weary sigh, Ara shook her head. She felt Lahvja's hand rest on her shoulder.

"I do not mean to discourage or scold you," Lahvja said. "But I know that some who consume the black fruit of fate immediately turn to the other tree and its fruit. Knowing one's fate and whether or not it can be changed is often devastating."

Ara reached up to clasp Lahvja's hand. "Yes. I understand that now."

She couldn't mask her disappointment. When they'd entered the woods and its comforting warmth, she'd felt relief and welcome. Now even the beautiful trees seemed ominous, laden with fruit that offered death on one hand, possible madness on the other.

A test, she suddenly realized. A way to press at the bruised and broken places inside her and reveal if she had faith enough in herself and the gods to forge on with no assurances.

"I'm sorry there isn't an easy way to know our path or divine our victory." Lahvja squeezed Ara's fingers, her gaze full of empathy. The summoner, Ara grasped, had known it was a test all along. "Just as I wish that our next steps were not so frightening."

Turning to face Lahvja, Ara gritted her teeth before asking, "What do you mean?"

With a sad smile, Lahvja said, "Follow me. The Well is near."

Lahvja's strange words and expression increased Ara's sense of unease as they walked deeper into the forest. It was as though she felt the weight of the fruit hanging from the branches and the coldness of the bones forever settled beneath the crystal boughs. Awareness of how separate the woods was from the human world tingled beneath her skin. She knew at least some pilgrims returned from their visit to the Well, but they couldn't have come to this place and left unchanged. How did they move through their lives afterward? How could they relate to those who had not touched the deep mysteries guarded by the Twins? It had to be difficult. Perhaps that was why so many who ventured here never left, even if they had originally intended to.

How will I be changed? Ara wondered.

In some ways she had already encountered the secrets of the gods. She had walked between worlds to reach the Loresmith Forge. She had spoken to not one but several deities and received their blessings.

And yet, as she approached the trial of Ayre and Syre, she was apprehensive. Eni's trial had been one of faith and loyalty amid the hardships of their journey, Ofrit's of reason in the face of fear and madness, and Nava's of compassion and strength to ward off grief and despair.

Considering what the Twins offered those pilgrims who reached these sacred heights, she wondered what they would demand of the Loresmith. What would be required to prove her worth as she had to the other gods?

With these questions at the forefront of her mind, she trailed after Lahvja. They'd walked only a short distance when Lahvja stopped in a small clearing amid the trees.

At first, Ara didn't understand why Lahvja had paused, but then she saw it. Barely raised from the ground was a circle of unassuming stones. Ara approached cautiously.

Compared to the ethereal beauty of the forest, the Well was almost laughably plain: a ring of gray rough-hewn stones about a foot high. Deep-green moss climbed up and around the stones, well on its way to engulfing them.

"The Well of the Twins," Lahvja said in a hushed, reverent voice. "Though I have longed to look upon it, I never expected to stand in this place." She turned to Ara. "I am blessed that the gods chose me to walk beside the Loresmith."

"And I am blessed to have your wisdom and friendship on this journey," Ara replied, smiling despite the lingering tension in her limbs.

Lahvja moved to the edge of the Well, and Ara went with her. Though the stones marking it were unobtrusive, the opening was wide, a great gaping hole in the earth that Ara estimated to be about six feet in diameter. She leaned carefully over the stones, looking down. Darkness rushed up to meet her gaze. There was no telling how deep the Well was. She couldn't see the bottom, nor could she hear the sloshing of water below. In truth, she wasn't certain this well was the sort that contained water. Its nature was indiscernible.

"Ayre and Syre have been calling to me since we stepped into their forest," Lahvja said, gazing into the Well's depths. "They wait for us."

Lahvja's face was pinched with tension. Ara had a sinking feeling.

"Not . . ." Ara had to draw a long breath. "Down there."

Lahvja smiled ruefully. "I'm afraid so."

This was the first Ara had heard of entering the Well. Pilgrims visited the sacred forest, paid respects at the structure of the Well, and didn't go farther. Ara backed up and cast about for any sign of a cave or tunnel by which they could enter the Well. She'd reached Ofrit in a cavern beneath the Tangle through a tunnel, so perhaps there was a hidden entrance somewhere in the woods. Lahvja stepped atop the ring of stones and gazed into the deep darkness below. Ara's heart dropped into her stomach.

"You mean we have to jump?" Ara asked, incredulous. "We'll die."

Lahvja sighed. "That is certainly possible."

Not just possible, Ara thought, *likely.* Should they survive the jump, they would still end up broken in ways that could end their journey.

"I thought you were afraid of heights," Ara said, watching as the summoner teetered on the ledge and remembering the way Lahvja had frozen midway across the Zeverin Gorge.

Lahvja's answering laugh was tight and high. "I am, but this is the way into the Well. Sometimes the gods require we confront that which we fear the most."

With those words, Lahvja closed her eyes and stepped off the stones. The summoner didn't scream; she fell in silence. Ara rushed to the Well and dropped to her knees. She peered over the ledge, searching the void.

"Lahvja!"

No sounds came from its depths, nor was there anything to see besides darkness. Ara continued to listen, straining to hear any sign that Lahvja had stopped falling—a splash or, Nava's mercy, a thud. But there was nothing. Lahvja was simply gone.

Ara slumped against the low stones.

Ayre and Syre have been calling to me since we stepped into their forest, Lahvja had said.

Lahvja's gods had spoken to her, and she had answered their summons.

But Ara hadn't heard anything. What she'd experienced of the Twins' sacred site she'd found disturbing. Now she was expected to make a leap of faith into the realm of gods whom she couldn't understand.

Pinching the bridge of her nose, Ara gave a little growl of frustration. Though she hadn't known what to expect from the Twins' trial, she had never imagined being asked to jump to her death as a possibility.

And yet Lahvja had stepped off the ledge without visible hesitation. Without question.

Ara wished the summoner had lingered a bit so they could have discussed the matter further, but maybe Lahvja hadn't dared wait lest doubts overcome her determination to join the Twins in their domain.

Sometimes the gods require we confront that which we fear the most.

Pushing herself up, Ara stood over the Well.

It wasn't fear of heights, she thought. *That was not what Lahvja meant.*

Ara looked at one of the black-leafed trees and its gleaming gold fruit. Fruit that offered the answer to life's greatest mystery, the mystery of death.

And wasn't death what every mortal being feared above all else?

Her pulse stuttered. To reach the Twins, she would have to risk death. Risk everything.

As her blood raced through her veins, roaring in her ears, Ara wondered if she could bring herself to jump into the Well. Her instincts screamed against it.

Survive, they chanted. *Live.*

The rational part of her brain joined the argument. How could she fulfill her destiny as Loresmith if she died?

But her journey had led here. If she stopped now, nothing she'd achieved to this point would matter.

A wrenching loneliness took hold of Ara. If only Lahvja had waited and taken her hand. They could have jumped together. It wouldn't have made the act easy, but it would have been easier.

That was the heart of the matter, though, wasn't it? This wasn't meant to be easy. This was a choice. She could walk off the ledge, knowing she might die or suffer a devastating injury; any other result was impossible.

Perhaps that was the key to this trial. Survival was improbable if not impossible, and it was in accepting that truth that Ara must embrace her fate.

Though her body was trembling, Ara climbed onto the Well's ledge. She clasped her hands together and rested them against her chest, above her heart. Closing her eyes, she thought of Joar and Huntress, waiting at the base of the pilgrim trail, of Nimhea with the rebels, of Teth in captivity, of Eamon, who was likely lost to them. She thought of Old Imgar and her grandmother. They were all counting on her. They needed her courage. If she considered only herself, she would never take the next step, but she could do this for them.

For a moment an image flashed through her mind. Fox running through the forest the night she'd met Teth. Ara chasing after. Following Eni down a path unknown.

She opened her eyes and jumped.

mgar hadn't expected to marry, much less become a father and raise a family, in the aftermath of the Vokkan conquest. Nor could he have anticipated how much joy a child would bring into his life. When he'd returned with the boy to the rebel hideout, he'd intended to find a home for the young one on a nearby farmstead or in a remote village. But as he'd hiked back through the woods, scrambling up hillsides and climbing over boulders, the child clung to him, at first shivering, then calming and at last falling asleep, wrapped in the warmth of Imgar's fur cloak. Though it defied reason, he couldn't push away the conviction that having found the boy, it was not only his duty but his destiny to watch over the child, to raise him.

And his realization—that some of Saetlund's children had escaped the Embrace—shifted Imgar's purpose. He'd learned of other surviving children and their whereabouts as he'd come into contact with other pockets of rebellion across the kingdom. With these rebels, Imgar devised a strategy of survival and endurance that might one day open a path for a true Resistance to rise again and drive the Vokkan empire from Saetlund. The time for ambushes of patrols and midnight raids on Vokkan military targets had passed. Instead it was necessary to fade and, if possible, be forgotten. And if not forgotten, dismissed.

In secrecy they would regroup, rebuild, and when the time was right, they would strike back at the conquerors with a force that had a chance at victory.

Imgar and the emerging Resistance leaders believed that the key to overcoming the Vokkans was to lure them into the same false sense of security that had been King Dentroth's downfall. And while the Resistance wouldn't disappear entirely—no, that would be too suspicious—they would instead behave like pestering gnats, striking here and there but doing no real harm.

It would be a long wait for their day of justice. Years. Perhaps a generation, until the Resistance reached the point where it could reveal itself. Maybe longer. Imgar could only hope that he would live to see the day of their uprising.

Time rolled on. The boy grew tall and strong, while Imgar's beard roughened and grayed. The Hawk existed only in secret correspondence with the Resistance leaders, who planted seeds throughout the kingdom. A garden to one day be harvested that would heal the broken land. But where his counterparts placed their hopes in strength of arms, Imgar knew that to defeat the Vokkans, a greater force than even the mightiest army would be needed. He kept faith in the gods and taught his son the old tales. He waited, looked for signs.

And, as happened so often in legends, the gods surprised him. First, they took his son—not the boy's life, but they set him on a path that led away from Imgar, on a journey to seek his own destiny. Though the separation grieved him, Imgar held fast to his beliefs, and when word came from another village, from an old friend in need, he saw the map the gods drew for his life and understood the reason his son was called away. For Imgar was likewise summoned to travel a new path. To make a new home, this time in the Fjeri Highlands, where there was a girl who needed to be kept safe and to be guided.

Because this girl might be a legend come to life. She could be the one to save them all.

9

imhea had never met a legend. Well, that wasn't precisely right, because as the Loresmith, Ara was a legend, but she was also younger than Nimhea and she hadn't actually been the Loresmith when they first met. She'd seemed like a normal, albeit very short, girl. It wasn't until much later that the wonders of Ara's power revealed themselves.

This meeting felt different. Anticipation filled Nimhea with the urge to bounce on her feet like a child expecting a gift. It was silly and she curbed the instinct, standing tall with the bearing of the future queen she was supposed to be.

Still, she couldn't wait to meet this man. Of the two royal siblings, Eamon had been the student of history, but when it came to battles and the conquest of Saetlund, Nimhea knew every detail. And nothing had stirred her like the story of the Hawk. The man who had waged a rebellion from the highlands of Fjeri even after Saetlund fell. Who had evaded every attempt the Vokkans made to capture him. He had stoked fervor and inspired followers, bringing supporters to the Resistance over the fifteen years that had passed since the conquest.

And today he was here, joining the Circle, because the next battle for Saetlund was drawing near. The Hawk would be the one to lead the Resistance army.

Activity stirred in the hall, announcing their storied guest's arrival, and in the next moment he strode into the room. Nimhea straightened, holding her head high, Nava's crown settled comfortably on her brow. Self-conscious of how much she craved this stranger's approval, she reminded herself that she *was* the heir to the River Throne and as deserving of his respect as he was of hers.

The Hawk was tall and barrel-chested, with arms so thick it was easy to imagine he'd be as effective in wrapping his arms around an opponent and crushing them as swinging the gleaming battle-ax strapped to his back. He walked with purpose, with the confidence that a path would be made for him. And it was. Curious onlookers melted out of his way, and furtive murmurs followed in his wake. Here was lore come to life, walking out of history to lead the Resistance forces into their long-awaited battle.

Though his face was largely obscured by his helm, the man's eyes made it clear he deserved his moniker: they were sharp, piercing, and ready to take in anything and everything around him. He strode toward the Circle, his bearing confident, almost surly, never glancing at the growing crowd around him. His gaze stayed on Nimhea.

The princess surveyed him as he approached, keeping her expression neutral. Despite her excitement, she had mixed feelings about his arrival. She'd become comfortable with the inner circle of the Resistance, especially Suli. The Solan woman had become her advisor and confidante. Nimhea had grown to trust her deeply. The Hawk, arguably, would play a greater role than Suli when it came to the final confrontation they'd been building toward since Nimhea's arrival in Saetlund. Suli had gathered the Resistance; her wisdom and efficiency held together its scattered members. But the man before her now would be the general of Nimhea's army. They would ride into battle together.

He a seasoned warrior, she facing the Vokkan forces for the first time.

The Hawk stood before her, gazing at her calmly for a moment before he bowed.

"Princess Nimhea, you have my allegiance."

He straightened, and when he removed his helmet, Nimhea drew a sharp breath of surprise. His ruddy, windburned face was familiar, deeply lined, and covered by a thick beard. The eyes framed by wildly bushy brows were shrewd yet glinted with mischief. She'd seen him before, met him even, she was certain. But where?

At her frown, the Hawk grinned. "Surprised to see me again, Your Highness?"

His rough tone and the challenging spark in his gaze were what allowed her to finally place him.

"But you're Ara's—" Nimhea stopped. This man had been at Ara's grandmother's house in Rill's Pass. Not her grandfather, but the village . . . blacksmith?

"As Imgar of Fjeri, I had the honor of teaching Ara the craft of smithing," he said, answering her unspoken questions. "A sometimes daunting task considering I knew she could one day become the Loresmith. It seems I didn't do too badly given that Saetlund can now claim three Loreknights among its allies."

"Ara is the strongest person I've ever known," Nimhea told him. "I believe in her."

But with growing disappointment, she knew she didn't believe in this man. The Hawk was supposed to be a legendary warrior; instead she stood face-to-face with a grizzled old man.

Imgar's eyes shone with emotion. "I thank the gods for that. I made a new life in Rill's Pass to see her safe and teach her what I could . . . but what I had to offer was so limited."

"Why didn't you reveal yourself?" Nimhea asked, curious about the man's long-hidden identity. "From what I saw, Ara knew you only as a friend and the blacksmith to whom she was apprenticed."

"One revelation was enough when you and your brother came for Ara," he replied. "She was, and still is, unaware of my connection to the Resistance. The fewer people who knew the blacksmith in Rill's Pass was also the Hawk, the safer Ara was from the Vokkans."

He rolled his bulky shoulders back. "I admit I'm a bit creaky in the joints of late, but I still have fight in me, and I look forward to reintroducing myself to Fauld's army."

Creaky indeed, Nimhea thought, impatience joining her frustration. Was Suli simply coddling this man's ego because of his history with the Resistance? If so, it was a waste of time they couldn't afford.

Nimhea made a short, noncommittal sound, eyeing the man with skepticism.

Imgar gave her a long look. "Let's take a walk, Your Highness. Show me where you've been training."

Frowning, Nimhea shot a questioning glance at Suli. The woman replied with a short nod.

"Very well." Nimhea exited the room, and Imgar fell in step beside her, the others trailing after, keeping a respectful distance.

"I was sorry to learn of your brother's alliance with the Vokkans," he said quietly. "Not only for the danger it poses to us, but because of the suffering it must cause you."

She was surprised by his acknowledgment of her pain at Eamon's absence, and reluctantly moved by it. "Thank you."

"Letting go of those we love so they may seek their own destinies is one of the hardest and most necessary acts of life," Imgar murmured.

Nimhea gave him an assessing look. "So Ara didn't know you're the

Hawk, but you always knew who she was. How was it that you were the one to teach the future Loresmith her craft?"

"Some would call it a series of lucky coincidences." The deep lines around Imgar's eyes crinkled. "But I believe it was the work of the gods."

They'd reached the paddock where Nimhea tested her skills against the best fighters of the Resistance. Imgar walked to the center of the ring and took up the war ax strapped to his back.

"Would you indulge me, Princess Nimhea?" Imgar brandished his ax, and her eyes went wide.

He couldn't be serious, yet he stood watching her expectantly. She even caught a glimpse of amusement in his crinkled gaze.

Very well; if he needed a lesson in humility, she would give it.

A crowd formed along the paddock railing as Nimhea drew her sword. She and the Hawk circled each other, studying, assessing.

"Suli!" Imgar called out. "I know there are matters you wish to discuss. Go ahead."

Nimhea couldn't stop her harsh laugh. Not only was the man arrogant, he was deluded. Carry on a conversation while fighting her? He'd be on the ground within seconds.

"Very well." Suli's easy reply shocked Nimhea further still. "Let's proceed."

She gestured to the small crowd gathered around the paddock, and it quickly dispersed, though Nimhea heard a few disappointed murmurs.

Once only the Circle, Nimhea, and the Hawk remained, Suli asked, "You bring news?"

While Suli waited for an answer, Nimhea made the first strike. She darted forward, blade slicing through the air, aiming low. It was a simple matter of throwing the old man off-balance. Once he was down, she could keep him there and end this nonsense.

"Mostly confirmation of what you already know," he replied to Suli while shocking Nimhea by stepping nimbly to the side and easily meeting her sword strike with his ax. "Our forces are beginning to gather in small groups. Most are in northern and eastern Kelden, but some are assembling near the border of Sola and Vijeri. When the time of the attack has been determined, the groups will merge according to the strategy we've settled upon."

The strength behind Imgar's defense reverberated up Nimhea's blade and into her arms. Luck. That was all it was. Gritting her teeth, she spun away and struck again. Was blocked again.

"You're dropping your shoulder before you swing, Princess," Ioth shouted. "He can see the blow coming. Imgar, have there been any actions among the Vokkans indicating they're aware of our movements?"

Imgar shook his head. "As always, we're extremely vigilant. The Dove has proven vital in providing intelligence about impending searches or attacks. And while the damage they've done to the Below is unfortunate, it has provided a distraction."

No sooner had he answered than Imgar launched a furious series of strikes against Nimhea. She dodged or deflected every blow, but the blacksmith drove her back until she was almost against the rail.

"And does the Dove agree with our assessment that the time to strike is very near?" Edram's dark skin gleamed like ebony beneath the strong afternoon sun.

"The Dove has deferred to our opinion," Imgar told him. He didn't have to catch his breath after the onslaught. When he struck again, Nimhea was forced to jump aside and roll along the ground to avoid being pinned between his ax and the railing.

"A deft escape, Your Highness." With a thin smile, Edram leaned forward, resting his elbows on the rail. "Imgar, do we know what those allies will do for us?"

Nimhea had begun to sweat. Her temper rose along with the heat in her blood. She lunged forward, dropping low when Imgar swung his ax. The blade whistled over her head. She swept her blade toward his shin, turning it so the flat would strike him. The bruises would hurt, but they wouldn't damage him the way a sharp edge could.

The Hawk answered as he leapt over her blade. "The Dove maintains that their role in the battle should not yet be revealed." Adding insult to injury, Imgar spun when he landed, planting a foot in her back and sending her tumbling through the dirt.

Silence followed as Nimhea pushed herself up and glared at Imgar.

"Again?" He smiled at her.

She nodded.

When the two fighters began to circle each other once more, Xeris let out a sharp breath. "That's hardly helpful information, Hawk. How can we gauge our own attack without knowing what kind of assistance we'll receive?"

"I agree with Xeris," Ioth said. "The Dove must tell us what kind of support their followers will give. Troops? Sabotage? Our strategy is flawed without that information."

"I don't disagree," Imgar replied. He hadn't attacked yet, but this time Nimhea was determined to wait the old man out. "At the same time, I can't force our friend to share what they choose not to."

"Are we still certain of the Dove's allegiance?" Xeris pressed. "If they turn against us in the middle of our attack, we have no way to retaliate."

At this Imgar stopped moving and turned to catch Xeris with a steely gaze. "The Dove risks as much as, if not more than, any of us with every breath they draw. Nothing they've brought us to this point has been false or misleading. If they've judged that revealing their martial assets is premature at this point, then it is."

Xeris looked ready to object again, but Suli raised a calming hand.

"Seeing as we have no real choice other than to accept the Dove's judgment, there's no use arguing about it."

Xeris slouched back, her frustration obvious, but remained silent.

As Imgar continued to watch the exchange, Nimhea couldn't pass up the opportunity to attack while he was distracted. She sprinted toward him, blade raised. But he moved so quickly, Nimhea hurtled past him without ever having the chance to swing her sword. Her momentum prevented her from turning immediately to face him, but Imgar didn't bring the follow-up attack she expected. She'd been vulnerable, but he'd remained in place. That infuriated her even more than if he'd knocked her down again.

When she finally turned to face him again, he came at her with another whirlwind of his ax blade. She was better prepared this time, ready for his attack style. Sword clashed with ax, but Nimhea was able to hold her ground. They parried for several minutes. He tried to sweep her legs from beneath her, but she jumped out of the way. She forced him back a few steps with a flurry of strikes, but then lost that ground when he brought his own fresh attack.

Nimhea was sweating now, but so was Imgar. The fight continued at a furious pace until Nimhea feinted, drawing an attack of opportunity that she knew she could use to finally bring the Hawk down. As he struck, she began to twist away as planned, but Imgar followed her, and she realized his own move had been a misdirection. Then he was behind her, and the flat of his ax blade caught her behind her knees.

For the second time, she was in the dirt.

Suli's voice sailed into the ring. "That's enough, Hawk. You proved your point."

Imgar walked over to where Nimhea crouched on the ground. "Have I, Your Highness?"

Nimhea was too angry to speak, but she offered a grudging nod. She accepted his outstretched hand and stood.

"You could have bested me if you hadn't presumed you'd win," the Hawk told her. "It distracted you the entire fight. Do you understand?"

Swallowing her pride, Nimhea answered, "Yes."

"That's the lesson for today," he said. "There will be more to learn if you do me the honor of letting me take over your training."

His offer set her back on her heels, and it took her a moment to reply. "I'd be a fool to refuse."

"I would have granted you stubborn over foolish," Imgar said with a mischievous smile that made him look much younger. "I'm glad neither word is required. The battle for Saetlund will be here soon enough. What we need to do now is wait and be ready."

There was a gleam in his eyes that prompted Nimhea to ask, "Is there something specific we're waiting for?"

"Of course," he said with a ready smile. "The return of the Loresmith."

10

he two guards who entered Eamon and Teth's cell carried shackles for both Teth and Eamon. The prisoners exchanged a puzzled look as their wrists were chained and they were led from the room.

Blood began to buzz in Teth's head when the guards led them down the spiral staircase rather than up. They weren't being taken to ArchWizard Zenar's office. While Teth didn't crave another conversation with Zenar, up to this point there had been no pain or bloodshed in the urbane confines of the ArchWizard's study or Eamon's simple cell. There was no such assurance in the bowels of the temple.

The deeper they progressed into the temple, the worse conditions became. An awful stench seeped into the air, sour and stale. A scent that told Teth he was about to encounter the sort of dungeon he'd expected to be thrown in. The hairs on his arms stood up, and a horrible crawling sensation wormed along his skin.

Again the unaccountable familiarity. Shadowed, cramped space. Hopelessness.

This is where they take the children, he thought. *Children who don't come back.*

Something dark twisted at the back of his mind, flashes of night and the press of sour-smelling bodies. Whimpers all around him. A wave of sickness made Teth shudder, and he gave his head a hard shake to chase away the strange vision.

The guards stopped in front of a nondescript door that they unlocked, and then took Teth and Eamon inside a room. It wasn't the kind of room one wanted to be in, not a cell but a chamber made for horror and suffering. The room was empty; its bare floor had darkened patches where some substance had saturated the stones and left permanent stains. Chains hung on the walls.

Teth and Eamon were taken to one of the walls, and said chains were attached to the shackles at their wrists, binding them to the wall.

While their restraints were being secured, another man entered the room. He was tall, his body clad in rope-like muscle. His clothing was that of a Vokkan soldier, but more elaborate, denoting his high rank. He looked to be on the younger edge of middle age. No silver threads chased through the deep amber strands of his hair. His face was cut at sharp angles that seemed somehow familiar to Teth. When the man fixed his stare on Eamon's face, his ice-blue eyes were bright with keen intelligence. The man's gaze shifted to Teth, sweeping over the chained young man in cursory assessment, then he turned to the guards who'd escorted them into the room.

"Leave us. I'll summon you when you're needed; until then we are not to be disturbed."

"Yes, Commander." The guards saluted and left the room.

"Commander, is it?" The chains binding Teth clinked as he gave a mocking mimic of the salute, having pieced together enough clues to guess the man's identity. "Prince Liran, I presume. What an honor to meet you. Forgive me if I don't bow. The shackles make it awkward."

Liran offered Teth a bland smile. He turned to Eamon and gave a short bow.

"Your Highness," he said. "It's good to see you looking well. I trust you're happy to be reunited with a lost friend—though admittedly the circumstances could be better."

Teth gave a snort. "Admittedly. Aren't you the keen observer?"

He could do nothing about his captivity, but he could rely on wry humor for strength in this place that had ghosts of long-buried memories plaguing him. He was surprised when Liran laughed at the comment.

"It is good." Eamon stole a glance at Teth and smiled slightly. "And I'm grateful neither you nor your brother have seen fit to harm him."

"Your gratitude might be premature, Eamon," Teth said dryly, casting a meaningful glance at their surroundings. "Things aren't exactly looking up."

Liran grimaced. "I apologize for your discomfort, but the ruse is necessary. My men are guarding the door and will ensure we aren't disturbed, but many in the temple are Zenar's creatures. I've used what influence I can to give you some measure of privacy. I'm your ally and will do what I can to keep you from harm."

"Forgive me if I maintain skepticism, Your Highness," Teth replied. He had no reason to trust the Vokkan prince, and Liran's assurances could easily be a trap.

Choosing to ignore Teth's gripe, Liran said to Eamon, "Prince Eamon, our last conversation convinced me that your greatest wish is to be redeemed in the eyes of your sister. Am I correct?"

Eamon's voice came out as a whisper. "Yes."

"Good." Liran nodded. "I'm going to help you with that."

Teth frowned, uneasy at Liran's unexpected friendliness. "Eamon, don't say anything else. You cannot forget he's Fauld's heir."

"Fauld doesn't have heirs." Liran rounded on him, eyes hard. "He has sons who die young, and then he has more sons who replace their namesakes. There have been forty-nine Lirans before me. No doubt my father expects that within a decade there will be a fiftieth."

Surprised by the fury in Liran's gaze, Teth nonetheless kept his tone cool. "I'd heard the emperor's children meet sudden and often mysterious ends. I could see how that would be disconcerting."

"It is rather," Liran replied with a self-mocking smile.

"That still doesn't mean we should put our lives in your hands," Teth said. "Why would you ally yourselves with a traitor prince and a thief?"

Eamon winced at Teth's description of him.

"It would perhaps be helpful that you know my other name," Liran said, giving Teth a long look. "Your friends call me the Dove."

Eamon gasped as Teth drew a hissing breath.

"I see you've heard of me," the commander said, smiling at them. "I admit I'm a bit surprised you didn't already know who I am, Teth. After all, your father is a Low King."

With a grimace, Teth replied, "Being a Low King, my father enjoys secrets. I'm not privy to all of them."

Liran gave a brief nod of acknowledgment.

"You're with the Resistance." Eamon's voice was filled with disbelief and a wild hope.

Though Teth knew how to mask his feelings, he had to admit his gut reaction was similar to Eamon's. He'd known the Dove held a high-ranking position, but he never would have guessed it could be Prince Liran. No wonder Lucket held his identity in such secrecy. If Liran was telling the truth, and Teth was inclined to believe he was, he and Eamon had gained a powerful ally. One who could be the only reason they wouldn't meet a horrible end in the bowels of Vokk's temple.

Proceeding with caution, Teth said, "From what I understand, you need to maintain your anonymity, so how exactly do you propose to help us? We're your brother's prisoners. I don't think he'd look kindly on your setting us free."

"No, I'm afraid that's not on the table," Liran admitted. "Though I hope that ultimately I will get you back to your friends."

Eamon sagged against the chains that held him, clearly overwhelmed. Teth wished he could move close enough to let Eamon lean against him. The impulse caught him off guard.

Liran was likewise watching Eamon with unveiled sympathy. "I'll do whatever I can to keep Zenar from harming you. Right now he doesn't appear inclined to do so. I'll do my best to make sure that doesn't change. He's decided Prince Eamon is useful, though he hasn't made clear exactly how."

"And you." His eyes narrowed at Teth. "I've been told you're a Loreknight."

Reading Liran's expression, Teth laughed. "I take it you're not a believer."

"I believe in Vokk," Liran replied. "Because I've seen him. I know his power."

"If you believe in Vokk," Eamon's tremulous voice asked, "and you've seen Zenar's magic, why would you doubt the existence of other magic, like the Loreknights?"

"I move in a world of blood and bone," Liran told him. "While I can speculate about the existence of supernatural forces, I prefer to deal with the material world, as I can actually do something about it."

With a troubled sigh, he went on. "I also know what happened to the Loreknights who rode out against the Vokkans fifteen years ago. It didn't end well for them."

"They weren't real Loreknights," Eamon argued.

"I've heard that," Liran said blandly. "And I hope for the sake of these new Loreknights and for the Resistance that you're right."

Teth heard the strain behind Liran's words. "Let me ask you this: You said you've seen Vokk and you know his power. Why then would you align yourself with the Resistance? After all, it's your god who's conquered the world."

Liran blanched, turning his face away. He was silent for several long moments, then took a long breath, let it out. "If Vokk only wished to conquer the world, perhaps I'd feel differently. But Vokk is the Devourer and can never be sated. His hunger will destroy the world if he's not stopped. There are words that all Vokkan children must commit to memory:

"To live is to hunger. To hunger is to live.

We are always hunger.

We will always live.

"Fauld the Ever-Living received these words from Vokk when the Devourer claimed my ancestors as his people, but the children of Fauld know another story . . ."

The commander grimaced, then looked at each of them in turn. "That of the beginning of the world and a starving people. A man of those people went in search of sustenance and found a god. A god who didn't promise food or to sate the gnawing ache in the man's belly, but instead taught him a new form of hunger. Hunger that was power. Craving that led to conquest. And in exchange for worship and fealty, the god made the man immortal and walked by his side as a starving people began to consume the world. That god was Vokk, and that man was Fauld. What began lifetimes ago is what we face now."

When Liran fell silent, his words hanging in the air, Teth realized all the hairs on his arms were standing on end. He had to swallow past the dryness in his throat before he could speak.

"You believe," Teth said quietly, "that the Fauld in that story is your father. Not some ancient relative."

Liran gave him a bleak look. "I know he is."

"There are many who claim," Teth persisted, "that Fauld's immortality is simply a story used to prop up the empire. That there has been a succession of Faulds over the centuries."

"My father has gained immortality," Liran told him. "I thought it was simply Vokk's will that prevented him from dying, but the truth is much, much worse. I only recently learned the true means by which my father achieves eternal life."

Eamon's voice came as a whisper. "The children."

Liran looked at him in surprise. "How did you know that?"

"I've been trying to understand why Zenar would be stealing children from across Saetlund and bringing them here," Eamon replied. "And when you first came to my cell and I asked about the children, you tried to hide your shock, but I saw it. You didn't know they were here . . . and now you know why they are . . ."

"Nothing has ever horrified me more," Liran admitted.

"The Embrace." Teth couldn't stop his own voice from shaking. He felt cold all over. "That's why the empire takes children with each conquest. Not to relocate them throughout the empire."

"Yes," Liran said.

"But how—" Eamon broke off.

"I don't know," Liran answered Eamon's unfinished question. "Zenar brought me to the dungeon where the children are kept. He explained that there is a magic by which the life force of children can be siphoned into another being. I can't begin to understand it. I don't want to. But it is happening and it needs to be stopped. That isn't possible without destroying the roots of Fauld's power. A primal hunger that can't be sated." Liran paced across the room, then back. "If we can't overcome that hunger, it will be the end of everything. Vokk devours. Destroys. The magic granting Fauld immortality will ultimately lead to oblivion."

He stopped in front of them and scrubbed a hand over his face. "I cannot serve that god."

Any doubts Teth had about Liran's sincerity had vanished. He'd never seen an expression like the one Liran wore: it was the mask of a condemned man, but one who would not balk at his fate, nor try to run from it. Prince Liran believed he would die because of his choice to turn against his father and his god. But he would still fight.

Seeming to recover himself, Liran said, "I've learned something that I hope we can exploit to our advantage."

Teth lifted his eyebrows with interest.

"My brother intends to challenge our father when he arrives in Saetlund."

"The emperor is coming here?" Teth blurted.

"Oh." Liran rubbed the back of his neck. "I skipped over that part. Sorry."

"If Emperor Fauld comes to Saetlund," Eamon said softly, "Vokk will come, too."

"I know," Liran said. "I'm trying not to think about that too much, but I have to warn the Resistance."

Eamon nodded even as he shuddered, his eyes wide.

Cold like a fist slammed into Teth's gut. A god of death and destruction whose greatest enemy was the woman he loved. How could he protect her, even if he wasn't imprisoned in the temple? What chance did any of them stand against Vokk?

"I'll join you in trying not to think about it," Teth said uneasily. A sick fear threatened to overwhelm him, and he couldn't let it. The only answer was to focus on the things he *could* fight. "Now, what were you saying about Zenar?"

"Zenar wants the throne," Liran told them. "He wants my support, so he's shown me more of his hand than he ever would have in the past. We don't exactly trust each other." He smiled ruefully before saying, "It's why he showed me the children and told me about discovering the secret to Fauld's immortality. Zenar believes he's become more powerful than our father. He wants to prove it to Vokk."

"Prove it to Vokk?" Eamon gasped.

"Vokk has been with Fauld since the beginning," Liran said. "Zenar believes if he can win Vokk's favor, then Fauld will be cast aside and my brother will take the throne."

"What happens to you after Zenar become Zenar the Ever-Living?" Teth asked.

With a dry laugh, Liran said, "I harbor no illusions about my brother's recent friendliness. He's likely planning to ship me off to put down uprisings in some far-flung territory. That's a best-case scenario; he might prefer to have me killed."

"I've been hearing about uprisings across the empire more and more frequently over the last few years," Teth observed, watching Liran for a reaction. "They matter, don't they?"

"Very much," Liran answered with hesitation. "If Saetlund can push back the empire, it will be a catalyst for other rebellions. The world is dying because of Vokk, but I believe there's still time to stop it, to heal the damage that's been done. It will take years, maybe generations, but I have to hope."

"We all have to," said Eamon.

Teth stayed quiet, but he agreed.

"I wish I could offer more," Liran told them. "But I had to simply let you know who I am. I'll be keeping a close eye on any plans Zenar hatches regarding you, and if there's a way to get you out of here without undermining my role in the Resistance, I'll make it happen."

"I believe you," Teth said, and Liran smiled slightly.

"I'll be in communication with you, but I might not always be able to come myself. There's someone else who can convey messages for me if necessary. One of the Below's agents. She's a young woman, petite, blond."

"Oh!" Eamon said. "She came to kill me."

Teth and Liran both looked at him with raised brows.

"But then she didn't," Eamon finished. "She was very polite about it."

"Petite, blond, assassin." Teth barked a laugh. The more he learned of his father's interventions here, the greater his belief in their chance of survival grew. "Dagger. Lucket sent Dagger. Suddenly, I'm in a much better mood."

For some reason, Liran frowned at Teth's grin. "You know her?"

"She's my father's best agent," Teth said wistfully. "It's nice to know he cares."

"How well do you know her?" Liran's frown deepened.

Teth started to answer, then gave him a long look. "Ah, I see. Not *that* well, Your Highness. You have nothing to worry about."

"I have no idea what you mean," Liran replied, dodging Teth's gaze.

"Of course you don't," Teth quipped, but couldn't resist adding, "She's very pretty."

Liran glowered at him.

"I didn't really think about it at the time," Eamon piped up. "Since I thought she would kill me. But I agree. She is very pretty. Scary, but pretty."

Liran held up a hand. "I believe we've exhausted this line of conversation." He looked at the door and then back at Teth. "Now . . ." He stopped, swore under his breath, then said, "This just became more awkward."

Regarding Liran's conflicted expression, Teth frowned, then gave a harsh laugh. "Hmm. I understand. You need to rough us up."

"Not Prince Eamon . . ." Liran replied.

"Because you're supposed to use me to intimidate him." Teth nodded, finishing Liran's thought. "That makes sense."

"If you have to hurt Teth, then hurt me, too," Eamon protested, and pulled against his shackles.

"That's very noble, Eamon." Teth smiled at him. "But it's not necessary. It's better if Liran does what Zenar wants."

"So it's clear," Liran said. "I don't want to hurt you, and I would prefer not to do this."

"Even though I said she was pretty?" Teth grinned at him. "Should I think of other things to say about her?"

"Are you trying to make it easier?" Liran laughed and shook his head.

"Maybe." Teth shrugged. "I'm starting to like you."

Liran walked up to Teth. "If it helps, I know how to make the damage look much worse than it actually is."

"I appreciate that."

"I really am sorry about this."

"I know."

Liran sighed, threw an apologetic glance at Eamon, then smashed his fist into Teth's face.

11

ra fell. She fell and fell and fell through the darkness.

Or at least she thought she was falling. She had to be. She'd jumped into the Well. But as the deep shadows swallowed her, there was no rushing of air around her body. The sensation was more like floating than falling, as if her being was suspended in a place where natural laws governing the movement of bodies, of weight and velocity, simply ceased to be.

Time lost meaning, as did any sense of place or space. Was she dying? Was this what death felt like?

And then she was somewhere else. She hadn't landed so much as she had simply stopped falling or floating.

In some ways it appeared to be nowhere. All around her was a strange mist that glowed and flickered like candlelight. She could trail her fingers through it, but it had no discernible substance. Other than the illuminating mist, there seemed to be nothing.

"Lahvja?"

"Loresmith." It was not Lahvja who answered.

The voice spoke in a range of timbres, like the layers of a chorus, ranging from soprano to deep bass. It came from nowhere and everywhere.

"I am here," Ara said, not sure where to direct her speech. She turned slowly, looking for a sign of who had joined her.

"Forgive our reticence," the voice said. "At this turn of the seasons, we are as brilliant as the sun, and to look upon us would damage your sight."

Of course. This close to midsummer, Ayre would dominate the Twins and would burn brighter than human eyes could bear.

"I understand," Ara said.

"We are pleased by your choice," Ayre/Syre said. "You embraced the possibility of death for the sake of those you love and for the future of Saetlund. We find you worthy to serve as Loresmith."

Ara bowed, though she felt a bit odd doing so. "I am honored."

Ayre/Syre laughed, and Ara felt it resonate in her bones, a pleasant sensation like a summer breeze swirling through her, enlivening her spirit.

"Come, Loresmith," Ayre/Syre said. "You must once again practice your art. Another Loreknight has been called and given our blessing."

"By your will," Ara said.

The mists surrounding Ara swirled, coalescing around her body until she stood at the center of a whirling vortex of light.

All at once it vanished, and Ara stood in the Loresmith Forge.

"Ara!" Lahvja ran toward her, opening her arms and catching Ara in an embrace. "You're here!"

"How is it that you're here?" Ara held Lahvja tightly then stepped back, puzzling over the summoner's presence. No other person had ever joined Ara at the Loresmith Forge, and she'd presumed that none ever would.

Ayre/Syre's voice sounded. "Lahvja is the only one of your companions who is tied to our realm. She moves beyond the mortal plane by way of her magic; thus, she can tarry with you here."

There was a pause, then the god continued, "Her presence is also required because we call upon her to perform a difficult task. A task for which only the Loresmith can prepare her."

Ara and Lahvja exchanged a confused look.

"Go to your forge, Loresmith," Ayre/Syre commanded. "We will speak with you anon."

Without warning, golden mist enveloped Lahvja, and a moment later, Ara was alone. Full of questions and wonder, she went to the worktable. Upon it she found ingots of godswood, as she expected, but alongside them were deep red gemstones, carnelians she thought, as well as tools she hadn't used up to this point but recognized.

Gathering the gemstones in one hand and taking an ingot in the other, Ara closed her eyes and let her mind float. An image began to form, an idea taking shape that developed into a set of instructions and then a plan of action.

When Ara opened her eyes again, she chewed on her lower lip, thoughtful. She'd never created a piece like that which she was about to attempt. It would be both strong and delicate, and possessed of a power she didn't fully grasp.

"I am the servant of the gods," she murmured, and went to work.

As always, Ara labored over her task for hours, possibly days. Always alone.

Only when she'd finished the piece commissioned by the Twins did the golden mist spill through the Loresmith Forge. Lahvja emerged from its swirling depths, a bemused expression on her face.

"Ara." The summoner approached slowly, but she was smiling. "How long have we been apart? In some ways I feel as though I just left you, in others I feel I've been gone for weeks."

Ara returned Lahvja's smile. "I can't answer that question. Time moves oddly here, and I am never sure how long it takes me to complete a piece."

"May I see it?" Lahvja appeared uncharacteristically shy. A blush crept up her cheeks.

"Of course." Ara laughed. "After all, it was made for you." She picked up the item she'd so carefully crafted. "Give me your hand."

Ara didn't have a precise word for the object she'd created for Lahvja. Four rings at one end and a bracelet at the other, the two sides joined by an array of delicate chain links that would overspread the back of her hand like a spray of fine lace. The piece was wrought entirely of godswood, with the exception of three gems, one featured on the ring of the middle finger, a second at the center of the glove, and a third at her wrist. They were deep red carnelian cabochons that gleamed, appearing almost liquid, when caught by the light.

Like blood, Ara thought.

Lahvja extended her hand, and Ara slid the rings onto the summoner's fingers, then smoothed the chain links over her skin, finally closing the bracelet around her wrist.

"This is the Whisper of Life." Ara frowned as she spoke the name. As she'd created the glove—she couldn't think of a better word for it—she'd been confident, but seeing it on Lahvja's hand filled her with trepidation.

Upon crafting the other pieces for her Loreknights, Ara had immediately understood their function and purpose. Not so with this piece. She had a vague sense that it was tied to the magic Lahvja already possessed, a link to the spirit world, but the specifics of its use eluded her.

"Lahvja," Ayre/Syre said. "You have served us loyally for many years. We have seen the way you strive to aid those in need while still maintaining the balance of the natural world. This equanimity you possess makes you the ideal vessel for our purpose."

Vessel? Ara didn't like the implications of that word. It robbed Lahvja of will, transforming her into an object to be used. Then again, was the role of the Loresmith any different?

If Lahvja was discomfited, she didn't show it. "As ever, I am your servant."

"Three gems for the three laws of the mortal realm: birth, life, death," the god intoned. "The gift we offer you through the craft of the Loresmith is, as she told you, the Whisper of Life. Its powers are two-fold. Its primary use is that it will allow you to walk, and bring others, through the eternal plane as a means to reach your fellow Loreknights at speeds impossible for mortals. The journey of a week will be completed in moments, but heed this warning: All who travel with you in this manner must be physically linked to you while you use your power. Should that connection be severed, your companions risk being lost forever beyond the veil."

Lahvja nodded, accepting the god's instruction, but Ara shifted on her feet. A sense of unease crept over her limbs. While the ability to break the rules of time and space by moving between mortal and ethereal planes was tempting, the idea that someone could be lost forever in that liminal space made her shudder.

"The second aspect of this gift may be used but once," the Twins said. "Your gift of summoning now reaches beyond the mortal plane. Therefore, you may commune with those who have crossed beyond the veil, and in a time of great need, you may call forth lost champions and complete the circle. But as we have said, you can perform this feat once and only once."

A cold fist tightened around Ara's heart. She couldn't think of any pleasant reason Lahvja had been granted this new power. In order to bring someone back to life, they had to die first.

Lost champions? Did they mean raise the dead?

And Saetlund's champions were the Loreknights. If the power could be used only once, did that mean Lahvja would have to choose who to save?

After Nava had named Nimhea Loreknight and gifted her the crown that would protect her fellow Loreknights from death, Ara had believed that no matter how difficult the battle ahead was, she wouldn't lose her friends. Now it seemed that might not be true. Maybe she misunderstood the power of Nimhea's crown. One could hardly call the magic of the gods predictable.

Each gift Saetlund's deities provided through Ara's work at the Loresmith Forge would play a pivotal role in driving the Vokkans from Saetlund. The first three pieces Ara had crafted made sense: Teth's bow that would shoot infinite arrows, Joar's axes that brought the power of winter to bear on his enemies, Nimhea's crown that protected her fellow Loreknights in battle.

Offense and defense, tools of warriors.

But this piece—chain links of godswood that appeared as delicate as lace, the ring and bracelet set with carnelians—did not follow the pattern that seemed to have been established through each of the gods' trials.

The Whisper of Life.

And completing the circle? Ara had no idea what the Twins meant by that.

Lahvja appeared equally disconcerted. "I am not a necromancer."

Her voice was halting. She seemed to be saying the words to herself as much as to Ara.

"I know that," Ara told her, feeling the need to offer some sort of assurance.

With a sigh, Lahvja lifted her hand, turning her wrist so the light glinted on the dark metal, the stones gleamed deep red.

"I don't understand," Lahvja murmured.

Ara bit her lip, wishing she had an explanation. Frustration simmered under her skin. At this juncture, she expected more clarity in her purpose, not fresh confusion.

"Be at peace, Summoner, Loresmith," Ayre/Syre said. "The mystery you contemplate will be resolved at the appointed time. The gods demand no feat you cannot accomplish."

Lahvja bowed, and Ara gave a little nod.

What else was there to do? She could only hope that their reassuring words held true.

Ayre/Syre said nothing more, and a sudden stillness in the Loresmith Forge convinced Ara that they were gone.

Sensing the same, Lahvja turned a slow circle, casting her gaze throughout the cavern. "How do you leave this place?"

"The gods have always returned me to our world," Ara said, frowning. "It seems this time they've elected not to do that, which is . . . interesting?"

"Another test?" Lahvja mused.

Ara shook her head. "I don't think so. The Twins told me I'd passed their trial, and that follows the pattern of the quest. No god brought me to the forge until I completed their trial."

Considering the situation for a moment, Ara slid her gaze to the bracelet covering Lahvja's hand. "Perhaps Ayre and Syre have offered the first opportunity for you to put your new power to use."

Raising her hand to admire the lace-like metal, Lahvja nodded. "Yes. That follows."

With a shy smile, she stretched her other hand to Ara. She blushed and gave a little laugh. "I confess I'm a bit nervous. The Twins described the power, but they offered no precise instructions about how to use it."

That made Ara a little anxious, too, but she didn't want Lahvja to doubt herself. Any such worries could easily hinder her ability to perform whatever magic was necessary to travel between mortal and divine planes.

"They said the Whisper of Life expands the power you already have, your summoning magic," Ara said as she took Lahvja's hand. "Maybe you should imagine a way to expand your magic and apply it to the task of moving between the spirit world and ours."

Lahvja gave Ara a considering look. "That's wise, Ara. Yes, I believe I can do that." She paused, then said, "I have not thanked you for your faith in me as we undertook this trial. The ways of the Twins are not easily understood and often frightening. I am honored by your friendship and trust."

Deeply moved, Ara stepped forward and wrapped Lahvja in an embrace. "Thank you." Releasing her friend with a smile, she added, "I hope you didn't say all that because you think we're going to be lost forever beyond the veil."

"No," Lahvja replied with a warm laugh; then she grinned. "Maybe a little."

"That's all right." Ara was laughing, too. "If you said absolutely not, I wouldn't believe you."

They donned the layers of clothing they'd shed in the warmth of the Forest of the Equinox, knowing that when they reached Joar, they'd be back in the cold climes of the mountains.

Still smiling, Lahvja took a deep breath and laced her fingers through Ara's, holding tight. "Now, let's find our way back to Joar."

The summoner closed her eyes, concentrating. Ara remained still and silent, all too aware that should she inadvertently break Lahvja's focus, it could put them in grave danger.

At first, nothing seemed to happen, but slowly the Loresmith Forge began to change. Its features undulated as if she were looking at it through warped glass or a swiftly flowing stream. The surroundings altered until they were unrecognizable, and Ara found herself in a place that was difficult to comprehend or describe. She had the slight sense of movement, but nothing so significant as to be jarring or dizzying. It was more that the space around her seemed to vibrate and ripple, a constant play of light and shadow and shifting colors, and there was a sound all around her like rushing water. Nothing seemed to linger. Occasionally a shape would form in her peripheral vision, as if trying to draw her attention, but her instincts whispered that whatever lurked in this space between mortal and spirit planes was best left unseen. Instead, she kept her gaze on Lahvja. The summoner's eyes remained closed, her face calm, and her grip on Ara's hands remained steady.

Ara felt a vague sense of time passing, but she could not have guessed how much. Then, without warning, the space around them gained definition. Colors separated and sharpened, the world took on curves and angles, and the rushing sound disappeared, replaced by gruff shouts and a sudden buzz that zipped past Ara's ear with a gust of air.

Lahvja cried out, her hands jerking free of Ara's as she fell back, clutching at her left arm. Struggling to gain her bearings, Ara turned, only to see a Vokkan soldier notching another arrow and taking aim at her.

Ara dove as he loosed the arrow, landing beside Lahvja on the ground.

A furious bellow filled the air, and a giant figure barreled into the Vokkan. The man went flying, his body slamming into the thick trunk of a pine tree. He slid to the ground and lay still.

"Stay down!" Joar shouted, already running toward them.

Ara obeyed. She flattened her body to the earth next to Lahvja, who likewise curled against the ground. A moment later, Joar leapt over both of them. Ara followed the hunter's trajectory. Her chest seized at the sight of more Vokkan soldiers, maybe a dozen, bracing for his charge, their weapons at the ready.

Two bowmen took shots at him, but with Joar came the wrath of StormSong—and a buffeting wind that knocked the advancing arrows off course. Joar didn't slow as he approached the soldiers. A few stumbled back as others were thrown into confusion by the whirlwind of ice and snow that lashed at them as Joar swung his axes.

One soldier lost his head with the first stroke; another was cleaved from shoulder to sternum. Even so, Joar was hard-pressed by the number of opponents he faced. The storm surrounding him kept the most timid at bay, at least for the moment, but others forced their way through the blizzard to meet Joar's attack.

Daring to look away from the fight, Ara turned her attention to Lahvja.

"You're hurt."

"It's not bad," Lahvja replied, though blood was seeping through her fingers where her hand was clamped over the wound on her arm. "The arrow caught the edge of my arm, but the cut isn't deep. I'll be fine."

Ara nodded, then bit her lip. "I don't know how to help Joar. I could try to defend him, but even entering the fray, I could be forced to attack and then . . ."

"You can't," Lahvja said without hesitation. "Even if you could fight them, you'd be putting yourself at too much risk. Help me bind my wound, and I may be able to give him aid."

Drawing her dagger, Ara cut a length of fabric from the wool head-wrapping she wore. She tied the cloth tightly around the cut on Lahvja's upper arm and tied it.

"Is that all right?" she asked, frowning. She didn't like giving such hasty, inexpert attention to a wound.

"It will do for now." Lahvja moved to a kneeling position and focused on the battle.

Joar had taken down another soldier, but it was taking all of his skill and stamina to hold the others off.

Lahvja bit her lower lip and pressed her palms to the ground. She began to whisper fervently.

A Vokkan soldier who'd been moving to flank Joar suddenly shouted with alarm.

As Ara watched, root-like strands of ice that had burst from the earth wrapped around the soldier's ankles and calves, locking him in place. Another soldier cried out as he was likewise trapped.

Ara glanced at Lahvja, only to see sweat beading on the summoner's forehead and her face contorted with strain.

"Lahvja," Ara murmured. "Don't hurt yourself. You've lost quite a bit of blood."

"I won't be able to hold many of them," Lahvja groaned, shuddering with the effort of the spell.

She'd trapped another soldier. The first two were hacking at the ice around their legs with their swords.

Joar was better managing the remaining attackers, but he was still outnumbered.

A howl rose in the air, coming from somewhere nearby in the forest. The wild cry made the hairs on the back of Ara's neck stand up.

Huntress, she thought. In the chaos of their arrival, she'd failed to note the ice wolf's absence.

Another howl sounded, then another. Many voices, many wolves.

The Vokkan soldiers faltered, backing away from Joar, their gazes searching the woods with alarm.

Joar seized on his advantage, cutting down another enemy, then wheeling to sweep the head from the shoulders of one of the soldiers Lahvja had bound in ice.

Growls and snarls sounded among the trees, followed by a flurry of movement and shadows hurtling from the forest. In the next moment, a pack of massive ice wolves raced out of the forest, setting themselves upon the Vokkan soldiers without hesitation, tearing into the enemy in a fury of claws and fangs. In a matter of seconds, it was the Vokkans who were outnumbered.

Fearful cries became screams as the soldiers were overwhelmed by the wolves' attack. Those that the wolves didn't take down fell to Joar's axes. Only a few minutes later, the battle was over. Slain Vokkans littered the ground, their blood soaking the earth.

The ice wolves lifted their crimson-stained muzzles and howled their triumph. In the midst of the pack, Ara spotted Huntress. Joar watched the wolves for some time, then as their howls faded and they began to jostle each other playfully, he turned away and walked to Ara and Lahvja.

Ara helped Lahvja to her feet.

"How is it that you are here?" Joar asked when he reached them.

"The Twins gave Lahvja a new power," Ara told him. "She is a Loreknight."

Joar regarded Lahvja solemnly. "You are injured."

"It's only a small cut," Lahvja said. "Once it's properly cleaned, I can apply a poultice and it will heal quickly."

"Good." Joar half turned so he could look again at the wolves.

Ara noticed that they were milling around one another and seemed to be paying particular attention to Huntress, nuzzling her, licking her, leaning against her.

"When we were set upon by the Vokkan patrol, Huntress knew I would need help," Joar said, his voice wondering. "She found her family and brought them here. She must have known they were nearby. I had no idea. If there were signs, I missed them, but then ice wolves are incredibly elusive. Almost impossible to track." There was a note of resignation in his voice. "It is a good thing that she is with them again. A good thing." He gazed at the wolves for another moment, then said, "We should go. They will not let a meal go to waste, and it is unsettling to see beasts feast on human flesh, no matter that it is a natural act."

Ara had no argument for that.

"The horses are tethered at our campsite, not too far from here," Joar told them as he began to walk in the opposite direction of the wolves. "We were hunting when we came upon the Vokkans."

Ara slid her arm around Lahvja's waist to give her weakened friend support as they walked.

The scrabble of rock came close behind them just before Huntress darted past in a flash of white fur. She came to a stop in front of Joar, who was startled into a halt.

Huntress sat on her haunches, looking up at Joar, and tilted her head as if in question as she regarded him. Joar dropped to a crouch. He reached out and rested one hand on the side of the ice wolf's face.

"It's all right, my friend," he said softly, his voice thick. "You have done more for me than I ever could have asked. I am thankful for the time we have spent in each other's company."

Huntress licked Joar's hand and whimpered. She stood up and trotted to the side, her gaze going past them to the wolves gathered around the fallen Vokkans. She stared at her pack for a long while, then looked at Joar again. Huntress turned around and butted her head against Joar's leg, then ran ahead of them on the path in the direction of their campsite.

Joar stared after her, his eyes wide. Sensing she wasn't being followed, Huntress stopped and looked over her shoulder at them. She wagged her tail and then continued forward.

"I did not—" Joar's voice broke as he began to walk. Gathering himself, he managed to say, "I do not understand why she has chosen to stay with me."

Ara used her free hand to take Joar's. "I think she's trying to tell you you're her family now."

Joar shook his head, and a few tears leaked out of his eyes. "I do not deserve such an honor."

"My dear friend." Ara squeezed his fingers. "Yes, you do."

Her eyes stung with unshed joyful tears. She understood both Joar's awe and the wolf's choice. Huntress and hunter shared a bond beyond the saving of a life, just as Ara's companions on her journey to become Loresmith were forever linked to her not only through the will of the gods, but because of love and loyalty.

Those ties were a gift beyond measure, but they also caused a chill of fear to sneak up Ara's spine. To lose any of her friends, her family, would be unbearable. The surprise of the Vokkan attack in this remote wilderness was a stark reminder of the unrelenting threat to their lives, the close brushes with broken hearts and sundered spirits. Teth's face leapt into her mind. She held the image there for but a moment, savoring it, offering a silent prayer for his safety, then put him and her fears aside.

The final trial awaited her in Senn's Fury. Should she prove herself to the gods there, a battle beyond imagining lay ahead. More risk. More fear. But greater than either: hope.

12

amon grimaced as Teth's wrists were shackled again, each of his arms taken by a guard as the thief was escorted from the cell. A moment later, two wizards entered, a man and a woman. Their robes distinguished them as Elders, the highest-ranking of wizards and the most powerful.

"I am Elder Byrtid," the woman spoke. She had dark hair streaked with white and olive skin. "My companion is Elder Tich."

The man alongside Elder Byrtid inclined his head ever so slightly. He had flowing white hair that brushed his shoulders and skin that was pale but slightly yellowed like parchment.

Both shared two startling traits—despite being obviously of advanced age, their faces were completely unlined, their skin unnaturally smooth, and their irises were large and so dark as to appear black, obscuring their pupils entirely. Eamon avoided meeting either of their gazes directly; looking into those fathomless eyes gave him the feeling that they could draw his life's very essence from his body into theirs.

"Our master bids you join him in the sacrificial chamber," Elder Tich said. "It is an honor to be invited to witness the ArchWizard perform this ceremony."

Elder Byrtid nodded. "The ArchWizard believes you possess the aptitude to thrive as a wizard. Today you will better understand the benefits reaped by becoming one of us. Then you must make your choice. Join us or wither away like all mortals."

Her words startled him. Though powerful, Vokk's wizards were still mortal.

Seeing Eamon's confusion, Elder Byrtid smiled condescendingly. "But for the ArchWizard's foresight and generosity, I would perish; he has discovered the secret to immortality."

Elder Tich took up the explanation. "Our emperor, Fauld the Ever-Living, has long possessed this magic, but always hoarded it for himself. ArchWizard Zenar has seen a new way, a better way, in which his followers will walk with him into eternity."

"I see," Eamon said. "And do all wizards enjoy such a long sojourn in the mortal realm?"

Elder Tich smirked at the question. "To reap the benefits of Vokk's deep magics, one must earn them. Powerful magic is demanding and dangerous. Most wizards die young."

Tich said this last with a pointed look that suggested he expected Eamon was likely to meet an early end.

"Prove your worth," Elder Byrtid cut in, shooting her companion a reproving glance that told Eamon that Zenar had provided a script he wanted these two to follow. "And the ArchWizard will look on you with favor."

Elder Tich returned her look with a bored gaze, then said to Eamon, "Come with us."

Eamon followed the elder wizards out of his cell and down the spiral staircase. As they descended, a familiar foul odor began to permeate the air. It was a miasma of sweat and decay, sour with human waste. His mind went to the children he'd seen marched, day after day, past his cell and into the depths of the temple, and his stomach twisted. Was that where the horrible scent came from?

Several floors below Eamon's cell, where the sickening odor of fear and neglect was awful but not yet intolerable—as Eamon knew it would be at its source—Elder Tich and Elder Byrtid led him into a chamber that was square in shape. The floor of the room sloped inward; a spiral had been carved into the floor that progressed from a wide arc to a tight coil at the center of the room. At the end of the spiral, in the lowest point of the floor, was a dead sapling. Its trunk was thin and twisting, its branches desiccated to the point where it appeared they would snap off at the lightest touch.

The Elders brought Eamon to one corner of the room. They stood to either side of him, attentive but silent. He forced himself not to react when he saw that Teth was positioned in the opposite corner, still bound with iron and flanked by guards rather than wizards.

What was the purpose of making him face off with his former companion? Perhaps Zenar wanted to make plain the disparity in their positions, Eamon free and seemingly counted among Zenar's followers, while Teth remained an outsider and a prisoner.

Eamon was uncertain about the ArchWizard's motives, but whatever they were, he sent a silent prayer to Saetlund's gods—and desperately hoped they were still willing to hear him—that the reason he'd been brought to this chamber was not to witness Teth's torment or death. Everything about this space was ominous. The room carried a sharp metallic scent that overpowered the stench coming from the bowels of the temple, and there were dark stains on the floor.

ArchWizard Zenar strode into the room, dressed in heavy, swirling robes of velvet and satin. He moved past Eamon to stand at the top of the spiral on the side of the room between Eamon and Teth.

Zenar raised his arms.

"The time has come to bear witness to the future of Saetlund and the empire, which nigh will rule the world without challenge. The uprisings will be quashed. Vokk will reign supreme, and none shall defy him or those who do his will."

Elders Tich and Byrtid dropped to one knee. Elder Tich caught Eamon with a hard stare until Eamon knelt with them. Across the room, the guards forced Teth to his knees as they moved to kneel.

Fixing his gaze on Teth, Zenar grinned, his lips stretching over his bared teeth in a gruesome expression. "My father's power wanes; thus, the enemies of Vokk have been allowed to gather in strength, have dared to oppose the inevitability of his reign. No more. I am about to ascend. The mantle of power that is my fated inheritance will rest upon my shoulders. All shall bow and tremble."

Teth glared in reply and looked like he had a rebuke ready in his mouth, but he held his tongue. Wisely, Eamon thought, as provoking the ArchWizard now would likely prove fatal. There was a wildness in Zenar's eyes Eamon hadn't seen before, a sheen of mad hunger begging to be loosed.

"Bring them!"

Eamon's heart was in his throat as six children filed into the room. A wizard instructed them to form a circle around the spiral and the tree in the center of the room and join hands. The children were wide-eyed as they obeyed, and horribly quiet. They followed instruction without question and seemed as if they were afraid to so much as whimper.

As soon as the children were finished, the wizard who'd led them in bowed to Zenar and moved to kneel beside the ArchWizard.

Eamon wanted desperately to flee the room. His soul screamed that he was about to experience something more horrifying than he could imagine or possibly bear while retaining his sanity.

He stole a glance at Zenar, and the ArchWizard smiled slowly, as if all too aware of Eamon's dread.

"Stay where you are, Your Highness," Zenar told him. "Do not move. Do not touch anything. You should do the same, Loreknight."

Eamon managed a nod, then looked at Teth. The thief's face was drawn into harsh lines of helpless fury.

Zenar drew a dagger from the folds of his robe, then shrugged off the heavy garment, which was quickly gathered up by the wizard beside him. The ArchWizard was bare to the waist, his torso and arms covered with writing and symbols—some in languages Eamon recognized, others in those that were unknown to him. The skin over his breastbone was marked with a scar in the shape of a spiral identical to that on the floor.

Putting the tip of the dagger to the center of the spiral on his chest, Zenar began to chant. As the words spilled from his lips, he pushed the dagger into his flesh. He moved the blade with agonizing slowness as it followed the lines of the scar, but he didn't so much as flinch, and his voice never faltered.

Blood flowed freely down Zenar's torso. It poured onto the floor, running into the grooves of the spiral, chasing down the slope toward its center. There was so much blood Eamon wondered how Zenar could stay upright, but the ArchWizard seemed unaffected by its loss.

A collective gasp from the children tore Eamon's gaze away from Zenar. Their eyes had changed, begun to glow with a white incandescence. Shining crystalline liquid spilled from the corners of their eyes like tears. It collected at their jaws and dripped to the floor.

The children didn't writhe or scream or even cry softly. They didn't move at all, though when he looked closely, Eamon could see their chests rise and fall with breath. While Eamon was grateful that they didn't show any outward signs of suffering, their absolute silence was terrifying.

The brilliant liquid pooled at the children's feet, then flowed down the slope and slid into the grooves of the spiral, mingling with Zenar's blood and following the channels that ran to the center of the room and the base of the dead tree.

The seemingly lifeless sapling shuddered when the combined liquids touched its roots. The bright substance disappeared, absorbed by the withered tree. Then it began to grow, its trunk thickening rapidly as its branches grew long and twisting. Gone were the desiccated limbs and dry bark. A new, wet substance seeped from within the tree to coat its surface. Dark, viscous, crawling. Familiar.

Eamon took a step back as he recognized the liquid to be the same that covered the walls of the temple, the slimy pulp that Zenar consumed with such relish. Eamon's stomach revolted, and he was thankful that he hadn't felt hungry enough to eat that morning.

The tree continued to grow, stretching up until its branches scratched the ceiling. They crawled along the surface, seeking, until they found openings in the stone, which they slipped into. Two branches slithered toward Zenar. The ArchWizard reached his hands toward them as if in welcome. The branches touched his hands, then wrapped around his wrists, growing along his arms and winding around his chest.

Thorns speared out from the branches, piercing Zenar's skin. Eamon drew a hissing breath of surprise at the sight, but Zenar threw his head back and closed his eyes in ecstasy. This went on and on until the ArchWizard's entire body was wrapped in branches and dripping black slime. Minutes passed that felt like an eternity as Zenar's flesh absorbed the dark liquid. At last his skin was clean again, and the spiral cut on his chest was healed.

Without making a sound, the six children dropped to the floor and lay unmoving.

"No!" Teth shouted.

Zenar grinned at him. "Yes."

With a retching sound, Teth collapsed to the floor, shaking and writhing as if in terrible pain.

Eamon felt sick. He wanted to scream, to cry, but he was locked in place, too shocked and horrified to move. And yet, beneath his revulsion, Eamon's mind began to spin, working furiously. Zenar had wanted him to witness this display of power. The Elders said it was meant to inspire him, to sway him to join Zenar's cause. The ArchWizard expected him to be both awed and cowed.

And in a way, he was. Zenar had shown an immense display of power, unlike anything Eamon could have imagined.

But he had also revealed the essence of himself, his ultimate goal . . . and possibly his only vulnerability.

Zenar looked over to where Teth was still retching.

"Take that one away," Zenar told the guards with a sneer. "Such weakness from a so-called champion of the gods."

Eamon forced himself to remain still as the guards lifted Teth's body between them and hauled him across the room. Teth was in no way weak, Eamon knew, but what had transpired in the chamber had undone him. Or could Zenar's magic have harmed him?

When the guards pulled Teth past him, Eamon had to clasp his hands together to keep himself from reaching out to his friend. He wanted to assure himself that Teth would recover, but couldn't risk revealing the depth of his concern. There would be time for that soon,

Eamon told himself. At present, he had to deal with Zenar.

The pulsing branches of the tree had begun to shrink, drawing away from the ceiling moment by moment as if time was turning back on itself. Minutes later the room had restored itself to its original state, the single stunted dead tree at its center, except for the ring of slain innocents that lay in silent testimony to the evil that had been committed.

The wizard who'd been attending Zenar helped the ArchWizard don his robes once more. Zenar handed the wizard the dagger he'd used in the ceremony. The wizard bowed deeply and left the room. Only Elders Byrtid and Tich, Eamon, and the ArchWizard remained.

After smoothing the folds of his robe, Zenar walked over to Eamon, his expression expectant.

"Why children?" Eamon asked, trying to sound curious rather than condemning. "Why not use prisoners of war?"

Zenar smiled and began to walk a slow circle around the bodies. He gazed upon each one in the manner of a parent watching a peacefully sleeping child rather than with the malice of the murderer he was. Eamon struggled to keep his expression neutral while his guts continued to churn.

"All children have pure, inherent magic." Zenar crouched beside a little boy, brushing his knuckles over the child's temple. "Very few are able to recognize their nascent power and cultivate it, much less learn to use it. The power wanes as a child grows; by the time they reach adulthood it's usually gone. When I have drained adults—yes, I thought it prudent to experiment—the magic wasn't nearly as potent, rather like a wine that's turned sour."

The comparison made Eamon want to wince, but he held on to his mask of passivity.

Straightening, Zenar stretched his arms out in front of him, regarding his hands as he flexed and stretched his long fingers. Eamon wondered if Zenar was looking for some particular change in his body, a sign of the power he'd . . . ingested.

At first, Eamon couldn't see any outward signs that the ArchWizard had been affected, but after a few moments he noticed a very subtle shimmering over the surface of Zenar's skin. A slow ripple moved through Zenar, making him grit his teeth and shudder. As Eamon watched, the ArchWizard's skin seemed to tighten over his bones, becoming even more pale and iridescent. Though his eyes had shrunk within over-prominent sockets, they burned with fanatical light.

Eamon had been grateful he hadn't eaten before Zenar's demonstration, but now he worried that his empty stomach didn't matter. Dry heaves threatened, but Eamon didn't want to show any weakness. He had to convince Zenar that he envied and desired the ArchWizard's power, that his greatest wish was to become Zenar's protégé. If Eamon wavered even a little, his plans would be quashed before they had a chance to begin.

Steeling himself, Eamon forced his expression into one of awe.

Zenar turned to face Eamon. "Power and immortality. These are the true gifts of Vokk. What his most faithful are rewarded with . . . if they can unlock the secret of how to obtain such vital magic, its true essence."

"And how did you?" Eamon asked, then quickly ducked his head. "If I may be so bold."

"Self-preservation is a powerful motivator," Zenar mused. "I will share what I have learned with no other, just as my father denied such knowledge to me so he alone could receive Vokk's gift of eternity." Regarding Eamon, he added, "But I will tell you why and how I came to possess it without his aid."

Zenar stepped over the bodies and made his way down the spiral on the sloping floor. He stopped in front of the stunted, dormant tree and grazed his fingertips over its branches.

"The tree is the vessel," Zenar said. "There must always be a vessel to siphon power and convey it from one being to another. This tree once grew in the desolate place my father was born, where he encountered Vokk and accepted the Devourer as his god. That was the beginning, and an echo of that beginning was required to re-create its magic."

Turning from the tree to look at Eamon, the ArchWizard held him with a burning gaze. "I have mastered this power, but unlike my father, I will share its boon with those whose devotion to me is unfaltering. Prove your worth to me, Prince Eamon, and you may join the ranks of my wizards. This is your chance to taste immortality."

An idea simmered in Eamon's mind, a nascent plan that brimmed with potential and equal danger. He looked at the tree, then at Zenar's face—a mask of greed and hubris. Here was a chance, possibly Eamon's only chance, to turn the ArchWizard's greatest advantage against him.

"How can I prove myself to you?" Eamon asked, daring to rise and return Zenar's gaze without flinching.

Zenar's mouth curved with approval. "I'm certain something will come up to which you are suited. For now, you must learn all you can of the Loreknight I hold captive. I must unlock the secret of his power."

Eamon bowed very low. "As you command."

13

mpatience and frustration—neither emotion was welcome, but Ara couldn't seem to fight them off. To reach Wuldr's Grove, they'd traveled near Rill's Pass, and the temptation to divert their journey to see to the safety of her grandmother and Old Imgar and the other villagers had been so tempting she was nearly sick with it.

She closed her eyes and rubbed them with the heels of her hands. How was she supposed to go on without knowing what was happening in her home? After the Vokkan patrol's ambush, it seemed inevitable that Zenar would send soldiers to Rill's Pass to find her. The weight of her family's unknown fate had pushed her heartache to an edge that was almost unbearable. Still, she hadn't stopped. They'd ridden away from the village instead of toward it. The Loresmith couldn't follow impulses driven by her personal desires, no matter how insistent they were.

"What do we do now?" Ara asked with a long sigh.

It had been hours since they'd settled into their camp alongside Wuldr's Grove. While the circle of sacred oaks was beautiful and serene, it offered no clues as to the location of Senn's Fury, at least not that she could find.

Joar and Huntress had gone off to hunt for half the day, returning with a young roe deer. Choice cuts of meat were now roasting over the fire, and Joar had created a second firepit, where he was smoking the remainder of the venison to supplement their provisions. While Ara couldn't fault his reasoning, she was unhappy at its implication—that they'd be traveling for many days, if not weeks, to come.

Joar looked up from where he was hanging strips of meat. "We wait."

"Wait," said Ara. "Shouldn't we try to find Senn's lair ourselves? Or at least look for signs as to where it might be?"

"You do not enter an animal's den without invitation," Joar said solemnly.

Ara laughed. "Are you saying you've been invited into dens before?"

"Once," Joar replied wistfully. "I was caught in a sudden winter storm. The winds were too fierce to build a shelter. But within the winds I heard a great howl, and I knew it was Senn calling to me. The howls led me to a cave where Senn bid me take rest with a hibernating bear."

"Are you joking?" Ara asked.

Joar shrugged. "Perhaps I am, perhaps I am not."

Lahvja shook her head and laughed softly as she basted the roasting pieces of venison.

When Ara looked at Joar again, he was grinning, and Huntress's tongue lolled out of the side of her mouth in a wolfish smile.

If Teth were here, Ara imagined, he would curse under his breath and stomp off to his tent.

All she could do was smile wanly at the giant warrior while her heart longed for the boy who wasn't there. The last thing she wanted to do was wait; she wanted to act. Needed to. The sooner she completed the final trial, the sooner they'd be able to find Nimhea and the Resistance, bringing the fight to take back the River Throne to the Vokkans after so many years in hiding.

Joar and Lahvja continued to banter, exchanging ideas about how to best season the venison and whether or not Joar should return to the forest to dig up savory roots he'd noticed while out hunting. Eventually Joar did wander off to collect the roots, leaving Ara and Lahvja to tend the fires. Huntress was on sentry duty, alert to any signs of intruders in the forest surrounding them.

Having noticed Ara's sullen mood, Lahvja offered a sympathetic smile. "I know it is difficult, but you must not lose hope. In the face of so much unknown, despair can find fertile ground in the mind, plant its seeds deep, and, if allowed, will grow wildly, until it rules you. You are strong, Ara, in heart, mind, and spirit. Remember that."

"I don't feel strong," Ara confessed. "What use am I if I can't protect those I love the most? If I can't help them?" Shaking her head, she paced beside the fire. "If anything, who I am is what put them in danger. Whatever has happened to them is my fault."

"It is no one's fault but the Vokkans'," Lahvja said in an uncharacteristically sharp voice. "Remember that this is but a single moment in a journey that has not ended, a drop of rain in the midst of a raging storm. The full story has not yet been told."

The firmness of Lahvja's tone and the intensity of her gaze shook Ara out of her self-pity.

"One puddle at a time," she murmured, recalling Old Imgar's words when she'd been about to begin her quest to become the Loresmith.

"I'm sorry?" Lahvja's brow crinkled.

With a genuine smile, Ara replied, "Just something a friend told me. Advice that I should consider right now." She came to Lahvja's side. "I'm sorry for my foul mood today."

"There's no need to apologize." Lahvja placed her hand on Ara's arm and gave a reassuring squeeze. "Fear and grief must be expressed in order to be released; the danger comes in clinging too long to those feelings and becoming lost in them."

Ara nodded. "I understand. Now, how can I be of help?"

Smiling, Lahvja said, "When Joar returns with the roots, you can help him clean and prepare them, but for now, check on his firepit and make sure enough smoke is reaching the meat."

Ara tended to the smoking venison while Lahvja continued to cook. A short time later, Joar reappeared with a small sack of thick, twisted roots. He and Ara set about washing them and stripping away the tough layer of skin. At Lahvja's direction they sliced the roots into small chunks and set them in a pot of water to parboil until they'd eventually be drained and fried with oil and herbs.

By the time their meal was ready, Ara's mood was much lighter, and she relished the delicious food as well as the conversation with her companions. After they'd eaten and cleaned up, Joar and Lahvja took turns singing songs of the Koelli and Eni's Children that Ara had never heard. Joar's rumbling baritone and Lahvja's exquisite soprano lulled her to contentment, and she tucked away the knowledge that in the midst of this difficult journey it was important to savor small moments of joy when they appeared.

Just before she sought her bedroll, Ara crept into Wuldr's Grove. Though the crackling campfire was close by, the ring of mighty broad-leafed trees seemed to silence all sounds from the outside, which she hadn't noticed before. Not only that, but looking up, Ara saw that within this space the night sky wasn't the lavender twilight it should have been, but instead the firmament above her was inky black sprinkled with stars. It looked exactly like the endless starry sky that surrounded the Loresmith Forge.

Should she reach Senn's Fury and pass the final trial, she would visit that sacred forge once more. Would it be the last time?

If she smithed another weapon or armor, was that the end of her work for the gods? The Loresmith quest set a path before her. After its completion, she didn't know her place in the next stage of the journey. She wasn't a warrior, but she couldn't imagine being a bystander when the battle for Saetlund came at last.

Taking all this in, Ara was reassured that her decision to come to the grove with her plea had been the right one.

"Wuldr, Great Hunter and god of my homeland," she whispered. "I seek your trial and ask that you guide me to the place where I may prove my worth to you."

For some inexplicable reason, her words lingered in the air, their echoes fluttering around the grove like butterflies before at last fading away. A little more at peace, Ara returned to the camp. To wait.

Ara's invitation came in the middle of the night.

Long twilight masked the stars as she stared up at the heavens. Sleep eluded her, and melancholy had crept back into her heart despite her attempts to repel it. Her mind returned again and again to Rill's Pass, to the Vokkans waiting in ambush there, to her grandmother's and Old Imgar's fates.

How was she supposed to complete a trial when all she could think about was finding out what happened to them? She wanted to leave this place immediately and search for one of Lucket's agents. The Low King was most likely to know what had happened at Rill's Pass.

But she knew finding anyone allied with the Below might be futile. The Low Kings had been run out of their lairs by the empire. All their agents were likely scattered, and any hiding places Ara was familiar with had to be compromised. To seek them out would be to hand herself over to the Vokkans.

No. The only thing to do was wait.

She ground her teeth in frustration, rolling onto her side. Worries about her family and friends weren't the only things plaguing her. That she was so close to reaching her goal should have filled her with hope. Instead she fought a new, growing fear. Senn's Fury held the final trial, but at each of the previous trials only one Loreknight had been called. If that pattern held, after this last trial a fifth Loreknight would be named by Wuldr.

Five Loreknights.

But there should be ten. When the gods first created the Loreknights, two had been called from each of Saetlund's five provinces. Ten Loreknights to defend Saetlund from its enemies.

So where were the other five?

Ara couldn't shake the feeling that she'd missed something important, but she didn't know what it could be. Nothing in the trials thus far or in the lore they'd been following spoke to the issue. And yet it had to be a problem, hadn't it? Was this yet another challenge, a demand of the gods that Nimhea prove herself a worthy queen by defeating the Vokkans with only half the champions they'd hoped for? Or perhaps this test was of Ara's skill, of all the pieces she'd forged. Would they be enough to overcome an army without five additional counterparts to support them?

The howl that broke the stillness of Wuldr's Grove made the hairs on her arms jump to attention. She sat up, looking to her companions, but Lahvja and Joar were quiet where they lay. Still fast asleep.

The howl came again, louder this time. Ara grabbed Ironbranch and scrambled from her bedroll. Neither of her friends stirred, but Huntress lifted her head, ears perked.

"You hear it, too?" Ara asked the wolf, and received a solemn gaze in reply.

Ara approached Huntress as she stood and shook any lingering sleep from her furry body.

"Will you show me the way?"

By way of answer, Huntress trotted away from the grove and into the forest. Ara followed.

The ice wolf didn't appear to be in a hurry; she moved at an easy gait that Ara had no trouble keeping up with. Senn's lair must be nearby. But as they walked, she noticed a strange quality in the air around her. It was a kind of shimmering. A blurriness of her surroundings.

Ara stopped, and the fuzzy quality of her environs cleared. As she looked around, her brow furrowed. The landscape had changed significantly. What had been a heavily deciduous forest surrounding Wuldr's Grove was now distinctly boreal, marked by pine trees.

She walked up to one of the trees, noting the lichen that clung to its bark. This lichen, she knew, only grew in places far north of where they'd made their camp. Somehow, she'd traveled a long distance in what seemed a very short time. Turning her gaze to the sky, Ara thought it appeared to still be the middle of the same night she'd been woken by the howl.

A soft growl brought her attention to Huntress. The ice wolf was looking over her shoulder at Ara, wearing an impatient expression.

"I'm coming," Ara said.

She fell back into step behind Huntress, and the world around her blurred once more.

They traveled for what felt like another quarter of an hour before Huntress came to a stop and their surroundings came into stark relief. Ara found herself still in the forest of dense pine, but a short distance ahead was a tall cliff face of dolomite, at the center of which was a yawning cavern entrance.

Senn's Fury.

She knew without question she'd arrived at Wuldr's hidden sacred site.

Huntress looked over her shoulder at Ara as if to make sure she understood their strange journey was over.

"Yes, I know," Ara said, and started toward the hunting hound's lair. Fear and excitement simmered in her veins.

At last. The hidden site. The final trial.

When she reached Huntress, the wolf walked beside her to the edge of the cliff face, at which point the ice wolf dropped to her haunches and fixed Ara with a steady gaze.

"I see." Ara regarded the wolf. "You're waiting here."

Huntress remained still, and that was answer enough. Ara wasn't surprised, since all but one of the trials had been a solitary endeavor. Still, as she crossed the threshold of the cave's mouth, she would have taken comfort in Huntress's company.

In mere moments, Ara was plunged into complete darkness. She had no torch or lantern, nor the means to create one, even should she return to the forest and find a branch or deadfall that could serve.

Her only choice was to proceed with cautious steps. Fortunately, the floor was dry and even. It seemed only to be sloping slightly downward. As she walked and the entrance to the cavern became smaller and smaller at her back until it completely disappeared from view, she began to question her decision to simply walk into the darkness.

You do not enter an animal's den without invitation.

That was what Joar had said.

Ara had taken Huntress's guidance as that invitation, but what if she'd been too hasty in making that determination?

This place was called Senn's Fury. It did not bear Wuldr's name.

What if she should have waited for the god's hunting hound to come to her and lead her inside?

She thought she had a good idea of what happened to those who entered an animal's den without invitation. She had no desire to continue onward only to be snapped in two by Senn's mighty jaws. There was a reason *Senn's teeth* was a common oath throughout Saetlund.

She was considering turning around when a sound caught her attention. It was coming from ahead, farther into the cave. Not a warning growl or some other animal noise. What she heard was voices. Many of them.

But how was that possible? Could it be that Senn's lair wasn't a cave, but a tunnel that led to some other place where the trial would occur?

Determined to investigate, Ara put aside her worries and continued forward. The voices grew louder, more distinct, separating into gruff, commanding tones and fearful cries.

What was happening?

Dim light joined the sound, illuminating the cave's shape and a wall ahead of her that curved sharply left. The light and voices seemed to be coming from beyond the curve.

Ara drew Ironbranch from its harness and quietly moved to the near wall, pressing her body close to it as she walked. With any luck, she'd be able to peer around the curve and assess the situation without being noticed.

Her progress was slow, and Ara felt impatience bubbling up, trying to compel her to move faster, but she clenched her jaw and maintained her cautious approach. When she finally peeked around the curve, the scene that spread out before her was so shocking she barely kept herself from dropping Ironbranch.

She had been walking through a tunnel, and on the other side of it she'd stumbled right into a Vokkan camp. It was occupied with not one patrol, but many. There had to be a hundred soldiers clustered around campfires.

How could this be? She must have made some mistake.

As she started to withdraw, a sudden commotion in the Vokkan camp stopped her. The soldiers were leaving their campfires quickly, moving as one with shouts of excitement toward some kind of structure that had been erected at the center of the camp. What was it?

Daring to creep forward, Ara peered ahead. Suddenly an immense bonfire flared to life, fully illuminating the structure and the soldiers grouped in front of it.

Ara's heart thudded hard against her ribs.

It was a gallows. And in a line alongside the steps leading up to the platform from which a noose hung were prisoners, their hands tied, their faces masks of fright.

Ara's blood turned to ice when she recognized two of the faces. Grandmother Elke and Old Imgar.

Nava's mercy. They had been taken captive, and they were about to be executed.

Ara swallowed a sob as she stood shaking, at a loss for what to do. She had no chance against that many soldiers. Even if she could attack them rather than just defend, she would still be overwhelmed in moments, killed on the spot or captured and brought to the gallows along with the others.

But she couldn't simply watch while her grandmother and mentor were killed.

As she watched, a hooded executioner climbed the steps to the scaffold, taking a moment to examine the rope and its noose before he called out.

"Bring the first!"

To Ara's horror, a soldier seized her grandmother's arm and began to drag her toward the gallows's steps. Something broke inside her. Her feet were moving, though she had no memory of deciding to charge the line of soldiers. Imgar shouted and struggled until two guards restrained him and a third dealt severe blows that had the blacksmith doubling over and ultimately sagging in his captors' grips.

Raw, primal rage rose up, forcing its way out of her throat in a scream.

One of the soldiers pivoted, staring at her.

She would not survive this fight. She knew that.

She didn't care. She ran toward them.

The moment she raised Ironbranch and swung it down to meet the blade of a Vokkan, she would no longer be the Loresmith.

It didn't matter.

Better to die than to stand and watch as the ones she loved were led to their doom. Better to forsake the gods than live without her family.

Her ears filled with the hiss of a hundred serpents as the soldiers' swords slithered from their scabbards. Steel reflected the orange and red glow of a massive bonfire near the gallows, throwing darts of flaming light at her. She blinked away the pain. She was still screaming, still running, getting closer and closer to the soldiers.

One hundred voices rose in a battle cry. Her steps did not falter.

Within the shouts of the Vokkan soldiers, another sound rose. Deep and cruel, but not a call to battle.

Laughter.

That sound made her stumble. Made her knees hit the ground.

She struggled up, expecting the Vokkans to be on her in the next breath.

But the soldiers hadn't charged. They stood still, the points of their swords leveled at her.

Snarling through her teeth, Ara began to run toward them again. The soldiers gave their mighty shout again. She was closing in on them. Thirty feet away. Twenty feet.

Dark laughs rolled over the battlefield like thunder. And within the rumbling laughs, Ara heard a sibilant whisper.

Yes, Loresmith. Vengeance shall be yours.

Ara stumbled again. She caught herself before she fell, but she did stop. The moment she stopped, the laughter stopped, too. The soldiers' call for blood died.

The line of prisoners moved forward again. Her grandmother had reached the foot of the gallows. She climbed one step.

Ara ran two.

Her grandmother stopped, turned, and looked at her with pleading eyes. A sweet, familiar voice echoed through her mind. *Save me. Save us all.*

Ara ran faster. Ten feet to the soldiers. Five.

The soldiers tipped their heads back and screamed, crying out for blood.

The laughter cracked through the air like a whip.

Yes. Come to me. Save them.

Ara didn't stumble this time. She stopped. She willed herself to be still.

Silence, again.

Then her grandmother began to weep as she climbed the remaining steps up the gallows. A breeze stirred, making the nooses swing.

Ara gripped Ironbranch so hard the skin of her hands mottled with strain. Her flesh ached, her bones shrieked. Her heart screamed for her to move.

But she couldn't risk that laugh again. That voice. Something about it was so very, very wrong.

The hooded executioner took her grandmother by the arms, forcing her to stand beneath the rope, putting the noose around her neck.

Ara dropped Ironbranch and wrapped her arms around herself as her stomach knotted with pain. She knew she would not attack, she would not fight. She would not save her family, her friends. She could not let the laughter triumph.

Though the words were futile, Ara sobbed, "Help me. I am so alone."

Her breath came in ragged gasps as her pulse pounded. How could she bear the sacrifice of those she loved the most? Yet she knew she must. And so she would.

A voice, deep and clear, reached through her heartbreak. "The Loresmith is never alone."

Ara gasped, taking a step back from the stranger who had appeared at her side. He was a tall man, his body wrought of lean muscle. His hair was the color of amber and his eyes pale blue, his face hewn in sharp angles. He wore armor and had the bearing of a soldier.

The man reached down and drew a sword. Grasping its hilt with both hands, he held it aloft, its silver blade gleaming in the firelight from the camp. As Ara watched, dark tendrils of shadow seemed to sprout from the hilt and climb up the blade. The shadows swirled and ebbed, in constant motion, circling the sword's length.

A collective groan flowed through the Vokkan soldiers like a wave. Every pair of eyes fixed upon the shadow-covered sword and the man wielding it.

Gazing at the man, Ara knew not who he was but what he was. The fifth Loreknight. And though she had never seen a sword such as he wielded, she knew it was her fate to forge it.

Ara bent to pick up Ironbranch and held it firmly, but this time not to attack. She moved alongside the stranger and prepared to defend him.

A snarl came from the gallows. Ara watched as her grandmother removed the noose from her neck. The executioner ignored her as she walked to the edge of the platform. Elke opened her mouth and snarled again. Her mouth began to expand and her body began to grow. She stretched to an impossible height. Her clothes ripped and fell away, revealing an emaciated body, gray skin stretched so tight over long bones. A mouth like a maelstrom dominated her narrow face. Circle upon circle of teeth stretched into the oblivion of that great maw.

Ara's grandmother was gone. Standing in her place was Vokk the Devourer.

The god roared and lunged at Ara and the stranger. The stranger lifted his sword and stood fast.

Ara looked at the warrior so willing to face a god.

"Today, I am your shield, Loreknight," she said, and stepped in front of him, filled with new purpose and unflinching resolve.

She stared at the mouth rushing toward her, a mouth taller and wider than her body. Than the warrior's body. The mouth filled with rings of dagger-like teeth.

For the first time, she understood that here was her true enemy. The creator of Fauld the Ever-Living. The force driving an insatiable empire. Brother to and betrayer of Saetlund's gods.

Vokk.

The truth flooded her with icy dread, yet she knew she could not surrender to its force.

"I am Ara of Rill's Pass!" she shouted. "I am the Loresmith. I serve the gods of Saetlund. I will never serve you."

Vokk screamed and his fetid breath hit her, knocking her back. Then the gaping mouth was upon her, the teeth surrounded her. Darkness fell as the Devourer swallowed her whole.

14

he guards had to drag Teth back to his cell. It was humiliating, but he couldn't help it. His body shook uncontrollably. He was unable to make his legs move, to put one foot in front of the other and walk. The guards swore as they hauled him up the spiral stairs and shoved him into the small room he shared with Eamon.

Teth didn't bother to crawl to the cot. He simply rolled onto his side, curling in on himself, trembling, as sickening wave after wave of emotions rolled through him.

"Teth." Eamon dropped to his knees beside his friend. "Teth, what happened?"

When Teth didn't respond, Eamon left him, returning a moment later, and Teth felt a cool, damp cloth press against his forehead. Then his jaw, easing the muscles there, which Teth hadn't realized were clenched tight.

Eamon murmured soothing words that pierced through the horrors ruling Teth's mind and memory. He could hear the fear in Eamon's voice even as the prince tried to comfort him, unable to understand what had provoked Teth's reaction. After all, Eamon had witnessed the same monstrosity as Teth, but was still upright, in control of his faculties.

But Eamon didn't know what Teth knew.

He lay there, shaking, while Eamon continued his kind ministrations with endless patience. After what could have been minutes or hours—any sense of time had abandoned Teth—the shaking subsided. His mind slowly cleared.

"Can you sit up now?" Eamon asked, helping him move until his back was supported by the wall. "Yes, that's it. Nava's mercy, Teth, that was frightening."

Teth rubbed his eyes, his temples. "I'm sorry. It couldn't be helped." He took a long breath, another. "I don't think it will happen again."

"Do you understand what happened?" Eamon asked with a frown.

Teth lifted his face to meet Eamon's searching gaze. "Yes. I remembered."

"Remembered," Eamon repeated. "I don't understand."

Teth looked away, gazing at the wall of the cell but seeing into the past. He knew what to expect now and could shield himself against it. His memories still wouldn't be pleasant, but they wouldn't consume him the way they had in that chamber.

"Before today, my earliest memories were of begging and stealing in Hunter's Rest," Teth said.

"The Fjerian capital." Eamon nodded. "Where Lucket found you?"

"That's right," Teth replied. "But ever since I was captured, I've been having these visions, flashes of what I realize now are memories. Memories of what happened to me before Lucket brought me into the Below."

Teth closed his eyes, gave his head a shake. It was hard not to sink into that fear again. Despite their distance, the memories were so visceral.

"I was like those children in the dungeon," Teth said, looking once more at Eamon. The compassion in the other boy's gaze steadied him.

"After the conquest, I was one of those taken in the Embrace."

Eamon swallowed hard. "You escaped."

"Yes. I don't remember being taken," Teth said quietly. "Only the rough road. How every crevice and bump shook the wagon. It creaked and groaned like it would fall to pieces at any moment, but no matter how much you wished it would, it didn't. You never had space. You were always touching someone else, bumping into them, falling against them. It was unbearably crowded, but I'd never felt so alone. The only familiar smells were awful ones. Sweat, excrement, vomit. Sadness and sickness all around me. And so much fear. I didn't know what was happening, but I knew wherever the wagon was taking me was a place I wouldn't survive."

Eamon listened, his features etched with sympathy. Teth's skin had a gray cast and was damp with sweat.

"There was another boy, older than me, though I'm not sure how much older. He managed to steal a key from one of the guards. Just lifted it from the guard's belt as he walked by. It was like magic. That night, when the guards slept, he opened the door. Of course, since the wagon was full of children, the sound of our escape was like a riot. All I could do was run. Somehow I wasn't caught. I'm sure most of the others weren't so lucky. I don't even know if the boy who stole the key made it."

With a shake of his head, Teth continued. "There were days and nights in the forest. Hungry days, cold nights. I knew I couldn't survive there, but towns and cities were dangerous. That was where the guards were, and I knew that if I was seen, I'd be taken again. But I also couldn't live in the forest; I didn't have the skill.

"Finally I had to risk sneaking into towns. I always went at night. At first I hunted through garbage for things to eat. I didn't always escape notice. Sometimes a person would see me. Because of the Embrace, everyone was afraid, too afraid, it seemed, to help me beyond offering a bit of food or a worn blanket.

"I seemed to instinctively know that staying in one place was too dangerous. That would make it easy to find me. I went from town to town. I got better at living in the wilderness, though my scavenging skills were poor. I couldn't hunt, and I didn't know what plants were safe to eat. I ate one berry that made me sick for two days and didn't risk unknown foods again."

He paused to rub his temples, then gave his body a violent shake as if to fight off creeping nightmares of memory.

"One thing stuck in my mind. The boy who stole the key. Without him, I would never have gotten out of that wagon, and that wagon was death. I wanted to be like that boy. To be able to save myself. So I taught myself how to steal. Learning to steal is mostly about watching people. Then it's about knowing how not to be seen.

"I was patient because I had to be, and because I was patient, I was able to become a good thief. Good enough that the only person who caught me was Lucket. When he grabbed me by the scruff of my neck, he said, 'You would have managed it, imp, if you weren't in dire need of a bath.'"

"He smelled you?" Eamon blinked with surprise at the turn in the story. "That's how you were caught."

Teth shrugged. "I'm sure I reeked like a cesspit. Bathing wasn't something I concerned myself with. I didn't know it mattered until Lucket made that observation. And that was the day my life began again. Of course, when he first caught me I thought I was done for. Lucket was well-dressed and well-spoken, someone who would surely turn me over to the empire. Instead, he brought me into the Below, and for reasons I still don't completely understand, he chose to become my father."

"The gods were guiding you both," Eamon said.

Teth touched his boot, where Eni's pendant was tied around his ankle. "I know that now."

"The world has changed for all of us," Eamon murmured.

They fell into silence. Teth fought to stay in the present moment, in this cell with a companion who was impossibly both enemy and friend. His mind wanted to drag him back to the ritual chamber, or further into the past to his own captivity.

He let his head drop back against the wall and reached for a strength beyond his own.

"My belief in Eni started as superstition." His words came out as a whisper. "Most agents of the Below tie themselves to one god or another for luck. Assassins have Ofrit and his poisons. Mercenaries like Wuldr's strength and Senn's ferocity. Thieves favor Eni because we're always moving, so no one place is home. When Ara found me, my regard for Eni was still mostly superstition, but obviously it's much more now. I've no doubt Eni was with me in that wagon and brought me to Lucket, just as they brought Ara to me. And now they've led me here. To the innocents who didn't escape."

Eamon sat quietly, searching Teth's face with a thoughtful gaze, then he simply nodded.

"You always had faith," Teth observed.

"I had faith that legends were actually history," Eamon replied sadly. "And I put all my hopes in magic. Magic for the sake of power, spells that could rid me of illness and pain. But if I'd had any real allegiance to Saetlund's gods, I wouldn't have made the choices I did. I used my beliefs as a map to find what I wanted, but I put my hopes in the wrong place. I've thought about it many times, and I don't understand why I wasn't killed by the butcher crows in the Bone Forest. They would have known my secrets; they should have judged me and killed me." He took a deep breath. "I suppose I was spared because they knew Ara needed my help to reach Ofrit's Apothecary and to read the scrolls."

Teth gave him a long look. "Or maybe the gods aren't done with you yet."

Eamon met Teth's gaze, then turned his face away, blinking rapidly.

"You've admitted you were wrong," Teth said. "That could be the first step along a new path."

"I know I was a fool to ever believe Zenar could be an ally," Eamon said. "But it was seeing the children marched past my cell that forced me to accept how wrong I was. He's truly evil."

Teth gave him a sardonic look but nodded.

"Above anything else"—Eamon drew a deep breath—"even more than seeing Nimhea again and begging for her forgiveness, I want to save them. I can't leave this place without trying to save them. If the gods allow it, that's the path I want to take."

Teth rubbed a hand over his face. "The question is: How are we going to help them? We'll enlist Dagger, of course, but she can't take down a force of guards and wizards on her own. Even if she freed us first and we could fight with her, our chances would be slim. Liran will help us, but he can't do anything that might reveal his collaboration with the Resistance."

"We can't do it on our own," Eamon said. "I believe their only chance of freedom is Zenar's downfall. His end would throw the temple into chaos; the confusion might provide an opportunity to free the children."

"So all we have to do is kill the ArchWizard?" Teth laughed dryly. "That should be easy enough."

Eamon gave him a sheepish look. "I know it seems insurmountable, but I have an idea."

Teth's eyebrows lifted. "You have the means to kill Vokk's most powerful wizard, the second son of the emperor?"

"I may," Eamon answered. "But I can't do it without you . . . and it might kill us both. Make that probably—it will probably kill us both."

"Wonderful," Teth muttered. "Perhaps you should explain what you have in mind."

As Eamon sketched out his idea, Teth's eyes narrowed, then widened. When Eamon finished describing his plan, Teth smiled ruefully.

"I can't believe I'm going to say this." Teth turned his gaze to the ceiling and sighed. "But that could actually work—mind you, you'll probably kill us in the attempt, but considering it could be our only chance to eliminate Zenar, I'm willing to risk it."

Eamon blinked several times before saying, "You trust me that much?"

"Not exactly," Teth replied.

"Okay," Eamon said, still reeling from the fact that Teth hadn't dismissed his idea out of hand.

"The question remains," Teth said. "How are you going to persuade the ArchWizard to cooperate?"

Eamon smiled coldly. "I won't have to. He's about to ask me to do exactly what we need. I'd bet my life on it."

"You *are* betting your life on it," Teth remarked.

"Yes," Eamon replied. "I suppose I am."

15

ra stirred to consciousness when something wet dragged over her arm. Remembering Vokk's horrifying mouth and rows of sharp teeth, she braced herself for terrible pain. It never came, but another slobbering swipe did.

Opening her eyes, Ara found herself staring at the nose and muzzle of a giant hound. She was lying on a soft mattress. When Senn's massive pink tongue licked her again, this time a little too close to her face, she sat up and scooted away.

"I'm awake. I'm awake."

It seemed like the right thing to say under the circumstances and had the desired effect. Senn wagged his tail, then trotted a short distance away to nudge his head beneath the hand of a tall, bearded hunter.

Wuldr turned, and when the god saw Ara sitting up on the bed, he smiled and approached her.

"Ara of Rill's Pass," his voice boomed. "You have made me proud. Of all the trials, I believe this may have been the most difficult, for it was rooted in your home and your heart."

Ara nodded, finding it difficult to speak.

It wasn't real. None of it had been real. The rush of relief she felt was quickly quelled, as while she hadn't witnessed her grandmother truly about to be executed by Vokkan soldiers, the fact remained that she had no idea where Elke was.

Wuldr's expression was sympathetic, but his words were firm. "Put your mind to the task at hand, Loresmith. Fear and doubt must be conquered for you to proceed."

"Yes," she replied, burying her worries into the deepest recesses of her heart.

Before she went to the forge, she dared to lift her hand and pat Senn's cheek. "Thank you for allowing me into your lair."

Senn's response was to lick her again before she could back out of reach.

Wuldr watched with laughing eyes and patted Senn's head. "He's very fond of you."

Ara nodded. Despite the slobbering, it was much better to be liked by Senn than the alternative.

Wiping her hands and forearms on her tunic, Ara made her way to the forge. She startled at the sight of Ofrit waiting for her there. His visage was again that of the scholar, dressed in neat robes, his gleaming dark skin a contrast against his shock of white hair.

"I have a puzzle for you, Loresmith." The god stroked his long beard. "Something to think on in the days ahead."

"A puzzle?" Ara frowned. It hardly seemed appropriate given the approaching conflict, which would surely consume all her time.

Ofrit clapped his hands, nodding with enthusiasm.

To find the end, begin again.

Fulfill the lore, as once before.

Restore the past, to rest at last.

"I . . . I don't understand," Ara said after a moment.

"Well, that's the point of a puzzle, isn't it?" Ofrit said gleefully.

There was no flash, no sound; the god simply vanished, leaving Ara to stare at the space where he'd been, caught between confusion and bewilderment. Though she couldn't fathom why Ofrit would have come to the Loresmith Forge simply to offer up a puzzle, Ara committed the words to heart.

Putting the strange episode aside, she gave her full attention to the forge. As always, ingots of godswood awaited her, but alongside them were three gemstones. Like the stones adorning the Whisper of Life, they were cabochons and blood red in hue, but at the heart of each was a jet-black star, its five arms curving out to the edges of the gem. Ara had never seen a gemstone of its like.

"Stones of oblivion," Wuldr's voice rumbled at her back.

Not having heard the god approach, Ara startled with a gasp.

"Apologies," Wuldr said kindly. "It was not my intent to frighten you."

Relaxing, Ara laughed. "Of course not."

Her gaze shifted back to the gemstones. "Stones of oblivion—what does that mean?"

She wanted to ask where they came from, but didn't know if Wuldr would be willing to share that information. Another part of her was afraid of what the answer might be if the god did tell her. Some mysteries were better kept that way.

Wuldr looked at her for a long time before answering. "There are some acts, those that verge on incomprehensible, that require that deepest, oldest of magics to be undertaken. The stones of oblivion are a conduit for such magics."

Ara pursed her lips, considering his words. "During your trial I saw a sword, and I know that weapon is what I shall forge here. The stones of oblivion, they will enable its purpose?"

"Yes."

Nodding, Ara turned, started to reach for one of the gemstones. She hesitated, her heart pounding.

The deepest, oldest of magics. Oblivion. What would happen to her should she touch one?

Once again sensing her feelings, Wuldr spoke. "No harm will come to you as you forge the sword. The stones are benign until the moment their power is called upon."

The tension that had hunched her shoulders eased.

"I will leave you to your task," Wuldr said, and like Ofrit had minutes before, he vanished.

To Ara's surprise, Senn remained, watching, but not in an ominous way. Whenever she glanced over at the gigantic hound, he thumped his tail against the floor, and his tongue lolled out in a jolly way. She sensed that, more than anything, he didn't want her to feel alone as she worked. Given the ominous purpose of the weapon she was about to forge, Ara appreciated the watchful presence and the way it assured her that she was safe, protected.

She turned her attention to the forge. It was already hot, so she melted the godswood down until it was malleable, and set to shaping the heated material. Hammering, folding, heating again, hammering again. Fire. Smoke. Strength. Patience. As hours passed, the blade and tang took shape. When at last she was satisfied, she quenched the blade to harden it, then returned it to heat to temper it. That step accomplished, she turned to the work of grinding and polishing. Meticulous, careful, requiring nothing less than perfection, she focused on transforming the blade from shaped godswood to incomparable weapon. Working with the material never failed to mesmerize her; in its luster she found infinite depths, mysteries that could not be untangled, nor should they be.

Unlike StormSong, the blade for the fifth yet unknown Loreknight called for no ornamentation. The vision she held in her mind was of a weapon brutal in its simplicity. Its only decoration would be the gems set into its hilt.

As she shifted her focus to creating the pieces of the hilt, she repeated Ofrit's strange word puzzle to herself.

To find the end, begin again.

Fulfill the lore, as once before.

Restore the past, to rest at last.

What could it mean?

With the riddle floating in the back of her mind, Ara crafted a simple bar for a cross guard, one that flared at each end to create a square that would accommodate a stone of oblivion. Likewise, the beveled disk pommel featured one of the stones at its center.

Despite Wuldr's reassurances, her fingers trembled as she picked up the gems and carefully worked them into the settings of the guard and pommel. She drew a startled breath when, as she settled the last stone into place, the hilt shuddered, then pulsed beneath her hand, as if it had its own heartbeat. As suddenly as the movement started, it was gone, leaving her to wonder if she'd simply let her imagination get the better of her.

Shaking off the strange sensation, Ara focused on joining the pieces of the hilt: the cross guard, the grip—which would ultimately be wrapped in leather—and the pommel. When that task was complete, she required fire, once more bringing hilt and blade together—the tang the bridge between the components.

When that final application of heat had abated, the pieces of the sword become one, Ara stared at the weapon she'd forged—a knight's longsword—and shivered.

Shadows slid over the surface of the blade, twisting around it like serpents. For the first time, Ara felt hesitation about what she'd created. The magics infusing this weapon were dark, turbulent. Perhaps too dangerous to exist in the mortal world. Though she'd crafted it, she didn't like holding it, abhorred feeling the cold fingers of its power crawl over her skin. She turned away from the forge to find Wuldr and Senn waiting nearby. She approached the god and went down on one knee, offering the hilt to the god. "I present this blade, forged for the Loreknight you have chosen." Wuldr took the blade from her. In his mighty hand it looked more like a dagger than a sword. Wuldr simply nodded. An unadorned scabbard appeared in the god's free hand and he slid the blade inside before returning the sword to Ara. Even sheathed, energy radiated from the weapon, pulsing in the depths of the dark star-cut gems set into the hilt.

"A fine weapon," Wuldr pronounced. "Worthy of the champion who will wield it. Rise, Loresmith, and know you have my blessing and my thanks. Without you, the work of the gods could not be completed."

Ara shifted her weight, hesitant to ask the question that wanted to spill from her lips.

"The sword has been made for a terrible purpose," Wuldr said gravely, seeming to read her thoughts. "You are right to fear it."

"Godsbane," Ara whispered. "Its name is Godsbane."

A terrible purpose. The death of a divine being. A task that myth and history had, to this point, deemed impossible.

And yet.

She looked at Wuldr and saw deep sorrow in the god's eyes. Beside him, Senn gave a low whine and pressed his muzzle into Wuldr's hand.

"You don't want him to die," she said. "Vokk."

"He is my brother; I would not see him slain," Wuldr answered. "But he will destroy the world, and that cannot come to pass."

The grief of a god must be so vast, so deep, Ara thought. Were all of

Saetlund's gods likewise balanced on a knifepoint of sorrow? They must be, and how awful for them.

Throughout her trials, she'd considered her own pain, her own losses and those of her friends, but she hadn't given thought to the way unfolding events affected the gods. They, too, must make a sacrifice to save Saetlund and its people, most of whom had abandoned them generations before. How deep must the gods' love be for the land and those who lived there that they would not simply forsake the kingdom, leaving it to reap the harvest of doom it had planted.

"I am sorry for your pain," Ara said to Wuldr, though the words felt terribly inadequate.

Wuldr simply nodded.

"The Loreknight meant to wield this sword." Ara spoke hesitantly. "He is a stranger."

"Indeed," Wuldr replied. "But he will not always be."

"Is it my task to find him then?" A great weariness washed over her. Another journey, another search? Her quest felt endless.

Wuldr smiled kindly. "Fear not, Loresmith. He will find you. You have completed the trials of the gods, and we deem you worthy. You are now truly Loresmith, and you may pass your gift to the next generation when that time comes."

Ara swayed a bit, both from relief that she didn't have to hunt down a mysterious warrior and at Wuldr's pronouncement.

I am the Loresmith, and a child of mine will be the next Loresmith.

It was too much to contemplate—a future, a family. Teth's face briefly flashed through her mind, and she closed her eyes against a surge of grief.

If that was indeed her fate, to live as Loresmith and pass on what she knew, she had yet to reach it. Between her and that hope was a battle. An emperor. A god.

"Go now, Loresmith," Wuldr told her. "And begin the end."

16

amon kept his fingers clasped together before his chest as he crossed ArchWizard Zenar's office. He hoped it appeared to be a supplicating gesture; in truth, it was the only way he could hide the terrible shaking of his hands. His weakness wasn't the result of fear alone. The strain of imprisonment and the constant weight of regret had brought on the worst symptoms of his chronic illness. The pain that was his daily companion burned with a new ferocity. His headaches often robbed him of any sleep, and his inability to rest only made the cycle worsen.

Zenar sat at his desk, watching Eamon approach. Elders Byrtid and Tich stood in flanking positions on either side of the ArchWizard's desk.

"Prince Eamon." Zenar smiled slightly. There was a hungry gleam in his eye that Eamon supposed could work in his favor or be a signal of his impending demise. "I was surprised when Elder Tich brought me your petition."

Eamon had to clear his throat before he could speak. "ArchWizard, I confess I've been conflicted about my place here. I failed to grasp the magnitude of your influence not only over the future of Saetlund but also over that of the world."

He worried his flattery might be too sycophantic, but Zenar appeared pleased.

"I hoped you would help my sister gain the throne," he continued.

⟵ 165 ⟶

"And that the illness I've suffered from childhood might be healed by your magic."

Zenar nodded. "As we agreed upon."

"I do still want those things," Eamon said, drawing a quick breath, then forging on to the heart of his plea. "But having spoken with your elder wizards and witnessing the . . . I have no words to describe the ritual you performed . . ."

That was a lie. He did have words, but they would only have conveyed his horror. The memory of the innocents' bodies limp upon the stones surged into his mind along with a sudden throbbing behind his eyes, and he struggled to continue.

When Zenar's eyes narrowed, Eamon forced himself to speak.

"I am awed, and know now that more than anything I want to serve you, to become your acolyte."

With a smirk, Zenar said, "Many covet the magic I possess, but tell me, Your Highness, why should I offer you a place among my followers? You've already given me what I wanted. Our deal is finished."

It was another test. Eamon had expected something like this. He knew Elders Tich and Byrtid wouldn't have approached him about joining the wizards without Zenar's approval. What Eamon had to say next was essential to his plan—if he failed, all would be lost.

"I know that as the Vokkan armies conquered kingdoms, your wizards mastered the magics of each people the empire claimed, making them your own," Eamon said. "But when you encountered the first Loreknight, Teth, that magic proved hostile to you."

Zenar leaned forward, and Eamon worried he'd crossed a line.

"All foreign magics offer initial resistance to being subsumed," the ArchWizard said. "Make no mistake, in time, the power of Saetlund's gods will belong to me."

With a quick nod, Eamon pressed, "I have no doubt, but I believe I know a way to help."

The wizards standing behind Zenar exchanged a look of surprise as their master regarded Eamon with new interest. "Pray tell."

"I may not be the eldest of Dentroth's children," Eamon said, "but the royal blood of Saetlund nonetheless runs through my veins. That blood is linked to this land and its magic. For years I've made study of the Loresmith and Loreknights. And—it may be possible to perform a ritual that would draw the innate power of the Loreknight Teth and transfer it to you, using my body and blood as a channel."

The ArchWizard rose and came around the desk to stand face-to-face with Eamon. He took Eamon's chin in his hand and stared into his eyes. "Prince Eamon, why in Vokk's name would you be able to manage such a feat? The magic demanded by a ritual of that nature would be taxing for the most advanced of wizards."

"You're right, of course," Eamon agreed, struggling to keep still. Zenar's hollow eyes and sunken features were nauseating up close. "But what I lack in experience, I will make up for in scholarship—and the power of my blood."

"Your studies revealed the ritual to transfer power?" Zenar asked, and though his face gave nothing away, Eamon heard eagerness in his voice.

Eamon took a breath, knowing he must tread lightly. "I understand the fundamental elements required, but there is a missing piece—one that I can only find by accessing a site of Saetlund's mystical power."

"One of the hidden sites sought by the Loresmith?" Zenar asked with a dry laugh. He was likely suspicious that Eamon was angling to reunite with Ara.

"No," Eamon replied, refusing to flinch under Zenar's gaze. "What

I need is inscribed on the five standing stones at the center of the Isle of the Gods."

Zenar went still. Behind him, Elder Byrtid edged over to Elder Tich and began whispering in an urgent undertone. When the ArchWizard turned to glare at them, they both shrank back, and their conversation ceased.

The ArchWizard searched Eamon's face, perhaps looking for guile or malice, then clasped his hands behind his back and began to pace in front of his desk.

"You've piqued my interested, Your Highness," Zenar told him.

Eamon held his breath, waiting for the ArchWizard's next words.

"Would it surprise you to learn that any Vokkans attempting to set foot upon the Isle of the Gods return seemingly unharmed, but are unable to speak of or write anything about their visit? They simply cannot . . . even if it would save their life to do so."

Eamon held back a shudder at Zenar's words.

"Yet, if I'm recalling my history correctly, you have actually visited the isle?"

Eamon nodded. "It was tradition for the monarchs of Saetlund to present their children to the gods by bringing them to the isle on their first birthday. Nimhea and I were taken, though I have no memory of it."

"Your memory or lack thereof is no matter," Zenar replied. "The bloodline you possess must give you access to the isle's secrets. Even if you fail to glean what is necessary for the ritual, you would still bring us invaluable information—that is, if you aren't affected the way my wizards have been."

Pulse racing, Eamon nodded. "With your permission I would visit the Isle of the Gods."

If Zenar agreed, Eamon's plan would be set in motion. There was no guarantee of its success, but without this first step he had no chance at all.

After what felt like ages, the ArchWizard nodded.

"I will send you to the isle. If what you find there unlocks the secret to claiming Saetlund's magic, you will have my favor and be initiated as an acolyte. What little power Saetlund's gods retain appears to be harnessed on that isle."

Eamon thought of several things he could say to counter the ArchWizard's assessment of the gods' power, particularly that if it happened to be so weak, why bother seeking it, but he kept his mouth shut. Zenar had granted his wish. Now he needed Saetlund's gods to hear his plea.

There was no wind the morning two guards rowed Eamon from a city dock to the Isle of the Gods. The guards were grim-faced and pale as they pulled their oars through the glassy waters of the lake. Its surface reflected the cloudless summer-blue sky. Gulls circled lazily above them, uttering shrill cries, while ducks and cormorants paddled through the calm waters, seeking sustenance.

Eamon gazed at the green island at the center of the lake. A perfect circle and a mile in diameter, the Isle of the Gods was small. Before the Vokkan conquest, it was tended by ceremonial priests and priestesses who served the king rather than the gods. Visitors were only permitted for ritual purposes, just as for Eamon and Nimhea's only visit.

When he'd told Zenar he had no memory of that ceremony or the isle, Eamon had been speaking the truth. Now as he stared at the approaching island, he searched for anything familiar. A landmark, a particular span of shoreline, but he found nothing that stirred his memory.

He had no idea what awaited him there today, if anything. It was possible that he was on a fool's errand, but the innermost part of his heart whispered to him that he was not.

Still, Eamon was afraid. While he came to the gods seeking redemption, forgiveness was not something he believed he deserved. When he asked Saetlund's gods for help, would they hear him, and if they did, would they listen to his plea?

In the shallows at the edge of the isle, the guards jumped out into the water and dragged the boat onto a sandy shore. There were no structures on the Isle of the Gods, and that included docks.

The guards had been silent for the entirety of the journey, but now one of them spoke as Eamon climbed out of the small boat.

"We'll wait for your return."

Both guards were eyeing the thick line of trees that rose like a wall behind the white sand beach, blocking the interior of the island from view, their faces drawn with apprehension.

Eamon nodded, and as he walked toward the trees, he heard the other guard mutter, "If he comes back."

Eamon could hardly resent the man's comment. When he'd offered to make this pilgrimage to the Isle of the Gods, he'd done so knowing that he might not return.

Eamon paused at the edge of the trees to gaze up at the towering, broad-leafed sentinels and was suffused by a feeling similar to that of when he'd stood at the border of the Bone Forest with its bleached trunks and branches grasping the sky like skeletal claws. Here was a place that belonged to the gods. Cross its threshold and be judged.

Part of Eamon wished he wasn't afraid; the other part knew any person about to face the gods who claimed to be fearless was a liar, a fool, or both. He drew a quick breath and stepped into the forest.

Beyond the first line of trees came more trees, a dense forest of deciduous trees and evergreens as well as flowering shrubs in full bloom. The soft, warm summer air carried an uplifting fragrance, both herbal and floral. Sunlight filtered gently through the trees, lending a quality of incandescence that offset the shadows thrown by the thick canopy of leaves.

Eamon walked in a straight line toward the center of the island, only because it seemed the best way to go. There were no paths or markers on the isle. Birdsong floated around him, and he caught sight of rabbits and squirrels before they dashed away from him to hide. As he progressed, his frayed nerves began to calm, and the burning in his limbs melted away. His vision, often blurred of late by the pain battering his skull, cleared. The relief nearly had him collapsing to his knees. He wanted nothing more than to lie beneath the trees, gazing up at the jade canopy. To simply feel without suffering.

But he couldn't. This island might offer succor, but he hadn't earned that reward, so he pressed forward.

He hadn't been walking long when he spied a tall object ahead. Drawing closer, he saw that it was a massive stone, roughly rectangular in shape. Something about it made his heart thud. As he approached, he noted the stone sat on the edge of a small clearing in the forest, and it was not alone. He could already see two other stones edging the clearing at short intervals from the first, and he knew when he reached the gap in the forest he would find five standing stones in all. One for each of Saetlund's gods.

Eamon reached the first stone and once again experienced the sensation he'd had before entering the forest, that of standing on a threshold. He could feel power radiating from the stone, and even though he should have been able to look across the glen to the stones on the opposite side from his vantage point, for some reason he couldn't. The air between the stones shimmered, obscuring what lay at the heart of the clearing. Eamon's pulse was thundering now.

"I have come," he whispered, unsure why those particular words came from his mouth, and stepped past the towering stone.

For a moment his body felt heavy, like he was wading through a mire, and then the sensation passed and he was standing in a clearing that was drenched in midsummer sunlight and circled by five monoliths, each one bearing a sign of Saetlund's deities.

Sitting at the center of the stones was Fox.

Eamon fell to his knees and wept.

17

ra didn't remember anything after Wuldr's parting words. She'd been standing beside the god, and in the next moment she was opening her eyes, her body safely tucked in her bedroll at the campsite, as if waking from a dream. When she emerged from her tent, she found the campsite drenched in morning light. Lahvja was preparing breakfast at the fire, and Joar lounged against a fallen log nearby, idly scratching Huntress between her ears.

At Ara's appearance the ice wolf stood and came to greet her. Ara knelt down and pressed her forehead to Huntress's muzzle.

"All is well," she told the wolf softly. "Thank you for your help."

Huntress poked her warm nose into Ara's cheek, wagged her tail, and went back to Joar.

Joar looked from Huntress to Ara and frowned. "Has something happened?"

"Quite a lot," Ara said, coming to sit opposite him. She laid Godsbane across her lap, and Joar's frown deepened. "But I could use some tea for the telling. I've had a long night."

Even as she said the words, she realized that despite their truth, she felt well rested.

Lahvja brought her the requested tea, and Ara curled her hands around the wooden cup, watching steam rise from its surface. She recounted the events of the night, pausing every so often to take sips of her tea. When she'd finished, Lahvja plucked the now empty cup from Ara's hands, refilled it, and gave it back to her, along with slices of bread toasted over the fire and a wedge of cheese.

"Thank you," Ara said.

With a slight smile and a nod, Lahvja prepared another breakfast plate for Joar.

"So you've returned with a sword, but no warrior to wield it," Joar said, taking the plate.

"Yes, but the sword isn't the only thing I brought from the Loresmith Forge," Ara told them. "Ofrit gave me a puzzle."

Lahvja replied with a quiet laugh. "Puzzles and riddles, ever Ofrit's domain. What did the clever god tell you?"

Ara recited:

"To find the end, begin again.

Fulfill the lore, as once before.

Restore the past, to rest at last."

Joar gave a snort of disgust. "Riddles. What rubbish."

"Do you think it's meant to help you find the Loreknight you saw in your vision?" Lahvja asked, sitting down with her own plate.

Ara took bites of bread and cheese, chewed and swallowed as she thought. "I don't believe so. Wuldr said he would find me. We're not meant to go searching for him."

"And you've completed the trials." Lahvja set her plate aside to fully focus on Ara. "You are the Loresmith."

Ara ducked her head, self-conscious of the way both her friends suddenly regarded her with wonder.

"I'm still me," she said quietly. "I'm still me."

"You will always be Ara of Rill's Pass," Lahvja said. "Just as you have always, from a certain perspective, been the Loresmith, only now you've crossed the final threshold."

Ara let those words settle into her as they finished breakfast. The Resistance awaited the Loresmith's arrival and she would follow that destiny to its end, but her heart demanded she undertake one more task before moving on from Fjeri's forests.

Ara's pulse fluttered like a hummingbird's wings as she stalked through the pines with Joar at her side. The hunter remained in a surly mood as they closed in on Rill's Pass. She was all too aware he thought they should be on their way to rejoin Nimhea and the Resistance. It stung that his irritation was justified, but after her vision of her grandmother and Imgar being marched to execution, Ara couldn't leave Fjeri without a glimpse at her home. She didn't deny that it was a risky decision, but she also knew that she'd be unable to reunite with Nimhea and the Resistance while fearing all was not well within her village.

Ara and Joar left Lahvja and Huntress with the horses in a deep forest glen Joar deemed safe enough. Then they made their way through the forest at a stealthy pace and approached Rill's Pass at dusk. This close to midsummer, the indigo of twilight didn't appear until the early hours of morning, and the low light would only remain for a short time.

The village was still. Heavy curtains covered every window, offering the only way to capture a few hours of sleep during the overlong days. Among the familiar buildings—small farmhouses, animal pens—her gaze fixed on her grandmother's home, and her chest pinched. Her grandmother was likely asleep, though Elke was often restless amid the days where the sun barely set. Perhaps she was sitting before the hearth with a cup of tea. Ara was overcome by a yearning for familiar things.

Waking to the sound of her grandmother singing sweetly as she prepared breakfast. The ringing sound of Imgar's hammer on steel calling her to the smithy each day.

Ara frowned at the smoke rising from the chimney of Old Imgar's smithy. It wasn't unusual for the blacksmith to work well into the night during the summer, but the smoke itself appeared unusual, curling into the air in thick, oily tendrils. Forge smoke shouldn't look like that.

"Something is wrong," Joar said quietly. "There are no animals in the pens. It is too quiet."

Turning her gaze on the pens that abutted most farmhouses, Ara found that Joar was right. No pigs or chickens, no shaggy cows or horned goats. In the harsh winter months, animals were often brought to shelter at night, but there was no need in this milder weather.

Ara forced herself to nod despite a reflexive response to deny it. As she watched the village, there was a movement at the drapes in her grandmother's house. The shape was too large to be her grandmother, too small to be Old Imgar. There was a stranger in her home.

"Joar—" she began.

"I saw him," he replied. "There are others, within the village buildings. And the smoke coming from the smithy smells off. That's not charcoal burning."

Ara glanced at him. "Can you tell what it is?"

"I am uncertain," he said with a grimace.

She had the sense he was holding something back, but dread kept her from pressing him further. There was no sense in stoking her fear when she could get answers for herself.

Keeping her belly to the ground, Ara began to crawl forward, heading toward the cover of a nearby tree. She'd barely moved when Joar clapped a large hand on her shoulder. His hold wasn't painful, but his obvious strength made it clear that she would go no farther without his assent.

Ara looked at the hunter over her shoulder. He gave a single shake of his head. Grinding her teeth, she pushed back until they were face-to-face.

"I have to know what's happened," Ara whispered. "My grand-mother, my friends . . ."

The scene from Senn's Fury reared up in her mind, filling her with dread and desperation to do something. Anything.

Joar shook his head again. "You will not serve them by entering that village. It is an ambush."

She wanted to argue that it might not be, but that would only serve to make her look like a fool. "Even so, if the Vokkans have captives, we need to free them."

"We cannot," he said with sadness. "The danger to you is too great. We must return to Lahvja."

"I can't." It was difficult for Ara not to raise her voice. "My only family is in that village."

The hand on Ara's shoulder gave a gentle squeeze. "You do not know that. We cannot know what transpired here. The Below or the Resistance could have picked up word of an imminent attack on your home village. The people here may have had warning and time to escape."

"I can't risk that," Ara snapped, and her eyes began to burn. In the back of her mind, a voice was telling her to listen to Joar, to accept that he was right. She ignored it. Her heart was breaking at what might have happened.

Joar gave her a long look, then nodded.

Ara turned away from him and looked toward the village once more.

Without warning, the hand Joar had placed on her shoulder reached around to clamp over her mouth. His other arm wrapped around her waist, drawing her against him as he dragged her back into the forest away from the village. She wasn't fool enough to shout, even with her mouth covered, but she did struggle. It quickly became clear there would be no escaping Joar's hold. He had pinned her arms to her sides; his muscles might as well have been molded steel.

When the trees thickened, closing them in and hiding the village, Joar stood up and turned in the direction of their camp. He didn't set Ara on her feet, nor did he loosen his grip even a little, trudging through the forest while her legs dangled a few feet off the ground.

Furious, Ara was tempted to kick him or bite his hand, but enough of her conscience prevailed so that she only thrashed her legs. Joar didn't try to soothe her. He didn't speak to her at all as he moved at a steady pace. Eventually she tired of fighting to no effect and slumped against Joar. When she did so, Joar removed his hand from her mouth. Ara wasn't sure if that was because he thought she wouldn't shout or because they were far enough from the village for it not to matter.

"You can put me down," she said.

Joar ignored her, and she knew it wasn't worth repeating herself. Apparently she would be carried all the way back to camp. As Joar walked, Ara's anger slowly ebbed as she accepted that he'd been right.

She'd pushed her friends enough by demanding to visit Rill's Pass. This small delay alone had been an indulgence. She hadn't found the reassurance she craved or hints of what had happened here, but at least she could take small comfort in knowing the next step in her journey would reunite her with Nimhea, and she could bring Saetlund's rightful queen the news that the Loresmith quest was complete. The time for warriors had arrived at last.

18

Eamon wasn't certain how long he wept, only that it was a release, a scouring of his soul that had been long coming. While his grief, his shame, his regret, poured out, Fox sat calmly, bright eyes fixed on him.

When he'd drawn the last ragged breath, calming himself enough to still his trembling limbs, Eamon swiped lingering tears from his cheeks and lifted his head to look at Fox. But it was no longer Fox in front of him. Instead, he stared up at the towering form of Eni, the Traveler, body garbed in cloaks that swirled wildly despite there being no wind. A broad-brimmed hat put Eni's face in perpetual shadow, disguising any distinguishing features.

"Eni," Eamon breathed. "I beg your mercy. The mercy of all Saetlund's gods. I know the wrongs I've done. I know I deserve no pity or forgiveness, but I beg you to give me the chance to atone."

Eni didn't answer. The god's eyes glowed beneath the brim of the hat.

"And how might you atone?" Eni asked.

"I'm sorry?" Eamon said, and in that moment he realized he'd expected direction, a setting down of terms by which he could restore himself in the eyes of the gods and, most of all, his sister.

"Surely if you believe there is a way you could be forgiven, you've given serious consideration to the path you must follow to do so."

Eamon balked, actually shrank into himself as if he were a turtle that could find protection in its shell.

"Don't limit yourself this way, Prince Eamon," Eni said, the varied timbres of their voice blending like a chorus. "Your mind is a gift which most souls never experience. Tell me. What is the way to atonement?"

Eamon had to draw several deep breaths before he could speak. "The children. The children must be saved." Shivering, he continued, "I love my sister more than anything. I did what I did because I thought it would protect her. I was wrong, so wrong. I still need to help Nimhea if I can, but it's the children who matter the most. We have to help them."

The nonexistent wind seemed to suddenly rise, tossing Eni's cloaks. "Yes. The children must be saved. And you believe you have a way to ensure their safety?"

"I cannot promise success," Eamon admitted. "But I will give everything I have, everything I am, to help them."

"And so," Eni prompted. "How is the ArchWizard to be defeated?"

Eamon replied, "His greed can be turned against him."

"True," Eni observed, then went silent, encouraging Eamon to continue.

"Above all else, he wants Saetlund's magic for his own, the power of the Loresmith and Loreknights, of the gods," said Eamon. "When he tried to reach it by using Teth's bow, the magic rejected him, caused him physical pain."

Eni nodded.

"But I don't think Zenar can control Saetlund's magic," he said. "Not because he hasn't found a way to seize it, but because it will always reject him. That power will never be his."

"Very astute, Prince Eamon." Approval and satisfaction rang in Eni's voice. "The magic innate to this kingdom, to its champions and its gods, was created in direct opposition to the source of all Zenar's power: Vokk the Devourer. When our brother asked to find his own people in another part of the world, and we assented, he swore an oath to leave Saetlund at peace. We knew he would break that oath. His nature made it an inevitability."

Eamon nodded thoughtfully, and Eni fell silent, but watchful, while he pondered the god's revelation.

He suddenly smiled. "Then what I want to do is possible."

"Indeed it is," Eni replied.

Eamon's pulse began to pound. "But will I be able to call on the magic? After what I've done?"

He paused, closing his eyes.

"Am I forgiven?" Eamon could barely voice the question; it came out as a rough whisper.

"A complex question with many answers," Eni replied in a gentle voice. "And the only answer over which you have power is whether you can forgive yourself."

Eamon opened his eyes.

"You have faith and hope," Eni continued. "Had you lacked either, I could not be here, and you must hold on to both in order to complete the task you've set for yourself."

The god reached into their billowing cloaks, withdrew a small object, and held it out. It was a small twig that, despite being broken from a tree, still maintained leaves of vibrant green.

"You will also need this."

Eamon took the twig from Eni. When his fingers wrapped around it, he could feel subtle vibrations.

"It is taken from a tree of this island," Eni told him. "Within it lives the essence of Saetlund's magic. Keep it safe. When the time comes, use its power for your purpose."

"Thank you."

"There is another task you must complete," Eni said. "I have a message for the Loresmith to be delivered by the Dove and only the Dove."

"Commander Liran?" Eamon gaped in surprise. "But he's in Five Rivers. I have no idea where Ara is. Does he know? Does the Resistance?"

"He will find his own way to her," Eni replied, amusement in their voice. "It is imperative that they meet before the coming battle."

Though he didn't understand, Eamon nodded. "The message?"

"The answer you seek lies in the Five Rivers catacombs."

Eamon repeated the words to himself, then looked at Eni with a puzzled frown. "What is the question?"

"The question belongs to the Loresmith. In this task you are only the messenger to the next messenger."

Eni seemed to be delighting in the strange request. Eamon decided not to press the matter any further.

"I will give the Dove the message."

"Good." Though Eni's face was hidden in shadow, Eamon sensed the god was smiling.

"I should thank you for calling me here. I enjoy this island," Eni said, and Eamon realized his time with the god had come to an end. "It has many plump rabbits."

With that, the tall, cloaked god vanished, and Fox stood in front of Eamon once more. Then, in a flash of red-and-silver fur, Fox darted out of the circle of stones and into the forest.

19

hen they'd broken down their campsite and were prepared to travel, Ara held out Godsbane to Joar. "I appreciate your taking care of this."

Joar solemnly accepted the sword, secured in its scabbard, from Ara. There was no question he'd be the one to carry it with them. Given Ara's short stature, if belted at her waist, the longsword would more than drag along the ground—it would likely bury itself and get stuck.

Ara, Lahvja, and Joar all looked at one another, their expressions caught between eager anticipation and anxious reluctance. Wuldr had said the trial marked an end and a beginning. What came next would be the first step of that new journey.

"I don't see any way around it," Ara admitted.

With the final trial completed and the fifth Loreknight's weapon forged, the time had come to reunite with Nimhea and the Resistance. But considering that the first, and only, time Lahvja and Ara had traveled between planes using the Whisper of Life had landed them in the middle of a Vokkan ambush, all three of them approached the prospect of traveling that way again with trepidation.

"We don't know where they are," Ara continued. "And we have no way to find them except through Lahvja. The Twins gave her this power for a reason. If we hesitate to use it, we're squandering that gift."

"The purpose of this power is to bring Loreknights together." Lahvja nodded her agreement. "But it comes with the inherent risk of traveling into an unknown situation."

Reading the doubt in Joar's expression, Ara said, "It's unlikely we'll run into trouble. Nimhea is with the Resistance, and they haven't mobilized against the Vokkans yet. They're *waiting* for us. We need to go to them. This is the way."

When he remained unconvinced, Lahvja said, "Our alternative is to head into Kelden, where we last knew Nimhea to be headed, and wander around until they find us or we find them. All while we know Vokkan patrols are out looking for us."

"She's right," Ara said.

Joar grumbled under his breath for a moment before asking, "Huntress and the horses can travel this way?"

"Yes," Lahvja said quickly. "So long as one of us is touching them. We cannot break contact during the journey. To do otherwise is dangerous."

As if to reassure him, Huntress sidled up to Joar and licked his hand.

"Very well," he said, looking at the wolf. "We will travel in this strange manner."

Ara and Lahvja mounted their horses and linked hands. Joar stayed on the ground. He'd guided his mount so it stood shoulder to shoulder with Lahvja's. They joined their hands and rested them on Joar's horse's withers. Joar kept his other hand buried in the fur at the scruff of Huntress's neck.

"Does it hurt?" Joar asked Ara as Lahvja bowed her head.

"No," Ara told him. "It's just very odd. Kind of tingly."

"Tingly?" Joar frowned.

"Quiet." Lahvja looked up and scolded them. "I'm trying to concentrate."

Ara and Joar exchanged a chagrined glance and held their tongues.

Giving each of them a final stern glare, Lahvja rolled her shoulders back, drew a long, slow breath, and closed her eyes.

The surrounding forest began to waver, becoming more and more indistinct until it slipped away entirely, replaced by the strange mélange of colors and shapes that composed the space between planes. Ara looked at Joar; his expression was a mix of wonder and discomfort. She was somewhat reassured his feelings seemed a mirror of her own. Even having traveled this way once before, she didn't feel any more at ease. Oddly, the horses and Huntress seemed less troubled about this mode of transportation than she and Joar did.

As before, it was impossible to gauge the passage of time. All she could do was wait in this ethereal, floating place, feeling unmoored all the while. Relief slipped over her when the watery, waving quality of the space around her began to take on the definition of objects. Something was moving close by, two somethings that were forming into what looked like people.

Ara focused her attention on them in case they turned out to be a threat.

"What the—" She heard the words followed by a sharp grunt just as the world around her came into sharp relief, and saw a foot connect with a man's chest. The blow sent him sprawling.

Ugh. They'd landed in the middle of another fight. Ara reached for Ironbranch, then froze when she recognized the man who was on his back, staring up at her with a frown.

"Ioth?"

"Loresmith?" Ioth gaped at her. "How?"

"Hello, Ara." A woman with bright blue and vivid ochre braids greeted her, her calm voice belying the shock on her face. "Who are your friends? And is that a wolf?"

·"Xeris." Ara slid from her horse's back. "Glad to see you're well, and you'll be pleased to know I've brought two Loreknights with me. Lahvja of Eni's Children and Joar of the Koelli."

Lahvja offered Xeris a warm smile.

Joar managed a grunt and a nod before deigning to say, "Huntress is my companion."

He made a show of patting the wolf's head. Huntress rolled her eyes up at him as if to convey that she had little patience with his patronizing performance.

"It's an honor," Xeris said, keeping a wary gaze on Huntress.

"Joar, Lahvja." Ioth smiled and started to elbow his way off the ground. "Good to see you again."

"You're down." Xeris put her foot in the center of Ioth's chest, pushing him flat against the earth. "I won."

"No," he protested. "I was distracted by the people who appeared out of nowhere. It doesn't count."

"Yes, it does."

"Fine," he said, but when Xeris smiled and relaxed her foot, Ioth grabbed her ankle with both hands and gave a hard jerk.

Xeris landed flat on her back beside him.

"There. That's better." He flipped to his feet and stood, side-stepping before Xeris could reach him.

"I still won," she muttered, pushing herself up.

"Keep telling yourself that." Ioth grinned at her, then said to the rest of them, "There are a lot of people who'll be thrilled you're here. You'd better come with me. Xeris will see to your horses."

"Of course she will." Xeris favored Ioth with a rude hand gesture.

Ara paused beside her before following Ioth. "You know he's only trying to ignore the fact that you beat him."

"Oh, I know." Xeris gave a throaty laugh. "And don't worry. I'll make him regret it soon enough."

Ara laughed with her, then continued after Ioth. Lahvja fell in step beside her while Joar and Huntress walked a few steps behind.

Ioth led them out of what looked like a horse paddock. Their surroundings were odd, and appeared to be ruined fortifications dug into a hillside.

As he opened a door that led underground, Ara asked, "Where are we?"

"Welcome to Drover's Redoubt," Ioth replied. "In western Kelden. Not the fanciest of places, but it's home . . . for now."

He took them inside what Ara decided were barracks. They walked down a hall and passed several smaller rooms until he turned to show the way into a large room that appeared to be a refectory. Several people were gathered around a long table.

Ioth loudly cleared his throat. "We have some visitors."

Ara heard a low cry and saw a blur of motion. A tall figure with fiery curls that streamed out flew past her into Lahvja's open arms.

"Thank Nava." Nimhea buried her face in Lahvja's neck.

Lahvja's eyes brimmed as she folded Nimhea in an embrace. "I've missed you, Princess."

Ara had barely followed their reunion because her gaze was fixed on the barrel-chested, bearded man who stared back at her from the far end of the table.

She didn't realize she was moving until she crashed into him, throwing her arms around his thick neck. "Imgar. Gods, what are you doing here?"

Old Imgar's voice was thick when he replied. "Long story, my dear. But you'll hear it. Now let me look at you. Are you well?"

"Very." Ara drew back to gaze up at him. The grizzled, familiar face made her heart swell with joy, then it contracted with fear. "My grandmother?"

"She's around here somewhere," he told her, then glanced over and gave a nod to Ioth, who immediately left the room. "Drover's Redoubt is a military site, and I wanted to send her to a place more suited to civilians, but she wouldn't hear of it, knowing you'd likely end up wherever the Circle was. You know it's impossible to argue with Elke once she's set her mind to something."

"Thank the gods." Ara gasped, so full of joy she fell like she'd burst into a million pieces at any moment.

Old Imgar reached out and cupped her cheek. "My Ara, the Loresmith. I knew you'd do it. Never had a doubt."

She had to swallow around the sudden lump in her throat. "Thank you. I couldn't have done it without you. You taught me so much. All the stories. I had no idea how much you were preparing me for the trials I'd have to face. Not to mention everything you taught me about smithing."

"I'd imagine the smithing you've done lately is a far cry from what happened at my forge," Imgar teased.

Ara laughed. "I can't wait to tell you about the Loresmith Forge, you won't believe—"

She broke off because Imgar's gaze had gone to the room's entrance, and in the same moment he'd become terribly still.

Ara turned to see Joar standing in the doorway, returning Imgar's intense stare.

"My boy . . ." Imgar's voice shook. He took a few steps forward. "They told me, but I couldn't let myself believe."

Joar wore a bewildered expression. "Father . . . why are you . . . ?"

Father? Ara looked from the Koelli hunter to Imgar in disbelief. No, it couldn't be.

Suddenly the confusion cleared from Joar's face, and he let out a booming laugh. "Of course! I see. The Hawk has returned to battle. I should have known. I had no doubt the time would come."

The two men strode toward each other. When they stood a foot apart, they stopped, each taking in their fill of the other before they embraced. Imgar wasn't a small man, but Joar still topped him by more than a foot.

When Old Imgar stepped back, his eyes were shining. "My son. When they told me . . . a Loreknight. I didn't want to let myself believe. Not until I saw you with my own eyes. All these years, I prayed Wuldr would keep you safe as you pursued the quest he gave you. That this was where the gods were leading you."

"It is an honor beyond words." Joar's voice was rough with emotion. "But there is no greater joy than being with you again. I have missed you, Father. So much. And I have tales to tell you. Many fires and mugs of ale are in our future."

"I can't wait." Imgar suddenly frowned and looked down where Huntress was enthusiastically licking his fingers. His eyes widened. "And who is this?"

Joar grinned and scratched between the wolf's ears. "This is Huntress. I saved her life, and she returned the favor many times. She has been my traveling companion and my closest friend. It seems she understands how important you are to me."

"I'm grateful she didn't think otherwise," Imgar observed. "Given the size of her teeth."

"She's very handy in a fight," Joar said. "And a hunt."

By this time, Ara had broken out of her stupor and made her way to the two men.

"Imgar," she blustered. "What in Wuldr's name is going on?"

Joar frowned at her, then at his father. "You know my father? And, Father, you know the Loresmith?"

"You could say that," Ara replied dryly.

Old Imgar scratched his beard, offering an abashed look to Ara, then Joar. "There are some explanations to be made."

"You have a son." Ara jabbed a finger at him. "And you're the Hawk? I can't . . . why . . . how?"

A pair of hands rested gently on Ara's shoulders. "I asked the same questions, my dear. Though you're maintaining a much more pleasant tone of voice. I'll admit I did some screeching when I found out."

Ara whirled and gazed into the kindest eyes she'd ever known. "Grandmother!"

She wrapped her arms around Elke's waist and was in turn enfolded in her grandmother's warm embrace. "Oh, my Ara. My love. Thank the gods for keeping you safe and for giving me the chance to hold you again."

Ara's face was wet with tears. Everything about her grandmother, her scent, her softness, it was home. She had known she missed all those things, but she hadn't begun to understand how much.

"Rill's Pass," she sobbed against her grandmother's shoulder. "I saw it. The Vokkans there. I was so afraid."

"Senn hunt down those Vokkans for taking our home," Elke said gently. "But we had warning. Imgar's . . . friends made sure we got out."

Ara made herself step back and swipe the tears from her cheeks.

Elke gave Ara's hands a squeeze before letting them go. "No need to cry, love. All is well."

Fixing a reproving gaze on Imgar, Elke added, "And this rogue has a fine explanation that he'll no doubt spin out for you by the fire some night."

"That's not fair, Elke," Imgar objected in a gruff voice. "I was the town blacksmith, there to ply my trade and help Ara along."

She ignored him. "All the while he was keeping his secrets and consorting with the Resistance, knowing that when the time came, he'd return to them as the Hawk."

"Is that really so bad?" Imgar asked.

Elke shook her finger at him. "You could have trusted me. I can't believe you kept such a secret."

"I would have told you eventually," Imgar said. "I promise."

He rubbed the back of his neck. Was he blushing?

"I told you I'm sorry, Elke," he said. "And I am. Are you ever going to let this go?"

"I'll let it go when I'm well and ready," she snapped. "Maybe I'd have let it go already if you hadn't tried to ship me off to some outlandish place where it would have been another year before I saw my granddaughter again."

"Senn's teeth," Imgar growled, all his humility gone. "I only wanted to keep you safe."

"Since when do you get to make that kind of decision for me?" Elke put her hands on her hips. "If I hadn't spoken to Suli, I would have been riding away without knowing why. And you would have been happy to see me go."

"I wouldn't have been happy," Imgar growled. "But I might have had some peace of mind."

Ara watched the back-and-forth—between the two people she'd always loved most—with growing fascination. Behind her grandmother's offense and Imgar's protests, she saw something very interesting, an affection that went beyond friendship. She realized it must have been there for a long time, but she'd been too young, or too self-involved, to notice it. But it was glaringly obvious now.

Suddenly giggles bubbled up from her chest. She tried to cover her mouth to muffle them but wasn't quick enough.

Elke rounded on her. "What's so funny, Ara? I'd think you'd be as irked with Imgar as I am."

Ara pressed her lips together, trying to stuff the giggles away, and ended up holding her breath.

Joar frowned at her. "Your face is getting red, Loresmith. Are you unwell?"

"Is he right, Ara?" Imgar asked, suddenly grim with concern. "Are you ill?"

She shook her head, his worry finally quelling her urge to laugh. "I'm fine. I promise. I just . . . there have been a lot of surprises."

"Enough to make you dizzy," Elke agreed, putting one arm around Ara's waist and giving Imgar a pointed look.

With a sigh, Imgar said to Ara, "I hope you know I wasn't deceiving you to be hurtful or because you weren't worthy of my trust. I only wanted to protect you."

"I know that, Imgar." Ara stepped to him and rose onto her tiptoes to kiss his cheek. "And I love you. I always have."

"Well," Imgar said, coughing to cover his sudden flush of emotion. "That's very kind."

"I'm still very confused," Joar interjected. "And I would like an ale."

"I can help you with that." Imgar took Joar by the elbow. "Let's go find some."

"Impossible man," Elke said under her breath as she watched father and son walk away.

Ara made a noncommittal sound and then smiled as Nimhea, Lahvja, and Suli came up to them.

Nimhea gave Ara a hug so tight it briefly stole her breath.

"It's so good to see you again, Ara."

"You too, Your Highness," Ara replied with a wide smile. "It looks like things are going well here."

"They have been," Nimhea said, returning the smile. "And even better now that you're here. It's all coming together. And . . ."

She paused, exchanging a look with Lahvja.

"What?" Ara said, suddenly wary.

"It's Eamon," Nimhea burst out. "Ara, he's not . . . he's helping us. Eamon is helping us. He's working against Zenar."

"Oh gods." Ara didn't realize her knees had gone weak until her grandmother leaned into her to give support. "Nimhea, that's wonderful. More than wonderful."

"It is," Nimhea said, her eyes shining. "I didn't dare hope . . . but it's true."

"And—" Lahvja nudged Nimhea with her elbow.

"Oh! Of course." Nimhea laughed. "Teth is safe . . . well, as safe as he can be. He's a prisoner, but all things considered he's doing very well. Lucket has an agent keeping an eye on things, and the Dove is helping. Eamon and Teth are working against the Vokkans from the inside. I really think they're going to be okay." Nimhea let out a gust of breath. "I can't believe I just said that, but it's true. Despite everything, they're going to be okay."

For a moment, Ara just stared at her.

"Ara?" Lahvja asked gently. "Are you okay?"

Ara began to nod, opened her mouth to reply.

All that came out was "Teth."

She burst into tears.

"Oh my goodness." Elke drew Ara's shaking form against her. "Perhaps you young ladies should explain to me exactly who this Teth person is."

20

enar leaned back in his chair, his fingers steepled at his chin, as he listened to Eamon's account of his visit to the Isle of the Gods. The story Eamon related bore little resemblance to what actually transpired, but if Zenar doubted its truth, he hid his skepticism well.

"When I laid my hands upon the stones, I felt their power—the magic of Saetlund," Eamon said, putting fervor into his voice. "It was . . . incredible."

A furrow appeared between Zenar's brows. "You sensed the power, that is one thing, but I see no reason it would indicate you can claim those magics for your own."

"Forgive me," Eamon said pleadingly. "I find it difficult to adequately describe what happened."

"Try harder." Zenar's frustration scratched through his words.

Eamon knew his performance required a precise balancing act: too much confidence and Zenar would dismiss him as naive; too little and the ArchWizard wouldn't believe him capable of the task he proposed.

"Forgive me for keeping this from you, ArchWizard," he spoke quickly, urgently. "But when I went to the island, I doubted I would return. I didn't expect to survive the journey."

Zenar went still, eyeing Eamon with sudden interest. "Is that so?"

Nodding, Eamon continued. "I didn't think my blood would be enough to maintain my connection to Saetlund's gods. I thought my attempt to tap into their power would not only fail, but would probably kill me.

"Instead, when I reached out for the magic harnessed in the standing stones, I not only felt its presence, I felt it welcome me. I understood that these magics are tied to my essence. I have no doubt I can channel that essence for your benefit."

Zenar tried to mask the gleam of desire in his eyes, but couldn't quite hide it.

"Prince Eamon." Zenar kept his voice cool. "While I admire your enthusiasm, by your own admission you are not adept with magic. Even if you can access this power, why would you be able to manipulate it to your purpose?"

Eamon's pulse jumped. This next bit was the crux of his plan. Clearing his throat and averting his gaze, as if embarrassed, Eamon said, "Actually, ArchWizard, it was . . . it was you who showed me the way."

There was a pause, simmering with surprise. "I?"

"Yes." Eamon risked a glance at Zenar, then averted his gaze again to show deference. "When you tapped into the life energy of the children and channeled it into yourself, it sparked an idea in my mind, and I realized there was a way to create a scenario in which you could draw Saetlund's power into yourself."

The ArchWizard's eyes were alight with greed. "How?"

"Forgive me if what I say next sounds like insolence," Eamon replied. "But you attempted to access the Loreknight's power, and it hurt you."

Anger flashed across Zenar's features, but he didn't interrupt.

"It's because you need a conduit. With the children, you use the tree from your homeland," Eamon continued. "To claim Saetlund's magic from the Loreknight, you need a willing channel. That channel is me."

"And what would you need to accomplish this feat?" Zenar's mouth was a tight line.

"To be in the same room with you, as you were with the children," Eamon told him. "Teth, the Loreknight, will also need to be there, as will his weapon—the bow and arrow."

"Nothing more? No blood sacrifice or herbal compounds? Elixirs?"

Eamon shook his head, then said haltingly, "In a manner, the Loreknight will be the blood sacrifice."

Though he knew he was lying, Eamon still found the words difficult to utter. He had to stop himself from shuddering at the mental image of Teth lying dead, the way the children had been, limp and lifeless on that stone floor.

Zenar's eyes widened slightly. Then, slowly, he smiled.

"Well, Prince Eamon," Zenar said, coming closer until he stood face-to-face with Eamon. "You've surprised and impressed me. Your reasoning is sound. And your timing is . . . fortuitous."

Eamon was puzzled. He'd expected Zenar to be pleased by the news, but it was clear that something else was driving Zenar's eagerness.

"My father's reign must come to an end," Zenar said. "And you will play a vital role in wresting power from the emperor. When he arrives, I will challenge him, and at the moment I command, you will complete the ritual to channel the Loreknight's power to me, a power that Fauld will have no defense against."

Dazed, Eamon needed a moment to gather his wits enough to reply. "Emperor Fauld is coming here?"

Liran had already given him and Teth that information, but the scenario Zenar offered had ramifications that made Eamon's pulse thunder. Because the magic he planned to use against Zenar could potentially bring down Fauld as well.

"Indeed." Zenar sounded almost bored. "My father is unhappy about the little revolt your sister is leading. He plans to crush it. Of course, I will do the same, but after I have dealt with my father and taken control of the empire."

"But you'll still keep my sister safe," Eamon blurted.

"Yes, yes." Zenar waved a dismissive hand. "Your sister will serve as a puppet monarch. She's the ideal figure for that role, provided she submits. If you cannot convince her to do so, I have no use for her, and you, Prince Eamon, will sit upon the River Throne."

Eamon bit his tongue to stop himself from blurting, *I don't want it.*

Instead, he managed to say, "I'll convince her."

"I hope so," Zenar replied. "But I don't want you to think you'll go without reward. It's hardly fair, your sister a queen when you've been the one to do me a great service."

Unsure where the ArchWizard was leading, Eamon stayed quiet.

"I told you that should you prove your worth to me, you'd be permitted to join my wizards as an acolyte," Zenar said, then waited until Eamon nodded.

"But that hardly seems a sufficient payment, should you give me the gift you've offered," Zenar continued. "A fitting reward, I think, would be this: when I become emperor, you will serve as my apprentice. That will spare you the petty politics and squabbles you'd face attempting to ascend the ranks of the wizards."

He waited for his words to settle upon Eamon. "Does that please you?"

Eamon was stunned, and felt a little sick. He dropped to one knee—both to hide his reaction and to please Zenar.

"I am deeply honored, ArchWizard." Eamon hoped the shaking in his voice conveyed humility rather than revulsion. "Nothing would please me more than to serve you and be your pupil."

"Yes." Zenar sounded smug. "I imagine so."

21

iran still couldn't believe he'd agreed to this ludicrous arrangement. As much as he'd been operating as a covert agent of the Resistance for many years, his role was to provide intelligence. From a safe distance.

Yet somehow he found himself out on a moonless night on his way to a secret meeting because Dagger, who'd been checking on Zenar's captives with some regularity, had brought him a message from Prince Eamon. A message that Liran was told had to be passed on to the Loresmith, by himself and no other, in person.

Liran wasn't accustomed to taking orders, and he was loath to follow a command he found foolish and seemingly unnecessary. He was neither spy nor assassin. He did not creep through the dark to accomplish his purpose.

Granted, he wasn't exactly sneaking through shadows to get there. With two of his lieutenants accompanying him, Liran had ridden out from Five Rivers at dusk. It was a lucky thing Liran was known for his habit of taking long rides into the countryside. Had he been able to choose his own vocation, Liran would have enjoyed spending his life training horses.

The purported reason for his ride out that night was to work with a horse that had become skittish in low light conditions. The flea-bitten gray he rode in the deepening twilight did need encouragement and reinforcement of training to overcome this fresh fear of the dark, but the horse also conveyed him along the shore of the Lake of the Gods until they reached a lone rider. The slight cloaked figure raised a black-gloved hand in greeting, but didn't speak. Liran gave a signal to his lieutenants, who brought their horses to a halt while he continued toward the other rider. The two of them followed the lakeshore at an unhurried pace.

When his men were out of earshot, Liran's guide turned to look at him.

"You cut a fine figure on a horse, Commander."

"It's nice to see you, too, Maira," he replied, settling his horse as it tried to spook.

Her only acknowledgment of his using her real name was a slight curve at one corner of her mouth.

They rode north until they reached a point where the sandy shore gave way to a steep rise. Over time, the wind had driven pounding surf into the rocky cliff until, millennia later, the water had carved through the rock.

A man bearing a torch emerged from the darkness where the water disappeared into the rock face. Liran's horse immediately balked, half rearing until Liran calmed him.

Dagger was already dismounting. "I'll keep watch over the horses."

When he'd jumped down from the saddle, Liran handed his reins over to Dagger. "You'll need a firm hold on him. He doesn't like the dark."

The man with the torch gestured for the commander to follow him into the opening. It was just tall enough that he didn't have to duck down to walk. There was about a foot on either side of the lapping water for them to traverse without soaking their boots. In the deeper recesses of the cavern, the space opened up, revealing an inner grotto with a shallow pool behind which was a wide, dry area. Torchlight flickered, making shadows dance along the walls and over the surface of the water, revealing seven people who stood watching his approach.

It was an odd assembly, Liran thought as he looked them over.

He had a good idea who the broad-shouldered, bearded man with war-weathered features was, and it was this man he was the most eager to meet. Beside him stood a tall Solan woman with a stance of rigid authority and a Daefritian man with dark skin who watched Liran with wise and wary eyes. A lanky Vijerian with braids colored by blue woad and ochre, who bore a bow and arrow she looked ready to use, pinned him with a gaze that verged on hostile. There was yet another Vijerian, but this woman had long, waving mahogany locks and wore the dress of the Wanderen. Standing close to her was a very tall young woman whose fiery curls made it easy to identify her: Nimhea, scion of the Flamecrowned Dynasty. She had the bearing of a queen. Seeing the heir to the River Throne in the flesh made Liran's skin prickle. If their cause triumphed, she was the future of Saetlund.

Next to Nimhea stood an even younger woman who was very short, even shorter than Dagger. She had pale skin, coal-dark hair, and dark eyes that seemed to reach inside him. He frowned at her. Though she was a stranger, something about her pulled at him. As if he should know her.

The Solan woman stepped forward. "Commander Liran. We were surprised you insisted on a face-to-face meeting, given these dangerous times. I am Suli, one who can speak for your allies in the Resistance."

Liran put a fist to his chest and bowed. "I thank you for granting my request. Believe me, I would have much preferred that we keep our exchanges at a distance, but I was given no choice in the matter."

"Is that so?" Suli lifted her eyebrows. "And who commands the commander?"

With a smirk, Liran pushed the hood of his cloak back, took another step forward, and replied, "Your gods do, it would seem."

The burly, bearded man beckoned to Liran, and he walked around the pool until he stood before the one he knew had to be his counterpart.

"Hawk." Liran's voice was one of respect and admiration.

The man's tone mirrored the commander's. "Dove."

By silent, mutual agreement, they clasped forearms in greeting.

"My friends call me Imgar," the man told him, a sudden grin splitting his face. "Sometimes Old Imgar."

"Liran," Liran replied. "No one's called me old yet. Though some days it feels like they should."

With a bark of a laugh, Imgar said, "You need a beard and joints that crack whenever you move to earn that title."

"I'll keep that in mind." Liran laughed as well.

"Now." Imgar clapped a hand on Liran's shoulder. "Let's take care of introductions. Suli spoke for herself, but the one whose eyes are trying to knife you is Xeris. And the man with the torch who brought you in here is Ioth."

"Your Highness." The Keldenese man offered Liran a brief nod.

Imgar's voice softened slightly when he gestured to the tall, flame-haired woman. "I'm certain you know who this is."

Liran bowed deeply. "Princess Nimhea. I'm honored."

"We are indebted to you, Commander," she replied. "You risk much to aid our cause. Thank you."

"I am at your service," Liran told her.

Imgar gave him an approving look, then smiled at the Vijerian woman who stood close to the princess.

"Lahvja of Eni's Children," Imgar said. "She is a summoner blessed with the gifts of Ayre and Syre . . . and she is a Loreknight."

Liran's gaze flicked from the woman to Imgar in surprise, and he couldn't stop himself from frowning. This woman, a soldier? The Hawk must be joking.

The short, younger woman whom Imgar had not yet introduced spoke in an amused voice.

"As you learn more of Saetlund's gods, Commander, you'll find they seem to delight in surprises."

22

When Eamon returned to his cell, Teth looked at him questioningly.

"I have good news and bad news," Eamon said with a shaky sigh.

"I know most people ask for the bad news first, but I like to flout convention." Teth was sitting cross-legged on the floor. "Tell me the good news."

"Zenar bought it," Eamon told him, feeling a surge of triumph. "He wants me to perform the ritual, and he wants it to happen as soon as the emperor arrives . . . and I think it might be possible to use the magic to defeat Fauld at the same time."

"The ArchWizard and the emperor. That is good news," Teth said, giving a low whistle. "When this is all over, I'll help you pursue a career in acting."

"Thanks," Eamon said with a quiet laugh.

"So what's the bad news?"

Eamon's smile faded as he answered hesitantly, "It will probably kill us both."

"I already knew that, and so did you," Teth replied. "But I can see there's something else."

Eamon frowned, then sighed. "There's no way to prepare for

Vokk. He's a god. He could stop the spell the moment I start it. We can't fight him."

"I see." Teth took a minute to digest that. "So we'll get an audience with the emperor, try to kill him and his son with unpredictable, untested magic, and a god who wants to protect them will be watching it all unfold."

"Um . . . yes, that about sums it up," Eamon told him.

They sat in uncomfortable silence.

Teth cleared his throat. "So, skipping over the problem of Vokk, what happens when Fauld gets here?"

Eamon had to tamp down another frenzy of panicked thoughts before he could answer. "Our good friends Elders Tich and Byrtid will bring us to the throne room, where we'll meet him with ArchWizard Zenar and Commander Liran."

"So the Dove will be there, too," Teth observed. "I wonder how he feels about that."

"I don't imagine he's been missing his father," Eamon said. "But he'll take it in stride. That's his way."

"I agree."

Both went quiet again.

"So this is it." Teth leaned back, resting his head against the wall. "Dagger told us that Ara completed the trials. She's the Loresmith, and the Loreknights will be on the battlefield. We'll be in the throne room with Zenar and Fauld. Maybe the gods intended for it to be this way. Seems like it's all coming together."

"Yes," Eamon murmured. "Except for Vokk."

"Then we don't think about Vokk," Teth pronounced abruptly. "We can't. We focus on Zenar and Fauld. Your plan is a long shot anyway, but it's all we have. Maybe all it will be is a diversion while Ara and the others do the real work on the battlefield, but maybe that's all it has to be."

Eamon nodded slowly. Teth was right. To focus on Vokk was to despair. It would take a miracle to gain an advantage over a god. But Eamon had witnessed miracles. Perhaps it wasn't futile to hope for just one more.

Teth pushed himself to his feet and crossed the small space to sit beside Eamon. He rested a hand on the prince's shoulder.

"Having said all that, are you sure you want to go through with this?"

When Eamon was quiet, Teth pressed on. "I could try to get us out of the cell tonight. I admit our chances of escape aren't good, but if we're here when they come tomorrow, there'll be no choice left, and our chance of living through a confrontation with Zenar and the emperor is probably even less than that of making an escape. You know that. I know that. We need to face it."

Eamon nodded and pinched the bridge of his nose between his fingers. "Do you want to run?"

Teth drew a long breath, let it out. "Honestly, I don't know. My instincts are usually reliable when it comes to my survival, but in this case I've got nothing."

"You should go," Eamon said after several beats. "If you go alone, you'll have a much better chance of escape. Maybe I can create some kind of distraction so that you'll have time to get to the children."

"What happens to you?"

Eamon looked away, didn't answer.

Teth ran a hand over his tufted hair. "No. If you stay, I'm not leaving. We're in this together."

"I—"

"And you need me to defeat Zenar and Fauld," Teth continued. "Even if we made it out of here . . . Eni gave you that stick for a reason."

Eamon laughed, but there was a hard edge to the sound. "Eni made it clear defeating Zenar is possible, but not that I'd be able to do it. There are no guarantees."

"There are never guarantees."

"True," Eamon replied. "It's decided then. We stay. When the time comes, do you understand what will happen?"

"Understand? No." Teth shoved his hands into his trouser pockets. "Can I play my part? Yes."

There was a long pause in which Eamon debated whether or not to ask the question he wanted to.

"Teth?"

"Yeah."

"What is it like to love the Loresmith?" Eamon braced himself for an angry reply.

But Teth slid him an assessing look, sat a little straighter, then said, "No. Because I'm not in love with the Loresmith—I'm in love with Ara. And loving Ara isn't easy or hard. It just is. I can't imagine not loving her."

"Oh" was all Eamon could say. Loving a legend, that was something he could hardly begin to wrap his mind around.

"Not that it hasn't been without complications," Teth admitted. "More on her part than mine."

"How so?" Eamon asked.

With a slight frown, Teth said, "At first she was worried that being the Loresmith meant she wasn't allowed to be in love with someone, especially a Loreknight. She thought it would interfere with her ability to treat all the Loreknights equally." He let out a rueful laugh. "We had quite a row about it, actually."

"You fought?"

"Yes." Teth's voice tightened a bit. "It was awful."

He turned his face away for a moment, drew in a long breath. "I've never loved someone the way I love Ara. And being so angry with someone I love that much—my head was spinning with it. Fortunately, she changed her mind about the whole no-falling-in-love thing."

"I'm glad," Eamon told him. "You deserve to be happy."

"I'm glad, too," Teth said with a slight smile. "And thanks. Now all I have to do is find a way back to her."

"You will," Eamon said.

When Teth raised his eyebrows, Eamon blushed.

"I mean . . . well, I don't know what I mean, except that I believe it. You will."

Teth chuckled. "I'll take it."

Eamon rolled onto his back on the cot and stared at the ceiling. He wondered if he'd ever fall in love. He'd always been a bit of a romantic, but there had never been anyone . . . Maybe when all this was over . . .

"If we survive, we should try to get to the catacombs beneath the palace," Eamon said.

Teth turned his head to look at his friend. "Why the catacombs?"

"Eni gave me a message for Liran to bring to Ara," Eamon replied. "The answer you seek lies in the Five Rivers catacombs."

"You think we'll find Ara there?"

"Possibly," Eamon said. "The Resistance army has arrived, and the battle will begin soon. I think Eni's message means Ara needs something that's in the catacombs. She'll come here, likely with the others."

"And the battle would offer a distraction that might allow her to enter the city without notice." Teth nodded. "There's a chance, I suppose. But the timing would have to be ridiculously serendipitous."

Eamon grinned bashfully. "I agree."

"And it's unlikely we'll live to escape," Teth added.

"There's that."

"But, if we do," Teth went on, "while it's unlikely we'll run into our friends among the dead, there is a strong possibility that the catacombs offer some access point to the cisterns running out of the city. And that's a way out for us."

"A smelly way." Eamon grimaced. "But it has merit."

"You'll have a new appreciation for sewers once they give you freedom," Teth said.

"I believe it."

23

hen the stranger lifted his hands and pushed back the hood of his cloak, Ara drew a sharp breath. She knew his face.

The Loresmith is never alone.

Standing before her was the man from the trial of Senn's Fury, the warrior who'd appeared at her side in her moment of deepest despair.

After her quip about the gods, the man fixed her with a puzzled look. His gaze searched her face as if he saw something familiar but couldn't place her. "Have we met?"

"In a way," she replied. "I am Ara of Rill's Pass, and I've been waiting for you."

His eyes widened slightly, and with a short, nervous laugh, he said, "That's interesting. I asked for this meeting because I have a message for you and was told it had to be given face-to-face."

Ara smiled, taking in his tall, strong form. His face was that of a person who'd borne witness to too much violence, but his pale blue eyes weren't dull or jaded in the way one might expect. Instead, his gaze was steady and flickered with a light of hope and determination.

Just as she was assessing him, Liran was looking over Ara with puzzlement. "So you're the Loresmith."

"Let me guess," Ara said. "You were expecting someone taller."

"I don't know what I was expecting," Liran said with a slight smile. "And you just told me your gods are full of surprises."

Ara nodded, becoming serious. "I'm afraid the surprise they have for you will be much greater than you ever could have anticipated."

Liran glanced at Imgar.

The grizzled warrior shrugged. "She hasn't shared this surprise with me."

"I didn't know it was Commander Liran I was looking for until I saw his face," she said. "I've seen him once before, during Wuldr's trial in Senn's lair."

Imgar stilled, and a frown notched between Liran's brows.

"Are you certain?" Imgar asked Ara quietly.

She nodded, then asked Liran, "Why did you request this meeting?"

"I have a message from your Prince Eamon," Liran said to Ara, still frowning.

Nimhea visibly started. "From my brother? But why?"

With a nod, Liran continued, "His request was strange . . . to say the least. The prince visited the Isle of the Gods at Zenar's behest. While there, he claims to have spoken to the god you call Eni, and it was this god who gave the message to Eamon with the instruction that I was to give this message to you."

Lahvja laughed. "Eni is also known as the Traveler, and likely enjoyed sending you on a journey."

"That's true," said Ara, smiling slightly. "But it likewise served an important purpose."

Liran watched her closely, waiting for her to elaborate.

Instead, she asked, "What is the message?"

"*The answer you seek lies in the Five Rivers catacombs*," Liran said.

Nimhea shot a puzzled look at Ara. "I don't understand it. Do you?"

"I'm not sure," Ara replied. "The catacombs. Why would I be looking for anything there? What are catacombs but a resting place for the dead?"

"I think," Lahvja interjected. "We must consider the phrasing of Eamon's message given that Commander Liran was instructed to repeat those precise words."

"The answer you seek lies in the Five Rivers catacombs." Ara turned to Liran. "That's all Eamon said?"

Liran nodded.

"The answer," Ara repeated. "But what is the question?"

"Yes," Lahvja murmured. "That is what we must determine."

"Is there a question that's been troubling you, Ara?" It was Old Imgar who'd asked. He'd been quiet, hovering, but now he held Ara's gaze. "A hidden question, perhaps? One you've been afraid to ask?"

Ara looked into his grizzled face, so familiar and comforting despite the shock of his new identity. Here was her oldest friend, her mentor. The teller of tales that in the past months had come to life: gods, monsters, myths.

She didn't understand the message's meaning, but that wasn't the question that plagued her. No, her query was more direct, and in her mind, more practical.

"Where are the other five Loreknights?" Ara asked Imgar. "That is the question. I completed the gods' trials, Wuldr said so. But only five Loreknights have been called by the gods. There should be ten."

Imgar stroked his beard. "Yes. That is an interesting problem."

"But what does it have to do with the Five Rivers catacombs?" Nimhea said, frustration rising in her voice. "If that even is the question."

"It is," Ara said firmly. Now that she'd spoken it aloud, she knew her worries about absent warriors were at the crux of this matter.

Where are the other five Loreknights?

Memories swirled around her, and Ofrit's riddle echoed in her thoughts.

To find the end, begin again.

Fulfill the lore, as once before.

Restore the past, to rest at last.

Shock suddenly rattled through Ara's bones. It was an appropriate sensation, as she'd realized that bones were exactly what Eamon's message was about.

Lahvja drew a hissing breath. When Ara's eyes met the summoner's, she knew Lahvja had reached the same conclusion. Ara's gaze shifted to the bracelet covering Lahvja's hand. Lahvja was already tracing the shape of the gems with her fingertips.

"Your gift," Ara whispered. "To be used only once."

Lahvja's voice was equally quiet. *"In a time of great need, you may call forth lost champions and complete the circle."*

Swallowing hard, Ara looked at Imgar. "Where were the original Loreknights buried? The first ten."

His eyebrows drew together. "Near their homes, I expect, wherever they came from. After all, there were always two Loreknights chosen from each province."

"That's not true," Edram spoke up. The Circle representative from Daefrit steepled his fingers. "At least not completely. I've studied Saetlund's history and the chronicles of the Loreknights. Some were returned to their homes to be buried, but five chose the honor that was offered by the king of resting beneath the Palace of Five Rivers."

"Beneath the palace," Ara said. "In the catacombs."

"Yes," Edram said, his eyes widening. "You can't mean . . ."

"Not I," Ara told him. Her hands were shaking. So were Lahvja's. "It is the will of the gods."

Nimhea went to Lahvja's side and rested a hand on her shoulder. "I don't understand. What's frightened you so?"

"The five remaining Loreknights to join us in this battle are waiting for us in the Five Rivers catacombs," Lahvja said.

"But they're dead!" Nimhea exclaimed.

"And it falls to me to call them forth," Lahvja replied. "That they may join us in the final fight."

"*Restore the past, to rest at last.*" Ara lifted her voice so the entire group would hear her. "Ofrit gave me a riddle. Only now do I understand it. Everything about my journey has been to join the past with the present. To complete the circle and restore Saetlund. The balance of the original champions and the new is required to defeat the Vokkans."

Liran shook his head, disbelieving. "You're talking about raising the dead."

"I don't know how the Loreknights will manifest themselves," Lahvja told him. "I have never attempted this kind of magic, but Ayre and Syre gave me this task, and I will fulfill it."

"Forgive me, but this is all a bit much," Liran said with a growl of frustration. "You claim I'll be fighting alongside ghosts?"

"Welcome to my world," Ara said, and laughed, surprising them all. She walked over to him and took his hand. "It is a bit much; it's too much for any person to comprehend or face alone. But you're not alone. I am with you. The other Loreknights—the living ones—are with you. The Resistance is with you. And I know this is difficult to accept, but the gods are with you as well."

"Well said," Imgar murmured, and she smiled at him.

Liran's face was a little wan, but he gripped her fingers tightly. "Why do I look in your eyes and believe despite the impossibility of everything you've said?"

"Because it's the truth," Ara told him. "And it's a truth you've been seeking."

"Yes." Liran's throat worked as he swallowed. "I think it is. Very well, Loresmith. If spirits are to join me on the battlefield, so be it."

"If I might interrupt." Lucket strolled forward, emerging from the far corner of the grotto, where he'd been hidden by shadows. "I believe I may be of assistance at this juncture."

Liran swore under his breath, obviously surprised by Lucket's sudden appearance.

Lucket swept into a graceful bow. "Lucket, Low King of Fjeri, at your service, Prince Liran."

Eyeing Lucket uncertainly, Liran said, "Your reputation precedes you."

With a lofty sniff, Lucket replied, "I should hope so."

"In what way can you help us?" Ara asked Lucket, ignoring the exchange.

"I know how to get you into the catacombs." He smiled at her. "You weren't planning to stroll through the city gates, I assume?"

"You can get us into the city without being detected?" Ara eyed him, always a bit suspicious of the Low King's motives. But he was right that the already fortified city of Five Rivers would be rife with Vokkan soldiers.

"I can and I shall." He folded his arms across his chest, sounding impatient and resolved. "And while you're chatting with dead knights, I'm going to save my son."

Imgar scratched his beard, considering Lucket's plan. "Very well. You'll go to the catacombs with Ara."

"Lahvja will need to come with me," Ara said.

"Do you need Joar and Nimhea?" Imgar asked her. "Because we could use them on the battlefield."

"I think they belong with you," Ara answered.

"I'll bring Dagger along," Lucket added. "Between the two of us, we should be able to deal with any trouble we run into. And for this type of operation, it's best if only a few of us are involved."

"Very well," Imgar said. "Commander Liran, we're ready for the attack when you are. Do you have a timeline ready?"

Liran hesitated before he replied. "Yes, but the reason behind it might not be welcome."

Imgar's bushy eyebrows lifted.

"Emperor Fauld is on his way to Saetlund with five battalions," Liran told them, and received a chorus of sharply drawn breaths in reply.

"A surprise, I know," Liran said. "But in the end, I believe his presence will work in our favor. If you can defeat the emperor, the effects of that victory will carry far beyond Saetlund. The empire claims its territories are ruled without challenge, but in recent years more and more unrest has cropped up. Fear of Fauld and his retribution holds most kingdoms in check, but should that threat be removed, people around the world will rise against Vokkan rule."

"Then we find a way to the emperor," Suli said.

Liran shook his head. "Ideally, that would be the strategy, but Fauld will not be on the battlefield, nor will he come to Saetlund alone."

"You've already told us he's bringing additional forces—"

"That's not what I mean," Liran interrupted. "When my father arrives in Saetlund, his god will be with him. Vokk the Devourer."

The room went very still.

"We cannot defeat a god," Suli said at last.

"With an army, no," Imgar said firmly. "But the Loreknights—"

"The Loreknights are still human," Xeris countered, alarm rising in her voice. "And they have never been tested."

"The Loreknights were created for this very purpose," Imgar argued. "Our gods knew their brother Vokk would not be able to resist the lure of Saetlund forever. They knew he would break his promise to them."

Ara gave Xeris a measured look. "Wuldr himself spoke to me of Vokk's part in the coming battle. While he could not assure victory, I also know our gods wouldn't send us into a hopeless fight. We can win, but we must keep faith."

"Commander Liran, our success hinges on your role in the coming battle." Suli's eyes narrowed at him. "Have you come here to tell us you're withdrawing your troops?"

Liran hesitated, then shook his head. "My father and Vokk will consume the world. It cannot stand. Saetlund is the last bastion against them. I will lead those loyal to me against the Vokkan forces with you."

"But can we go forward?" Xeris asked, her features drawn. She threw a wary glance at Ara as if expecting another objection.

"You're asking for assurances that are impossible for anyone to offer." Ara folded her arms across her chest, growing impatient with the conversation. They could talk in circles around this question until the end of time.

"If we go up against Vokk and fail, there will be no coming back from it," Suli said, nodding at Xeris. "It will be a slaughter."

Ara noticed Nimhea and Lahvja exchange a glance. Lahvja gave the princess a slight nod. The pair of them moved forward so they stood in front of the group.

Nimhea stepped close to the summoner and drew her sword. "I love you."

Lahvja smiled. "And I trust you."

Nimhea drew a quick breath and ran Lahvja through. The tip of Nimhea's sword slid out of Lahvja's back, dripping crimson.

Chaos exploded all around them. Someone screamed. Shouts and cries filled the cavern.

Xeris darted toward Lahvja while Suli moved as if to seize Nimhea.

Out of the corner of her eye, Ara saw that Old Imgar remained still, watchful.

"Do not touch them!" Ara's voice rang out.

Lahvja drew a long, shuddering breath, all the while holding Nimhea's gaze. "Go ahead."

Nimhea jerked her longsword free of Lahvja's body and stepped back.

Ara knew the others in the room were waiting for Lahvja to crumple, to fall to the floor and fade from this world as her life's blood spilled from her body.

But Lahvja did not fall. She didn't so much as sway on her feet.

"All right?" Nimhea asked.

Lahvja smiled, then threw back her head and laughed. A deep, rich sound, full of joy and power. She took the edges of the tear the sword had made in her clothing and ripped it further open, turning so that everyone could see the wound Nimhea had made slowly close, then disappear.

"It's a shame," Lahvja said. "I was very fond of this dress."

Xeris drew a hissing breath. "What manner of trick is this?"

"No trick," Ara answered. "Only the will of the gods."

Nimhea took a moment to sweep the room with her gaze, ensuring she had the full attention of all present. "Hear the words of Nava, goddess of life and mercy. Words spoken to me after the Loresmith crafted this crown, that when it sits upon my head and I am at their side, the Loreknights will not come to harm, no weapon will touch them, nor spell assault them."

A hush fell over the cavern; the only sound was the gentle lapping of water upon rock.

Suli was the first to break the silence. "Impossible."

"And yet . . ." Imgar came to Nimhea's side. "A brave show of faith, Your Highness."

"A necessary one," Nimhea replied firmly.

"I'll be the first to admit that was impressive. Miraculous, in fact," Xeris said. "But do you know if this magic can withstand the power of another god?"

"Are you looking for excuses to run?" Imgar's voice rumbled, accusing and disappointed.

Xeris glared at him. "I'm simply pointing out the truth. We have never faced a god—no one has. How can we go forward with our attack when it could mean certain defeat?"

Suli looked from Xeris to Imgar. "Fighting among ourselves gets us nowhere."

"I can't lead cowards who'll balk at the first sign of trouble into battle," Imgar growled.

Xeris's eyes flared with rage. "I am no coward!"

"Easy now." Ioth put his hands on her shoulders. "We're all friends here."

Imgar regarded Xeris with barely veiled contempt. She tried to lunge at him, but Ioth held her back.

"Enough!" Ara pushed between them. "The battle is coming and the gods have laid before us the path to victory, but we must follow it. To give in to doubt, to fear, is to surrender to the Vokkans before the first blow has been dealt."

"The Loresmith speaks true." Ara was surprised that Commander Liran was the first to come to her side. "I fear Vokk more than anyone in this room. I have stood in the presence of this god and know his power, his cruelty. Yet I will not let my terror of his evil rule me. I am not one of you, but I will lay my life down for Saetlund. For I believe, without a doubt, that the fight for Saetlund is the fight that will save the world."

Imgar and Xeris both stared at Liran, obviously as taken aback as Ara by his intervention.

Ara gave Liran a long look and bit her lip. She'd hoped to find a moment to take him aside, to give him quiet and space to learn and accept that he'd been chosen by the gods. That he was a Loreknight. Now, she realized, that privacy wasn't an option.

"Commander." She addressed him but raised her voice so all could hear. "Your words are truer than you realize. The reason I recognized you is because I've seen your face before. You appeared to me in the final trial presented by Saetlund's gods."

He frowned at her, puzzled.

"You are the fifth Loreknight." Ara looked to Lahvja and beckoned her forward. "Your face was shown to me by Wuldr, the Hunter. He has called you to serve the gods as champion of Saetlund."

Understanding, Lahvja came close, unbelting the scabbard at her waist. Joar had transferred the sword to her care when it was decided he would remain at the rebel hideout so the rest of the group could use Lahvja's power to travel to and from the meeting with Liran.

"Surely you jest." Liran shook his head. "How can I be a Loreknight? I'm not of this land. I'm the enemy."

Smiling slightly, Ara said, "If you were the enemy, you would not be here. The gods' choices are often surprising, but never wrong. You are a Loreknight."

She took the scabbard from Lahvja and held the weapon out to Liran so its hilt faced him. The dark stars at the heart of the red gemstones pulsed as if with their own heartbeat, seeming to recognize and welcome the commander.

Ara watched Liran's throat work.

"Saetlund's gods are not my gods," Liran protested.

"And yet they've chosen you," Ara said while he gazed at the sword.

Hesitantly he reached out until his fingertips rested against the gem set into the pommel. When his skin made contact with the stone, he shivered, and Ara felt a surge of power flowing from the sword into the Vokkan commander.

"The Dark Star," Liran whispered. His hand moved over the hilt, tracing the shape of all three star-cut gems. "This sword is mine."

"Yes," Ara said, watching as emotions battled on Liran's face. "I forged it for you and you alone." She paused, then said, the words escaping on a sigh she couldn't stop, "Its name is Godsbane."

He jerked his hand away from the sword and stared at her. "Godsbane?"

Ara could only offer him a solemn nod. How could she give voice to a task that any reasonable person would consider not only impossible, but suicidal? It became obvious from Liran's expression that he didn't need her to explain.

"No," he said, blanching. "I cannot."

"You must," Ara told him, and offered him the sword once more. "Only one of Vokk's people can defeat him, and Saetlund's gods have called you to fulfill that destiny."

Liran bowed his head, his hands clenching into fists at his sides. He drew a long, shuddering breath, released it. He reached for the sword, wrapping his hand around the grip. The blade hissed out of the scabbard. When Liran lifted it, shadows climbed its length, swirling around its sharp edges, embracing it.

Everyone who'd been watching took a step back. Ara could sense the shudders traveling around the room. Despite being its creator, Ara still had a difficult time keeping her eyes on the weapon.

But the aversion others felt didn't seem to affect Liran. He gazed at the sword with rapt attention, unflinching. His head tilted slightly as if he could hear something the rest of them could not.

His mouth tightened in a grim line, and he said, "If it must be, it must be."

He reached toward Ara with his free hand, and she gave him the scabbard. He sheathed the sword and belted it around his waist.

There was a palpable easing of tension in the room now that the sword was hidden away.

As Liran looked at Ara, one corner of his mouth tilted in a wry smile. "It seems I'm following your orders now, Loresmith."

24

amon knew he must have visited the throne room of the Palace of Five Rivers during the first three years of his life, but he had no memory of it. More than opulent, the gilt and glittering room testified to the excesses of King Dentroth and his predecessors. Their proclivities had invited corruption and led directly to Saetlund's downfall.

What would he and Nimhea have been like if they'd been raised in the wealth and privilege of this court rather than in exile? Eamon wondered.

He didn't like to think that they would have unquestioningly repeated the mistakes of their father, but it was impossible to know. All he had was the present and the choices he made with each new day. Mistakes had brought him to this place, this moment, but he would use those mistakes to repair the damage he'd done and, if possible, to change the course of history.

The two Vokkan princes stood to one side of the dais that held the River Throne. Four guards were posted at the door, two palace guards and two soldiers who had arrived with Liran from the barracks.

A few feet away, Eamon and Teth waited. Eamon was free while Teth was shackled, flanked by Elders Tich and Byrtid. Elder Byrtid held Tears of the Traitor, the bow in one hand, the quiver in the other. Zenar trusted Eamon enough to have the Loreknight's weapons in the room, but not in his possession. That almost made Eamon want to laugh. He hardly had the strength to draw Teth's bow, much less the skill to accurately aim it. The atmosphere of the throne room brimmed with the crackling energy of a coming storm, but none of the pomp or celebration that often marked the arrival of a visiting monarch. The simmering tension made it difficult for Eamon to keep still, not to mention that very soon he would face the most important, most defining moment of his life. He wanted to fidget, move, but he forced himself to keep a calm facade.

Though Commander Liran kept his gaze on the throne room doors, he said to Zenar, "You're certain there's nothing else you need from me?"

"I will deal with Father," Zenar replied coolly, likewise keeping his eyes fixed on the doorway. "And I trust you will see to the other situation."

"Indeed," Liran murmured. "I admit, your confidence impresses me."

Zenar's smile made Eamon shudder inwardly. "If I was not certain of my success, I would never attempt a coup."

Liran made a noncommittal sound by way of reply.

Teth leaned toward Eamon. "I love family reunions, don't you?"

"Quiet," Elder Tich snapped. "Speak again and I'll have you gagged."

But Eamon thought he caught the corner of Liran's mouth twitch with wry amusement.

The sound of marching feet came from the hall, and the throne room's tall doors swung open.

A man dressed in swirling red robes stepped inside and shouted in a shrill voice, "All hail Emperor Fauld, the Ever-Living, the Eternal, Defier of Death, Beloved of Vokk the Devourer, He Who Consumes the World. May we tremble at his presence."

The man flung himself to the ground, his body prone, his face pressed to the rug, then scrambled aside in a rather undignified manner to make way for the small retinue who had arrived with the emperor.

A pair of guards swept into the room wearing red-feather-plumed helmets and armor of shining silver. Their spears were encrusted with jewels and appeared to be tipped by diamonds. Behind the soldiers came a quartet of men whose faces were covered with golden masks, but who wore robes marking them as Wizards of Vokk. Eamon watched them with growing curiosity.

As ArchWizard, Zenar ostensibly controlled all the lesser Wizards of Vokk, but had he managed to bring all the Vokkan mages to his side, or would his attempt to overthrow his father pit him against some of them? Eamon had never seen the wizards in the temple don golden masks, and he wondered if that ornament set them apart from their peers in some way. Considering the politics of power that no doubt pervaded the empire, it wasn't hard to imagine rival factions of wizards forming and jockeying for control. On the other hand, the masks might simply be imperial pomp.

Behind the wizards came the emperor himself. He was clothed in robes of a similar style to those of the wizards, but his were of sump-tuous purple silk embroidered with silver thread and piped with black velvet at the hems. He wore no crown, but a talisman hung from his neck, suspended on a long gold chain. The talisman had been wrought from gold and silver strands that were twisted together, the twined strands forming a spiral—the symbol of eternity with which Eamon had become all too familiar—that rested against the emperor's breast-bone. The center of the spiral was mounted with a black opal, within which a multitude of colors glittered, shifted, and swirled.

Emperor Fauld was taller than either of his sons, but Eamon saw that Zenar had inherited more of his father's features than Liran had. Like Zenar, Fauld had a face made of sharp angles and pale skin that stretched too tightly over his skull, but in the emperor that effect was even more striking.

Eamon found it difficult to look directly at Fauld's face, not because he feared the man, but because of how repulsive his visage was. His skin shared that strange near-translucent quality of Zenar's to a more extreme degree. Eamon thought he could actually see bone beneath the thin veil of flesh covering the emperor's skull, and he began to wonder if those physical traits were the result of the magic used to sustain life beyond its natural limit. The emperor's robes were voluminous, but he suspected their bulk hid a ravaged, emaciated body.

Was the price of immortality a slow eradication of vitality? Fauld's and Zenar's bodies seemed to strain for existence rather than flourish. Their faces had become masks of death, a reflection of the fate they sought to defy. Perhaps mortality could never truly be denied, only twisted into a warped state of being.

Eamon understood the lure of eternal life, but staring at its cost made the reality of wielding such power much less appealing.

Though Emperor Fauld held the room's attention, Eamon was plagued by an uneasy sensation that something else had entered the room with the Vokkan ruler. It was as though a presence flickered on the edge of Eamon's vision, perceptible but always out of focus. Looming, but elusive. It left Eamon feeling like insects were skittering over his arms, and he fought the urge to scratch at his skin.

He glanced at Liran and Zenar, but they showed no signs of being affected by whatever troubled Eamon. Perhaps it was simply the emperor's presence. He possessed power beyond any Eamon had encountered.

The emperor paused when he was a few feet away from his sons. He lifted a hand, and the doors to the throne room slammed shut, making Eamon jump.

Liran crossed his arms over his chest and went down on one knee. "Emperor, Father."

Eamon quickly mimicked the commander's action. He glanced up very cautiously to watch as Zenar stayed on his feet, bowing his head but offering no other sign of subservience. Teth remained standing, too, but that was hardly a surprise.

Shocked by Zenar's show of defiance, Eamon glanced up at Fauld to see the emperor's reaction. Fauld simply lifted one eyebrow, then turned his attention to Liran.

"My son, my soldier, rise," Fauld said.

Liran stood, but kept his eyes respectfully downcast—though Eamon suspected that perhaps it was not respect, but revulsion like his own, that chased Liran's gaze away from the emperor's face.

"The battle awaits," Fauld continued. "And I have brought reinforcements so that you may not only quell this rebellion, but humiliate those who dare rise up against me."

"As my emperor commands," Liran said. He bowed and started for the door.

"Liran—" Fauld's voice stopped Liran short, and he half turned toward his father.

The emperor spoke slowly, putting weight in each word. "You have served me long and well. Perhaps I have not shown my gratitude. I find myself desirous of a greater legacy than that of conquest. After this final battle, I believe it is time that I have a grandson, don't you?"

Though Eamon could tell Liran tried to hold off any reaction, he couldn't stop himself from staggering slightly at Fauld's declaration. The emperor smiled at his elder son's shock.

Clearing his throat, Liran said, "Your will, as ever."

"Go with my blessing and with the might of the Devourer," Fauld intoned. Liran bowed again, obviously shaken, and left the room.

Eamon stared after him, deeply troubled. He knew that Liran's decision to break with the empire stemmed largely from the fact that Fauld had never allowed his offspring to live beyond middle age, much less have a spouse and children. Could the emperor have sensed Liran's imminent betrayal? Was this a ploy to draw Liran back into the fold at a critical moment? Without Liran's support on the battlefield, the Resistance had little chance of success.

Feeling helpless, Eamon looked at Zenar. The ArchWizard was livid, glaring at his father with unconcealed hatred. His father smiled back at him, his expression placid but his eyes alight with satisfaction, and Eamon allowed himself to feel a trickle of relief. The offer to Liran, it seemed, was more likely a means to twist a dagger in Zenar's gut than to manipulate Liran. At least Eamon hoped that was the case.

Zenar's hands shook at his sides, his fingers curled like claws. Blue and purple shadows leaked from his fingertips, swirling over his skin. The emperor noticed.

"Has the time finally come, Zenar?" Fauld's voice was a dry rasp. "Do you truly believe yourself powerful enough to challenge me?"

Zenar lifted his head. All signs of fealty to his father had vanished. "Step aside, Father. Abdicate to me, and I shall suffer your existence. Live in comfort while I rule as emperor."

"What comfort is there without power?" Fauld laughed, a crackling, bitter sound. "You are not such a fool." He gave a snort of disgust. "And mercy doesn't suit one who aspires to my throne. Your attempt at such a pitiful emotion insults the very station you claim to deserve."

"Mercy?" What was left of Zenar's thin lips curled back. "I merely thought it entertainment to see you squirm and wither while I become more than you ever could have hoped to be."

"Better." Fauld spat out the word. "But you will not usurp me, Zenar, no matter what magics you think you have mastered."

Zenar laughed, a shrill, barking sound. "It is not for you to judge my worthiness or my power, Father."

Raising his arms, Zenar shouted, "I call to you, Vokk, my god, the Devourer, Conqueror of the World, whose hunger is never sated. Witness what I have wrought in your name! See my devotion!"

There was a sudden flickering in the space behind Fauld, a play of shadow and light. The hairs on Eamon's arms stood on edge as he felt a new presence spill into the room that radiated unspeakable power. The flickering slowed, and a shape took form, stretching toward the ceiling.

"Nava's mercy," Teth whispered, taking a step back.

Eamon would have uttered something similar, but he couldn't speak. His throat was closed, and his heart slammed against his breast-bone as he watched Vokk the Devourer materialize.

Eamon had been in the presence of gods before, had been awed by their immensity and all that was unfathomable about their divinity.

Vokk didn't inspire awe, but terror. Not wonder, only horror. His very being seemed to make the room hum with imminent violence.

The Vokkan god's body was skeletally thin and covered in gray leathery skin. His long fingers were tipped with claws. He bent so as to keep his head from brushing the ceiling. Eamon didn't know if Vokk had eyes, because all he could see was the immense mouth that seemed to take up all of the god's face. A gaping maw filled with ring after ring of razor-sharp teeth.

"Blasphemer!" Fauld screeched at Zenar. "You dare call upon Vokk when I am his favored child, his chosen one?"

Zenar ignored the emperor, instead fixing a maniacal gaze upon Vokk. "Lord and master, I beg your leave to demonstrate my power, to show my strength of purpose and will, all that I have done to honor you."

He tore off his robe, revealing the spiral scar on his chest. Fauld snarled at the sight and took a step back. Zenar's fingers began to weave an intricate pattern in the air, and the ceiling above his head shuddered. He spoke a single word, and the ceiling began to weep the viscous black liquid that covered the temple walls. The dark substance fell in thick drips on his head and shoulders. It moved over his skin, sometimes sliding and at others seeming to crawl, always seeking the spiral on his chest, where it burrowed inside his body.

"No," Fauld growled.

"Yes," Zenar snarled. "It cannot be denied. It is my destiny."

"I am pleased by your hunger." Vokk's voice rasped through the room, like dry leaves skittering across parched earth. "The challenge may proceed. He who triumphs shall have my favor. He who fails will become my feast, as will any who interfere with this contest."

Fauld visibly winced at Vokk's last words. Eamon saw that the emperor considered himself both infallible and untouchable. Fauld found it near impossible to reconcile his assumptions with this fresh challenge.

The emperor's retinue was likewise cowed. Almost immediately, they abandoned their positions around Fauld, scuttling backward against the room's walls, cowering as if desperate to avoid Vokk's notice. Yet all appeared too afraid of their master's wrath to flee the chamber.

"I will rip you to shreds!" Fauld screamed at Zenar.

"You will try." Zenar smiled.

Father and son faced off, glaring at each other. If affection had ever existed between them, there was no sign of it now. Eamon had no doubt that neither of them would hesitate to destroy the other.

"What are the chances they'll kill us while they're trying to kill each other?" Teth asked quietly.

Eamon slid a glance at him, then returned his focus to Zenar and Fauld without answering.

"Thanks," Teth muttered. "I feel much better."

auld's reinforcements filled the road that stretched toward the eastern coast. A dark river of black armor with rapids of glinting steel. Five battalions in total, according to the Dove.

A formidable addition to the Vokkans' standing army in Saetlund, thought Imgar, bolstering their numbers again by half. But it wasn't enough to make a Resistance victory impossible, even accepting the fact that the Vokkans boasted twice the soldiers as the rebels. But that was before Liran's cavalry and troops would reveal their true loyalties. It fell to the Loreknights to make up for the remaining disparity, and Imgar believed they would.

But even still, Vokk the Devourer had arrived with the new troops. And there was no real way to factor a god into the situation, at least not if one wanted to maintain one's sanity.

As soon as his scouts sighted Liran's cavalry coming through the city gates on the eastern horizon and sent up signal flares, Imgar's troops would move out from behind the hills where they lay in wait, and Xeris's archers would begin their volleys. Then the Hawk's two battalions would be unleashed on the center of the Vokkan troops, striking from the north. At the same time, Ioth's cavalry would attack the rear of the column from the northeast, while two more battalions led by Suli would make their charge from the south.

Waiting was one of the hardest parts of war, Imgar knew. As hours stretched out, one's mind flirted with doubts and second-guesses. And in this situation, there were so many moving pieces that had to fall exactly into place.

No one knew what to expect of the emperor. What orders would he give his son? Could he somehow prevent Liran from leaving the city, choosing to trust that his own reinforcements would complete the task of putting down the rebellion?

That would be disastrous.

But Imgar knew he couldn't dwell on all the ways the Resistance could fail. That was a sure way to invite defeat.

No, he must remain steadfast. Trusting the plan. Trusting his allies. Including Liran.

Yes, that was the only way forward.

Imgar felt the peace of that resolve settle into his bones.

Even so, an hour later, when fiery arrows crested in the eastern skies, Imgar thanked the gods.

26

amon had no way to mark the passing of time, but he was sure hours had passed since the battle between Zenar and Fauld began. It had taken a minute or two after they'd shouted at each other for Eamon to realize the magical battle was already underway. The two men had fallen silent, staring at each other, eyes locked.

At first, Eamon hadn't understood—then he noticed sweat beading on the emperor's forehead. A moment later, Zenar winced and Fauld smiled. They were waging a silent internal war against each other. For a long while, it didn't spill beyond the two men, but as the intensity of the magic increased, it began to burst whatever bounds held it in check as finally both emperor and prince lost control.

Zenar broke from his statue-like concentration first, lashing his hands out. Without warning, a marble column cracked, then exploded in a blast as dagger-like shards flew outward across the room. Eamon heard a high-pitched whistle and felt a shock of heat as debris flew past him, then a punch in the gut as Teth slammed into him, sending them both to the ground. There was a cry as a stone shard impaled a guard on a wall behind them. Teth had saved him.

Fauld whispered something too quiet to understand, and the shards that would have struck him fell harmlessly to the ground. He raised his arms, and flames danced on his fingertips. The tapestries on the walls burst into flame and leapt from the walls to hurtle toward Zenar. But Zenar made a sweeping motion with his arms, and a whirlwind burst into life, sending the burning tapestries spinning. One struck Elder Tich, who screamed when it wrapped around him. The fire flared white. Eamon covered his eyes for a moment, and when he blinked all that remained of cloth and man was a pile of ash. A second tapestry brushed past a guard, who narrowly escaped being trapped inside the burning fabric, running from the throne room with his arm scorched and smoking. The remaining two fiery tapestries slammed into the walls, flared white, and crumbled to ash, leaving the walls painted with black soot.

Eamon and Teth took cover behind a stone bench that had toppled onto its side.

"How long can they keep this up?" Teth hissed through his teeth as a mirror behind them shattered.

"It won't end until one of them is dead." Eamon dared to peer over the top of the bench.

Fauld let out a string of unintelligible words, each emerging with dark power. Eamon's heart twisted at the sound. Then, in an instant, Elder Byrtid suddenly swelled, her skin rippling as her body burst, splattering blood and hunks of flesh on the floor and walls. Teth's bow and quiver clattered to the floor, resting in a pool of the wizard's blood.

A moment later, Zenar retaliated, turning one of the emperor's retinue to stone. The rest of the attendants ran, abandoning all deference in hope of their own survival. The surviving guards remained, demonstrating an admirable, if foolish, degree of loyalty, but still they crouched behind whatever defenses they could find.

As time passed, Fauld and Zenar were both drenched in sweat, breathing in harsh gasps. They unleashed magic with increasingly violent physical gestures. Sweeping arms and clawing hands. They cursed each other in spits and snarls.

All the while, Vokk flickered in and out of sight, his presence making Eamon's pulse pound even more than the violent magic that swirled all around them.

The problem of Vokk chased through Eamon's mind. When he'd imagined defeating Zenar, he hadn't considered that the enemy's god would be present. Eamon was certain that as soon as he began his plan—invoking powerful magic that would harm Zenar—Vokk would simply intervene and destroy him, and Teth alongside him. Eamon had no idea how to overcome this—how could he outwit a god? He only had a chance if the effects of the spell were instantaneous, but Eamon knew that wasn't possible.

Thus far, the battle between the ArchWizard and the emperor seemed a stalemate, but eventually Zenar would call upon Eamon for his part. To give him the edge needed to defeat Fauld, siphoning magic from Teth to unleash against the emperor.

Eamon saw that Zenar wouldn't be able to fight on his own much longer. Lines of strain pulled at his face. Twice now he'd staggered back, struck by some invisible blow.

Fauld showed signs of tiring as well, but they were not as severe. He stood taller than his son, and when a hit landed, he flinched rather than stumbled back. Where Zenar grimaced, Fauld simply smiled.

Then a cry of pain flew from Zenar's throat and his eyes widened, as if surprised he'd made the sound himself. Fauld laughed, the sound curdling. Eamon saw Teth grimace beside him. They watched as Zenar glanced over his shoulder, searching the room until his eyes met Eamon's.

It would be soon.

"My lord! My lord!" Frantic shouts spilled into the throne room a moment before a Vokkan soldier appeared, stumbling over rubble. He froze when he saw the wrecked chamber, and his eyes bulged when they fixed on the ArchWizard and emperor facing off on the other side of the room.

"Who dares?" Fauld turned blazing eyes upon the now trembling man.

"Loreknights, my lord!" The man's strangled cry emerged. "An urgent message from the field sent by falcon. Loreknights have joined the battle and are using their magic against our forces. They are led by Dentroth's heir!"

Another sound suddenly filled the room, one no human could have made. A whisper carried on a snarl, riding a thousand echoes.

"Loreknights."

Without warning, Vokk materialized beside the soldier who brought the message. The man didn't have time to scream before his god's teeth sank into his body and the Devourer swallowed him in long, squelching gulps.

Teth retched, and Eamon stared in sick disbelief as the man disappeared and blood slicked the floor.

Vokk raised his spindly arms, his talons scraping the ceiling, and shrieked. Simultaneously shrill and deep, the sound stabbed into Eamon's ears until he covered them to try to stop the pain. The palace shuddered. Eamon wondered how long the building would stand the quaking before coming down around them.

Emperor Fauld lost his balance, falling on one knee.

Vokk's form blurred, then shimmered into nothing. As quickly as it began, the horrible noise stopped, and the building ceased shuddering. The throne room felt lighter, emptier.

Everyone in the room had been stunned by Vokk's violent departure, but the ArchWizard recovered his wits before the emperor. Seeing his father on the ground, Zenar gave a shout of glee.

"Now, Eamon!" Zenar hissed.

Fighting off the lingering haze of Vokk's power, Eamon struggled to his feet, dragging Teth up with him.

Regaining his dignity and his feet, Fauld watched without fear, his mouth twisting in derision, making it clear he had no doubt victory lay in his grasp. "Have you found a new toy to play with, Zenar? How foolish. Your puppet is no threat to me."

Zenar ignored his father's taunts, his eyes boring into Eamon.

Eamon's fear of what he was about to do cut deeply, making him tremble. The magic at work could kill Teth easily if Eamon made even the slightest mistake. He drew the dagger from his belt, then the twig from the Isle of the Gods. His hands shook.

A growl rumbled from Teth's throat. "Do it."

Eamon lifted his eyes to meet Teth's hard gaze, and where he expected to find fear and doubt, he instead discovered resolve and, more than that, trust. There was no greater gift Teth could have offered Eamon in that moment. It sent a surge of strength through him. With a swift nod, Eamon sliced through the flesh of his palm, then Teth's. He clasped their hands together, the twig pressed between the two wounds. Their blood flowed, mingled, and the twig trembled. Heat blazed from their palms as the twig grew, becoming a branch that sprouted leaves. New branches shot out, winding around their arms.

Eamon began to speak, his words fevered. "Gods of Saetlund, who chose this land and blessed its people, hear your child now, son of Dentroth, heir to the lost kingdom. Witness your champion, the Loreknight, calling to you. Our blood flows in search of your power. Wuldr, Hunter; Ofrit, Alchemist; Nava, Sower; Ayre/Syre, Twins; Eni,

Traveler. Zenar the Betrayer reaps life from your children. He twists the mortal coil to the point of breaking. Let his corruption end. Let our blood be the cleansing fire that burns his evil from this kingdom forever."

Teth's eyes were closed; his lips moved in a silent echo of Eamon's chant. It wasn't necessary, but Eamon was grateful for Teth's commitment to the spell.

Branches crawled across the room, overspreading the floor and the ceiling. Zenar saw the tree forming, coming toward him, and threw his head back, releasing a triumphant laugh.

"Your doom comes, Father!"

Eamon sucked in a sharp breath of relief at Zenar's shout. The ArchWizard hadn't noticed the differences between the shadowed and tar-like tree that sprouted in the dungeon and the vital, sharp green growth that spilled into the room now. Zenar was too immersed in his fight for dominance to realize treachery was afoot.

Red-faced and sweating, Fauld scowled at the vines and leaves closing in. He raised his hand, and a ball of fire manifested in his palm.

Teth gave a muffled shout of alarm as Fauld hurled the fireball at the branches closest to him. The flames hit, and the branches crackled and shrunk back.

Eamon and Teth screamed as the blood on their hands burned, and the spell wavered. Eamon gritted his teeth and chanted again, throwing all his will into his words. His body shook with the effort. Teth gripped his hand more tightly. It was painful, but it gave him strength. The spell held fast.

Zenar shrieked at Fauld. "No! You cannot stop it! You shall not."

The branches on the floor reached Zenar's back. Eamon thrust his free hand up to the ceiling, and the branches coiled together, joining, erupting into a single trunk that grew and grew until a tree stood behind the ArchWizard, its branches overspreading the room.

Eamon watched, breathless. So close. It was almost time.

"Yes!" Zenar's eyes were wild with glee as the branches stretched over him. "You fool of an old man. I have claimed a power the likes of which you have never known. You will feel its wrath."

The branches surrounding Zenar grew longer, leaves sprouting along them, then buds swelled on newly appearing, slender, thorn-laden branches and turned into blooms that perfumed the air with the sweet scent of spring. Of rebirth.

Tears slipped from Eamon's eyes. It was working. They could win. But one last thing was required. Zenar had to listen to him. To do what he said. Eamon prayed he would.

With a derisive laugh, Fauld said, "You have no such power. What child's trick is this? Do you expect to defeat me while tripping over roots and stopping to sniff flowers?"

Fauld lifted both his hands, spreading his fingers wide. Lightning crackled at his fingertips. His eyes narrowed, and his focus moved past Zenar to where Eamon and Teth crouched in the corner.

Eamon swallowed hard. Fauld realized striking at the source of Zenar's new power was the key to defeating him. Eamon could only hope that Zenar would stop Fauld's attack before it destroyed them.

Ready to deal the fatal strike Eamon had promised, Zenar howled a battle cry and threw himself on his father. Fauld gave a shout of alarm, utterly stunned that his son would resort to a physical attack rather than magic. The force of Zenar's blow sent both men sprawling. They rolled along the floor, spitting and hurling curses at each other, locked in a death grip.

Eamon's heart leapt. Zenar had inadvertently done exactly what

Eamon needed—come into direct contact with the emperor. The men came to a thudding stop against the tree in the center of the room. The emperor gained the advantage, pinning Zenar to the trunk. His hands closed over his son's throat while Zenar clawed at his father's face.

"Take the power now, ArchWizard!" Eamon shouted over the snarls of the two grappling men. "Grasp the thorns on the tree! The power of the Loreknight's blood must flow through you!"

Zenar turned his gaze on Eamon and grinned. Eamon's heart was in his throat as he watched Zenar's hands reach up.

Fauld's eyes narrowed as he glanced up at the tree in full bloom. He drew a sharp breath just as Zenar's fingers closed around a thorn-tipped branch.

"At last," Zenar hissed, and the emperor's face blanched.

"No! You FOOL!" Fauld dragged Zenar's hand away from the tree, but Zenar's fingers came away bright with blood. The thorn had pierced his skin.

Fauld scrambled away from his son. "What have you done?"

No! Eamon's mind shouted. *Don't let him go!* Fauld had to be in Zenar's grasp.

Panic gripped Eamon. If the magic failed, they'd have little chance of surviving.

Then Eamon caught sight of something glinting amid the ruin of flesh that had been Elder Byrtid. A key ring. He scrambled to retrieve it, then started trying each key in the shackles that bound Teth's wrists.

Zenar dragged himself to his feet, flexing his bleeding hand. "I have done what you never had the strength to imagine. The power of Saetlund's gods is mine now. Mine. You can never hope to defeat me."

"The power of a god cannot be taken." Fauld shook his head, eyeing Zenar with increasing alarm. "It can only be given."

"No." Zenar laughed, baring his teeth. "I have taken what was meant to be mine. You should be afraid, old man. Your magics are nothing compared with what I now wield. I—"

Zenar broke off, staring at his hand with a frown.

"All you have wrought is your own doom," Fauld whispered.

With a cry of horror, Zenar watched as his palm split apart and branches shot out from the remains of his hand. Not the black, desiccated branches of his tree in the depths of the temple, but a living branch, with brown bark the hue of fertile earth and verdant leaves sprouting where they willed. He screamed as the branches grew, tearing the skin at his wrist, up his arm, shattering his elbow. Blood sprayed his face and body. Gobs of his flesh dropped to the floor, hitting with heavy, wet squelches.

He turned to stare at Eamon in horror. "What have you done?"

But just at that moment, Eamon fitted the right key into Teth's shackles. The lock clicked and Teth's bonds opened. Teth shook his arms, and the shackles dropped to the floor. But Zenar took no notice, his stare locked on Eamon.

He screeched again, "What have you done?!"

Eamon didn't answer the ArchWizard, but simply watched him, sickened but stoic, as the spell shredded Zenar's upper arm and rent apart his shoulder.

Mad with pain and fear, Zenar wheeled around and lurched toward the emperor. "Father! Help me!"

"No!" Fauld stumbled back, raising his hands. Fire sparked in his palms. A warning. "Do not touch me."

"Please!" Zenar wept, reaching out with his arms, both flesh and branch, the latter of which continued to grow, shooting out toward Fauld. "Have mercy!"

"No!" Fauld screamed, and fire shot out from his hands, hitting Zenar full in the chest.

Zenar shrieked, but fell forward rather than back, tumbling into his father. With shrieks and sobs, he fell to his knees, wrapping his arms around Fauld's waist.

The emperor struck at Zenar, struggling in his grasp, but it was too late. The branches that had once been Zenar's arm latched on to Fauld, climbing from his waist up his back. Fauld twisted and fought, then stared in horror as Zenar opened his mouth in a silent, agonized wail before his jaw split apart, branches surging up from his throat and spearing through his eye sockets.

Zenar's silence was replaced by Fauld's shouts, which quickly turned into screams when the branches overtaking his son's body wrapped around his chest and wound about his throat. They climbed up his face, seeking, prodding.

Wrenching his body around, desperate for escape, Fauld's wild gaze landed on Eamon and Teth. The emperor's eyes gained a terrible focus as he took in the source of the spell and saw one final chance for his own salvation.

"You." He brought his hands together, one hand fisted, the other clasped around it, even as branches snaked around his arms. Lightning crackled over his tightly joined hands. "Release me!"

A bolt of electricity shot toward them.

"No!" Eamon cried.

He ripped his hand free of Teth's and threw himself in front of the bolt. It hit him full in the chest, hurling him past Teth and into the wall. His body slammed against the stone with a sickening crack and dropped to the floor.

It shouldn't be this hard to breathe, Eamon thought as he heard Teth shout his name, the sound far away though the thief was right beside him. Eamon's body felt as though he'd been scorched from the inside. He was stunned, but he peered across the room through blurred vision, waiting for Fauld to send another bolt. There would be nothing Eamon could do to save Teth. He had failed.

But no bright light shot across the room. There were only screams, groans, and then gurgles as the emperor collapsed, branches twining around his body, spiking through his flesh. And finally silence.

Eamon let his eyes close. He sighed a wheezing breath and began to slip toward the stillness of oblivion. And in that space between consciousness and darkness, he felt himself falling, and then, suddenly, he wasn't. Strong arms held him, and a powerful wind swirled all around him. He heard the rustling of a many-layered cloak.

"I have you," Eni said. "Rest, Prince Eamon. Rest now. All is well."

27

eth saw death coming for him and decided he was ready. He had to be.

Though he knew there was more he'd hoped for, more he longed for.

Ara. Especially Ara. Teth had always been one to live in the moment. There was no point in the long view. Now was all that mattered.

But in Ara he couldn't help but see something more. Not only because she was the Loresmith, a legend that stretched back to the beginnings of Saetlund and promised a future of hope. No, what Teth saw in Ara was not the myth, but the woman. Her dark, bright eyes. Her wit. Her laughter. Her strength. He saw things in her he never thought he could imagine for himself. For his life. For their life together.

At least he'd met her, known her. It would have to be enough. It was enough.

What is it like to love the Loresmith? Eamon's question whispered through Teth's mind.

He should have answered, *It's everything.*

Teth watched the crackling bolt fly toward him and accepted his fate.

But Eamon didn't.

Teth heard the prince's shout. "No!"

He saw Eamon's body fill the space between Fauld's deadly bolt and himself, stood helplessly as the power of that spell flung Eamon into the wall. The prince's limp form slid to the stone floor.

Teth's word echoed Eamon's, but emerged from his throat as a hoarse whisper.

"No."

With a glance across the room to ensure the fight was truly over, Teth ran to Eamon's side. He carefully rolled the prince onto his back. Teth's heart lurched when he saw the dull, gray cast that had overtaken Eamon's bronze skin.

He bent down, gently pressing his ear to Eamon's chest. He could find no heartbeat. There was no rise and fall of breath.

"Eamon, please." Teth groaned. "Don't do this to me."

He took Eamon's face in his hands. "Eamon!"

There was no response. Teth grabbed Eamon's shoulders, giving him a hard shake. "Senn's teeth, wake up! Wake up, Eamon!"

Teth didn't want to notice the warmth leaching from Eamon's body, the absence of breath. With a desperate cry, he balled his hands into fists and brought them down into the center of Eamon's chest. Once. Twice.

Nothing.

He buried his hands in his hair, pulling at the roots. "Nava, please, no."

He waited. Watched.

But Eamon was gone.

Teth covered his face with his hands and screamed. Once. Only once. Then he drew a shaking breath.

Stumbling across the room, he gazed down at the ruined bodies of ArchWizard Zenar and Emperor Fauld.

Eamon had done that. The prince of Saetlund had laid low the two most powerful men in the world. No matter what was happening in the battle outside the palace, this victory was extraordinary. It was hard to believe it was real.

But it is, Teth told himself. *I saw it. I saw everything.*

He took it all in one last time, then closed his eyes and steeled himself.

He had to get out of the palace. He'd take his own advice and head for the catacombs. The fight between Zenar and Fauld had driven most from the throne room. The remaining guards fled when Eamon had cast his spell.

Teth anticipated little resistance, if any, as he made his way out of the palace. He had no doubt he'd escape. He would make his way back to Ara and the other Loreknights.

But not without Eamon.

He knelt to pick up Tears of the Traitor, slinging the bow and quiver over one shoulder, then gathered Eamon's body close, shifting the limp form onto his other shoulder so Eamon's torso hung over his back and Teth could wrap one arm around Eamon's legs for counter-leverage.

"Sorry this isn't more dignified, my friend," Teth said as he stood. "But I have to get us both out of here as soon as possible."

Teth knew there should be an entrance somewhere in the throne room. Tucked away, but accessible for entombing monarchs when they passed. Teth searched the room, keeping his eyes carefully averted from the mangled bodies of Fauld and Zenar. Both men had earned their gruesome deaths, but Teth had no desire to look at them again. He'd seen more than enough to give him nightmares.

He found the door hidden by the sole surviving tapestry on the wall behind the thrones. Though he was sure he could have figured out a way to pick the lock, he was thrilled to discover he wouldn't need to. The hinges squeaked from lack of use, but the door swung open, revealing stairs that were quickly swallowed up by darkness.

At the moment, Teth was relying on a candlelabra he'd picked up off the throne room floor for light, and he was happy to trade it for a torch he found in one of the wall sconces. It took only a moment to light the torch using his candles.

The chamber at the base of the stairs was clearly the home of long-dead kings and queens. He passed through it quickly and into a narrow hallway that soon opened into another chamber, this one five-sided with some sort of monument at its center. He passed through it as well and into a long hallway lined with the dead on both sides.

Every so often he would pause to listen for the sound of running water. Somewhere in the catacombs would be a way into the cistern, and the cistern was a way out of Five Rivers. It didn't take long for Teth to reach an access point. He laid Eamon's body against one wall of the catacombs and used Eamon's dagger to weaken the mortar around the rusted iron grate in the floor until he could jerk it free.

Teth dragged Eamon's body to the opening and lowered it as far as possible before letting it fall. He dropped himself through a moment later, got his bearings, and picked Eamon up again. The flow of water showed the way out of the cistern, but when Teth reached a major junction he hesitated. He'd been careful to keep track of his direction from the moment he left the throne room, and he knew he stood at a cross-point of the cistern where one tunnel led out of the city, and the other stretched between the palace and the temple.

He drew a long breath, then said softly to Eamon, "We made a promise, didn't we?"

After adjusting Eamon's weight more securely on his shoulder, Teth turned and made his way into the tunnel that would lead him beneath the temple.

28

ra stared at the mouth of the cistern, tension building in her limbs. This would be the second time in her life she went searching in tunnels underneath a city. Considering her previous experience, she wasn't eager to plunge into the waiting darkness.

"The smell is unpleasant, but not overwhelming . . . most of the time," Dagger said, gauging Ara's pensiveness.

With a small shake of her head, Ara replied, "It's not the smell I'm worried about."

Dagger lifted a questioning brow.

"The last time I went into catacombs, they collapsed," Ara said, remembering the groan of the tunnel walls and the roar of cascading debris that had almost buried her during her escape from Nava's temple beneath the Great Market.

"So you're a frequent visitor to catacombs?" Dagger asked. "Interesting hobby."

"Not by choice." Ara sighed.

"If it helps, I haven't seen evidence to suggest that these catacombs are structurally compromised," Dagger offered in a friendly voice. "And I've been spending quite a bit of time traveling through them recently."

Ara nodded. "It helps."

"I don't remember a part of the plan that involved dawdling," Lucket said, striding past Ara and Dagger.

In a single lithe movement, the Low King hoisted himself up and into the cistern, disappearing into the darkness.

Dagger grinned and gestured for Ara to follow. "After you."

"Thanks," Ara muttered. She approached the opening and wrinkled her nose. Gods, it was a terrible smell. Then, gauging the cistern's height, she looked back at Dagger. "I think I need a leg up."

"Always happy to help," Dagger said, and cupped her hands.

Ara stepped into Dagger's grip and was boosted up until she could haul herself into the dripping tunnel. She scrambled to her feet and quickly turned to offer Dagger her hand, only to see, to her chagrin, that the woman who was barely taller than her had vaulted into the cistern with ease.

"I've had a lot of practice," Dagger said apologetically.

"I'm sure," Ara replied.

Dagger leaned over the edge of the cistern's lip to help Lahvja climb up. When the summoner got to her feet, she frowned at the damp stains on the front of her dress.

"That wasn't a favorite frock, was it?" Dagger remarked.

Lahvja sighed. "Not anymore."

After winding her way through the tunnels of the cistern, Ara couldn't decide if she was getting used to the smell or not. While it wasn't making her as acutely nauseated as before, her headache felt worse. But maybe that was from squinting into the darkness. Lucket carried a hooded lantern, but it offered only a slim band of light as they made slow progress forward.

"Hold a moment," Lucket called.

They'd reached another juncture. Whenever the cistern split in more than one direction, the Low King called a halt to establish what tunnel they should follow. It had happened several times now, and the only difference Ara could discern from when they'd first entered the tunnels was that there was no longer any sign of light from the outside world at their backs.

Dagger stopped beside Lucket, and the two of them conversed in hushed tones. Lahvja paused beside them, listening. Ara knew she should wait for Lucket's instructions, but she'd learned that impatience made her crabby, too. She didn't want to stand still. She wanted to find the burial chamber, and more than that she wanted to find Teth. It couldn't hurt to move a little farther into the tunnel; she wouldn't let the others out of sight.

As Ara leaned forward to peer around the next corner, a shape came hurtling at her from the shadows. She wheeled around and dropped to a crouch, raising Ironbranch at the same time. The attacker landed on her, their hands latching on to Ironbranch and knocking her back. She kept a tight hold on her stave and used the momentum of the fall to draw her assailant into a roll, flipping them onto their back. She kept them pinned to the ground with Ironbranch pushed against their chest to hold them in place.

"I see you haven't forgotten our lessons."

Ara's heart stuttered at the familiar voice.

"Teth?"

Lahvja came running and whispered a few words. A ball of light bloomed in her palm, revealing Teth's grinning face.

"As soon as I touched Ironbranch, I knew it was you," he said.

Ara gave a little cry. She pushed the stave away and wrapped her arms around him, burying her face against his neck. "Oh gods. It's really you."

Teth held her tightly. "To say I've missed you would be an understatement of epic proportions."

She lifted her face, and he brought up one of his hands to brush away the tears she hadn't realized were coursing down her cheeks. His other hand slid around the nape of her neck, and he pulled her down to kiss her. She returned the kiss, losing herself in the warmth of his skin and the feeling of his breath on her lips.

He's alive. He's here.

Her body was shaking with relief. She never wanted to stop kissing him, touching him, desperate for the reassurance that he was alive and with her once more.

The clearing of someone's throat brought her back from the place where only she and Teth existed.

Ara was too full of relief and joy to even blush, but she reluctantly rolled to the side, picking up Ironbranch before she stood. Teth got to his feet.

"Sorry for attacking you," he said to her. "I didn't know who was coming around the corner and thought it best not to take any chances."

Lahvja rushed forward to embrace Teth.

"Thank the gods you're all right," she told him. "We feared the worst."

"It's good to see you, Lahvja," he said, smiling. As he looked past her toward Dagger and Lucket, his smile vanished, and his eyes widened slightly.

Teth moved away from Lahvja, his eyes fixed on Lucket.

Lucket stared at Teth, his expression unreadable. The Low King drew a sharp breath, then slowly released it.

"Son." Lucket stepped forward, placing his hands on Teth's shoulders.

Teth swallowed hard, emotions flying across his face. Disbelief, surprise, wonder. "Father."

Lucket took another step, then pulled Teth into his arms, hugging Teth tight to his chest.

Startled, Teth went still for a moment, then wrapped his arms around Lucket's back, returning the embrace.

Tears welled in Ara's eyes again, and beside her Lahvja sniffed and swiped at her cheeks.

"Isn't this lovely," Dagger observed. "I didn't know you had a soft side, Lucket."

With a dry laugh, Lucket released Teth. "Exceptional circumstances."

"Exactly," Teth agreed. "Don't worry, I'll deny this ever happened as long as you do, too."

"I was about to suggest that very thing," Lucket said, laughing.

Dagger nodded at Teth. "It's been a long time. You look well . . . all things considered."

"Neither of my eyes is swollen shut at the moment," Teth replied. "So I can't complain."

Dagger's eyes narrowed slightly. "How is it that you're here? Lucket and I were coming to help you escape, but it seems you managed on your own."

Mirth vanished from Teth's expression, his mouth setting in a grim line. "Not on my own. Wait here."

Teth moved away from them back into the shadows. Ara heard shuffling and a quiet grunt. When Teth stepped back into the torchlight, she gasped at the sight of Eamon's limp body. The rich bronze of his skin had faded to a gray pallor, and there was no rise and fall of his chest with breath. Ara knew with a wrench of her stomach that he was gone.

With a low cry, Lahvja ran forward. She placed one hand on Eamon's chest, the other on the side of his neck.

"Oh no," she whispered. "Oh, Eamon."

A fist had closed around Ara's heart, but she forced herself to speak. "What happened?"

"He saved me." Teth's voice was thick. "He saved us all."

Teth drew a shuddering breath, then related all that had happened in the throne room and during his subsequent escape into the catacombs.

"Zenar and Fauld?" Lucket spoke in an awed hush. "How is that possible?"

Shaking his head, Teth replied, "I couldn't begin to explain it, but Eamon was able to turn Zenar's magic against him. He channeled the power of Saetlund's gods through my body and his, and that magic somehow became a weapon that took down the ArchWizard and the emperor."

Teth looked down at Eamon's still face. "It should have been me who died. Fauld hurled a bolt of power at me, but Eamon threw himself in front of it. That's what killed him." He released a long sigh. "I couldn't leave him there, so I carried him with me."

Lahvja wept quietly, and Ara went to her, sliding an arm around her shoulders. Gazing at Eamon's lifeless body, Ara struggled with a storm of emotions that battled against one another. Sorrow at his death. Joy that he had abandoned Zenar to fight for Saetlund. In the end, he'd been one of them again. Nimhea would be so proud, though her heart would be shattered.

Dagger stepped forward and took one of Eamon's hands in both of hers.

"You did well, Prince Eamon," she said softly. "You did very well."

Releasing his hand, she stepped back and made a small sound of surprise.

Ara followed Dagger's gaze to a furtive movement behind Teth. A small boy crept from the dark passageway where Teth had been hidden.

"Is it all right?"

Teth looked over his shoulder at the boy. "Yes. You can bring the others."

The boy turned back toward the passage and made a beckoning motion. A group of children cautiously emerged, joining the first boy. They were all wide-eyed and covered in grime. Ara could scarcely breathe at the heartbreaking sight.

The children huddled together, keeping close to Teth.

Slowly, Lucket came forward. He paused beside Teth and said softly, "The missing children. Well done."

"Thank you," Teth murmured in reply. "I only wish I could have saved more, but these were all that were left after Zenar . . ." He broke off. "It's a story for another time."

"I understand," Lucket said. "Why don't you introduce me, so we're all a little more comfortable."

Teth nodded, half turning toward the children. "This is my father. His name is Lucket, and he is going to help you leave this place and take you somewhere safe."

The boy, who appeared to be the appointed leader of the children, looked at Lucket. "Hello."

"Hello." Lucket smiled gently at him. "What's your name?"

"Foeren," the boy answered.

"I'm pleased to meet you, Foeren," Lucket said, and he carefully approached and crouched in front of the boy.

He continued in a quiet conversation with the boy, and Ara was deeply moved to see the way the Low King patiently engaged with him, working to establish trust. Other children began to move closer as their fear lessened.

Keeping her voice low, Ara asked Teth, "Were you followed? Do you expect guards to come looking for the children?"

They'd reached a juncture in this mission, and whether or not there was a fight ahead would guide her next decision.

"No," Teth replied. "It's absolute chaos in the palace. The wizards are panicked. I didn't encounter any palace guards on my way to the catacombs, and only two at the dungeons."

"Good," Ara said. "Lahvja and I need to find the resting place of five of the original Loreknights. Their sarcophagi are somewhere in the catacombs."

With a thin smile, Teth spoke, "*The answer you seek lies in the Five Rivers catacombs.*"

"You knew the message?" Ara asked in surprise.

Teth nodded. "I was there when Eamon gave it to Commander Liran, though I had no idea what it meant. Why are you trying to find the graves of Loreknights?"

"Lahvja is going to ask them to help us," Ara told him. "And we hope they'll say yes."

"Okay," Teth said slowly. "I'm going to just let that lie and see how things turn out."

"That's probably wise." Ara smiled and brushed her fingers over his, earning a flash of a grin from him.

"And I think I know where to find the Loreknights," Teth told her.

Turning to Dagger, Ara said, "This is where we part ways. You and Lucket should take the children, then make your way out of the city."

"Yes," Teth agreed. "The children should be taken out of here as soon as possible. They're malnourished, and a few are ill. They need care."

Lucket said something to Foeren that Ara didn't catch, but the boy nodded and began to speak to the other children as Lucket returned to Teth's side. "We'll see them to safety."

"Where Lucket goes, I go," Dagger added. "At least until he tells me otherwise."

Lucket looked at Teth.

"My place is with the Loresmith, but I'm touched by your concern," Teth replied to the unspoken question with a wry smile.

"Let me take him from you," Lucket said to Teth, and gestured at Eamon's body. "I'll make sure he's properly seen to until he can be put to rest."

Teth passed Eamon's body into Lucket's arms, and Teth murmured a rough thanks to the Low King.

Lucket nodded. "No sense in lingering. We'll get the children to safety. Gods go with you."

"And you." Teth rested his hand on Lucket's shoulder briefly.

"Foeren," Lucket called to the boy. "It's time to go. Please follow me."

Foeren nodded, but before he went after Lucket, he stopped to hug Teth's legs—he was only as tall as Teth's waist.

Teth ruffled his hair. "I'll see you again soon, Foeren."

Foeren smiled up at him, then trotted after Lucket, the other children trailing after him.

"Till we meet again," Dagger said to Ara, Lahvja, and Teth. "Good luck with your ghosts."

29

stride his favored battle mount, a Keldenese bay gelding, Liran surveyed the lines of Vokkan troops in the valley below. With the arrival of Emperor Fauld's reinforcements, the infantry loyal to Liran were now outnumbered two to one, a disadvantage that weighed heavily on him as he anticipated entering the battle. The Resistance forces and Fauld's battalions were fully engaged; even at this distance, Liran could easily hear the clangs of steel, roars of fury, and cries of pain. Soon, Liran and his troops would be in the fray.

Liran's greatest asset and most guarded secret was this: the Vokkan cavalry was his and had long been so. Since the conquest, he'd also gained the loyalty of more than half the Vokkan infantry commanders, and while the contribution of these foot soldiers would be pivotal, it was the shock force of the mounted troops that would shift the balance of the battle to the Resistance's favor.

Once he'd risen to command, Liran had dedicated his military career to honing the cavalry into a precise, devastating weapon that struck in two waves. The first attack came from heavy destriers bearing knights in plate armor. Their arrival on the battlefront was always cataclysmic; they were akin to a thunderstorm and an earthquake combined. These knights and their warhorses plowed through an enemy's front lines, not only trampling attackers but also throwing well-ordered battalions into disarray.

In the wake of that chaos, Liran unleashed his second wave of horsemen. These soldiers were lightly armored, bearing weapons designed for speed and improvisation. They surged into the fray, and their riders wreaked havoc amid the confused ranks of the enemy lines. This act of the bloody battle play was the one that brought about the most casualties. Liran himself rode with the light cavalry.

While the light cavalry engaged the enemy, the initial onslaught of warhorses and heavily armored knights regrouped and, if possible, flanked their adversaries, trapping enemy soldiers between the two mounted attacks. Liran was betting on the fact that the realization that his cavalry was now fighting for the rebels would unleash insurmountable confusion that led to a complete breakdown of order as well as loss of morale.

In order to distinguish Liran's soldiers from the other Vokkan troops, they'd been given a bladder of blue paint. When the attack began, Liran's troops would slather the bright sky-blue color over the standard imperial tabard to mark themselves as fighting for the Resistance. In the chaos of battle, there would be mistakes. Unnecessary losses, but he hoped they would be limited.

Though he would need to push all distractions aside and focus on the impending charge, Liran remained shaken by his father's pronouncement:

After this final battle, I believe it is time that I have a grandson, don't you?

The lure, both Liran and his father knew, was not so much that of a family, but the promise of a future.

The question had shocked him, but he felt only disgust at his father's attempted manipulation, and a surprising wave of pity that a person could be so devoid of love. He had no doubt that Fauld's promises were empty, just as Zenar's were. They were only dangled in a time of need and would be withdrawn the moment Liran's usefulness had played out.

In the distance, Liran watched the final volley of arrows arc up and sail down into the center ranks of the Vokkan battalions. He signaled his lieutenants to begin the forward march.

The front line of Fauld's reinforcements saw Liran's cavalry crest the hill that lay before them. A great cheer rose to welcome them. For a moment, Liran's heart clenched with remorse for the bloodshed to come. Then he set his jaw and gave a second signal to the captain of the heavy cavalry. A moment later, the thunder of hooves filled the air, and Liran watched as the storm of destriers crashed into the shocked Vokkan battalion at the bottom of the slope.

30

eth led them at a fast clip through narrow corridors, the dead tucked into hollows on either side. As they hurried forward, Ara's mind spun from one thought to the next: the thrill of being reunited with Teth, the hope and worry she held close for Lucket and Dagger's mission to rescue the children, and the sense of time she didn't have slipping away even as they drew closer to their goal.

What was happening aboveground, outside the city? Were the Vokkan and Resistance armies still marching toward each other, or was the battle already underway? And how long would they last without the full complement of Loreknights?

Teth slowed when the corridor opened into a broad chamber. "This is it."

The room was the shape of a pentagon. Along each wall sat a sarcophagus carved in elaborate detail with the likeness of the person at rest within.

"There are still torches in some of the wall sconces," Lahvja observed, and set about lighting them until the space was lit with dancing hues of orange and gold.

An obelisk rose from the floor at the center of the room. Ara approached to read aloud the words carved into its base.

"*Honor to these champions of Saetlund, matchless in courage and character.*"

Lahvja came to stand beside Ara. "Champions. Lying in eternal rest."

"*The answer you seek lies in the Five Rivers catacombs,*" Ara said in reply. "Do you know what to do?"

"Not precisely," Lahvja said with a shy smile. "But neither was I certain of how to make us travel between planes, and I managed that."

"I have no doubt you'll succeed." Ara rested her hand on the summoner's shoulder. "What should the rest of us do?"

Lahvja pressed her lips together, pondering, then said, "You and Teth should return to the corridor while I perform the spell."

While Ara and Teth retreated, Lahvja walked in a slow circle through the room, touching each sarcophagus as she passed it. When she completed her turn through the space, she began again.

Ara and Teth watched from the edge of the chamber, their fingers threaded together. Ara could feel the pulse at his wrist, and each heartbeat was a comforting reminder that he was alive, with her once more. She never wanted to let him go.

Lahvja made her circle around the room five times. Then she returned to the obelisk and knelt before it, pressing her palms flat against the base.

Now Ara could hear her own heartbeat as it drummed steadily, then faster.

Let us be right. Let this be the answer.

If they were mistaken, she didn't know what they could do.

"Champions of old, I call upon thee in our time of need. Give us your blessing, your aid, so that we might begin the cycle anew."

Ara's breath became shallow, and Teth released her hand to wrap his arm around her waist, drawing her close. She could feel the tautness of his limbs. He understood as well as she did what was at stake.

Lahvja stood and walked to one of the sarcophagi, laying her hands upon it. A gleam drew Ara's gaze to the Whisper of Life. The blood-red gemstones.

"Champions, I name you: Ursina of Fjeri, bring us your strength."

She moved to the next entombed Loreknight. "Nathor of Daefrit, lend us your will."

Lahvja continued her circle: "Mirix of Vijeri, supply us your ingenuity."

And again: "Turhea of Sola, we plead for your relentlessness."

Finally: "Resek of Kelden, we ask for your agility."

Returning to the obelisk, Lahvja knelt once more and placed her hands upon its base. "Champions, I summon thee in the name of Saetlund's gods. Our enemies approach; remember your sacred oaths and defend your kingdom."

Lahvja bowed her head. Even from the corridor, Ara could see that she was shaking with the effort of the deep magics she drew upon. Until that moment, Ara's thoughts had centered on raising the knights and bringing them to the battle. She hadn't considered the cost to Lahvja, and she suddenly feared for her friend's well-being.

She didn't realize she'd tried to take a step toward Lahvja until Teth's grip tightened around her waist, holding her back.

"No," he whispered. "We can't interfere."

Ara gritted her teeth, knowing he was right, but wanting to run to Lahvja and help the summoner in any way she could.

Lahvja had fallen silent. She continued to kneel before the obelisk, in the quiet. Ara held her breath, waiting. But nothing stirred in the chamber. Still nothing. Ara let her breath out slowly and felt her soul begin to quake.

Nothing. Only quiet.

They were wrong. Whatever answer waited for them in the catacombs, it wasn't here.

Fury and frustration surged in Ara's chest. She wrestled free of Teth's grasp and started toward Lahvja.

Every torch in the room went out, cloaking the chamber in shadow.

Ara froze, and in the next moment she felt Teth beside her, his fingers resting lightly on her arm. A simple yet vital reminder that he was with her.

Something stirred in the darkness. Not movement but sound, the barest of vibrations. Then the vibrations became a murmur. Gathering. Growing. Another sound came, and with it a soft, warm wind that stirred Ara's hair, slid over the back of her neck, like the slow release of a breath.

New lights appeared in the chamber. Sparks of pure white, twinkling like stars, floated before each of the five sarcophagi. The sparks expanded, the intensity of their light increased, brighter, brighter, until Ara had to look away. Brilliance like a shock wave pulsed through the chamber, then receded, and Ara dared to return her gaze to Lahvja.

What she saw made her gasp. Five warriors now stood with Lahvja, who was slowly rising on shaking limbs. Lahvja reached for the obelisk, leaning on it for support, and Ara rushed forward to help steady her friend. Teth matched her movement from the summoner's opposite side.

Even as she braced Lahvja against her body, Ara sensed one of the risen Loreknights coming toward them.

I shouldn't be afraid, she told herself. *They're on our side.*

She shivered, unable to hold back the frisson of cold that flowed over her as she watched the tall woman clad in heavy armor, the one Lahvja had named Ursina of Fjeri, approach. Ara could see the expertise in the finely wrought armor the Loreknight wore, but most distinctive was her helm. It had been forged in the shape of a roaring bear; the top of the bear's jaw rested at the woman's temple, its lower jaw aligning with her own. Only a master craftsman could have created such a wonder. *The first Loresmith forged that armor*, Ara thought with awe. Oddly, Ursina carried no weapons.

"Summoner." Ursina's voice had a strange echo. "Why have you raised us from our slumber? Our time in the mortal realm is long past."

Lahvja straightened, but Ara kept her arm tightly around her waist, and Teth did the same.

"The gods bid me call upon you." Lahvja spoke in clear tones despite the trembling of her body. "Saetlund is in crisis. Vokk the Devourer approaches; his empire consumes the world. It lies with us to stop him lest he destroy it."

"How has this come to pass?" Another risen Loreknight, Nathor of Daefrit, ebony-skinned and bearing two wickedly curved swords that were coated in a vivid green substance. "Surely Saetlund's protectors have not been defeated."

Lahvja hesitated.

"It's a long story." Teth spoke up. "But we don't really have the time to tell it."

A third Loreknight, Mirix of Vijeri, whose long blue and yellow braids swung as she walked, cracked a spiked whip in the air, drawing the room's focus.

"You think we do not deserve an explanation?"

"Of course you do," Ara hurried to say. "But there are five new Loreknights, called to save Saetlund, who cannot succeed without your help. They may already be engaged in battle, and we must go to them without delay."

"I wouldn't say no to a good fight." Turhea of Sola, with gleaming bronze skin and a cloud of dark hair crowning her head, brandished her sword and shield.

"That's the spirit," Teth said, then checked himself. "So to speak, begging your pardon."

Ursina's eyes narrowed as she gazed at Teth. "The mouthy one is a Loreknight. What strange times you live in."

"The strangest," Teth agreed.

"He's very good with a bow," Ara interjected, feeling defensive.

"As am I."

Ara started at the sound of hooves clattering on stone, but she turned to see Resek of Kelden astride a roan horse. A crossbow was strapped to his back.

He shot a gaze that pierced like a bolt at Ara. "Loresmith. You have the eyes of your ancestors."

Her first instinct was to say, *I do?* But she checked herself and replied, "Thank you."

The moment Resek named Ara Loresmith, every risen Loreknight in the chamber focused on her.

"Yes, I am the Loresmith. I wish we had time to explain all that's happened, but what you need to know is this: Some time ago, the kings and queens of Saetlund strayed from their fealty to the gods, and the roles of the Loreknights and Loresmith were sullied, stripped of all the old magics. Because of this, Emperor Fauld, servant of Vokk the Devourer, sent armies to Saetlund's shores that easily conquered our kingdom. Only now has the opportunity arisen to drive back those armies and restore Saetlund to the purpose the gods intended. But we cannot drive the Vokkans from the kingdom without you. Ofrit, the Alchemist, spoke these words to me:

"To find the end, begin again.

Fulfill the lore, as once before.

Restore the past, to rest at last."

Ara paused, then continued, "Five new Loreknights have been called, but it is you who complete the circle. Join us."

Resek regarded her for several heartbeats, then said, "Truth lives in your words, Loresmith."

"Indeed," Ursina said. "As the gods will it, we will fight once more for Saetlund."

A murmur of agreement passed among the remaining Loreknights.

Ara turned her head to look at Lahvja. "Can you bring us to the others?"

Lahvja nodded, but Ara wasn't convinced.

"Are you certain?" she pressed. "You seem tired. I don't want you to harm yourself."

"I am tired," Lahvja admitted. "I've never attempted, much less accomplished, anything like the magics required to summon the dead. But I can, and will, take us to the battle. It's where we are needed."

"If you're sure." Ara chewed her lower lip, worried for her friend.

"I'm sure," Lahvja replied. As if to prove her point, she shook Ara and Teth off and walked toward the risen Loreknights, who'd formed a half circle opposite the three of them. To her credit, she didn't so much as wobble.

"The gods have granted me the power to travel between the mortal and spirit worlds," Lahvja told the Loreknights. "Join hands."

The five Loreknights linked hands, but Teth hesitated.

"How does this work?" he asked.

"I will carry us between the planes to reach Nimhea," Lahvja answered.

"But Nimhea is probably fighting." Teth frowned. "Where exactly do you expect us to land?"

Ara and Lahvja exchanged a look.

"There's no way to be certain," Lahvja admitted. "But we don't have another choice. If we left through the cistern, it would take far too long to reach the others. We must use my power."

"If we arrive in the midst of a battle, which is likely, we know that Nimhea's crown will protect the Loreknights," Ara said to Teth. "You won't come to harm."

"But you could," Teth cautioned.

"Then I'll stand at the center of the circle," Ara offered. "That should keep me safe enough."

Teth looked doubtful but had to concede. "It's probably the best we can do."

Ara smiled and leaned in to kiss him on the cheek. "Have a little faith."

"I've had to have a lot of it lately," Teth replied with a roll of his eyes.

Lahvja directed all the Loreknights to form a circle around Ara. When their hands were linked, Ara wrapped her fingers around Lahvja's wrist and held tight.

"We should crouch," Lahvja suggested. "That way if there are arrows flying and swords slashing, we're less likely to be struck."

"Good idea," Ara said, though the vision of said arrows and swords made her jaw clench.

"Wait," said Teth, eyes narrowing. "Are you saying this because you did this before and were hit by an arrow or a sword?"

Lahvja grinned at him. "It was nothing. Barely noticeable."

Teth swore under his breath as they all crouched.

"I like your spirit, Summoner," Ursina said with a rumbling chuckle.

Nathor snickered. "I think the thief's question is apt."

"You would," Ursina replied.

"Oh, stop." Mirix rolled her eyes. "We've barely returned from the dead and you two are already griping at each other."

Resek laughed. "But, Mirix, how would you know they were truly themselves if they weren't bickering?"

"Hush, all of you," Turhea said firmly. "We go where we are needed, when we are needed. Let the summoner work her magic."

After a few chastened glances and furtive smiles, they all fell silent.

Lahvja closed her eyes, and the burial chamber slowly faded from view.

31

nother long shriek stabbed Nimhea's ears while a spray of hot blood hit her face. She didn't pause, but waded farther into the fray, baring her teeth as she swung her sword, striking true again. The Vokkan soldier fell at her feet. She moved on.

The screaming had begun some time ago—it was difficult to gauge the passing of time in battle. Nimhea didn't know what was making the awful sound, only that it didn't come from wounded or dying fighters. It was unnatural, frightening, and she'd noticed that it had a much greater effect on the Resistance warriors than it did on herself and Joar. Some of her allies in arms fell to their knees at the cries, shaking with fear. Others began to bleed from their ears and eyeballs.

It was some evil. Some magic.

She refused to think about the possibilities, knowing there was nothing she could do about it but try to protect those more vulnerable to the strange assault from being overrun and fight on.

To her left, Joar's blades made deep sweeps through the enemy ranks while a blizzard raged around him. The shock of the cold and sting-ing ice had the Vokkans stumbling back, giving Joar endless openings for attack. The song ringing around him seemed to rise in triumph with each adversary felled. It was stunning to witness, but equally sobering.

In all the imaginings Nimhea had indulged in as a child, longing for glory, dreaming of battles that would bring her the River Throne, she'd never considered the banality of warfare. It was relentless, bloody butchery. Driving the enemy back, shielding yourself from attack, wading through bodies.

The stench could easily overwhelm a person. It wasn't only blood that spilled out from someone who'd been disemboweled. The wails of the wounded clawed at your heart.

The only choice was to block all of it out. War required singular focus. Slay the enemy. Survive. Press on.

Before she'd charged alongside the Hawk into a wall of Vokkan soldiers, Nimhea hadn't grasped the reason Saetlund's gods had created the Loreknights. Champions to defend the kingdom, but never to chase their own glory. The purpose of a Loreknight's power stood in direct opposition to Fauld's. The Vokkan emperor wanted, needed violence.

The essence of an empire is violence, Nimhea understood. It is consuming and destroying. It asks everything and gives nothing, even when it claims benevolence. The promises it offers are never without poison.

Saetlund was meant to stand against all of that. For centuries, it had; the kingdom had flourished in peace, enjoyed prosperity. And then all that goodness was squandered.

It had happened by degrees, Nimhea knew. Cracks in the foundation that had been laid. Flaws that could have been repaired, but were instead ignored. So they widened, deepened. Generations of monarchs refused to see the damage, excused it or denied its presence, until ultimately convincing themselves that the altered structure had been that way all along, unwilling to accept that at the slightest tremor it would all come crashing down upon them.

And it had. The earthquake had arrived in the form of the Vokkan empire, and Saetlund had collapsed.

Nimhea had always believed the River Throne should belong to her, but she saw now that it would be bought at a terrible price.

Plowing through another two attackers, Nimhea was surprised by a sudden break in the assault. There were still Vokkan soldiers in front of her, but a number of them had backed off. She wondered if they finally noticed that any strike managing to hit her had no effect. But the wide-eyed Vokkans weren't gaping at her; their gazes were fixed on something behind her.

Nimhea whirled to face whatever had captured the Vokkans' attention. Her own mouth dropped open as Lahvja leapt forward, beaming at Nimhea.

"Where did you come from?"

"The catacombs," Ara replied, striding forward with a smile.

Nimhea's eyes widened as she caught sight of the warriors who flanked the summoner and the Loresmith.

"You raised the five," Nimhea gasped. "You did it."

Ara nodded.

"Did you doubt me?" Lahvja asked in a teasing voice.

Nimhea took a moment to press her lips to Lahvja's temple, then whispered into her ear, "Never."

Grinning, Lahvja stepped back from Nimhea and lifted her hands, her voice rising above the din of battle. "Loreknights, the enemies of Saetlund stand before you. Drive them from these shores as the gods have willed it."

The five risen Loreknights raised their voices as one in a battle cry. "For Saetlund!"

Lahvja, Nimhea, Teth, and Joar joined the call. "For Saetlund!"

"On me, Loreknights!" Nimhea cried. Raising her sword, she pointed it toward a figure on horseback in the distance. "Our goal lies there. Drive the enemy to Commander Liran's cavalry, where they will be trapped between our advancing forces!"

Another rousing shout followed Nimhea's orders, and with the princess driving ahead, her sword slashing, six fellow Loreknights fell in step behind her. Lahvja and Teth held back, their particular skills better suited to distance than close combat.

For several moments, Ara watched mesmerized as the five risen Loreknights launched themselves into the fray. A roar rattled her bones and made all the hairs on her arms stand to attention. Where the heavily armored Ursina had just stood, an enormous bear rose on its hind legs. It lumbered forward, knocking Vokkan soldiers aside with heavy swipes of its arms, its long claws shredding throats. A handful of enemy fighters were so terrified by her transformation, they fled rather than holding their ground.

A flurry of flashing silver moved alongside the bear as Nathor's two swords sliced through the Vokkan ranks like a deadly whirlwind. Shouts of surprise followed the cracks of Mirix's whip, which snaked forward to jerk soldiers off their feet or rip weapons from their grasp. Alternating shield bashes and deadly sword slashes, Turhea advanced at a steady, relentless pace. And a few paces behind the wall of his fellow Loreknights, Resek raced back and forth through the rear of their line on his swift, nimble roan, his crossbow bolts buzzing out at a dizzying speed to fell enemies beyond the reach of his friends, further clearing a path forward.

It was an incredible sight, witnessing the Loreknights surge ahead.

Ara's heart pounded as she watched the promise of Saetlund's gods come to life. The Loreknights could not be slowed, nor stopped. They plowed ahead, cutting, bashing, driving the enemy back. Only a little time passed before the Vokkans began to comprehend that this new group of enemies, while only the smallest fraction of the force that opposed them, were an army unto themselves.

Grasping their slipping odds of victory against these fresh foes, the Vokkans split into a chaos of reactions. Some fought on with grim, despairing determination. Others retreated, and while not quitting the field, ran off to find less formidable adversaries somewhere else in the battle. Still others threw down their weapons and attempted to surrender.

Ara struggled to determine where she belonged in the midst of a pitched battle. She couldn't attack the enemy, making her useless as a fighter, and because of Nimhea's crown, the Loreknights couldn't be harmed, rendering her need to defend them obsolete. She briefly wondered if it would have been wiser for her to retreat behind the lines. Perhaps that was the more rational choice, but she couldn't imagine being anywhere other than with her Loreknights.

Ultimately, Ara resolved to stay close to Lahvja. The summoner couldn't be harmed by Vokkan attacks, but she required concentration to cast spells. With Ara defending her against advancing soldiers, Lahvja would have the necessary time and focus to work her rituals.

While Ara remained beside Lahvja, it seemed Teth had resolved to stay close to Ara. Tears of the Traitor sent off arrow after arrow, keeping most of the Vokkans who approached at bay. A part of Ara wondered if she should tell him to take his archery skills elsewhere, but her more persuasive inner voice convinced her that his presence wasn't unwarranted. She could defend Lahvja against Vokkan soldiers who got too close, but without Teth's arrows driving the majority of the enemy back, she could easily have been overwhelmed.

Ara heard Lahvja begin to chant behind her as she deflected the blows of a charging soldier. The twang of Teth's bow sounded at steady intervals, picking off the Vokkans Ara tangled with as well as others who found their way around the Loreknights. Absolutely no one made it through them.

At the telltale blaze of heat hitting her back, Ara crouched even before Lahvja shouted, "Down!"

"Senn's teeth," Teth exclaimed, bringing a smile to Ara's lips, even as Lahvja's fireballs began to sail over her head.

32

iran watched the Vokkan lines begin to break with grim satisfaction. His troops—joined with the Resistance battalions—had been slowly pushing the enemy back, but with the arrival of the Loresmith and her Loreknights, what had been a trial of endurance was becoming an incredible show of force. They were on the verge of overwhelming Vokk's battalions.

Nimhea and her companions had finally fought their way through the enemy to him. They were an array of warriors too astonishing to grasp. He even thought he glimpsed a bear charging into the Vokkan lines. But that couldn't be right . . . Then there was the matter of the blizzard that whirled around one giant of a man.

Princess Nimhea greeted him with a grin, and at once, they continued the battle as a united front.

A surge of triumph set fire to Liran's blood. Victory was almost in their grasp. He shouted a command and led the light cavalry fighting alongside him in another charge that crashed through enemy soldiers in a devastating flood of blades and hooves. His own blade, Godsbane, had danced in graceful, macabre steps through the field. The sword was nigh weightless in his grip, its balance perfect, as if it were an extension of his own body.

Panic had set in among the Vokkans. Their commanders had lost control of the action, and chaos reigned throughout their faltering ranks.

Liran regrouped his cavalry for another charge, but before he could give the order to attack, a piercing shriek filled the air. It wasn't the first unnatural cry that had sailed over the battlefield that day, but this one was different. Louder and longer. The sound stabbed into his ears, and he brought up his hands to cover them even as the ground trembled from the force of the awful sound.

Liran's horse reared, squealing with fright, and lost its balance. Time seemed to slow as the gelding tipped over backward. Liran threw himself from the saddle and hit the ground, rolling away before he was crushed beneath the horse's weight. He came to a crouch and was relieved to see his mount recover, shaking itself, then rising to its hooves.

The earsplitting screech came again and again, and his horse bolted. The rest of the cavalry's mounts shook off their riders, and as a herd they stampeded from the battlefield.

Quickly scanning the ranks of his soldiers, Liran saw most were on their feet, or getting there, while a few had been injured when the horses panicked, and remained on the ground.

"Healers! Get to the fallen," Liran shouted. "The rest of you, to me!"

As his soldiers closed ranks around him, he searched the field for the source of the cry.

He found it in the midst of the first and second Vokkan battalions, which had long since blended into one confused force. Taller than all the soldiers around it and skeletally thin, the figure stretched long arms toward the sky. Liran could see the talons tipping its fingers.

Vokk.

While Liran had known it was beyond foolish to hope the god wouldn't reach the battlefield, he still quaked at his first glimpse of the

Devourer. This was the god of his people. The being who had led the Vokkans on a campaign of conquest set on devouring the world. It had almost succeeded. Might still.

Here was the last stand.

It fell to Liran to end the god's eternal hunger, if such a thing was possible.

Godsbane was suddenly heavy in his hand—not physically, but its significance, its purpose. His fate. Magical or not, it was still a weapon wielded by a human, and Liran found it difficult to believe that he could kill a divine being, much less one as powerful as Vokk the Devourer.

For his entire life, Liran had lived in fear of Vokk—the source of the empire's power, the same power that was the key to Emperor Fauld's immortality. The task before him seemed insurmountable. Who could challenge a god and survive? The enchantment on Princess Nimhea's crown protected him from injury at the hands of mortals, but Liran doubted it would shield him from Vokk's attacks.

As he stared at the god towering over the Vokkan troops, Liran's every instinct screamed that he should save himself, turn and chase after the horses. But to do that would be to spend the rest of his life running, hiding, to be a man cowering in the shadows, waiting for the inevitable moment when Vokk finally found him and punished him for his betrayal.

No. He could not run.

Taking his sword in both hands, Liran brought the pommel to the center of his chest, the blade pointing toward the earth. Toward Saetlund. This land, its people, had convinced him to turn away from the empire and seek a better future. Somehow that choice had brought him not only into an alliance with the Resistance but into communion with the very gods of this place. He'd neither expected nor wanted to be named champion of the gods along with Saetlund's storied Loreknights; nonetheless, here he was. It was time to fully embrace his fate.

Around him, shouts of alarm became screams of fear. Something had changed in the Vokkan ranks. Where there had been disorganization and signs of a burgeoning retreat, there was a sudden stillness, as if as one, the enemy soldiers had fallen under a trance. Then a low, rippling moan sounded, rising steadily into the air, sending spikes of dread into Liran's heart.

The broken battalions Liran's forces had driven back now charged forward, running with reckless abandon into a fresh attack. They hurled themselves on their enemies with snarls and mindless cries.

The shocking force of the assault caught the Resistance fighters off guard, taking many down in the first charge. Liran watched, stunned, as the enemy not only overwhelmed his allies, but literally began to rip them apart.

"Nava's mercy," he heard Nimhea cry out, a sick note in her voice. "They aren't just attacking, they're eating people, tearing into them while they're still alive."

A shriek to Liran's right drew his attention. One of his soldiers had run through a Vokkan attacker, but instead of falling, the Vokkan grabbed the soldier by the shoulders and jerked his body forward. The sword slid deeper, but the Vokkan paid it no mind, sinking his teeth into the soldier's neck. Blood sprayed when the Vokkan lifted his head, painting his face in bright crimson. His jaw worked in a steady rhythm. He was chewing.

The soldier went down, succumbing to massive blood loss, and the Vokkan went with him, tearing another chunk of flesh from the dying soldier's neck.

With a strangled shout, Liran rushed the Vokkan. He grabbed his enemy around the waist with one arm and pulled up, lifting him off the sword and throwing him to the ground. The Vokkan should have stayed down. His wound was fatal. But he rolled into a crouch and hissed at Liran.

Liran swung his sword, shearing the Vokkan's head from his neck. The headless body collapsed and lay unmoving. He stared at the corpse, wanting to deny the proof before him. He'd heard the tales of how the Vokkans first overcame more powerful adversaries—a gift from Vokk himself, insatiable hunger made into a weapon. The ravening, it was called. Men become monsters. The terror they drove into their enemies was as effective as their thirst for blood and flesh.

He'd thought the stories embellishments, but now he witnessed the horror of Vokk's blessing at work.

"What's happening?" Princess Nimhea shouted as she hacked the limbs from a soldier who snapped his jaws at her face before she drove him back.

"The ravening!" Liran told Nimhea. "We're no longer fighting human beings. They're mad with hunger. Their minds are gone."

With a broad sweep of his sword, he cleaved another attacker in half.

"The only way to stop them is to dismember or behead them," Liran called to his nearby allies. "Spread the word."

"Well, that's just lovely," Nimhea said through clenched teeth even as she cleanly severed a ravening Vokkan's head from his body.

She began to shout orders, and her fellow Loreknights fanned out on the field to meet the onslaught as best they could.

Liran swore and continued his attack against soldiers that threw themselves at him with hissing and gnashing teeth. Even as Saetlund's fighters learned how to put down the raveners, this enemy would bring catastrophic casualties. It had to be stopped. Liran was filled with the awful realization that he was the one who could put an end to this terror.

He gazed across the field to the god who towered above the Vokkan army. Vokk's bellows filled the air, each cry sending a new frenzy of bloodlust through his troops.

With a sickening twist in his gut, Liran understood the only way to break the spell was to destroy its creator, but he couldn't see how he could reach Vokk. The god was at the center of the Vokkan forces, while enemy soldiers crowded Liran and his companions, slavering and chomping wildly. He struck them down methodically, but it made no difference. There were always more. Mindless and relentless, they climbed over the bodies of their fallen peers that were quickly piling up. Soon there would be a wall of corpses separating Liran and Vokk.

Gritting his teeth, he hacked his way through the horde, making little progress. It was hopeless.

33

ra was forced down to one knee. She clenched her jaw and held strong, pushing back against the onslaught. Vacant-eyed Vokkan soldiers clawed at her, held back by Ironbranch, but she doubted she'd be able to keep them at bay for long.

"Lahvja!" Whatever the summoner was attempting, Ara needed it to happen now, or they'd be overrun.

She fought to retain her grasp on Ironbranch as a soldier wrapped his hands around it, trying to tear the stave from her hand. A buzzing sound ripped past Ara's ear, followed by a wet thunk as an arrow buried deep in the eye socket of the soldier. The Vokkan soldier shuddered and fell back, dropping to the ground. Another arrow struck nearby, then another, until Ara's assailants lay dead at her feet.

She rose and turned, searching for the archer who'd come to her aid. When she met the amber gaze fixed on her, a cry rose in her throat.

"Teth!"

When Vokk appeared on the field, the frenzied attack of ravening soldiers had driven them apart. Now he was moving toward her, loosing Tears of the Traitor as he wove through a maze of embattled fighters and broken bodies. His never-ending supply of arrows felled soldiers without pause.

At Ara's flank, Lahvja gave a shout, drawing Ara's attention. The summoner thrust her arms forward. Her fingers curved like grasping talons. The earth in front of the summoner rippled as a tangle of roots erupted from the soil. The roots surged toward the Vokkan ranks like a horde of serpents. The Vokkan soldiers tripped over thick, writhing wood and then were trapped as the ever-searching roots wrapped around their ankles and legs, holding them fast.

Ara glanced at Lahvja and gave a quick approving nod. Then Teth was at her side, and her pulse leapt. He released one more arrow, then lowered his bow, turning toward her.

With the enemy trapped for at least a moment, Ara let herself reach for him. Teth wrapped his free hand around her waist, drawing her against his chest.

"Thank the gods," she sobbed, unable to stop herself from weeping with relief.

She was touching him; she could her his heart beating.

His lips brushed the crown of her head. "My sentiments exactly. What in Eni's name is happening to the Vokkans?"

"Vokk must have done something," Ara said.

Teth shuddered. "I can feel him. His magic. Like it's trying to crawl under my skin and tear me apart from the inside."

Ara nodded, trying hard to ignore that same insidious feeling of being corrupted. She had known Vokk would pose the greatest threat in this fight, but she hadn't been prepared for the sickening wave of energy that hit her when he manifested amid his troops. And she knew it would only get worse.

Whatever magic the Devourer had unleashed upon his troops had rendered them mad and mindless but for the need to attack. The soldiers trapped by Lahvja's spell clawed at the roots binding them, even cutting and slashing at their own limbs in the attempt to get free. The soldiers behind the bound Vokkans didn't stop to help their fellows, instead clambering over them to rush at Lahvja and Ara.

Lahvja dug her fingers into the ground again, whispering fervently, but the enemy was coming too fast. Teth loosed his arrows, aiming for eye sockets, as only direct hits to the brain seemed to stop the ensorcelled Vokkans.

Ara bit her lip, fighting a surge of terror and despair. There were too many. Crazed with bloodlust. She closed her eyes.

Where was Liran? Vokk had to be stopped.

"What the—"

Teth's exclamation made her gaze fly up. She glanced at him, then followed his wide-eyed stare to the giant shape hurtling toward them. Huge paws dug furrows in the earth as the beast ran. Its jaws snatched up frenzied Vokkans, snapping them in half. In less than a minute, the soldiers who'd been charging toward them were scattered, most in pieces.

Senn lifted his muzzle and let out a baying cry that shook the earth.

The air beside Ara shimmered, and she turned to see Wuldr looking down at her.

"I have an errand for you, Loresmith."

34

howl rose above the din of battle, raising the hairs on Liran's arms. He'd never heard a sound like that, so primal and preternatural. No creature of this world could have made it.

Liran turned, steeling himself to face whatever monstrosity Vokk had raised to join his ravening army. His eyes widened at the massive shape that barreled toward him.

It was a wolf. No, a hound, long limbed and wiry haired like the most coveted of hunting dogs, but it was unnaturally large, twice the size of a warhorse.

He raised his sword as the beast drew closer, frowning as he saw another shape rising on its back. Not rising, riding. There was a person astride the great hound.

"Commander!" The shout came as the giant dog slowed its approach.

The voice was familiar, but no, it couldn't be, and yet it was. He gaped in disbelief at the sight of the small young woman astride the hound. It was the Loresmith.

"Liran!" Ara called to him. "Come! Senn will carry you to Vokk. It's time."

The beast crouched, and Liran vaulted onto its back, sitting behind the Loresmith.

"He doesn't have the smoothest gait," Ara advised. "So I'd grab on to his fur if I were you. He doesn't seem to mind."

Though hesitant to do so, as he didn't want the hound's jaws snapping at him, Liran did as she urged, taking fistfuls of fur as the hunting dog rose to its feet. He was glad he had when the beast surged forward, trampling the Vokkan lines as it ran.

"It's called Senn?" Liran shouted as wind rushed over them.

"Yes," Ara called back. "Senn is Wuldr's hunting hound. Wuldr asked him to help us reach Vokk."

Liran didn't have a reply to that revelation. Wuldr, if he recalled correctly, was one of Saetlund's gods, associated with the northern provinces of the kingdom and also known as the Hunter. And apparently he had a giant hound as a companion.

Briefly closing his eyes, Liran promised himself that if he lived through the battle, he'd set aside time to do some serious theological study. Considering that he was acting as an agent of Saetlund's gods, whose existence he had far too much proof of, committing himself to a better understanding of the divine and its place in his life seemed imperative. The gods of this land would be his gods, perhaps already were his gods, because with each of Senn's long strides, he was borne closer to his fate: to slay the only deity he'd ever known.

The instrument of his fate was already gripped tight in his hand.

Godsbane, his sword was called, so the Loresmith told him. For his sake and for Saetlund's, he prayed the weapon lived up to its name.

Liran's gaze fixed on the young woman in front of him. She rode fearlessly, her gaze fixed on the looming figure of Vokk. Ara was so small in stature, yet she was the force that had changed the world.

When Liran allied himself with Saetlund's Resistance, he'd never heard of the Loresmith, nor had he imagined that gods and magic would ultimately shape his fate. It was clear now that without Ara, the rebels would have had no chance at defeating the empire. Their army would have been crushed by Vokk's power. Only with the return of the Loreknights did Saetlund have a chance at victory. And it was yet to be seen if they would have that victory.

Now it fell to him, Prince Liran, eldest son of Fauld, the Dark Star.

They were a short distance from Vokk when Senn slowed and bent his head. He snarled, knocking aside soldiers with his muzzle. The Vokkans struck at him with their weapons and clawed and bit at him, but the hound seemed oblivious.

"There's our path." Ara pointed, and Liran saw that Senn's attacks had cleared the way for them.

"Our path?" Liran stared as the Loresmith looked at him expectantly. Surely she wasn't coming with him.

"My place is at your side," she told him without so much as a blink. "Senn and I will do our best to keep the Vokkan troops away from you while you face Vokk."

"You can't fight," Liran objected.

"I can defend," Ara replied. "And that's what I will do. And don't worry; if Senn can't protect me should I get into trouble, I doubt anyone can."

It took less than a heartbeat to see from her steely gaze that there would be no arguing further.

In moments they'd closed in on the god. Liran leapt from the hound's back, allowing himself one glance to ensure that Senn and Ara wouldn't be overwhelmed by the ravening troops behind them. But it was immediately apparent that they were a far greater threat to the Vokkan soldiers than the opposite. Senn was impervious to harm, tossing aside attackers like rag dolls, while astride him, the Loresmith blocked incoming strikes with her stave.

"Vokk!" Liran braced himself and lifted his sword. Shadows slithered up Godsbane's blade, and Liran felt an echoing power swirling in his blood.

Baleful eyes fixed on him, and Vokk's rasping voice surrounded him. "Son of Fauld, what folly is this? You cannot mean to defy me, the god of your father. Of your people."

"Devourer, you will not destroy this world," Liran shouted. "I will not allow it."

"Allow it?" Vokk snarled, then laughed. "Fool. You must be eager for death. Let me fulfill your wish."

Almost lazily, Vokk slashed at Liran with his many-clawed hand. Liran swung Godsbane, meeting the attack. When the god's hand met his blade, Liran partly expected the sword to shatter and to simply be cut to ribbons by Vokk. But Godsbane sank into Vokk's leathery flesh, slicing deep into the god's palm. Vokk shrieked and jerked away from Liran, clasping his injured hand with the other, staring at the wound in disbelief.

Liran's pulse pounded. Vokk was bleeding. The sword in Liran's grip had the power to render a god mortal.

Liran drew a shuddering breath, truly believing for the first time that he could defeat Vokk.

Vokk threw his head back and screamed with outrage. Liran charged, hoping to strike while the god bellowed his fury, but Vokk was preternaturally fast and easily met Liran's attack. He blocked the blow Liran had aimed at his chest, but Godsbane bit into Vokk's forearm, leaving a deep gash.

This time Vokk didn't pause to rage; instead he bore down on Liran in a ferocious assault. Liran dodged the swipe of one clawed hand and blocked another. The force of Vokk's blows sent him reeling back, but he sliced into the god's other hand. Blood streamed from both of Vokk's hands now.

Rearing back, Vokk opened his massive jaws and bellowed. Along with the horrible, shaking cry came a storm of wasps, pouring out of the god's mouth in a deadly cloud that surged toward Liran.

The commander's eyes widened in horror as the swarm moved to engulf him, but the shadows sliding over Godsbane's blade suddenly lashed out, sweeping through the wasps and flaring with bouts of pure white flame that engulfed the buzzing cloud until it was nothing but ash that floated harmlessly to the earth.

Vokk hissed, a furious sound, but edged with something Liran thought was fear. The god opened his mouth and bellowed again. This time a noxious green fog spilled forth, billowing toward Liran. Liran had no doubt that one breath of that poisoned air would kill him.

But once again the shadows that writhed around his blade flew out, this time forming a net around the cloud, capturing it and burning it away.

"Impossible," Vokk snarled.

Liran pressed his advantage, whirling to the right and bringing Godsbane up in a swift, broad arc that Vokk didn't anticipate quickly enough. The blade sliced across Vokk's chest and shoulder, opening a wide gash.

Vokk screeched and lurched back.

"Son of Fauld." He kept moving, staying beyond Liran's reach, as he spoke. "Why do you ally yourself with this tiny, pitiful kingdom? The world is mine, and I would share it with you."

"I don't want the world." Liran lunged and Vokk dodged, Godsbane whistling past his arm.

"Only because you never imagined it could be yours," Vokk pressed. "But hear me now. Your father is dead. Your brother is slain. You are the only heir to my empire. Abandon this foolish path. Claim your destiny at my side."

Vokk's words stunned Liran into stillness.

Fauld and Zenar dead? He could hear the truth of it in the god's desperation. But how? They must have destroyed each other in that throne room. Liran shuddered, and while it wasn't quite sorrow that he felt, there was a brief, gnawing emptiness. His father and brother had been nightmarish beings, but they were still his blood, and that connection meant something.

Liran was a heartbeat too late to realize his shock had given Vokk an opening. The god threw his body into Liran's, knocking the commander onto this back. The breath spewed painfully from his chest as Godsbane flew from his grasp. Liran wheezed, struggling to draw air back into his body, but he rolled away instantly, just before Vokk's claws buried themselves in the earth where he'd lain a moment before. The god screamed in outrage and raised his hands to strike again.

Liran gathered himself into a crouch, breathing raggedly, and tracked Vokk's movements. He anticipated the next attack, launching himself away and somersaulting to escape the sweep of Vokk's arm, but not quickly enough to avoid the slash of a claw along his back. He gritted his teeth against the wave of pain. It wasn't a deep cut. He could still rely on the muscles of his back and shoulders, but it was bleeding profusely. He already felt warm liquid soaking into his shirt. Pushing the pain from his mind, he readied himself to face the next attack.

This time Vokk lunged, opening his giant maw with its rings of teeth. The sight of that gaping darkness lined with dagger-like fangs almost froze Liran in place. But instead he sprinted away, hearing Vokk's jaws snap at his back and the rush of hot, fetid breath surrounding him. His stomach lurched, but he ran without faltering.

He turned, searching the ground. He had to get to his sword. His blood went cold when he spotted the weapon and realized Vokk had been driving him away from it. The only way he could recover the sword now would be to run straight at Vokk, an act that was tantamount to suicide.

Vokk reared back, and a twisted form of laughter spilled out of his mouth, as if he saw the thoughts in Liran's mind and knew his frustration.

Suddenly the god's terrible laughter choked off, becoming a snarl of annoyance. Vokk pivoted, his burning eyes searching for . . . what?

Liran caught sight of a small figure, tumbling along the ground on the opposite side of the god from where he stood. Not the Loresmith, no; Ara was behind him with Senn. Whoever this was, they moved with incredible speed as sharp projectiles flew from their hands. Throwing knives. Vokk swatted the blades away as if they were flies. Doing little harm, this new attack was merely an annoyance. A distraction.

A distraction.

Liran would be a fool not to seize it. And he was no fool. He charged forward, running straight at Vokk, who had turned away from him. Liran made it past him and dove for his sword. As his hand closed around the hilt, he could sense Vokk turning.

Rolling to his feet, Liran lifted his blade and understood that the god hadn't seen him move.

He only had seconds, and he had to take them.

Vokk was already pivoting toward him, but Liran gritted his teeth and charged forward. The god's mouth opened wide, those teeth rushing at Liran once more. Primal fear screamed at him to dodge, to flee, but instead he drove forward, pushing himself even faster.

Vokk struck, lunging down, and Liran dove, catapulting himself beyond and beneath the jaws that closed on the ground inches behind him. Liran rolled over, crouched, and then pushed up from the earth with all the force he could muster, at the same time thrusting his sword straight up. The blade pierced Vokk's throat, and Liran drove it deeper still, then wrenched it hard, tearing flesh. Vokk's throat split open and blood gushed out. Godsbane was buried deep. Liran jumped, closing both hands around the sword's hilt, using his body weight to drag the blade down Vokk's neck.

What started as a scream became a sickening gargle as the wound lengthened, widened, and then gaped. Liran's feet hit the ground, and still he drew the blade down, forcing it through muscle and tendon until he hit bone.

Maddened by pain, Vokk reached wildly for the man who'd stolen beneath him to wreak havoc on the god's body. Liran jerked his sword free and swung hard at the claws coming at him, severing long fingers.

Vokk lurched away from Liran, swaying on his long, spindly legs. He struck at Liran one last time, but he was already falling backward. The god sprawled on the earth, shuddering, wet breaths coming at longer and longer intervals.

Liran approached warily, but Vokk's eyes had glazed over.

Standing over his fallen god, Liran lifted Godsbane one last time. "The world will not be yours."

Liran drove his blade down, deep into Vokk's heart. Vokk gave a final, terrible shudder and was still.

Pulling Godsbane from the god's chest, Liran stumbled backward and fell to his knees as exhaustion overwhelmed him. He was vaguely aware of shocked cries rising from the battlefield and then shouts of triumph.

He suddenly sensed a presence on his right, but he had no strength left to fight if an attack was coming. He closed his eyes, resigned to whatever fate held for him. But instead of a blow, he felt hands cupping his jaw.

He lifted his eyelids, and a familiar face came into focus.

Dagger searched his face with concern. "That was impressive, Commander. It's not every day I see a man kill a god. Even if I had to give you a little help. Now, tell me, how badly are you hurt?"

It took a minute for Liran's brain to sort through her words and understand that she had been responsible for the flurry of knives that briefly drew Vokk's focus away from him.

"It was you. You attacked Vokk." Liran stared at his petite savior in disbelief. "Where did you come from?"

"I've been lurking," Dagger replied with a sly smile. "I thought you might need me."

He gave her a long look. "I suspect I'll always need you."

Her lips parted in surprise at his words, and he seized the opportunity to draw her close, delighted that he at last had the chance to catch her in a kiss she wasn't expecting, as she'd done so many times to him.

When Liran released her, they were both breathless, but smiling. The Loresmith was nearby, gazing at Dagger with astonishment.

Dagger smiled up at Ara and Senn as she curled one arm around Liran's waist and snuggled into him. It was an absurd thing to do in the middle of a battlefield, but he found it inexplicably pleasing.

Ara watched them for a moment, then shook her head and laughed. "Your timing is impeccable."

"I know," Dagger replied.

Liran bent his head to whisper in her ear. "You may come to regret that, because you're stuck with me now."

She looked up at him, grinning. "Oh, Commander, surely you see that was the plan all along."

"That's a happy coincidence," he said, pressing his lips to her temple. "Because I seem to be quite fond of you, Maira."

He was gratified by the subtle blush that washed over her cheeks when he said her name.

"Now let's get you to a healer," Dagger quipped. "You're bleeding all over me."

She looked past Liran to the Loresmith still astride a god's hunting hound.

"That's a very big dog you have," she said to Ara. "Do you think he'd give us a ride?"

35

he final battle had brought the end, Ara thought, and yet another beginning.

Despite Dagger's suggestion, Senn hadn't carried the assassin, the commander, and the Loresmith away from Vokk's body. Moments after Dagger made her jest, a wind rose, spilling softly over the battlefield like a heaving sigh.

When it passed over Ara, she felt a wrenching loss followed by a deep calm. Perfect peace. She turned, her gaze following the strange wind as it rippled outward over the embattled soldiers. As it struck them, the spell-cursed Vokkans toppled, limp as rag dolls, to the ground, and sounds of pitched battle fell away, leaving a hollow silence in its wake as warriors who'd been fighting for their lives abruptly found themselves without opponents.

The quiet settled, a collective holding of breath. Then a single shout shattered the silence.

"Saetlund!"

Cries, cheers, more shouts swelled to a thunderous roar of victory. Amid the cacophony, Ara could pick out words that made her heart drum out its own joyous tattoo:

"Nimhea!"

"For the Queen!"

"Hail the Loreknights!"

She closed her eyes and let the sounds lift her up and set her spirit soaring. Only when she sensed a shift in the air around her did she open her eyes again, drawing a quick breath as she discovered she no longer stood on the plains of Sola, but in the Loreknights' burial chamber in the catacombs beneath the Palace of Five Rivers.

Standing alongside her, five on each side, were the Loreknights. To her left, the risen warriors: Ursina, Nathor, Mirix, Turhea, and Resek. On her right, her friends: Teth, Joar, Nimhea, Lahvja, and Liran.

Ara barely stifled a gasp as before them rose the awesome forms of Saetlund's gods. Eni in their swirling cloaks; Ofrit stroking his long white beard; Nava's bountiful curves and warm eyes; the nebulous, shifting light and dark of Ayre/Syre; and mighty Wuldr with Senn at his side.

"Heroes of Saetlund," Nava spoke, her voice ringing with joy. "You have honored your home and your gods. We thank you and offer our blessing."

To the five Loreknights Lahvja had called from the grave, Nava said, "Warriors of legend, first champions, you answered the call when Saetlund most needed you."

The risen warriors bowed to the goddess of Sola.

Ayre/Syre's chorus-like voice spoke. "As you were called, so now are you returned. Be at peace once more."

As Ara watched, the Loreknights to her left blurred, as if obscured by a shimmering fog, and then were gone. A pang of regret caught her by surprise. She would have liked to know them.

Nava beckoned to Nimhea. "My daughter."

Nimhea came forward, and Nava took her hands. "Today you claimed the greatest victory, but it was not without sacrifice."

The gods parted, a subtle movement like the lifting of a veil, to reveal a marble sarcophagus that had not yet been sealed. A hard stone lodged in Ara's throat as Nava led Nimhea to the sarcophagus.

Looking down at her brother's still form, Nimhea whispered, "Eamon." Her hands covered her mouth as her breath hitched. "Oh, my brother . . . why . . ."

Ara felt a light touch, then Teth's fingers laced with hers. She clasped his hand tightly as tears spilled down her cheeks.

Nimhea trembled, her shoulders beginning to shake, and Lahvja stepped forward, then hesitated.

"Come, Summoner," Nava said. "It is the time for comfort and remembrance."

Lahvja hurried to Nimhea's side and wrapped her arms around Nimhea, who was breathing raggedly, but had yet to weep.

"Your brother gave his life for your sake," Nava told Nimhea in a quiet voice. "For the sake of this kingdom. Without him, Saetlund would be lost. For that he will rest in this place of heroes and kings, as is his due."

"Eamon," Nimhea whispered again, and rested her hand on Eamon's cheek. "I wish . . . I love you, brother. Thank you."

Only then did she turn and bury her face in Lahvja's shoulder. Lahvja stroked Nimhea's hair, murmuring soft words.

"We will leave you to your grief." Nava turned to the rest of them. "Know that until you leave this place, time does not move in the world outside. That is our gift to you, that you may share your sorrow and honor your friend. When you are ready, return to the field, where you are needed to restore order and begin the work of rebuilding a kingdom. Farewell, champions of Saetlund."

And the gods were gone.

Ara and Teth joined Nimhea and Lahvja at the sarcophagus. Together they wept for their friend, who had been lost and was now restored to them, but not in the way any of them would have wished. Liran and Joar kept a respectful distance, but when Ara glanced at them, Joar's gaze was full of admiration, while Liran's eyes held the sheen of tears. He'd known Eamon as well, she realized, if only briefly.

There would never be time enough to say goodbye, Ara knew. And they would return to this tomb, to visit Eamon's resting place, as individuals or together. For now, they offered one another what comfort they could until they gained some small measure of peace with the loss.

But this moment, Ara thought, joined the beginning to the end. This farewell completed the circle of her journey to become the Loresmith. Without Eamon, she would never have taken the first step.

A hush fell over the assembled guests in the Five Rivers throne room as Nimhea climbed the steps of the dais. She stood before the throne and turned to face the crowd.

The Circle was present, along with Imgar and Liran and the commander's lieutenants. Ara and the other Loreknights stood closest to the throne. In time, five more would be added to their number.

As part of Nimhea's reign, the kingdom would return to the practice of choosing a Loreknight from each of Saetlund's provinces to serve with those the gods had already chosen.

Suli approached the dais, bearing the crown Ara had forged when Nava named Nimhea Loreknight. Nimhea knelt before the leader of the Circle.

"Princess Nimhea, you led your people in battle, proving your valor." Suli spoke in a clear, ringing voice. "You and your companions defeated the conquerors and have restored the kingdom. Do you swear to protect Saetlund and its people, to stay true to the gods of this land and honor them, for all the days of your life?"

"I do," Nimhea said.

Suli placed the crown on Nimhea's head. "Rise, Queen Nimhea."

Nimhea stood and lifted her face.

"Queen Nimhea!" Suli shouted.

Every voice in the room echoed her joyful cry: "Queen Nimhea!"

❖ ❖ ❖

A week had passed between the defeat of the Vokkans and Nimhea's coronation, days that were mostly devoted to sorting through the chaos that reigned in the immediate aftermath of the battle. When Lahvja's magic returned them to the battlefield, as Nava promised, nothing had altered from the moment of their departure—with the exception that Senn was no longer available to carry Ara, Liran, and Dagger back to their friends. And Vokk's body had vanished.

Despite the chaos all around, they quickly discovered there was no danger. In the wake of Vokk's death, the spell that had turned his soldiers into crazed, flesh-eating creatures had broken. When Vokk's hold had vanished, the soldiers had suddenly dropped to the ground, their bodies and minds utterly ravaged by the power of the magic that had controlled them. Some died; others were reduced to gibbering husks of human beings. Vokk's army was no more.

There were still soldiers loyal to Fauld in other parts of Saetlund, but they were significantly outnumbered. In the coming days, Nimhea and Liran would send detachments to quell whatever factions rose up against the new queen of Saetlund. News of Fauld's and Zenar's deaths, as well as Vokk's, was already spreading like wildfire throughout the kingdom, and with it the expectation that the desire to fight for a dead emperor would quickly fade, particularly given Commander Liran's continued presence in the kingdom. In the stories that were repeated from town to town, Liran was most frequently known as the Godslayer, a name he did not care for but could do little about.

Liran did revel in the knowledge that Vokk's demise and the liberation of Saetlund would be the catalyst for the empire's destruction throughout the world. Nascent and ongoing uprisings in other conquered territories would grow in strength. Years of strife lay ahead, and it would take decades for the earth to recover from being ravaged by Vokk's insatiable hunger, but hope for the future thrived. Watching Nimhea stand before the River Throne filled Ara with the unshakable belief that the world would heal.

The night before the coronation, Ara had woken from a deep sleep to find herself in the Loresmith Forge.

"Ara, come join us." Eni's crinkle-faced old woman sat at a table that held a plate of cookies, a steaming pot of tea, and three cups. There were three chairs at the table; two of them were occupied.

Ara's pulse sped up as she approached.

"Hello, Ara." Eamon smiled at her. "May I pour you some tea?"

"Oh, I'll do that, Your Highness." Eni batted Eamon's hand away from the pot. "You just have another cookie. I know they're your favorite."

With a blush, Eamon picked up a cookie.

"They are really good," he said to Ara.

A little dazed, Ara sank into the chair between Eni and Eamon. "You're here."

Still looking bashful, Eamon nodded. "I asked Eni if we could talk one last time. I want you to know that I'm okay, more than okay. And I hope you will tell Nimhea."

"Eamon." Ara's throat wanted to close. "What you did . . . you saved Saetlund."

Eamon quickly shook his head. "No. I did my part, that's all."

"Humility is well and good, Prince Eamon," Eni tsk'd, pushing a filled teacup in front of Ara. "But your part was vital. No one else could have managed it."

"I had to." Eamon ducked his head to avoid Eni's piercing gaze. "Ara, I'm so sorry I betrayed you, I didn't—"

"Don't." Ara covered Eamon's hand with hers. "You don't have to say anything. None of that matters."

"Thank you," Eamon said, turning his palm up so he could clasp her fingers.

Eni nodded approvingly.

"You saved Teth," Ara said softly. "There aren't words for how much that means to me."

At that, Eamon smiled. "He loves you."

Ara felt herself blushing. "I know."

She picked up her teacup and took a sip, trying to find a way to word the question she wanted to ask.

"It's all right," Eamon said, seeming to understand her hesitation. "I died. It must be strange to see me here, to talk to me."

With a grateful laugh, Ara said, "It is. Are you . . . What happens to you now?"

Eamon glanced at Eni, who gave a little nod.

"Eni has shown me that there is more to discover in the universe than I ever could have dreamed. An eternity of knowledge is ready for me to explore. I . . . . I'm happy."

Ara bit her lip as tears threatened to well in her throat. She wanted to speak, but could only nod. For a few minutes, she had to focus on her tea and the cookies to keep from falling to pieces.

"I'm so glad you're well, Eamon," Ara said when she found her voice again.

"Tell Nimhea I love her and I know she'll be a wonderful queen," Eamon said.

"I will," Ara replied. "I promise."

"Thank you," he said to Ara, then he looked at Eni. "And thank you. So much."

Eni smiled, and as Ara watched, the old woman's face and body blurred, and then Fox was sitting on the chair.

Fox hopped to the ground and gave Eamon an expectant look. Eamon nodded and stood. He leaned down and hugged Ara.

"Be well, Loresmith. I always believed in you, and I always will."

Ara turned in her chair to watch Fox and Eamon walk to the edge of the Loresmith Forge. Her breath caught when Fox leapt into the darkness. Eamon looked over his shoulder and gave a little wave, smiling at her. Then he turned and walked off the edge. The outline of his body began to shine, and shimmering light spread inward until Eamon's form was composed entirely of dancing lights that sped toward the distant stars.

Ara had shared the vision with Nimhea shortly before the coronation ceremony began and watched the cast of haunted grief fade from the princess's eyes. Now, as Ara cheered along with the others, she scanned the crowd, smiling when she caught sight of Lucket and Dagger watching from a far corner of the room, half-hidden by shadows. Neither joined the celebratory shouts, but they wore identical expressions of cool satisfaction.

Nimhea hadn't wanted it that way. The princess had called Ara to a meeting with Teth and Lucket. Even now the memory of that conversation made laughter bubble up and spill out along with her cheers.

"No." Lucket served up a serene smile in response to Nimhea's incredulous expression.

"What do you mean, no?" Nimhea scoffed. "I'm offering you a great honor."

"I neither need nor want honors, Your Highness," Lucket replied coolly, "but I appreciate the gesture."

"But our alliance has been so fruitful," Nimhea argued. "Why not extend it? You can come out of the shadows, make your enterprises legitimate in cooperation with the crown."

Lucket coughed delicately. "Princess Nimhea, how precisely do you propose to make thievery, assassination, and sundry criminal activities legitimate?"

Nimhea lifted her chin and placed her hands on her hips. "Obviously there would need to be reforms within the Below."

"Ah." Lucket clucked his tongue. "Therein lies the problem. The very essence of the Below is contained in its name. We are the undercurrent, the hidden. The darkness is where we thrive."

"But you're criminals," Nimhea insisted. "If you return to your old ways, I'll have no choice but to pursue your agents, to arrest and jail them. No matter how much you helped the Resistance, I can't ignore illegal activities."

"I'd expect nothing less," Lucket replied with a polite nod. "The endless hunt makes what I do all the more rewarding. I've no doubt your monarchy will serve as worthy adversaries."

Nimhea stared at him. "I thought we were friends."

"We are, Your Highness," Lucket said gently. "And there will be times when we'll cooperate, covertly, but for the most part we must remain independent and at odds."

When Nimhea started to speak again, Teth placed a staying hand on her shoulder. "He won't change his mind."

"And where will you end up in this arrangement, Teth?" Nimhea glared at him. "Thief or Loreknight?"

Lucket raised his eyebrows, turning to Teth to wait for his response. Ara's curiosity heightened as well, accompanied by a spike of nerves. She and Teth hadn't spoken about what came next yet. Until this moment, she'd assumed it was because they'd been too caught up restoring order to the kingdom, but she suddenly wondered if they'd both been avoiding the subject.

"I prefer flexibility over rigid definitions." Teth shrugged. "Don't worry, Your Highness, I'll find my way."

Nimhea muttered an oath and stalked out of the room.

Ara waited until she was certain the princess was out of earshot, then said, "Poor Nimhea. Couldn't you at least have allowed her to pin a medal on you, Lucket?"

"Don't be ridiculous," Lucket replied, smoothing his coat as if to reassure himself no shiny objects had manifested there against his will. "I'd be the laughingstock of the Below."

Teth slid his arm around Ara's waist. "My father's right. It's better if the Low Kings are well separated from the monarchy."

"Of course I'm right." Lucket flashed a grin at his son. "Besides, Nimhea will be an exceptional queen. I can't make it too easy for her."

Ara felt she should scold Lucket on Nimhea's behalf, but when she opened her mouth, all she could do was laugh. Now Ara watched as amid the cheers, the Low King and assassin slipped quietly from the room, leaving her to wonder when, possibly if, she'd see them again. When the throne room emptied and the celebrants began making their way to a grand hall where a banquet with a much larger number of guests would be held in the Queen's honor, Teth took Ara's hand and held her back until they were the only two left in the room.

"What now, Loresmith?" Teth asked, his arms encircling her. "The future is stretching out before you, and you can choose to walk any number of roads. You know I'll follow you anywhere. Or, as a Loreknight, am I meant to spend the rest of my days in court, as our new queen would prefer?"

He spoke these last words with a hint of distaste. Ara didn't blame him for a moment.

"The Loreknights defended Saetlund in times of need," Ara said, turning to look at him. "But they returned to their homes in times of peace, lived their lives as they chose. Obviously, as Saetlund's queen, Nimhea will remain in Five Rivers, and where Nimhea is, Lahvja wants to be. But I see no reason the other Loreknights should be confined to life at court."

"Interesting." Teth made a show of thoughtfully stroking his chin. "So how would you feel about this Loreknight returning to his former life of crime?"

Ara smiled up at him. "I fell in love with a thief. It hardly seems fair to expect you to abandon a profession you're so fond of, not to mention skilled at . . . sometimes. I did catch you in the act."

"Not my finest moment, I confess. But I'm also a prince." Teth grinned at her. "Don't forget that."

"Prince of the Below." Ara laughed. "How could I forget?"

He bowed with a flourish, then snatched her hand and pressed his lips to her fingers.

"Very gallant," she said, still laughing. "Speaking of gallant, Nimhea has asked Liran to remain in Saetlund as commander of the military."

Teth nodded. "I overheard Liran and Imgar arguing about it. Liran thought it should be Imgar or Suli, but Suli is overseeing a special task force focusing on the restoration of Sola, and Imgar insists he's retiring."

"You overheard this conversation?" Ara frowned at him. "It sounds awfully private."

"I was curious." He shrugged. "And I'm very good at finding creative ways to overhear conversations I'm curious about."

"You spied on them."

He slid an arm around her waist, drawing her closer. "You make that sound like a bad thing."

"I'm inclined to think it is." She gave him a light jab with her elbow.

"Ow." He rubbed at his ribs. "If you're not nice to me, I won't tell you about the other conversation I overheard. This one was between the Hawk and your grandmother."

Ara elbowed him harder this time. "I know that was a private conversation. My grandmother told me about it. Imgar's going back to Rill's Pass with her, and that's none of your business."

"I stopped listening before they started kissing," Teth objected.

"If that's true, how do you know they started kissing?" Ara scowled at him, blushing on her grandmother's behalf.

"I meant to stay I stopped listening once it was obvious they were kissing instead of talking," Teth told her, and jumped aside before she could elbow him again. "I think it's time for you to stop attacking me so we can be happy for them together."

He stole behind her and wrapped his arms around her waist, nuzzling her neck. "And then you can tell me what would make you happy."

Surrendering the field, Ara leaned back into him. "I'm already happy."

"Good," Teth said. "But not helpful. What do you want, Ara? I'll give it to you if I can."

"Is that so?"

"Thief's honor."

She smiled at him thoughtfully. "Before Nimhea and Eamon found me, I'd spent nearly all my life in Rill's Pass. And I'd never set foot outside Fjeri. The Loresmith quest took me to each of Saetlund's provinces, but it wasn't as if I was able to explore them."

"I suppose I could think of a few places I'd like to show you," Teth said. "And Lucket asked if I'd be willing to help him reestablish the Below's network of hideouts and caches. If I agree, it would involve a lot of traveling."

"That sounds like an adventure." Ara turned in his arms.

He bent his head to kiss her lightly. "You're sure you haven't had too much adventure lately?"

"I'm sure," she replied. "But I want to go with Imgar and Elke to Rill's Pass first. I need to see that everything is safe and settled there."

"I'd like to see your home," Teth said warmly.

"Joar's traveling with them, too. Before going off into the wilderness with Huntress, he wants to spend time with Imgar first. We can all travel together."

Teth let out an exaggerated groan. "So I've proposed a romantic adventure, and now we're traveling with Joar and your family as chaperones? Clearly my plan went awry somewhere."

"We'll be on our own soon enough." Ara poked him in the chest, then kissed his cheek. "But I suspect Imgar is going to convince my grandmother to marry him the minute they're back in Rill's Pass. I don't want to miss that."

"Then that's where we'll go first." Teth looked at her a long time, his amber eyes intense. "It's a good thing Eni likes me, because I can't wait to walk every road in Saetlund with you." He suddenly laughed. "I wouldn't be surprised if Fox shows up to keep us company every so often."

"Neither would I," Ara said, laughing with him.

She had no doubt that wherever Eni was, the god was laughing, too.

ACKNOWLEDGMENTS

Concluding a series is always a bittersweet endeavor. This particular trilogy's journey was deeply meaningful because it began with my return to writing after learning how to cope with chronic illness and continued as we all struggled through the pandemic. I am so grateful to all those who cheered Ara and the Loreknights on to their victory. For over a decade, Philomel and Penguin Young Readers have been my authorial home. I couldn't have wished for a more wonderful writing family. Thank you to Kenneth Wright and Jill Santopolo, as well as Eileen Kreit, for everything you do to bring amazing books to readers. Kelsey Murphy's sharp eye and brilliant contributions shaped this novel in wonderful ways. Krista Ahlberg never fails to astonish me with her superpowers of copyediting. Thank you to all the hard work of the publicity and marketing teams at PYR, especially Tessa Meischeid and Felicity Vallence. The beautiful covers that so perfectly capture the spirit of this series are courtesy of Katt Phatt and Jessica Jenkins. Charlie Olsen, agent extraordinaire: you're the best. The Robertson and Otremba families give me respite and joy amid the chaos of the world. I'm especially grateful to my parents for their love and support and owe an extra shout-out to my dad, who planned a trip to Norway to visit my great-grandparents' homes, which served as the inspiration for this series. My husband, Eric, is simply a wonderful human, whom I adore and am grateful to for not minding when I ignore him for days while I'm drafting. Lastly, in 2010, I began a new journey with my first novel, *Nightshade*, and the captain of that series and all my subsequent books was Jill Santopolo. Her editorial skills are pure magic, and I am so grateful for her guidance and patience through every book we've created together. The next chapter of adventures is afoot for both of us, and I can't wait to see what life's new pages bring. Thank you, Jill, for everything.